PRAISE FOR LOUISE PHILLIPS

'A gripping, suspenseful story peopled with well-drawn characters'
Irish Independent

'A satisfyingly chilling yet enthralling read that had
me turning around checking I was home alone'
Woman's Way

'A deliciously dark thriller … the writing is truly spectacular'
Writing.ie

'Phillips goes from strength to strength … the pace is excellent, the
characters well drawn and believable … Highly recommended'
Belfast Telegraph

'Unusual and unsettling' *Irish Times*

'Among the best crime writing in the world – a top notch thriller'
BBC Radio Ulster

'As fast-paced and thrilling as a rollercoaster' Jane Casey

'A page-turning, gut-wrenching thriller which will undoubtedly
earn Phillips further accolades and hordes of new fans'
Lisa Reads Books

'Fast-paced, dark and intriguing – and well worth reading'
Novelicious

'This book is superb! Chilling and original … it has an
ending that you just can't see coming'
Eurocrime

'It was dark, it was deep, it was scary, it chilled me

Dublin-born crime author Louise Phillips won the Ireland AM Crime Fiction Book of the Year Award for *The Doll's House*, her bestselling second novel, in 2013. *Red Ribbons* (2012) and *Last Kiss* (2014), which also feature criminal psychologist Dr Kate Pearson and DI O'Connor, were each shortlisted for this award.

Louise's work has been published as part of various anthologies and literary journals. She has won the Jonathan Swift Award, was a winner in the Irish Writers' Centre Lonely Voice platform, and her writing has been shortlisted for prizes such as the Molly Keane Memorial Award and Bridport UK. In 2015, she was awarded a writing residency at the Cill Rialaig Artists' Retreat in Kerry and was also a judge on the Irish panel for the EU Literary Award.

The Game Changer is her fourth novel.

www.louise-phillips.com
@LouiseMPhillips

ALSO BY LOUISE PHILLIPS
Last Kiss
The Doll's House
Red Ribbons

LOUISE PHILLIPS

THE GAME CHANGER

HACHETTE
BOOKS
IRELAND

First published in Ireland in 2015 by HACHETTE BOOKS IRELAND

1

Cataloguing in Publication Data is available from the British Library

ISBN 978 1 4447 8940 9

Typeset in Bembo Book Standard by Bookends Publishing Services
Printed and bound in Great Britain by Clays Ltd, St Ives plc.

Hachette Books Ireland policy is to use papers that are natural, renewable
and recyclable products and made from wood grown in sustainable forests.
The logging and manufacturing processes are expected to conform to the
environmental regulations of the country of origin.

Hachette Books Ireland
8 Castlecourt Centre, Castleknock, Dublin 15, Ireland

A division of Hachette UK Ltd
Carmelite House, 50 Victoria Embankment, London EC4Y 0DZ

www.hachette.ie

For Mum and Dad

'When we step into the family, by the act of being born, we step into a world which is incalculable, into a world which has its own strange laws, into a world which could do without us, into a world we have not made. In other words, when we step into the family, we step into a fairy-tale.'

G.K. Chesterton

November 1988

DUBLIN

THE SMOG HAD BEEN HEAVY FOR DAYS, DUBLIN CITY falling into darkness by late afternoon. The poison billowing from the chimneys attacked the throat and lungs as it crept menacingly through doors and windows. Some of those who ventured outside wore masks in an effort to stop the sickening blackness, while politicians argued in government buildings about speeding up the transfer to smokeless fuels, and another black Dublin winter took its toll. The mood on the streets was sombre, the air choking, as if the city was partially buried.

It was after midnight when Valentine Pearson strolled past the town-hall clock in the suburb of Rathmines, then turned around and went back in the opposite direction. The repeated solitary movement, up and down the footpath, fought off the night chill and the edge to his mood. He wore a long grey overcoat with a black silk scarf wrapped around his nose and mouth, his collar raised, his black trilby tilted downwards, keeping his eyes in shadow. He listened as the clock chimed a quarter past midnight, his irritation and impatience at the late hour forming a tight knot in his chest. He swallowed hard. The man he was due to meet was now fifteen minutes late. He kicked a stray beer can with more force than he'd intended as a lone car crawled past him with its fog lights on. The rest of the street was deserted, apart from some teenagers, a few moments earlier, falling out of the late-night chip shop further up the street.

He gripped the envelope that contained the tightly bundled cash in his pocket, ten thousand pounds in large notes, and the term *guilt money* came to mind. He stopped walking, retreating instead under the town-hall archway. Out of sight, his eyes fixed on Leinster Road, opposite him, second-guessing the direction from which his late rendezvous would come. The wrought-iron amber streetlamps created circular pockets of light on the ground.

He heard the man's footsteps before he saw him, disappearing and reappearing within the circles of orange light, the encounter getting closer with each step. It would be over soon, he told himself. Give him the money and that would be it. He recognised his co-conspirator before he saw his face, crossing Rathmines Road with apparent arrogance as Valentine pulled further into the dark. The man was barely half his age, early twenties, with the swagger that younger males possess, a confidence born of ignorance and too much testosterone. Still, he thought, any port in a storm. He clenched his fists, part of him wanting to hit out at someone, anyone. He hated feeling vulnerable, and the sense that the power was in the hands of another.

As the men came face to face, they kept their silence for a couple of seconds, the younger man waiting as the older one finally stepped out from the darkness onto the smog-filled street.

'Lovely night,' the younger man said, with too much vigour for Valentine's liking.

Valentine pulled the scarf down from his face. 'You took your time,' he said, sounding cold and indignant.

'I told you I'd be here, and here I am.'

'You told me a lot of things.'

'Don't shoot the messenger.' The young man coughed, covering his mouth with his hand.

'Is that what you are now, Malcolm, a messenger?'

'Do you have the cash?'

'I do.'

'If you want things sorted, you'll need to pay.'

'Can we trust them?'

'To stay quiet, you mean?'

'Yes.'

'Would you prefer to run the risk of not paying?'

'No.' Valentine took out the envelope of cash and handed it to his collaborator. 'We won't be discussing this again. Do you understand?'

'I do.'

May 2015

NEW YORK

GLITTERING MOONLIGHT CAUGHT A FERRYBOAT travelling along the East River, the light cutting through nightfall as the streetlights of the Lower East Side and the interconnecting city exit roads and highways danced in the remaining darkness.

It had been a killing like no other, Detective Lee Fisher had reflected for the umpteenth time. The bloodied room holding the chopped-up remains of Tom Mason was one of the worst crime scenes he had ever witnessed. He used to think he had seen too many goddam killings for any of them to be extraordinary, but he had been wrong-footed this time, nothing surer.

He liked to walk at night. The exercise always helped him to think during a difficult investigation, when the city felt like an extension of his mind, pensive, partly mysterious, full of urban mutterings and capable of surprising itself. Soon, he would take the thirty-minute subway ride home to Brooklyn, but for now, he breathed in deep, the smell of nicotine lingering in the air. Smoking was one of his guilty pleasures, but he only ever lit up at night and outdoors. More than once, people had referred to him as bohemian: he was tall and slender, with near-shoulder-length curly dark-chestnut hair, a tight-cut beard, and the air of a wise rebel.

Two months earlier, when he had arrived at the corner of Orchard and Rivington Street, he was unaware that the 911 call would result in something more horrific than he had ever witnessed. The building he had stood in front of was six storeys high with a red stone façade and an upscale trendy boutique at the bottom. Access to the upper floors had been via a communal hallway to the side, with a fire exit at the back on each floor. He remembered a time when that part of the Lower East Side was filled with immigrants, a working-class neighbourhood. Rapid gentrification in the mid-2000s meant the place had changed, with inhabitants possessing far bigger bank balances.

The victim was male, Irish, late sixties, unmarried and retired. He had lived in the US since '92, an ex-small-time local politician who had stayed well away from politics in Manhattan, from what Lee could gather. Instead, he had concentrated on working as a financial adviser and part-owner of a chain of boutiques, including the one located on the ground floor of the building. There was nothing particularly interesting about Tom Mason, described as a quiet man who kept himself to himself. The official cause of death was heart failure, brought on by loss of blood and shock, but the attacker had wanted more than the victim's death: they had wanted to ensure maximum pain by chopping him to pieces. According to the medical examiner, the killer had started with the victim's fingers, then severed both arms. The toes were next, the heart finally packing in before both legs were amputated from the upper thigh.

The term 'in bits' seemed to fall short of an accurate description, but 'in bits' was how Lee saw the investigation, a chaotic cocktail of anger, determination and the ability to administer pain with clinical and methodical application, necessitating a calm head on the part of whoever had butchered the man's body. The victim had been gagged, but other than some neighbours reporting a loud version of what Lee had later discovered to be Beethoven's Symphony No 5, Op. 67 (first movement), playing and replaying from the music centre in the apartment, nobody had noticed anything unusual. The vast array of blood, guts and body parts found at the scene, coupled with the putrid smell of death – Tom Mason's body had been discovered two days after he was slaughtered – was like an ocean in comparison to the tiny droplets of forensic evidence they had found. Everything at the scene had been traced back to the victim, or the home help, who had discovered the body after the weekend – everything, that was, except one tiny unidentified swab taken from the tip of a pen used to create the incision lines.

Lee had been long enough in the game to realise that some investigations had the hallmark of being unsolved right from the beginning, although on this occasion the killer had left a note. Scrawled in blood on the bathroom mirror, using the severed index finger of the deceased, were the words: 'HE SAW THE LIGHT'. A religious fanatic, they had surmised, but either way, as Lee inhaled the last of his cigarette, there was one thing he was sure of. Solving this crime would take another killing or killings. It was simply a question of who the next victim would be, and where and when the crime would take place.

Part One

September 2015
DUBLIN

Kate

KATE AWOKE AS SOON AS SHE HEARD ADAM'S MOBILE phone ringing. It was a few hours since the two of them had made love, and it still felt good lying close to him. As he reached out to take the call, coldness set in between them: she watched his body turn away from her, the room dark except for the light from the streetlamp outside. As he moved, she saw shadows bounce from one side of the room to the other, and for the briefest moment, he reminded her of her late father, Valentine. Both were complicated men, but poles apart in so many ways.

The next sound she heard was the creaking of branches, the tentacles of the whitethorn tree, sporadically tipping the apartment window. She checked her own phone – 2 a.m. The time could mean only one thing: an emergency call from Harcourt Street Special Detective Unit. She didn't say anything, at least not at first, observing Adam as he got dressed on autopilot, pulling his white shirt over his head. He only ever opened the cuff and top two front buttons – all shortcuts to save time. With his back hunched, he pulled up his trousers, closing the belt tight as he straightened before attaching the gun belt across his chest, like a silent shadow in the dark. She couldn't even hear him breathe.

'It's all right,' she said, sitting up in the bed. 'I'm already awake.' Her voice was low and croaky from sleep.

His shadow shifted, and the streetlamp caught his smile. He whispered in her ear, 'Two light sleepers living together may not be the best of plans.'

She had already switched on the bedside light. 'You're the one who told me planning was overrated.' It was her turn to smile.

'What's up?' She'd kept her voice low, not wanting to wake seven-year-old Charlie, in the other room.

'Some guy has topped himself.' He said it so matter-of-factly that she wondered if, after years in the police force, death was eventually diluted for everyone. Standing at the end of the bed, he raised his shirt collar to wrap his tie around his neck, still going through the motions, like a fireman putting on his uniform with no time to waste.

'What else do you know?' She was now curious.

'He isn't any guy.' He pulled the tie tight. 'It's the chief super's brother-in-law – or, rather, late brother-in-law.'

'Do they think it's suspicious?'

'Too early to tell, but one way or another, Kate, it means trouble.' He kissed her softly on the lips.

'Be careful,' she murmured.

'Try to get some sleep. I won't be long.' His words sounded reassuring as he pulled the bedroom door closed.

Turning off the light, she listened to his car pull away from the kerb, the rest of the quiet Ranelagh suburb long since fast asleep. She thought about the other partners of police officers out there, especially those with families. What a different life it was from any other.

A few moments later, when she heard the low whimper, she thought it was a stray cat outside, but as it got louder, she sat up again: it was coming from Charlie's bedroom. She bounded down the hallway and opened his door, her voice gentle as she entered. He was still half asleep. 'It's okay, honey. Mum's here.'

She didn't switch on his light, hoping he would settle. Even in the darkness she could make out his small shape, his knees raised to his chest. He was wearing his favourite Spider-Man pyjamas.

'Shush, honey.' Her right hand touched his hot cheek. The other rubbed his shoulder in the familiar motion she used to lull him back to sleep. 'It's okay, sweetheart, you were only dreaming.'

She climbed into his bed, her words seeming to ease whatever had frightened him. His face became less troubled, turning into her, the way children do. All she could think of was him as a baby, round and soft, with wisps of hair, and that intoxicating baby smell, the one that grabbed you like no other and never let you go. Examining the contours of his face, his small hands, the fingers clenched in sleep, she felt as if she was reliving every day of the last seven years – she'd never known she could love anyone so much.

Within the stillness, she also knew she would stay awake now, listening out for Adam coming home. At first, she'd been hesitant about him moving in, apprehensive about taking that next step. They had agreed to try it one day at a time. Four months in, she wondered where the time had gone. It had started with him staying over only at weekends, then towards the end of the summer, with Charlie taking it so well, it had made sense to create a more permanent living arrangement. So far it had worked out, and even Declan, Charlie's father, had accepted that she and Adam were now on a more permanent footing.

She also thought about her decision to take a step back from work, partly wanting to spend more time with Charlie. It had been one of the best choices she had made. She'd known she would enjoy being at home, even for a short while, but another part of her was surprised by it. Ocean House, where she operated her psychology practice, understood her reducing her hours, although it hadn't been her work there that had put her life at risk. That had been down to Adam, and the Special Detective Unit. Kate had spent three years profiling killers for the police, which had opened up a world that previously she couldn't have imagined. The scars of the last case were still there, and the biggest one, how close she had come to losing her life and leaving Charlie without a mother, still played on her mind. Adam had encouraged her decision to step back, both of them knowing she needed this time.

The main players at Harcourt Street were fine about it too, and with Adam working there, she was still in touch with things, even if it was at arm's length. The officers who had finished their profiling training were doing well – at least, as far as she had heard from Adam. She was suspicious that he was telling her what she wanted to hear, but for now, she was happy to go with the flow.

She stroked Charlie's hair, the only sound in the bedroom the ticking of his Mickey Mouse alarm clock. Not working with Adam, she thought, had probably made it easier for their relationship to move forward. But it was good that they both understood the pressure of two or three critical investigations landing on your desk at once. She looked at the clock: 3 a.m. Hopefully, Adam would be back soon and able to grab some sleep.

The last few months had been hectic for him too, and the long nights hadn't helped his erratic relationship with his estranged teenage son. He had the same first name as his father, initially confusing when he and Charlie were first introduced. But young Adam didn't show the same hostility towards Charlie that he displayed towards his father, instead telling Charlie to call him Addy, like his friends did.

Adam was so different from her ex-husband, Declan, and even though some of her friends thought Declan was more in tune with his emotions, and that Adam was like the proverbial bull in a china shop, Kate knew otherwise. After all, it was Adam who had supported her decision to take things easier. Declan's reaction had surprised her, until she understood that, the more time she spent with their son, the more Declan fretted that his relationship with Charlie would lessen, especially with him working permanently in Birmingham.

Sometimes she felt as if she was constantly trying to manage others: Declan's anxieties, Adam's failure to make things work with Addy, or Charlie coping with his world being turned upside down. Life was messy, and her running away from things in the past hadn't served her well. Everything felt less hectic now. Small things that she hadn't had time for before, like chatting with the neighbours, going to the park with Charlie or catching up with old acquaintances, brought a new normality. She was especially glad to connect with Malcolm again.

He had been so close to her father, but also to her. When she'd met up with him at the Dyadic Developmental Psychotherapy lecture earlier that year, it was only then that she fully realised the important role he had played in her younger life. He had been like the older brother she'd never had, and she took it as another warning sign that she had allowed important parts of her life to slip, failing to link up with him during the ten years since her father's death. The fact that they both worked in the area of psychology added to their revived mutual bond. In some ways, Malcolm's work had influenced her choice to study it: he helped others to function in this world, and she wanted to do the same. Somewhere along the way though, she had lost sight of her own mental well-being, working long hours and not spending enough time with Charlie. It was certainly good to have someone else in her life that she could trust.

The Game Changer

THE WALL TEMPERATURE CONTROL UNIT DISPLAYED seventeen degrees, an optimum level for communication. The room wasn't a large one, no more than sixteen metres square, with brilliant white walls and off-white parquet flooring. Matching venetian blinds covered the two windows opposite the office-type white door. There were eight chrome down-lighters in the white ceiling, should any light, other than daylight, be required. The area was devoid of excess furnishings or anything deemed unnecessary for a successful self-enlightenment session. There were no candles, soft music, muted lightings or fragrant burners. Two thin white plastic chairs, with curved seats to support the inner thighs and angled to optimise blood flow to the lower leg, were positioned opposite each other. To the side, there was a white-granite plastic folding table, narrow but appropriate for the various sheets and handouts. In the corner, to the right of the door as a person entered, the black video camera was positioned on an aluminium tripod.

Lisa Redmond had booked the 7 a.m. self-enlightenment session. Webcam sex with her clients, or camers, as she liked to call them, was particularly slack at that time of the morning. She was in her mid-twenties, medium height, slim, attractive and ambitious. Wearing a classic charcoal figure-hugging suit, with a pencil skirt finishing above the knee, a sheer white cotton blouse, and Manolo Blahnik ankle-strap maroon sandals, she felt composed and looked forward to making further progress within the self-enlightenment programme. Placing her designer olive patent handbag on the floor beside her, she sat in the white chair opposite the door, the camera ready to record their conversation.

'Good morning, Lisa.'

'Morning.'

'Can you hold on for a second while I switch on the camera? Are you feeling relaxed?'

'Yes.' She flicked back her shoulder-length honey-brown hair.

'Good. What would you like to talk about today?'

'I've been thinking about this current step from the programme.'

'The one called "Finding a New Way", Lisa. That is the step you're currently on?'

'Yes.' She crossed her long, tanned legs, resting both hands on her knees, her fingers intertwined, her nails French-polished.

'Are you having some difficulty with it, Lisa?'

'Being part of the programme, and my sessions at the Centre of Lightness, has helped me a great deal. I mean, I spend most of my life talking to the camers. That's what I call my clients, the ones who watch me on camera.' She trailed off.

'Lisa, it's good to talk about any difficulties you might be having. Why don't you pretend I'm not here, and that you're simply thinking out loud to the camera?'

'I've decided I'm not going to humiliate my clients any more, no matter how much they want me to. Some of them love that. They enjoy being sexually degraded.' Her face showed strain: disgusted by her clients' desires.

'Carry on.'

'They beg me to call them horrible names. It frees up their sexual inhibitions, you see. That's why they want me to do it.'

'And why, Lisa, are you going to discontinue this? Especially if it's something they want from you.'

'I realise I need to apply boundaries, work out the lines I'm not prepared to cross. Doing things I don't like, well, it doesn't make me feel good about myself.'

'Feeling good about yourself is important, Lisa. How long have you been turning those camers away?'

'Only a few days – I've still been busy, though. There are always others to take their place.'

'Because, Lisa, you're in demand. You've managed to build up a successful business and a large amount of money over the last few years. You must be proud of yourself.'

'The money isn't important to me, not any more.'

'No? That's interesting. What is important to you, Lisa?'

'Being happy is important, and I'm going to stop doing things I don't want to do, especially when I don't need to.'

'That's very commendable, Lisa, but if you say the money is no longer of any importance to you, why do you need so much of it?'

'I don't.' She stood up, walking closer to the camera. 'I have a plan for the money.'

'Planning is good, Lisa. It puts you back in the driving seat.'

'I only need half of it, and I probably don't even need that. I've decided I'm only going to hold on to fifty thousand euros. The rest can be put to better use.'

'Do you feel that parting with some of the money will help you, Lisa?'

'Yes, I do.' She kept looking at the camera, as if she was talking to herself. 'I realise it doesn't matter how much money I have. Whether it's ninety-five thousand or nine hundred and fifty thousand, I'm still trapped by it. It doesn't mean anything, not really.'

'Lisa, you are more important than the money. You understand that too, don't you?'

'I'm beginning to, but it can be daunting finding a new way.'

'I know that, which is why you must take one step at a time. When you are ready for the next step, you will know.'

Turning from the camera, she sat down again on the chair, lifting her handbag on to her lap, taking out a chequebook. Everything about her body and the expression on her face reflected determination. She believed she was the one in control. Folding the cheque, she got up and placed it on the narrow wall table, then returned to her chair.

'Now,' she said, sounding confident, 'I'm ready for the next step.'

'You'll like it, Lisa. It's called "Continuous Self-motivation". You can pick up a package at the desk outside before you leave. There are motivational discs in it for you to listen to. Try to play them at least three times a day, in the car or if you're relaxing at home in the evening. Make sure to give yourself time. You owe it to yourself now that you have reached Step Eight.'

'Thank you.'

'Terrific, Lisa, you've done very well.'

Kate

HEARING ADAM'S KEY TURN IN THE DOOR, KATE looked at the Mickey Mouse alarm clock – 7.30 a.m. In the hallway, she immediately saw the tiredness in his eyes.

'Is the little man okay?' he whispered.

'He's fine. He was unsettled after you left. I think it was a bad dream.' Stretching and yawning, she asked, 'How did it go in Harcourt Street?'

Putting his arms around her waist, he brought her closer to him. 'Did I ever tell you how sexy you look in the morning?'

'Once or twice.' She kissed him on the lips. 'You look like you've had a tough night.'

'I'm okay.'

'So, what happened to the chief superintendent's brother-in-law?'

'Carbon-monoxide poisoning.'

'Intentional or accidental?'

'It's not looking like an accident.'

'Why not?'

'A few things.'

'Let's go into the bedroom,' she said. 'I'll need to wake Charlie for school in a little while.'

They sat at the end of the bed and he kicked off his shoes, letting out a loud 'Argh', then flopped backwards. She lay down beside him. 'So, why not an accident?'

'The guy locked the garage door for one thing. He put the key on a workbench, and placed padding in the areas that might have allowed in leaks of air. At least, at this point we're assuming it was him.'

'Do you think someone else was involved?'

'Hard to know. His car was still running when his wife found him.' He turned to her. 'More than likely, he didn't suffer.'

'Why do you say that?'

'Some people call it the beautiful death. According to the pathologist, the body prefers carbon monoxide to oxygen. Apparently, it sucks it in willingly.'

'I didn't realise. Is Morrison on this one?'

'Nothing but the best for a relation of the chief super.'

'Anything else important?'

'Are you sure you want to hear all this crap?'

She punched his shoulder. 'Of course I do. I take an active interest in your work.' She didn't attempt to hide the sarcasm.

'Right, you asked for it.' He propped himself on his elbow. 'The skin typically turns cherry red or pink with carbon-monoxide poisoning. As I said, it may be a relatively painless death, but it's not always pretty. A victim can go into convulsions. We'll know more once Morrison has done the full autopsy, but there's a lot about the case I don't like.'

'Go on.'

'It feels too neat, and you know how I hate neatness. Plus, no one has found a suicide note.'

'People don't always …'

'I know that, but the guy was a teacher, or at least a retired one. Before that, he lectured on social policy at Trinity.'

'So?'

'You'd imagine he'd want to leave a few words.'

'Not if he was suicidal – that changes everything.'

'I didn't like the position of the body either.'

'Where was it?'

'On the floor of the garage – that wouldn't be a problem if the body had convulsed. It could have caused the movement, but I don't know. The thing feels staged to me. Either way, Morrison says he would have died quickly.'

She rested a hand on his chest. 'Adam?'

'Yeah?'

'I knew someone who died that way. It was a long time ago.'

'And?'

'I don't know. I guess it always kind of stayed with me. He was a neighbour. The family hadn't been living in the area long when it happened.' She let out a low laugh. 'I remember having a crush on him.'

'You have my interest now.' He sounded more upbeat than he had earlier.

'I was twelve. He was fourteen. He seemed very grown-up at the time. It was stupid, really.'

'What happened?'

'A plastic bag went up the chimney. My father was full of information about it, telling me how the bag had blocked out the supply of oxygen, and a load of other scientific stuff I didn't care about. Dad always liked to sound knowledgeable when it came to these things. None of it mattered. What mattered was that a fourteen-year-old boy had died.' She put her fingers through her hair, staring at the ceiling. 'I used to imagine the way they found him, lying on the floor in the front sitting room, perhaps with earphones on, listening to music.'

'It's no wonder you developed an active interest in the cheerful side of life.'

'Very funny.'

'What was his name, this guy?'

'Kevin. I think my infatuation grew when he was gone. He became the ultimate unattainable love.'

'And now you're stuck with me.'

'I like being stuck with you.'

He leaned in to kiss her, but she held his shoulders, keeping him at arm's length. 'What was the guy's name – the brother-in-law of the chief super?'

'It's time to stop the questions. I need sleep.'

'Humour me.'

'Michael O'Neill.' He lay down. 'Apparently, he couldn't come to terms with being retired.'

'Strange.'

'What is?'

'That was Kevin's surname too, or at least the name of the family he was living with. I think he was fostered.'

'O'Neill?'

'Yeah – I suppose it's a common enough name. Did the O'Neills have any children?'

'Not unless you include the ones he watched in the schoolyard.'

'Was he ...?'

'I'm told by the chief super it was nothing like that. Apparently, he simply couldn't cope with not being there, but it made some of the parents uneasy.'

'I'm sure the school wasn't happy about it either.' She frowned.

'You okay?'

'Yeah, I'm fine, but it must be difficult for his wife, now that's she on her own.'

'I know, and here's the thing, Kate. A guy spends his whole life teaching, helping others, and when it's his turn to live a little, he ends it all.'

'These things can be hard to understand.'

'There's something else.'

'What?'

'Over the last few months, his wife says he's been going to some kind of meetings. He wouldn't say who he was seeing. He kept it all very secretive. I think she partly blames herself.'

'She wasn't to know. A person intent on dying by suicide can keep it from those closest to them.'

'Maybe – but there'll be plenty of digging now, although it will have to be handled sensitively.'

'Sensitively?'

'Being related to the chief super.'

'I see,' she said, unimpressed.

'It's not like that, Kate. It's just that he'll be closely involved. Everything we find out will have to be run by him.'

'Isn't that normal?'

'More or less, but we're talking *everything*.' He waited a few moments, then asked, 'What do you think?'

'About what? The chief super or the investigation?'

'The investigation, of course – the chief super I can handle. Let's say for a second this wasn't a suicide. Other than redirecting blame, why would anyone set it up like that?'

'Was there any sign of forced entry?'

'No.'

'And you've no way of knowing if a second key was used to lock the door on the other side?'

'I guess not.'

'The crime scene always tells you more than you can see.'

'I'm listening.'

'The means of killing is certainly important, but if a potential perpetrator got that close without using any force, assuming another party was involved, then more than likely, they meant something to each other. It's the first marker.'

'Marker for what?'

'The relationship between the killer and their victim.'

The Game Changer

AFTER LISA'S APPOINTMENT, HER CHEQUE FOR forty-five thousand euros, donated to help others within the programme, was locked away in the safe. Lisa believed that separating herself from the money had helped her along the path to self-enlightenment and therefore greater happiness. The Game Changer knew she would progress with speed.

That evening, the only sound in the room was the steady, hypnotic rhythm of tapping on the laptop keyboard as the member/player records were brought up to date.

CENTRE OF LIGHTNESS
20 Steps to Self-enlightenment Programme

Player: Lisa Redmond – Evaluation 7
Attributes: Ambitious and attractive
Career: Webcam sex
Current Bank Balance: €50,000
Step 7: Completed

Money is a form of validation for Lisa. It tells her people will pay for what she is prepared to give them. It also tells her that she is successful and in many ways special. Overall, she doesn't want to perform webcam sex; neither are her actions solely based on a desire to do things well, she being something of a perfectionist. The money is her gold star. Like the cheap paper gold stars her teachers gave her when she behaved well in school (see earlier notes).

Lisa maintained composure throughout the camera interview, but alterations in eye movement were indicative of an exaggeration of her disdain regarding her camers/clients. She sat provocatively with her legs crossed, using sex as a tool. Always impeccably dressed, her appearance and sexual appeal are components in her evaluation of self-worth.

(Page 1 of 2)

CENTRE OF LIGHTNESS
20 Steps to Self-enlightenment Programme

Player: Lisa Redmond – Evaluation 7 continued

As with earlier interviews, Lisa was forthcoming with information about her life. In part, this is because she spends a large proportion of her time lying to massage the ego of her camers/clients.

Step 7 has resulted in the realisation that she doesn't need money to give value to her life, and that, as a person, she is better than the money she possesses.

She enjoys these confessional-type conversations. She also enjoys the repetition of her name. It brings a form of intimacy with a *lock–in* effect, making her think she is special, that she is talking to someone close to her, someone who cares about her health and well-being.

Progression:
Step 8 – Continuous Self-motivation
Desired Outcome – Transfer to group location
Action required
Apply continued pressure to the evaluation of self, emphasising a necessity to be away from the familiar, constituting a change of environment.

(Page 2 of 2)

Sarah

SARAH SINCLAIR STARED AT HER REFLECTION IN THE bathroom mirror, waiting for her husband, John, to close the front door behind him. Her long black hair was a tangled mess, with unruly strands covering her face, almost as if she'd put on a wig the wrong way around. Forty wasn't old, she told herself, but she felt every bit of it.

Lately she'd made a point of getting out of bed only after John had left for work, but today, standing with bare feet in her powder-pink nightdress and dressing gown, she felt excited about the day's possibilities. Everything, she thought, was so much easier when she was alone, especially when she needed to read or listen to her material from Saka and the Centre of Lightness. Pulling the tangled strands off her face, she thought of what Saka had told her about the importance of being *selfish*. Contrary to the term's negative connotations, being selfish was a good thing: it was part of our human survival mechanism.

She had been apprehensive about it at first, indoctrinated by Catholicism as a child, and although she was no longer a believer, a part of her still felt bitter about the restrictions within her early beliefs. Self-sacrifice had been rated too highly, putting others before yourself. Blessed are the meek for they shall inherit the earth. Good girls do as they're told. Never question, keep the faith.

Saka had explained that being influenced by things we no longer believe in was an element of our mind's reluctance to take on new ideas. Sarah could see that now, and the words *selfish* and *survival* finally made sense. Furiously brushing her teeth, she remembered a time when she hadn't wanted to survive, and the thought of that still scared her. With the help of the Centre of Lightness, over time, she had come to realise that those thoughts were temporary. Decisions,

29

or entrenched points of view, were of the moment, and not worth risking a whole lifetime for.

She had never met anyone who could explain things the way Saka could. He allowed her to find her own answers, and it was to him, not John, that she finally admitted her suicidal thoughts. He didn't judge her, he listened. She didn't even mind when the camera was on, or that sometimes Saka's assistant, Jessica, took his place. In some ways the camera helped. It was as if she was talking to herself, clearing the negative thoughts from her mind. Unlike John, Saka wasn't quick to criticise. He didn't look at her as if she was a fool, or as if she had somehow disappointed or annoyed him. John got so angry when she ignored him, but the more she tried to explain about the value of the programme, the more hostile he became. Saka had said, 'Some people will never understand,' and she certainly wasn't going to allow John to upset her today.

When she'd listened to the CD the previous night, it had explained how everyone was on the earth for specific reasons, and that the key to finding out those reasons was inside our minds, waiting to be discovered. She knew she had a lifetime of social conditioning to undo, the kind that made you put other people first. At the last sub-group session, Jessica had explained how we need to seek out the things that others feel are unacceptable. A couple of people had thought this was odd, but Sarah understood what Jessica meant. Plenty of beliefs, Sarah had told them, would have horrified people twenty years ago but were considered perfectly reasonable today. Saka had been there too, and he was proud of her when she'd said that. He didn't say so, but she knew.

Tying her hair in a long side plait, she told herself it was time to go downstairs. She was apprehensive, but she knew she had put off the moment for far too long. It was over half an hour since she'd heard the postman deliver the package. There were no guarantees it was the parcel she was waiting for, but a part of her felt that today would be the day.

Seeing the cardboard box on the kitchen table, she let out a shriek of excitement noticing the foreign stamps. From the size, it couldn't be anything else, could it? Would John have noticed the postmark? Would he have wondered about the contents? She didn't care: she needed to remain focused. Her hands were shaking, a mixture of joy and fear, but she did the breathing exercises Saka had suggested, all the while keeping her eyes on the parcel. 'I want the moment to be perfect,' she said out loud, looking around her to see if anyone else was listening.

For the first time in months, Sarah smiled, thinking about the future. When she lifted the box, it was lighter than she'd imagined, and holding it up to her nose, all she could get was the smell of cardboard. She put it down, took a small knife out of the drawer and used it to rip the adhesive tape, careful not to damage the contents. Folding back all four sides at the top, she paused, wondering if she would be disappointed when she removed the white polystyrene packing beads. She dug her hands in deep, the beads falling like large snowflakes across the kitchen table and spilling on to the floor. She couldn't wait any longer. It didn't matter if she wasn't as Sarah had imagined: once she saw her, she knew she would want to hold her, and love her. She felt a small arm, and again, she let out a tiny cry of joy. She concentrated on the breathing exercises again, telling herself not to rush things. Saka said our minds are amazing receptors of information, yet we miss so many things in our rush to get from point A to point B. She chided herself to take her time, closing her eyes tight as she dug in deeper, reaching for the baby doll, stroking her small arms, then her tiny fingers, touching all ten toes, until finally she lifted Lily out of the box. The baby's blue eyes blinked at her, and in her heart, Sarah knew she had done the right thing.

The Babygro was perfect too, soft white cotton, an exact replica of the one her daughter had worn in the hospital. Unable to restrain herself any longer, she pulled the doll close to her chest, snuggling her, stroking her face, her cheeks and her wisps of hair, which were exactly as Sarah remembered them. She was so beautiful, she thought. Lily was everything Sarah had hoped she would be. 'Forgive Mummy,' she whispered, 'for waiting so long to find you.'

Kate

IT HAD BEEN MORE THAN A WEEK SINCE MICHAEL O'Neill's death, and although Kate knew she had nothing to do with the investigation, it had churned up the old memory of Kevin. Her mind kept drifting back to her early adolescence, a particular sentence repeating itself in her head. Walking towards her study, she muttered, 'The things you can't remember are the very things your mind wants you to forget.' She hadn't been sleeping well either, and her dreams, like that sentence, felt caught in repeat mode, as if trapped.

The previous night, she'd dreamed her father was standing outside their old house. It was late in the evening. He was facing another man, who had looked familiar but she didn't know why. Her father wore his hat down low, shadowing his face, but she was sure he was angry. Every now and then, she'd hear a dog barking, loud and threatening, then lowering to a whimpering wail. She had felt cold, and even though it didn't make any sense, with the streets empty of cars, she kept hearing traffic. There was something about a room, one she couldn't get out of, and it was when she was in that room that she felt the bitter cold, but then the dream skipped. One minute she was looking at her father, the next she wasn't at home. She was staring out of another window, but all she could see was darkness. She could hear the dog barking again and traffic zooming in and out. There was something else, but she couldn't remember what it was. The missing piece of the dream felt close, but beyond her grasp. It was only after she closed the study door that she thought about another afternoon, when her twelve-year-old self was looking out of her bedroom window: she had seen

Kevin talking to a girl, and a man she didn't know. Who were they? She repeated the words again, 'The things you can't remember are the very things your mind wants you to forget.'

She thought about the dog barking again, feeling uneasy. What was wrong with her? Maybe she had too much time on her hands. There had been moments lately, especially in the mornings, with Charlie at school and the chores done, that she'd found herself without a task that she *had* to do. It had never happened when she was working full time. It had been the very opposite, always trying to balance work and personal life, the two overlapping in ways that didn't do justice to either.

The one and only appointment she had at Ocean House that day was after she had dropped Charlie off at school, at 10 a.m. It felt good, she thought, being able to maintain a tentative hold on what had been, until recently, her full-time job. The session had been a positive one too, an ex-abuse victim on the mend, with a fuller, happier and better life. She had been surprised when she bumped into Aoife Copland afterwards. For a few moments, she had wondered if Aoife, an ex-patient of hers, was seeing another psychologist at Ocean House. The girl had seemed a little embarrassed too, blurting out that she was attending meditation sessions. There was no need for her to feel awkward, or to appear to be in an almighty rush to get away. Kate already knew Aoife was in a long-term relationship with Adam's son, Addy. Maybe that was the cause of her awkwardness, but it shouldn't have been. Their connection went back long before that. Anorexia had been a serious problem for Aoife from early puberty but, thankfully, years of counselling had made a difference. Adam might have had issues with Addy, but it seemed to Kate, from listening to the boy himself talk about Aoife, that he had really stood by the girl, especially when the pressure had intensified during her Leaving Certificate and first-year college exams. It was probably a good thing Aoife was now doing meditation. It all fed into a more holistic and balanced approach to life.

Once she had finished at Ocean House, driving home across the city, with the sun shining and autumn crispness in the air, Kate had looked at the myriad shades of the leaves and made up her mind to go for a run at some point that day. Now, unable to think clearly, she felt that a run was exactly the right thing to do, and within ten minutes, she had changed into her gear, the town-hall clock striking midday. At that time, it was relatively laidback in Ranelagh. Children were at school, the commuter traffic had eased, but there was still a bustling hub of village life. The cafés seemed endlessly full, and with the Luas stop only metres from the centre, people coming and going gave the impression of a transient, somewhat cosmopolitan community.

As she headed in the direction of Palmerston Park, the rhythm of her movements got steadier the further up Palmerston Road she went. Part of the footpath was still damp from a shower half an hour earlier and, as if she was a child again, she went out of her way to find pockets of dry leaves that she could crunch – she remembered stomping from one leaf to the next on her way to school.

Before reaching the park she turned left onto Cowper Road, taking a right at the T-junction at Merton Avenue, then ran on to Springfield Road. Their apartment was only a few minutes from her old home, but it had been a long time since she had passed the house. Perhaps it was because of the dreams that she wanted to see her old home again, or maybe it was connecting with Malcolm after all this time, especially his inclination to talk about things that had happened years before. It was only natural, she supposed, for him to enjoy revisiting old times, like friends who hadn't seen each other for years reliving events they had shared. However, their last conversation had caused her to reflect. There had been a sharp slant to his words when he spoke about her father that she hadn't noticed before. She realised that, even though she was a grown woman, she still looked up to him – not, as she had originally thought, like an older brother, but as some kind of surrogate father figure. She found herself unwilling to contradict or challenge him, behaving with a level of shyness, indicative of how she had been as a child. She had always thought that Malcolm and her father were close, but something had been bubbling below the surface, she was sure of it. She increased her pace: suddenly, getting to the house seemed more important than ever. She was breathless when she arrived, not realising she had pushed herself so hard. She stood on the opposite side of the road, not wanting to encroach on the family living there.

There were no cars in the drive, and her mind drifted to when she and her friends had played chasing out the front. She had been an only child, which had meant the company of others outside the house was often far more interesting and nicer than that inside. She had hated those afternoons when the atmosphere felt hostile and threatening, and although she had made peace with her father long before his death, there were emotional bonds that could never be rebuilt in adulthood. That was partly why she understood how hard it was for Addy to accept Adam. These things took time, but time couldn't cure everything.

Leaning back against the railings, she stared at the stone walls of her old home, thinking about her father, what an angry man he could be. Her mother hadn't encouraged his behaviour, or in the early years tried to avert it. At some point, though, during Kate's late teens, her father had withdrawn into himself, and the angry outbursts had subsided. She had asked her mother about it, but all she ever said was that people could change once they had the right motivation. Kate used to wonder about his name too. Valentine, symbolising love, although at times he was certainly a far cry from that.

Lost in thought, she didn't notice an old woman out walking her dog until they were close upon her, and all of a sudden, Kate felt self-conscious about staring at someone else's house. Let them pass, she told herself, but the nearer they got to her, she saw that the dog, a dachshund, was readying itself to attack. With its short legs and elongated body, it pulled hard on the lead, snarling, its lips drawn back, showing its teeth. She reminded herself, he's on a lead, but even so, she pulled in closer to the railings. What if the woman couldn't control the dog? What if it was too strong for her? And as if the animal sensed her fear, it barked loudly, menacingly.

'Stop it, Roger,' the woman roared, pulling the lead shorter. Kate didn't move, waiting for the dog and its owner to walk on. Her heart was thumping, her palms were sweaty and the skin around her ankle tingled. Pull yourself together, she told herself, it's only a dog, but the fear was almost palpable. Something similar had happened to her during a previous conversation with Malcolm. He had mentioned the way her father used to flick his keys from one hand to the other. She hadn't been able to work out why the flash of memory upset her. Now, looking at the house again, she wondered if any of that old stuff was worth obsessing about. She was happy, wasn't she? Why couldn't she forget the past, move on? She bit her bottom lip. Meeting Malcolm after all this time had intensified her questions about the year she was attacked, when she was twelve; even though she repeated in her mind the words she had said to herself many times, *Let it go.*

It was only after she had decided to start back home that she noticed a curtain move in one of the front windows of her old house, that of her parents' bedroom. It happened so quickly that she wasn't sure if she had imagined it. On the spur of the moment she crossed the road, opened the small wrought-iron gate and walked up to the front door, now painted a bright canary yellow. She rang the doorbell, and waited.

She thought about the dog again, its jaws ready to tear at her skin, as she stood back to check for any more movement inside, wondering if this was such a good idea after all. Like earlier, when she had detoured to run this way, the desire to walk around the rooms that held her past was immediate and strong. She told herself people were sympathetic about such things, and although she knew it was a long shot, she also knew that it was important to her to be inside the house.

When the door wasn't answered on the second ring, she stepped back once more. What was it about the house that was unsettling her? Why did she have the feeling that she was being watched? She turned, looking behind her, but other than some passing cars, the street was empty. She rang the doorbell a third time. Again, there was no response, and reluctantly she was forced to walk away. It was only as she opened the gate to leave, and turned to look at the house for the last time that she realised the sensation of being watched had been with her ever since she had crossed the road. Could someone be watching her from inside?

The Game Changer

Beethoven's Symphony No 5, Op. 67 (first movement) was playing at low volume from the sound system. It was a recent favourite of the Game Changer, adding greater energy to the completion of records, player evaluations, progress reports, prescribed readings, seminar content and confidential material under the 20 Steps to Self-enlightenment Programme.

CENTRE OF LIGHTNESS
20 Steps to Self-enlightenment Programme

Confidential Record: 119

Knowledge separates you from the ignorant and followers of social norms.

Outside stimuli, including a person's connection to others, will influence their thoughts and, ultimately, their choices. They can be cajoled, manipulated, convinced of things that they may not otherwise have believed or desired.

Commonplace Examples:

A sales assistant convincing a potential customer they should buy a product, or subliminal advertising creating pathways for things that can easily be done without – altering status from possible desire to essential.

Evaluation of players/members should reflect individual and group benefits, and/or the Game Changer's decision as to whether they should live or die.

(Page 1 of 2)

CENTRE OF LIGHTNESS
20 Steps to Self-enlightenment Programme

Other Notes

1. Parting with money is emotional. A great many people will part with large sums, and continued indoctrination within the programme is essential before moving to STAGE 2.

2. This will primarily be done without the use of blackmail or any other form of obvious coercion. Members will be convinced that what they are doing they are doing of their own free will.

3. Human beings are adaptable. A person can change lifelong habits once they're prepared to invest the time, energy and know-how into changing them. Shock can be useful too. It speeds up the process, but positive methods, praise, good humour, charm, consistent attention, or even physical desire, will assist the process of winning them over.

4. Drip feeding of information into someone's mind will produce a reaction unique to them, but if handled correctly, a person can be convinced that a belief was self-created.

5. Nothing is ever fully guaranteed where human beings are concerned, but group people together (STAGE 2), lead them towards a certain belief and a mighty beast can be created, one that can be blinded in many ways, yet capable of doing things that individually would be impossible.

6. The process is the key: 20 Steps to Self-enlightenment has gone under other names, but the name is immaterial. A name is merely a title – nothing more.

ADDENDUM 09-175:

The killing of people is frequently required. Acceptance of this means everything else is viewed within it – an emotion-free zone where the messy business of morals and other complications no longer applies. Each human being is capable of killing, although some are more adept at it than others.

(Page 2 of 2)

Sarah

EVEN THOUGH IT HAD BEEN A WEEK SINCE LILY'S arrival, Sarah worried that everything must feel so strange and new to her. Yet, she was being so good, never crying or making a fuss. Cuddling her close to her chest, Sarah told her about the box of baby clothes at the bottom of the wardrobe. Part of her knew Lily was too young to understand what she was saying, but she hoped she could sense how happy her mother was, and how much she loved her.

'The clothes have been waiting for you, Lily,' she murmured, 'waiting for you to come home.'

Laying Lily in the centre of the bed, she said, 'Mummy will get you dressed in something nice. Mummy understands that all of this is very new for you. It must have been so dark and scary inside that cardboard box. You had to travel a very long distance on your own, but you're not alone now, and that makes Mummy very happy.'

The doll stared at her, but Sarah didn't mind, energised, rummaging through the clothes, trying to decide on the right outfit. It was the first time she had opened the box of baby clothes in years, and as she felt their softness, a sharp pain hit her in the chest as she thought of all the joy that had been taken from her. She remembered picking out each and every item as if it had happened last week, not five years earlier. None of that darkness mattered now. What mattered, she told herself, was that, at long last, her darling Lily was with her.

Before removing the white Babygro, Sarah checked the radiators were hot enough in the room. She didn't want Lily to catch a chill. Gently manoeuvring the clothes off the doll's arms and legs, even though she was all fingers and thumbs, she kept telling Lily how much she had missed her, and that Mummy would never let her go away again. It didn't take long to change Lily into her coming-home clothes, the ones she'd never had a chance to wear, the ones with the clowns and the bright primary colours. John had said it looked more like an outfit for a boy than a girl, but that was part of his conditioning too, blue for a boy, pink for a girl. He probably wanted Lily to wear something with a princess on the front – more nonsense that the world used to warp thoughts.

After Lily was dressed, Sarah wrapped her in a cream blanket, holding her close and sitting on the rocking chair. It felt completely natural to open her blouse and snuggle Lily to her right breast. At first, she was unresponsive, but then Sarah got that tingling sensation, and they both relaxed some more. Soon Lily closed her eyes, falling into sleep. Sarah waited a long time before moving. When she stood up, the rocking chair creaked but, thankfully, the sound didn't wake Lily as she took her into her bed.

Sarah knew John wouldn't be happy about Lily being in their bed. He'd say Sarah was starting a bad habit and that she should be putting the baby in her cot. As if any of that nonsense mattered. Nobody ever said they wished they hadn't held or loved their baby quite so much. They said the very opposite. Lily could sleep with her for as long as she wanted to. She would try her in the Moses basket later on, in case she preferred it. It was in the storage cupboard downstairs. She would put the cot together too. John's tools were in the garage. It shouldn't be too hard to follow the instructions.

John had wanted to get rid of everything, to pretend Lily had never existed, that her life hadn't happened. Sarah wasn't having any of that, not any more. Her love was too strong. It was the pain of trying to hide it that messed up her head. You had to be a mother to understand these things. Her life had changed the moment Lily was born. Nothing would ever be the same – she didn't want it to be.

Sarah hadn't cried since the day they told her how sick Lily was. She wouldn't allow herself to cry, but in her heart she knew that Lily would never leave her, and now they were together again, and she had had her first proper feed. Neither John nor anyone else was going to spoil that. For the first time in five years, she allowed the tears to flow.

Pulling a blanket over both of them, she thought how lucky she was to have her darling Lily beside her. She remembered Saka's words, about taking it one step at a time, and how each step would bring her closer to where she needed to be.

Kate

THE RUN BACK TO THE APARTMENT HELPED KATE TO settle her thoughts, her steady breathing easing her anxiety. When she turned the key in the front door, she heard the phone ring and saw from the caller ID that it was Malcolm.

'Hello,' she said, sounding as upbeat as she could.

'Are we still okay for later on? I've booked the restaurant for eight thirty.'

She could hear traffic noises at the other end of the line. Darn it, she'd forgotten they were due to meet for dinner. 'Sure. If Adam gets back on time that should be fine. He's working on a new investigation, so I can't be a hundred per cent. I can let you know later.'

'What's the case about?'

'A suspected suicide.'

'Suspected?'

'You know how these things are.'

'Actually, I don't, Kate. Why don't you explain them to me?'

'All sudden deaths are investigated, and this one was a little unusual.'

'I suppose it can pay to have a suspicious mind.'

'I guess it can, Malcolm.'

'Are you still writing in your journals as I suggested? It's a great way to free the mind. I know it certainly helps me.'

'Yes, but ...' She thought about what had happened earlier, her feeling of being watched, and her reaction to the dog. 'I'm writing about old stuff.'

'You can put anything you want in the journal, Kate. It's your call.'

She wondered should she tell him about the repeating dream, and how that sentence kept going around in her head. She wasn't seeing him professionally, but at times it was as if he was treating her like a client, or was it her? Was she depending on him more than she knew? 'The writing seems to be triggering a reaction of sorts, that and other things.'

'What other things? What kind of reaction?'

She had no intention of telling him that he was part of it. At least, not yet. Instead, she said, 'It's weird. I mean, I've never been happier than I am now, spending time with Charlie, taking a step back from work, being with Adam, living a less hectic existence. I'm even getting to know my neighbours.' She laughed.

'So what's the problem?'

Be honest, she told herself. He's only trying to help. Isn't that a good thing? 'The problem is that every now and then I'm getting this negative feeling, a kind of fear, I guess.'

'What are you afraid of?'

'Different things. Like today, when I was out running, I was terrified by a dog. That hasn't happened to me in years. I got over that phobia a long time ago.'

'The journal writing could be a factor, Kate, depending on what you're writing about.'

'You sound like you're psychoanalysing me, Malcolm.'

'Sorry, force of habit.'

'No need to apologise. It's fine. I know you want to help.'

'So, if it's not a big secret, Kate, what exactly are you writing about?'

'As I said, most of it seems to be focused on years ago, my childhood, things about my parents and other stuff.'

'It's not unusual to look backwards, but I suppose it depends on whether or not there's a particular area of concentration.'

She didn't respond.

'Kate, if you don't want to talk to me about it, you don't have to.'

'No, it's not that. It feels strange talking about it out loud, that's all.'

'Now you know how our clients feel.'

'I guess.'

'Kate, are you still worried about those memory gaps? You know it's perfectly normal for everyone to have them.'

'It's not only that.' She wondered whether she should be more specific.

'Kate, are you still there?'

'Yes, I'm here ... I keep going back to that time I was attacked.'

'When you were twelve?'

'Yes.'

'Maybe there are still some unresolved issues around it. I don't need to tell you how the mind works.'

'Perhaps I have too much time on my hands.'

Kate wasn't sure why, but all of a sudden, she didn't feel like talking about it any more. 'Look, Malcolm, I'm really sorry, but I've only just arrived back at the apartment, and there's a few things I need to do. We can talk later.' She heard a police siren down the phone line.

'That's up to you, Kate.'

'Where are you by the way?'

'I'm out having a stroll. I'm not as energetic as you are – no running as of yet.'

'You know the mantra, Malcolm. Thirty minutes a day to keep the body healthy.'

'That's what they say.'

'Look, I'd better go.'

'Can I ask you one last question, Kate?'

'Sure.'

'Have you written anything specific about your mystery attacker?'

'Why do you ask?'

'I'm concerned, that's all, or perhaps concerned is too strong a word.'

'What do you mean?'

'Sometimes a physical reference can conjure up all sorts of possibilities that may or may not be reliable. Sorry, I don't mean to pry.'

'You're not prying. And thanks for the warning. As I said, it's probably nothing more than having too much time on my hands.'

'Call me if you need anything.'

Hanging up, she checked her watch. It was two o'clock. She needed to pick Charlie up in less than an hour. Why had she held back with Malcolm? Maybe a part of her didn't want to share the information until things made more sense to her.

Taking out her journal, she recorded her visit to the house, along with the feeling that someone had been watching her, wondering whether she had imagined the curtain moving in what used to be her parents' bedroom. It was only then that she heard the footsteps walking towards the front door of the apartment. Putting down her pen, she closed the journal and went out to the hall. The footsteps had stopped. She was about to go back inside when she saw the large white envelope on the hall floor. It must have been slid under the door. Picking it up, she looked at the front – it was blank. Perhaps it was meant for Adam, but either way, she tore it open, finding what looked like cut-up newspaper clippings inside.

Walking into the living room, she laid them flat on the coffee table, realising the cut-out shapes were joined, each one forming an individual letter. They combined to make a sentence. She stared at the words, hardly believing what she was reading, and at the same time wondering what the message – 'I REMEMBER YOU KATE' – actually meant. The edges had been cut using pinking shears, a line of small triangles on each of the sides. Who remembered her? It couldn't be him. Could it? Not after all this time, surely.

She contemplated phoning Adam, but what could he add that her own two eyes didn't tell her?

It was then that she wondered if someone had followed her from her old house. She looked through the peep-hole in the front door, but didn't see anything out of the ordinary. Nervous, she opened the door, looking left and right, jumping when she heard movement in the apartment above, her heart skipping, relieved that the communal hall was empty. But someone had been there. Someone had put that envelope under the door. It hadn't been there when she arrived. It had to have been delivered when she'd heard the footsteps. How had someone managed to get into the building without a code? It didn't make sense. But no matter how she thought about it, there was no denying one simple fact. Whoever had created the message knew where she lived.

The Game Changer

DACNOMANIA: AN OBSESSION WITH KILLING, encompassing the method used, the level of terror and agony felt, including specific details of density of wound or wounds, and the length of time it takes a person to die.

CENTRE OF LIGHTNESS
20 Steps to Self-enlightenment Programme

OBSERVATIONAL TARGET: Kate Pearson
Visit to Apartment, 7 September 2015

The boy, Charlie, delayed picking up his bag for school, and while the target was distracted at the front door, access was achieved. A momentary turn of her head facilitated the opportunity.

The main bedroom was in mid-flux, the sheets and duvet half hanging off the bed, her discarded T-shirt and underwear still on the floor. The blinds were down, and the room was in semi-darkness. There were strands of her hair on a pillow. It smelt of jasmine. On rolling the hair like a miniature fluff-ball, her presence felt close.

More smells were noted. She and her partner had made love at some point in the last twenty-four hours. The study door was locked, and a prolonged visit will be necessary to locate the key.

(Page 1 of 2)

CENTRE OF LIGHTNESS
20 Steps to Self-enlightenment Programme

OBSERVATIONAL TARGET: Kate Pearson continued …

Trust is where the true power game lies. Trust ensures minds will behave as the Game Changer wants them to.

Scepticism, as always, is commonplace, but uncertainty feeds into the illusion of free choice. Ultimately, if people get what they want, or what they think they want, their initial scepticism will serve as proof that they have come to a conclusion on their own terms – and a shift in perspective will be achieved.

The first note has been delivered to the target. This will send her in all kinds of directions. Doubt, uncertainty, unanswered questions are a distraction, and will feed into the overall objective. The subject will become further absorbed in the note and the identity of the sender.

Action required:
1) Revisit apartment
2) Gain access to study
3) Continue close observation
4) Step up emotional pressure

(Page 2 of 2)

Addy

ADDY KEPT HIS HANDS TUCKED DEEP INSIDE THE pockets of his grey hoody as he listened to 'Work Song' by Hozier on his iPod. He crossed the road at the mini-shopping centre near his house in Templeogue, an area made up of a series of interconnecting housing estates built in the early seventies, predominately occupied by middle-class families.

Looking at his reflection in the newsagent's window, he smiled – every afternoon after school he'd used the glass to check his height. There was a time when his reflection barely reached the Slush Puppie machine in the window. As a kid he'd used it to measure any gains in height. His growth had been limited from the age of thirteen, but that changed after his fifteenth birthday when he'd shot up. His copper brown hair had become longer over the summer and, much to his mother's annoyance, he wore it in a man bun with unruly strands constantly fighting to get free.

He checked the time on his phone. It was an hour since he'd had the text from Aoife, asking him to call over. Addy liked the way he didn't have to pretend with her. She didn't go on like his mother did about giving Adam a chance. Aoife understood his hurt, and how being ignored by your father for your whole goddam life, especially one living in the same goddam city, made you feel like shit. Adam wasn't anything like Addy had thought he would be. Addy had seen all those programmes on television about lost family members being reunited and how, when they met, there was an instant bond between them. As far as he was concerned, Adam might as well have been landed on the earth by aliens for all they had in common. He had called Addy on the mobile earlier, but Addy hadn't answered, not keen on having another of those strained, meaningless conversations.

Leaving the newsagent's, he texted Aoife to say he'd be there in ten minutes. She lived on the other side of a large communal green, and on the way there, he worried that something was up. She'd been a bit elusive lately, and he had to admit, he preferred it when she depended on him more. Then, he felt on safer ground.

Reaching her house, a three-bed semi-detached identical to his own, with cream pebbledash and large windows, he pulled his earphones out, ringing the doorbell, more convinced than ever that things mightn't be as cool as he wanted them to be. A couple of alarm bells were going off in his head, like how she'd been acting differently recently, and the fear of her dumping him had crossed his mind more than once. Sure, he knew he'd been a bit needy, but he'd been there for her when things were tough. Still, he told himself, best not to go on about Adam just in case.

'Hiya,' he said, as she opened the door. He bent to kiss her.

'Stop.' She giggled. 'Come in, before the neighbours see you.'

He stepped inside.

'I was meditating.'

'Is everything okay? Your text sounded a bit urgent.'

'No, everything's fine,' she said. 'Couldn't be better.'

That sounded hopeful. 'So what's with the "come straight over"?'

'Mum and Dad are out so we can talk freely.' He followed her into the living room, and when they were both sitting down, she said, 'Addy, I don't want to upset you.'

Shit, he thought, this is it. After all this time, she's going to dump me.

She was staring at his socks. 'Why don't you ever wear a matching pair?'

'Things don't need to match. My mother loves things that match. Socks are socks, you know. You can work hard, or work smart.'

'You're nuts.'

'I'm not. You were saying … about not wanting to upset me.' Keep it cool, he told himself.

'That's why I was meditating. Saka says it's the best way to find the right words for things.'

'I don't like that guy. I mean, it's not even his real name.'

'It is his real name if he wants it to be. People get hung up on things that are of no importance, ignoring what really matters.'

'So what does matter?'

'What matters is the kind of person you are, not a label, but if you really want to know, the reason he uses it is because it reflects a deep inner desire for love, and to work with others to achieve peace and harmony.'

'He told you this, did he?'

'You can look it up for yourself, if you don't believe me. It's an Indian word. Anyway, you've never met him. You shouldn't judge people you've never met.'

'I'm not judging him.' He was pushing it, he knew, but he wasn't going to turn into a whimpering mouse, even if his neck was on the line. She gave him one of her disappointed looks.

'Is he Irish, this Saka guy?'

'Yeah, he's a bit like my dad.'

'That's kind of weird, don't you think?'

'Stop being stupid.'

It was his turn to give her a look.

'You don't have to be so angry, Addy.'

'I'm not angry, but I don't like being called stupid.' He checked the time on his mobile.

'Are you in a hurry?' An element of hurt had entered her voice.

'I promised Carl I'd meet him for a game of pool, but it's okay, he'll wait.' Putting his arm around her shoulders, his voice sounding sympathetic, he said, 'Come on, tell me what's bugging you.'

She took a deep breath. 'Remember I was explaining about the steps in the programme, how each one brings you closer to the person you really need to be?'

'Sure.'

'I was really proud of myself today.' Her voice quivered. 'Even Saka said to get to step five this fast is amazing for someone as young as me.'

'You're nineteen.' He felt insulted. It was his age too.

'To him, that's young.'

'I guess when you're old, everyone is young.'

'He's only fiftyish, younger than my dad, and he's really fit.'

He didn't want to visualise an image of a fit fifty-something, especially one *helping* his girlfriend, and it was then he heard the voice coming from upstairs. 'Who's that?'

'Oh, don't worry. It's only a recording. I listen to Saka's voice during the day now. It's part of the meditation. The more familiar I am with it, the quicker I can relax.'

'Do you have to go to this guy?'

'He's helping me.'

'Okay, but turn your man off. It's creeping me out.'

When she darted upstairs, he texted Carl, telling him he'd be a while. He wasn't happy about Aoife listening to recordings at home. She had tried to play a CD in his mum's car too: relaxation CDs and driving weren't a good combo.

Coming back into the room, she picked up where she'd left off. 'Step five is about looking at your life in a scientific and logistical way.'

'That's how they study mice in an experiment, isn't it?'

She ignored his question. 'It's about examining the things you do, and logically working out the reasons *why* you do them. Saka says we all do things for a reason, but sometimes our choices are made out of habit rather than desire. Some things that might have seemed important to you when you were younger may not be important any more.'

'So?'

'So, even though they're not right for you any more, you still do them. It's called *repeat behaviour*, striving to reach something you don't really want or that's no longer necessary.'

'The point?'

She let out a long sigh. 'It's why at times you need to take a step back and work out if you're doing them out of habit or desire.'

'Meaning what exactly?' His concern about her dumping him was coming back.

'I'm not like you, Addy. I don't have all the answers.'

'I never said I did.'

'Look.' She took his hand.

This is it, he thought. She's going to do it now.

'All I'm saying is that I've had to work out a certain amount of crap over the last while.'

If she says, *It's not you, it's me*, he made up his mind he wouldn't even bother answering. He would bolt out of the door before she could say any more.

'You see, Addy, I often do things to please others.'

Maybe this is all about her parents, he thought. Probably best not to jump in too soon.

'I conform too easily.'

'No, you don't.'

'You don't know what I'm like around my parents. It's suffocating.'

Right – good. He wasn't the target. 'We all conform, Aoife. You'd want to hear my mother going on about my room. Christ, like it matters a shit. The amount of times I want to tell her to chill out and ...'

'It's not about stupid things like that. It's about the big stuff.' Tears welled in her eyes.

'Go on, then.'

'I started to ask myself why I chose to go to college in Dublin, and not Glasgow.'

He had thought it was to stay near him, but he didn't say anything.

'Sure, I knew it would cost my parents more, but they said they could manage it. I didn't want to be a burden ...'

'That's fair enough.'

'No, it's not. Saka says if you want something, if you really want it, you have to make it happen.'

'Yeah, well, it isn't always that easy.'

'No, Addy, you're wrong.'

'You're not going to start quoting that positivity stuff?'

'Saka says that by repeat visualisation, concentrating on the idea or the goal that is important to you, you're taking the first step to making your hope become a reality.'

'Saka says a lot.'

Looking at her reaction, he knew his last remark was a mistake. She would either go all quiet now, or she'd do that thing that drove him mad: go back to the beginning and explain it all over again. When his phone bleeped with a text message, he picked it up quickly. 'It's only Carl,' he said. 'Ignore him.'

The rejection of Carl seemed to earn him some Brownie points. Maybe he was still on safe ground.

'I came to a decision this morning, Addy.'

'Decision?'

'I have to start considering what I really want out of life, and not allow anything else to get in the way. If you believe in something, it's more likely to happen.' The last sentence sounded as if she was trying to convince herself.

'Okay, okay, I get you, I think.'

He could see she was about to cry. So much, he thought, for everything being great. Maybe he should hug her, but what if she was dumping him? He'd look like a right fool if he did.

'I made a mistake in deciding not to go to Glasgow. I compromised my needs and wants by convincing my parents it was the right decision because I didn't want them to pay out any more money.'

'Then tell them you changed your mind.'

'It's too late.'

'It's not. There's always next year. Finish the year at UCD, and then start over.'

'I'm leaving college.'

'You can't.'

'I can. Saka says we all need *time out* to work out the next part of our life.'

'Can we stop talking about your man?'

Again she gave him a look. 'Saka says some people live their lives like speed trains, doing things they think they're supposed to do because they don't take the time out to stop and ask the right questions.'

'You think you've been on a speed train?'

'Yes.'

'So get off it, but do the year, then apply for Glasgow in the meantime. Your parents will be grand. It'll make more sense that way.'

'It's not about what makes sense to them, it's about what makes sense to me.'

'I know that.'

'What's the point in jumping from one thing straight into another? I need time to reflect. Anyhow, Saka said I can go to the island for a while.'

'You can't be serious? I mean, think about this for a minute.'

'I have thought about it. I've done nothing but think about it. You can come too if you want.'

'What? Go to a retreat house? Plant vegetables and pick stones off a beach?'

'Among other things – I've asked Saka about it already.'

'Asked him what?'

'About you coming for a while – he was fine about it. He said there were always plenty of chores that needed doing and an extra hand would be great.'

'I'm not going to any island, and neither are you. This is nuts.' He realised he was shouting, and a couple of milliseconds later that she was looking at him as if he was the one who'd lost his mind.

'I thought you'd understand. Saka said it might be like this, that lots of people would criticise, but that none of it matters. What matters is that I'm sure.'

'He's brainwashed you.'

'No, he hasn't.'

'Listening to CDs and messing with your head.'

His phone rang. It was Carl again. His timing was always bloody awful. 'Carl, I'll ring you back.' But by the time he'd hung up, Aoife had already adopted the *I'm okay, I don't need you* stance. He decided on a change of approach. Keep a level head. 'Look, Aoife, I'm not saying you're wrong. All I'm saying is that it's a bit drastic. What do you know about this guy? He could be a serial killer.'

'Now you're being daft.'

He moved in closer. 'I'm mad about you, Aoife, you know that.'

She smiled, her strained facial muscles easing. 'I know you care about me, Addy. Why do you think I asked Saka about you coming? The commune is very careful about who they invite.'

She's really serious, he thought. She's actually going to an island off the south coast to join a crowd of nutcases.

'I haven't told my parents. Not yet.'

He felt relief flooding in. There was still a chance she'd change her mind.

'I wanted to tell you first.'

'When are you going to talk to them?' He sounded as nervous as he felt.

'This evening.'

'I can meet you afterwards.'

She kissed him on the cheek. 'No, that's okay, Addy. I've booked a seat on a late bus. I'll need to get organised. I won't be packing a lot but ... '

'Your parents won't let you go.' He'd raised his voice again.

For a few seconds she didn't respond. Then she said, 'I'm an adult. My parents can't stop me.'

'Then I won't let you go.'

'You can't stop me either. Don't you get it? I need to do this. I've never been more serious or determined about anything in my life. I'm going to the island, Addy, and that's final.'

Kate

DRIVING BACK FROM SCHOOL WITH CHARLIE, KATE couldn't get the newspaper-cutting note out of her mind. The 'who' and the 'why' had kicked in fast, quickly followed by how threatening she should consider it to be. Its delivery to the apartment was an infringement of personal space, which was never a good thing, especially with a form of menace attached. Someone had an agenda, otherwise why stay anonymous?

It could be a disgruntled ex-client, someone who had followed her home from Ocean House. Neither could she discount the possibility that it was connected to an old police investigation, or even her own distant past. Each one was a strong contender, but no matter which way she turned it around, the sender had crossed the line, and once someone did that, they could do more. They knew where she lived, and they potentially knew the code to her apartment building. They were also telling her that, if they wanted to, they could take it a step further.

'What's wrong, Mum?' Charlie asked, from the back seat.

'Nothing, sweetheart.' She glanced at him in the rear-view mirror, realising he looked anxious. 'There's nothing wrong, honey. I'm trying to work something out, and not doing a very good job.' Smiling, she asked, 'How were your friends at school?'

'They're good. There were two boys and one girl out sick today.'

'Who?'

'Carla, Shay and Alex.'

'No doubt they'll be back soon. What did the teacher say about practising for the school play?' Keep it normal, she told herself, keep talking. There's no point in letting things get out of proportion.

'We've to practise *all the time*.' The last three words came slowly, as if he was copying his teacher's voice.

'Did anything exciting happen?' Kate indicated to turn left.

'We got to watch *A Bug's Life*. It was cool.'

Pressing her foot on the brake, slowing down because of the backlog of school traffic, she asked, 'What did you like most about it?'

'I liked the way one ant stood up for the other ants, and then at the end, the smaller ant saved the day.'

'I like that too.'

'Mum, I'm starving.'

'I know you are. We won't be long.'

'Can we go to McDonald's?'

What's the harm? she thought. One trip to McDonald's isn't going to be the end of the world. Changing direction, she turned the car right on to Rathmines Road.

'Yay!' Charlie roared. 'I want large fries this time.'

It felt good holding his hand crossing the road. A part of her was still getting used to doing things on the spur of the moment. On the way to McDonald's, Charlie talked and talked. Marbles was the latest craze at school, and collecting match cards of football players was high on the list too.

'Some cards, Mum, are harder to get than others. They're rarer.'

'I see.'

'If I got two Wayne Rooneys, I could swap him for five different ones. Dad's getting me a book for the match cards, so I can keep track of the ones I want to keep and the ones I have for swaps.'

'That's good.'

'Can Patrick come over on Saturday? His dad is getting him a match book too.'

She remembered the note: others coming to the apartment didn't seem like such a good plan. 'I'll have a chat with his mum.'

'Patrick's dad supports Manchester United.'

'That's good.'

'Patrick's going to play in the Premier League when he's bigger.' His words tumbled out. 'For his birthday, he got new boots. They cost a lot of money, but his mum says they're an investment. What's an investment, Mum?'

'Hmm, it's sort of like doing something today for a reward in the future.'

'Do you mean like practising my singing for the school concert?'

'Yes, the more you practise, the better you'll be.'

'Some people, like my friend Ella, are brilliant already. She doesn't have to practise, even though the teacher tells her to.'

She raised her eyebrows, but Charlie took no notice. He kept on talking, and the only time he stopped was when he had a fistful of chips in his mouth. She liked listening to him, to how contented he sounded.

Before she left the apartment, she had locked the newspaper-cutting note in her study, not wanting Charlie to see it when they got back. As he ate his chips, another thought crossed her mind. What if whoever had left the note was watching them now? She did a quick survey of the people in the various booths: two teenage schoolgirls chatting away, and what looked like a grandmother with her grandson, a mother with a baby asleep in a buggy beside her and a toddler stuffing a burger into his mouth. None of them looked out of the ordinary. Behind her, she saw a woman sitting on her own, reading a book. She was about the same age as Kate, attractive with similar hair colouring. There was something familiar about her, but Kate couldn't work out what it was. Maybe she'd seen her before at the school, or out and about. She was forced to turn away, embarrassed, when the woman caught her eye.

This, Kate thought, was exactly what the person who left the note had wanted, for her to be uneasy, apprehensive, jumping to conclusions about innocent people. Determined she wasn't going to give anyone the satisfaction of messing with her head, she kept on talking to Charlie, as if everything was perfectly fine. As he licked the salty cardboard of the chip packet, she finally said, 'Come on, we've homework to do before it gets late, not to mention singing practice.'

'Ah, Mum.'

Not so long ago, she mused, she would have been up to her neck in case files. She knew she'd have to talk to Adam about the note. How seriously should she take it? Perhaps it was a one-off, somebody's idea of a joke, but what if it wasn't? What then? As if he had read her mind, when they reached the car her phone rang, and it was him.

'Hi, Adam,' she answered, still holding Charlie's hand. 'What's up?'

'My son is what's up.'

'Oh?'

'He won't return my calls.'

'He will. Give him time.'

'Sorry, that's not why I rang.'

'Hold on a second, I need to put Charlie in the car.'

'Okay.'

Once Charlie was safely buckled in, she decided against putting the phone on the hands-free set, instead stepping outside the car to ask again, 'What's up?'

'It's the Michael O'Neill case.'

'Has something turned up?'

'You could say that.'

'Go on.'

'I know you're not on the case, and I don't want to be pulling you into—'

'It's fine. If you have a question, ask it.'

'I've been contacted by a Detective Lee Fisher from NYPD.'

'What? New York?'

'That's right. It seems they have unidentified DNA from a murder scene in Manhattan a few months back.'

'So?'

'Fisher sounds like a needle-in-a-haystack kind of guy. The victim in New York was Irish. He got it into his head that there could be more to the Irish connection.'

'And?'

'Interpol in Washington contacted our Interpol division in the Phoenix Park. The principal impetus behind the enquiry was vis-à-vis murders or suspicious deaths in Ireland, those with a similar gender, age, social profile and, of course, nationality as the New York victim. Fisher didn't think the killing was a one-off.'

'Okay.'

'With the suspicion behind O'Neill's death, for DNA purposes we quarantined the lengths of tape used to seal off the area around the air vents. We needed to establish whether or not O'Neill had done it. We managed to extract sweat marks, probably from the victim's fingers. Long story short, they were his, but only after we pulled a full DNA profile from the victim.'

'That was fast.'

'No comment.'

'I'm sure the chief super was very close to his late brother-in-law. He must be very pleased with the efficiency.'

'Let it go, Kate.'

'Fine, but the results from the tape will only add credence to it being a suicide. I'm still not getting how this is connected with Fisher's case.'

'That's what we thought initially, but the DNA profile was sent to our guys in the Park.'

'And?'

'It turns out they've found a match with the Manhattan case.'

'I didn't think the US and Ireland could share that kind of information, what with jurisdictional boundaries, international data confidentiality, et cetera.'

'No, but with both victims being from Dublin, and the other similarities, it was enough to legitimise the contact. There is a good relationship between the two countries. We were able to exchange the information on an intelligence basis.'

'I see.'

'If it goes any further, Kate, and by that I mean if the US wants something admissible in court, they'll have to produce their own sample. Information collected using intelligence isn't admissible in court proceedings.'

'Meaning they'd have to come over here to produce their own DNA profile.'

'Or have it brought to them for analysis.'

'You said they found a match? What details do you have? Was O'Neill's DNA found at the Manhattan killing?'

'The killing was vicious. The victim had parts of his body amputated. The unidentified DNA is from a pen they believe the killer used to mark the incision lines. The sample was taken in the same way as in the O'Neill case, from palm or finger sweat. It's O'Neill's DNA on the pen.'

'You can't be serious?'

'Never more, but it gets better.'

'How?'

'O'Neill has never been to New York, and certainly not when the murder happened. He hadn't left the country in the last twelve months – and get this, when Mason was being chopped up, O'Neill was with the chief super all weekend, playing golf.'

'Mason?'

'That's the victim's name, Tom Mason.'

'The politician?'

'Ex-politician. Why? Did you know him?'

'My father knew someone by that name a long time ago.' Kate leaned into the car. 'Sorry, honey, Mum needs another couple of minutes.'

'Don't be long.'

'I won't – promise.'

Once the car door was closed, she picked up her conversation.

'None of this is making any sense, Adam. If O'Neill wasn't in New York, does Fisher think the DNA was planted?'

'He does, and he's not the only one.'

'But even if someone wanted to frame O'Neill, they'd know that if he hadn't left the country, he'd be cleared.'

'Which is why, Kate, I'm phoning you to ask you what you make of it.'

Kate didn't know what to think, but if it was the same Tom Mason, he'd have been a close friend of her father. Malcolm would know him too. 'I assume you're looking at other connections between Mason and O'Neill.'

'Yes, but Mason had been living in New York for over twenty years.'

'Well, if the plant of the DNA was deliberate, it could be a message of sorts.'

'What kind of message?'

'I don't know, but if it wasn't to shift the blame to O'Neill, then either it's a cryptic form of communication designed to lead someone away from or to the truth, or …'

'Or what?'

'Someone is playing a power game.'

'I'm not getting you.'

'They want people to know they're controlling things, that they're capable of a lot more than murder.'

'So you're saying they have a set plan.'

'Could be. If Fisher's hunch is correct, about it not being a one-off killing, it brings O'Neill's death into the mix as another potential victim.'

'It's a completely different MO, Kate.'

'I know that, but it doesn't mean the same person didn't orchestrate both deaths. Even if O'Neill sealed the air vents, we can't be sure he didn't do so under duress. Potentially, all it's telling us is that the killer is capable of varying their method.'

'Meaning?'

'Don't underestimate them.'

'I won't.'

'Adam, there's something else.'

'What?'

She knew there was no other way of saying it. She gave Charlie a reassuring look. 'I got an anonymous note. It was sent to the apartment.'

'When?' His tone was sharper, snappier.

'About an hour ago.'

'What did it say?'

'It said, "I remember you Kate."'

'Jesus.'

'It could be someone's idea of a joke.'

'I'm not laughing.'

'Neither am I. It was created using old newspaper clippings. It could be an ex-client. It could be anyone.'

'Do you have the note with you?'

'No, it's back in the apartment.'

'We'll need to get it checked.'

'I know that.'

'Have you any idea what it means?'

'That's the thing, Adam, it could be almost anything.'

Getting back into the car, a number of miniature explosions were going off in her mind. Even though she hadn't said it to Adam, it was as if everything was pointing her in one direction. The dreams, the repetitive sentence, her journal writing, the similarities between Michael O'Neill's death and Kevin's, the note and now Tom Mason. Could it all be coincidence? She had enough life experience to know it could, and that the easiest thing in the world was to jump to conclusions, forming an incorrect or incomplete analysis. When had her life started to become a mini-investigation? But the note was important. There was no denying that.

312a Atlantic Avenue, Brooklyn, New York

THE LOFT APARTMENT OF LEE FISHER WAS LOCATED on the ninth floor of a seventies apartment building that was only a stone's throw from Brooklyn Detention Center, but also close to the Atlantic Terminal on Hanson Place. Apart from the steel balconies attached to the lower units, the building looked more like an office complex than a residential block. Still, that high up, the view was better, even if the neighbourhood had some downsides.

It had been a long day. Lee walked along the upper corridor, with its tiled impersonal cream walls and floor, and went into his apartment. Inside he had a better sense of self. Ten years earlier, he'd moved into the blank canvas with white walls and wooden flooring, but the minimalist look hadn't lasted. Lee was a hoarder of anything useful, including old newspapers, books, ashtrays, glass, cutlery that didn't match, and containers in all shapes and sizes. The largest object, other than the retro upholstered black and maroon striped sofa, with four seats, was a red vintage double-fronted Westinghouse fridge. Lee liked to cook, and he liked his fridge. He also liked living alone. The four seats accommodated stretching, nothing more.

He flicked on the television, a modern flat-screen with high resolution. There was a cup with stale coffee in it to the side. Picking it up, he poured the contents down the plughole of the enamel white kitchen sink. WABC-TV Eyewitness News was talking about a doctor who had removed a huge tumour from a three-day-old infant girl. It didn't matter what was on, because Lee was only half paying attention.

His eyes felt gritty, his body tired. The breakthrough on the Tom

Mason investigation would take some time to unravel, although there was no denying the link with the suicide in Ireland. The Irish detective had been helpful, and right now, it was over to him to search for other connections. The DNA found at the scene allied the dead men as closely as if they'd been married. The big question was what it all meant, and who else was swimming in this murky pond. Mason had lived in Manhattan for a couple of decades, long enough for Lee to grasp that, if the same killer linked the two men, ancient history could be playing a part.

He took a cold beer out of the fridge, then fired his scuffed leather jacket onto the far end of the sofa. History, he thought, usually meant old grudges, scores to be settled that had been simmering for some time, and simmering was never a good thing, at least not as far as murder was concerned.

Addy

LYING IN HIS BEDROOM, ADDY IGNORED THE CALLS from Carl and Adam. All he could think about was Aoife. He hadn't put any music on, despite his mother constantly knocking on the door asking him if he was okay. He was far from okay, but he wasn't going to share that with anyone.

Carl rang again. He let it ring out. Carl had been the first in his class to lose his virginity. It had happened one night after the local disco. The event sort of turned him into something of a celebrity within the group, and somehow his raised status still existed. The only girl Addy had ever been with was Aoife. They had been going out together for more than a year before it had happened, and he hadn't told anyone about it. It was none of their damn business.

When his mother knocked on the door again, asking him if he wanted any supper, his answer was one word: 'No.' He waited until he heard her walk down the stairs before he relaxed a little. The first time he had met Aoife, she had been wearing dark skinny jeans and a baggy green jumper. It was only afterwards that he discovered the jumper was to cover up her body shape. Her vulnerability, if anything, made her more attractive to him. He didn't have all the answers, but he wanted to protect her, to make her well.

Damn her and her 20 Step Programme, he thought, but at the same moment he wondered if he should go with her. It couldn't be any worse than being trapped inside his bedroom. College wouldn't start for another six weeks. He could still follow her.

She had given him a small booklet. The words on the opening page said: 'If you WANT something, you can HAVE it.' Inside, the contents were full of suggestions for bettering your life. What was the harm in swapping one crap situation for another?

Everything felt messed up. Aoife hadn't said she was finishing with him, but if she cared that much, she wouldn't leave. Would she?

He thought again of how they had been together since the end of fifth year. At the end of the school term, they had celebrated in town, a whole gang of them, but she had been the one person in the crowd who had stood out. It wasn't just her laughing at his jokes or how attractive she was to him: it was the way she could turn serious all of a sudden, becoming so enthusiastic about stuff.

Even if this whole self-improvement lark wasn't his kind of thing, at least she'd had the courage to go for it. What was he like? What was he trying to prove? Lying on a comfortable bed in a warm house, his mother hovering, making sure he didn't do anything stupid ... It wasn't exactly living life on the edge.

He thought about Carl and his other friends. None of them had done any real living. Most were still at home, their parents doing everything for them. What was the harm in going to the island? Aoife had said he could help out around the place. He would be fed, have a place to stay ... The prospect seemed more appealing when his mum knocked on the door again.

'Addy, are you sure you're okay?'

'I'm fine, honest.' This time his tone sounded less hostile. It wasn't her fault. Unlike Adam, she had always been there for him. It had been a long time since he'd thought about the summer he'd spent with Carl's parents at their house in Cork. He couldn't have been any more than nine years old at the time. Carl's father was putting up a wooden fence around the site. Addy had watched him as he worked, Carl's mother, every now and then, bringing her husband cold drinks. Addy remembered staring at Carl's father's Adam's apple, as he swallowed the liquid fast. There had been a kind of primitive power about the man, the kind he wished he had in his life. He didn't dwell on not having a father, but when he and Carl were given the job of carrying the wooden stakes over one by one, and Carl's father patted Carl on the head, he wished he'd had a dad.

Now, with Aoife going away, he felt left behind. He'd have to start taking risks, and if that meant going to the island, then that was what he was going to do.

Kate

IT WAS LATE BY THE TIME KATE PUT CHARLIE TO BED.
She regretted having to cancel her dinner with Malcolm, especially
as it had been less than an hour before they were due to meet, but
with Adam working, getting in a babysitter at such short notice felt
like too much hassle. And the note wasn't far from her mind. It
seemed sinister, imposing on her, calling out to her from behind the
locked study door, pulling her thoughts like a magnet. Adam had
promised he would have it checked for prints and DNA, but part of
her already knew he wouldn't find anything.

Malcolm, it turned out, had already heard about Mason's death.
Such a dreadful tragedy, he had said. They weren't close, and she
wasn't sure, but something about the way he had described Mason's
relationship with her father as professional, rather than social, irked
her. Was he alluding to something? Her father had been a lecturer:
what could he possibly have had professionally in common with a
politician? And, for some reason, she felt Malcolm wanted her to
ask more, which was partly why she hadn't. She was being childish,
she knew, but she couldn't help herself.

'Mum.' Charlie rubbed his eyes as she closed *The Chamber of
Secrets*, his second Harry Potter book.

'Yes, honey.'

'Why don't Adam and Addy like each other?'

'It's not that, Charlie. It's just that sometimes when people care
about each other deep down, they need to work stuff out.'

'I like Addy.'

'I know you do, and he likes you.' She pulled the duvet up before
leaning down to kiss him on the forehead.

'Mum, what's your favourite insect?'

'I don't know. I've never thought about it.'

'Think, then.'

'Okay, let's see … It would have to be a butterfly.'

'Why?'

'Because they're beautiful, and they have lots of different colours and patterns, and they're gentle, and they remind me of summer.'

'That's a lot of reasons. Do you have any more?'

She knew he was buying time. 'Just one.'

'Tell me.'

'Because they start life one way, and then they become beautiful.'

'A caterpillar, you mean?'

'Yes.'

'Mum, they have to eat themselves first. They make this cocoon, and then they eat all the bits. At first it turns into soup, but the protein in the soup makes them grow fast, and that's when they get eyes and legs and wings.'

'And how do you know all this?'

'I learned it in school, but a butterfly isn't my favourite. Everyone picks a butterfly.'

'So what's your favourite?' She checked the time on the Mickey Mouse clock. It was nearly nine thirty, and Adam still hadn't called.

'A firefly.'

'Why?'

'Because a firefly reminds me of Addy,' he said triumphantly.

'Addy?'

'They shine from the inside. Teacher says, not everyone can see their light, but I do when Addy plays with me, which is why I like him even though Adam doesn't see the good bits.'

'He does, sweetheart.'

'No, he doesn't, but that's not his fault.'

'Oh?'

'Addy doesn't show them to him, so it's hard.'

'I see. At least, I think I do.'

'It's all right, Mum, don't look so worried. Some day Addy will let him see them, and they won't argue any more.'

She rubbed his cheek. 'I hope you're right, clever clogs. Now, settle down or you'll be falling asleep in school tomorrow.'

'Night, Mum. Love you.'

'Love you too.' Then, changing her tone from soft to serious, she said, 'Now go to sleep.'

He turned his back to her, pulling the duvet over his head as she closed the door. She turned on the light in the hall, knowing he liked to see the light coming under the door at night.

She checked the time again, deciding she would give Adam another half an hour before phoning him. As she walked into the study and took the note from the desk drawer, she decided to concentrate on the articles that formed parts of it, rather than the cut-out words, but the columns didn't make any sense. Each sentence had been tapered off before the finish, and whoever had cut out the shapes had been careful not to reveal which newspaper it was either, or any other detail, including a publication date. Her training told her that everything about it, including the envelope it came in, mattered. She also knew Adam wouldn't be impressed with her touching it without wearing protective gloves, but her reaction earlier on, when she was taken by surprise, would have eradicated any worthwhile forensic evidence. She would need to be more careful next time, if there was a next time.

When she heard the knock at the apartment door, she assumed it was Adam, having forgotten his key, but leaving the study, she hesitated before opening the door, looking through the peep-hole instead. She was surprised to see Malcolm on the other side. Opening the door, she stood back, staring at him.

'Are you okay, Kate?'

'Yes, I'm fine.'

'I was concerned about you. Earlier on, you seemed frazzled.'

'Did I?' She realised he was looking beyond her, towards the study.

'Doing extra homework?' he asked.

'I guess you could call it that.' Turning, she closed the study door.

'Can I come in?'

'Sorry. Of course – how rude of me.' She stood back to let him pass.

He walked towards the living area, and as she shut the front door, she asked, 'How did you get into the communal hallway?'

'Someone was leaving so I slipped in. Why?'

'No reason. I just wanted to make sure the key code pad was still working.'

'You shouldn't rely on that for security, Kate.'

'Why not?'

They stood face to face in the living room.

'It isn't reliable.' He removed his coat, placing it over the couch's arm rest, and sat down. 'Most people use number association or both, as part of their passwords. We have so many logins these days that it's not unusual for a person to use the same password or a similar one for all kinds of things.'

She sat down opposite. 'I don't get you.'

'I could be mistaken, Kate, but for all your expertise, I doubt you're very different from others when it comes to creating codes. People will use the same words or numbers for their computer login, alarm code, bank cash card, or anything else that requires digits. It's too difficult to keep a range of different ones in our heads, and writing them down can be risky.'

'So, you're assuming I use the same code for everything.'

'Most people do.'

'Well, even if I did, it would be my code.'

'Yes, but then there's the use of association too. You know the kind of thing, names of people, places or the year we were born. These are all important in how we remember things.'

'Go on.'

'Is that really necessary, Kate? I'm sorry now I brought it up.'

'Humour me. I'm interested.'

'Fine.' He leaned back in the couch. 'If you insist.'

'I do.'

'What people don't realise is that our fingers, as well as our brains, remember these codes. It's called muscle memory, and it's not surprising, considering how many times we use the same combination over and over again. I can work out codes simply by watching how a person uses their keyboard, and you'd be surprised how many people choose their own name or the words *pass* or *login*.'

'That's very observant of you, Malcolm.'

'Being observant is useful in my profession, as it is in yours.'

Kate made a mental note to change the code as soon as Adam got home. 'Sorry, Malcolm, I don't mean to sound critical. It's been a tough day.'

'I understand.'

'Malcolm, I was thinking about what you said earlier on.'

'About what?'

'How creating physical references can conjure up all sorts of possibilities that may not exist.'

'Indeed.'

'You know a lot about my dad?'

'Your father, Kate, was a bit of an enigma.'

There it was again, that critical tone. 'How do you mean?'

'He was fond of puzzles. It was one of his survival tactics, not letting others know what he was really thinking.'

'Survival – that's a rather strong word.'

'Perhaps, but it sums up how he used to be, always wanting to keep others guessing. I doubt even your mother knew him fully.'

Kate wasn't sure why, but Malcolm's last sentence made sense to her. How much did she know about her father?

She was still lost in thought when he asked, 'Are you happy?'

'Yes, I think so.'

'Then let sleeping dogs lie.'

'You're not usually a man for clichés.'

'Sometimes they're appropriate.'

'I guess.'

He stood up, walked over to sit beside her on the couch and took her hand. 'Kate, you do know you're very important to me?'

'Yes.'

'If anything is troubling you, I want you to know that you can trust me.'

'Thanks, Malcolm. That means a lot.'

'You're very like him, you know.'

'My father, you mean?'

'Yes. He was often far too stubborn for his own good. '

'Do you think I'm stubborn?'

'At times, yes, I do. It's the fighter in you.'

'That's partly an act, you know.'

'I doubt it, Kate.'

'I don't know. There's been times lately when I've felt strong and others, when I've not been so sure.'

'You're only human. I've always watched out for you. You do know that?'

'I do, but it's all the bits I don't know that trouble me most.'

The Game Changer

Kate

A NOISE MADE KATE BOLT UPRIGHT ON THE COUCH. She must have fallen asleep. A small table lamp lit one corner of the living room. She heard the noise again. Someone was turning a key in the front door but it was jamming. The door to the hall was open, and she could see Charlie's door.

What if the sender of the note was taking it a step further? What if they had somehow managed to get a copy of the key? It was then that she heard the front door creaking, as if in slow motion. She jumped up from the couch, seeing the front door opening a few inches at a time. She'd never make it to Charlie's room in time. Looking around her, she grabbed the first thing resembling a weapon: a glass paperweight from the coffee table. Hiding behind the living-room door, she heard the front door close. The intruder switched off the light in the hall. Christ, she thought, someone is actually breaking in, they are actually inside the apartment, and as she thought this, she also realised that they would see the lamp on in the living room. She held her breath, ready to bring the paperweight down as hard as she could as soon as they passed the door. But there were no footsteps, only the sound of another door opening. Charlie's. Jesus, she screamed inside her head and, like a wild person, she ran out into the hall.

'Christ, Kate, what are you doing?'

At first she didn't say anything, taking in Adam's large frame. 'Why did you turn out the light?' she barked.

'I thought you were asleep. I was checking in on Charlie.'

'But the hall light is always left on.'

'Okay, okay – calm down,' he whispered. 'I forgot.'

She rubbed her eyes. 'I must have had a bad dream.'

'You think?'

'I remember someone was chasing me, but then when I looked around, I couldn't see them. They'd disappeared.' She rubbed her eyes again.

He took the paperweight out of her hand, gesturing for her to go back into the living room. He followed, asking, 'What else happened in this dream?'

'I don't know. I can't remember much more of it.' She turned to him, asking out of the blue, 'Did you have any luck contacting Addy?' It felt such a random, yet oddly normal thing to ask.

'Kate, are you sure you're all right?'

'Yes, yes, I'm fine.'

'Let's put on another couple of lights.'

Initially, the brightness felt oddly intrusive to her, at odds with her half-dream state, but then her mind settled. What she had feared didn't exist, it was only a dream.

'That's what I call a close encounter,' he joked, gesturing at the paperweight.

'Sorry.'

'Don't be.'

'And Addy? I was asking you about Addy.'

'It seems, Kate, I've made a career of putting people into prison, while my son is intent on locking himself into one. According to his mother, he's been in his bedroom for most of the day.'

'He'll come round. Give him time.'

'Maybe,' he replied, 'but right now, I need a hug.'

It was him, rather than her, who did the hugging, and Kate felt as if he was trying to hold on to her for too long. Almost as if he knew something he wasn't saying. The moment she thought this, she chided herself. Why was she suspicious of everyone?

'How's the Michael O'Neill case going?' she asked instead.

'It gets more complicated by the hour.'

'Do you have any more information on his mysterious meetings?'

'Not so far, but the guy certainly knew a lot of people.'

'I don't suppose you get to his age without gaining a number of acquaintances along the way.'

'Or enemies, Kate.'

'How do you mean?'

'As of late this afternoon, we've been looking at potential blackmail.'

'Really?'

'Michael O'Neill made large cash withdrawals from his bank account over the last few months – they added up to a hundred thousand euros to be exact.'

'Cash?'

'Yeah, multiples of five thousand – the bank should have noticed it, but each time it was below the threshold for irregular transactions. There were a few questions asked, mainly because they thought he had plans for investing the money elsewhere.'

'And did he?'

'Not that we know of.'

'It's sounding like one of those investigations that keep gaining legs.'

'I know.' He paused. 'You're very pale.'

'Am I? Sorry, it must be tiredness.'

'Or that note?'

'Wait there,' she said, 'I'll get it.'

A moment later she was back, placing the envelope and the note on the table. She watched as he took in the message, then asked, 'Any more ideas on what it means, Kate?'

'As I said earlier, it might be a disgruntled client or someone connected to one of the investigations.'

'Whoever it is, they know where you live.' He kept his words deadpan.

'That's not all.'

'What?'

'I think they know the code to the building. The envelope was put under the door from the communal corridor.'

'They could have slipped in when someone was going in or out.'

'Maybe.'

'You look like you have a theory, Kate. Spit it out.'

'I can't help thinking it's connected to when I was attacked all those years ago. I know it's a long shot, and I'm probably only linking it because ...'

'Because what?'

'It's been playing on my mind.'

'Kate, can I ask you something?'

'You're putting on your detective voice.'

'Am I? I didn't know I had one.'

'Well, you do. What is it?'

'When was the last time you saw Malcolm Madden?'

'This evening, why?'

'Are you sure you can trust him?' He leaned back in the chair.

'Of course. I've known him my whole life.' She stared at him, sensing he was still holding something back, then blurted out, 'What is it? What are you getting at?'

'He knew Michael O'Neill.'

'So? You said yourself a great many people knew him.'

'I'm only telling you to be careful. Don't shoot the messenger.' He leaned forward to take her hand, just as Malcolm had done earlier. 'It might be nothing, but even if their mutual acquaintance means nothing ...' he paused, looking down at the note '... that means something.'

'I know it does.' She sounded more downbeat than ever.

'Look, Kate, I'll take it to the guys in the lab in the morning.'

'The techies have enough to do. Anyhow, you won't get anything off it now.'

'I'm owed a few favours. Leave it to me. Look, you're the one taking time out, so step back and let me deal with it.'

'That's the thing, Adam. Stepping back doesn't feel like an option any more.'

The Game Changer

PLANS HAD TO BE REARRANGED TO FACILITATE Sarah's request for an urgent meeting outside of Ocean House. Luckily, the Game Changer now had a more private venue set up, one closer to Kate, both physically and personally.

If things worked out, the session with Sarah would prove to be a profitable one. Like many in the programme, for her, the concept of Saka and all he represented was seductive: she saw Saka as the great hero, the one who echoed the ethos of the programme, creating whatever illusions best met her needs, and the Game Changer had every intention of reaffirming her delusion. People, like Sarah, who had never experienced financial worries, and didn't have enough respect for money or its power, deserved to be punished.

∞

'Nice to see you again, Sarah. Why don't you take a seat with Lily in front of the camera? Make sure you're comfortable before you begin.'

Nervously Sarah wrapped the blanket around the baby doll. 'John has refused to touch Lily.' Her voice was close to a whisper, covering the doll's ear on the side not held tight to her chest. 'I wasn't sure how he would react, but I hadn't expected that. He keeps looking at me as if I'm deranged and no matter how much I explain to him about Lily, and that she means the world to me, he won't accept her.'

'He might need more time, Sarah. Do you think that could be the problem?'

'I don't know. I don't understand him any more. I can't deny her.'

'What about work? How did they react to your change of plans?'

'They were sympathetic. I told them I needed time off for a personal matter.'

'So, Sarah, you're saying John is the real problem.'

'Yes, and it was awful last night. After he'd stopped shouting and stomping around, he stood in the bedroom where I lay with Lily, and there was a crazy look in his eyes. He asked if I wanted him to get help for me, saying our GP could recommend someone. He's so bloody-minded at times. He thinks one cure fits all.'

'Do you think his mind is completely closed to accepting Lily?'

'Yes. He can't see past living his life like everyone else. What's so terrible about me wanting Lily in my life, if it makes me happy?'

'Happiness is important, Sarah.'

'In the end, I built up the courage to ask him why he was staring at us, and if he didn't love us any more.'

'And what did he say?'

'He didn't answer. Instead he walked around the room, his arms folded tight to his chest, like he wanted to squeeze some torment out of himself.'

'That doesn't sound good, Sarah.'

'I pleaded with him. I told him we didn't have to follow other people's concepts of what's okay.'

'And what was his response to that?'

Sarah looked down at Lily, making sure she was still fast asleep, then said, her voice low and strained, 'He roared at me that Lily was nothing more than a damn doll. I couldn't believe it. He should have known that she was more than that to me. If he wasn't so pig-headed, he'd understand.'

'I can appreciate your hurt, Sarah.'

'When I told him I had no intention of going back to work, he was even more annoyed. I hadn't said it categorically to my employer, you see. I didn't want anyone asking too many questions. It wasn't like typing other people's letters was a major career. It was only a part-time job, and we certainly didn't need the money.'

'But the job helped you for a while?'

'Yes, it did. It helped me to pretend my life could get back to normal, but that was before I realised that being normal was society's way of not letting me be the person I wanted to be.'

'It's tough, Sarah. There's no denying that.'

'After John left the room,' she paused, wiping her tears away, 'I pulled the curtains closed so it would be easier for Lily to fall asleep. I told her that Daddy would understand soon, and I don't know how long we slept for, but when I saw John standing in the doorway, I knew by the way he held himself that he'd been crying. I waited in silence as he walked over to the bed and sat on the edge. I thought he didn't want to disturb Lily, and for the first time in a long time, it felt like we were a family again.'

'I can see why that would be important, Sarah. You have a lot of love to give.'

'He said my name, softer, more relaxed than he was before. He told me that he loved me, and I could feel my spirits lift, and I thought maybe this wouldn't be as difficult as I had first envisaged. It was then that he suggested I should get dressed. He wanted us to go for a walk, to spend some quiet time together. I assumed he meant with Lily. I mean, I couldn't possibly leave her behind, but when ...'

'When what, Sarah?'

'He looked at me so strangely when I told him I needed to change Lily into warm clothes so she wouldn't get a chill. I knew then he didn't love her, but his words hurt so much, delivered with such coldness, when he said, "That thing is not my daughter."'

'Do you need a few moments, Sarah, to compose yourself?'

'No, it's fine. I turned my back on John, but he kept on talking, saying she wasn't real. I knew it was hopeless then. He was never going to accept her, no matter how important she was to me.'

'That must have hurt you.'

'I told him, I practically spat at him, that she's real to me. I told him I wasn't going to let him ruin my happiness, not for the second time. He lost it completely then, and I knew why.'

'I don't quite understand, Sarah.'

'He still blames himself for Lily's sickness. He delayed bringing us to the hospital, you see, saying first labours always lasted for hours and hours, and wouldn't it be better to stay at home for as long as possible. He wasn't to know he was putting her life, and mine, at risk. But last night, when he was denying her, prepared to exclude her from our lives, I wanted to hurt him more than anything. I told him I wouldn't allow him to harm her or me ever again.'

'That must have been harsh for him to hear.'

'I meant every word of it.'

'I know you did, Sarah.'

'He went out then for the walk on his own. When he came back, he did that staring thing again, watching me as I attached the new teddy-bear mobile over the cot, before covering Lily up for her night's sleep. That was when I knew for sure he hated us.'

'Hate is a very strong word.'

'You didn't see how he looked at us.'

'No, Sarah, I didn't. What do you want to do?'

'I need to be somewhere else.'

'That's completely understandable.'

'Can you help me?'

'Of course – the group is all about supporting one another.'

'I know the work done at the commune is important, and with a new baby, I wouldn't be much use on the island. I don't want to be a burden.'

'Don't worry about that. However, going to the island is a big step. Sarah, you need to be sure.'

'I've never been more sure of anything in my life, or at least, not for a very long time. I know there is a lot to sort out.'

'Don't worry about incidentals, Sarah. Your well-being is what's paramount.'

'And Lily's?'

'Lily is important to you. Anyone can see that.'

The Game Changer walked over to Sarah, who was now rocking the baby doll. 'It's okay, Sarah. Things will work out fine for everyone, you'll see.'

'I'm sure about going to the island, but I'll only go under one condition.'

'What's that, Sarah?'

'I want to pay my way. I'll take the money out of the bank tomorrow. I don't know how long I'll need to stay for, but I don't want charity.'

'You're a proud woman, Sarah. I respect you for that.'

CENTRE OF LIGHTNESS
20 Steps to Self-enlightenment Programme

Player: Sarah Sinclair – Evaluation 11
Attributes: Loss of daughter magnifies her vulnerability and ease of manipulation, along with her protected social class and scant regard for money.
Current Bank Balance: €95,000
Step 10: Completed

A change in routine has a dramatic effect on our cognitive process. The unfamiliar can make us susceptible, apprehensive, and can cause all kinds of spikes in our emotions. It is also when we are at our most flexible.

Behaviour, as is the case for Sarah, can also be based on required reward/payback. The value of a reward to a recipient can be increased or decreased within their perception. Expected rewards can reduce motivation; surprise rewards will increase it. Giving Sarah an alternative to her current environment allows her to feed into her illusion of happiness and denial.

The isolation of the island will have a two-fold effect. First, once Lily is accepted, it will make it increasingly difficult for Sarah to return to her current domestic arrangement. Second, becoming more dependent on the group, her mind will continue to find ways to reaffirm the group's beliefs, thereby indoctrinating her further.

(Page 1 of 1)

Kate

THE FOLLOWING MORNING, MALCOLM HAD LEFT A message on Kate's voicemail, but as yet she hadn't replied. Even if his association with Michael O'Neill was innocent, there was no getting away from the fact that Adam had sown a seed of doubt in her mind. Why hadn't Malcolm connected the suicide case she'd spoken to him about with Michael O'Neill's death, especially if he knew him? He might have thought she was talking about someone else – she hadn't mentioned any names – but even so.

The note was still rattling her. She had quizzed Adam earlier about what Sam Miller, the profiler attached to the case, had come up with on O'Neill. According to Sam, the victim had shown numerous tell-tale signs of inability to cope since his retirement, shutting out his wife and other lifelong friends. There were other signs of depression too – calling to the school uninvited, allowing his appearance to deteriorate – and although his form had improved a couple of weeks before his death, the latter, as Sam had pointed out, was not unusual, especially if the deceased had already made the decision to take his own life. A planned suicide often acted as a release valve, with many victims appearing happier before they died. There would have been a feeling of contentment, knowing that whatever troubled them in life soon wouldn't be able to harm them. The potential blackmail scenario might have compounded matters, all of which pointed in one direction: suicide.

The police still hadn't any idea where the money had gone. And, although Michael O'Neill's widow would receive her husband's life-assurance payment, her financial situation was a lot worse than it should have been. The profile that Sam Miller had drawn up on the late Michael O'Neill was of a man who was careful, reliable and conservative, at odds with the disappearance of the money, unless blackmail had been at play. It was impossible to work out in retrospect what a person had on their mind before death, and for some reason, this thought brought her back to her reaction the day before, standing outside her old home, thinking someone inside was watching her. Too many questions were floating around in her head, but were her questions feeding into a form of paranoia, making her jittery?

Walking into the study, she pinned a large sheet of white paper to the wall opposite the door, and began to create a variety of mind maps, almost as if she was turning her past life into some kind of investigation. On the first, she wrote Kevin's name in the subset of friends, then added two question marks, the first after 'girl', and the second after 'man', thinking about the memory she had of seeing them together from her bedroom window. She kept adding sets under various headings, and more subsets, until the whole sheet was covered. Twiddling the pen, her palms became sweaty. The mind maps didn't give her any answers, but somehow she felt more certain about one thing: although they held a lot of information, gaps existed.

She pinned up another sheet of white paper, equal in size to the previous one, then another and another, until the whole wall was taken up with them. Some were linked to her life at school, others to her life at home, the friends she used to hang out with, friends of her parents, relations, all the people known to her back then, especially around the time of the attack.

When her mobile phone rang, she saw immediately it was Adam. The call felt almost like a distraction.

'Hi,' she said, sounding more together than she felt. 'Did you get anything on the newspaper clipping?'

'That's the bad news, Kate. The techies couldn't find anything, other than your own prints.'

'That was stupid of me.'

'Don't beat yourself up.'

'I know, but still … What about Malcolm and the late Michael O'Neill? Have you found out any more about their connection?'

'I spoke to Malcolm Madden half an hour ago. According to him, he hadn't seen Michael O'Neill for a couple of months. They met at Golf Classic last year, and although O'Neill wasn't a client, Madden admitted speaking to him about his low moods. The conversation hadn't gone down well with O'Neill, and because of that, they had ceased contact.'

'Seems reasonable … Adam?'

'Yeah?'

'I was wondering about visiting Michael O'Neill's widow.'

'That's a bit out of the blue, Kate, especially as you're not part of the investigation.'

'I know, but I'd feel better if I did. It's not that I don't think Sam Miller is capable, but what harm can it do?'

'I don't like it, Kate. I mean, with the chief super and everything, visiting Ethel O'Neill sounds a little …'

'A little what?'

'Odd.'

'Look, I'll play it easy. Ethel O'Neill was the closest person to the victim, meaning she was also the most likely person to know which of her late husband's friends or contacts were important to him.'

'Are you digging because of the Malcolm connection?'

'It's not only that. I've been thinking about the other killing, the one in Manhattan, and how the killer planted evidence linking O'Neill.'

'Go on, I'm listening.'

'If it is a power game, and they're playing clever, it feeds into a narcissist-type mind-set.'

'Meaning?'

'Meaning people's motivations are complicated. There's often more than one scenario influencing events.'

'You're talking about the different MO?'

'In part, yes, that is important, but I'm sure there's more than that happening here.'

'You're supposed to be off work, remember?'

'Do you want to hear my thoughts, or don't you?'

'Sure.'

'To kill Tom Mason in the manner Fisher described required a form of detachment. If power and ego are at play, then the killer may see the victim or victims as a form of collateral damage, unimportant, except in so far as they impinge on the killer's desires.'

'And someone capable of inflicting great pain.'

'Yes, but they also wanted to leave a calling card.'

'As you said, Kate, ego could be an influencer.'

'If that's the case, especially if we're dealing with a narcissistically motivated individual, the reasons behind the killing are not always straightforward. Minor or major past events could be a factor.'

'I'm not getting you, Kate.'

'Look, all I'm saying is that normal rules don't apply where narcissism is concerned. All sorts of nuances can influence a killer's behaviour.'

'Go on.'

'The heightened narcissism or egotistical beliefs are essentially false, and are often linked to a suppressed low self-esteem. One that can be seriously undermined by rejection, for example, resulting in elevated levels of hatred or jealousy. What one person might take as a slight against their character, a narcissist will see as something else entirely.'

'Why is that?'

'To the narcissist, the slight or the offence threatens their grandiose perception. They can also link two totally obscure motivations easier than others, and once they're connected, their ego will do the rest. They'll see it all as part of some grand plan they need to control.'

'So what you're saying, Kate, is that the Mason case is telling us more about the killer than the O'Neill case, assuming they are connected.'

'They're connected all right, it's just a question of how. And, yes, the Mason case illustrates that the killer likes to play games, exhibiting their intelligence, or their belief that they're one step ahead of everyone else, exposing a side of their personality that may be useful.'

'Kate, I don't know about you talking to Ethel O'Neill. I mean, we've already interviewed her. She's very forgetful. I don't think you're going to get anything more out of her.'

'Let me try.'

'I don't like this, what with the note and how you've been lately.'

'What do you mean?'

'The last week or so you haven't been yourself. You've seemed preoccupied, distracted.'

'It's just lack of sleep, that's all.'

'Lack of sleep didn't cause the delivery of the note.'

'I know that, but I can't let it turn me into a house hostage either. It could be nothing more than a prank. I've worked with a few oddballs in my day.' She looked at the mind maps on the wall. Was someone on those maps capable of sending her that note and, if so, why?

'All right, but remember, you're supposed to be concentrating on other things right now.'

'I know that too.'

Addy

WHEN ADDY LEFT HIS BEDROOM, HE SENSED HIS mother's relief straight away. She had purposely delayed going to work when she realised he had locked himself in because of Aoife. She said she understood how he felt, and that even though he and Aoife had been seeing each other for a while, it wasn't uncommon for early relationships to run their course.

He let her do all the talking, figuring that when he finally confided his plan to her, she would be more understanding. 'Mum, I've another few weeks before I start back in college.'

'So?'

'I was thinking about going on a short break.'

'Where?'

'Some of the lads were talking about going to Corfu.'

'Corfu?'

'Yeah. The nightclubs there are great.'

'I see ...' she sounded less than approving '... and where do you plan on getting the money to go to Corfu?'

'That's the thing. I've enough saved from the bar job in Flanagan's, but I don't fancy it, not really.'

'Why not?'

'I don't know. I'm not into it. I was thinking of going to see Aoife instead.'

'Are you sure about that? I mean, if she gave you the brush-off—'

He stopped her in mid-sentence. 'Look, Mum, I know what you said about us being too young, and you're probably right, but I need to get this sorted. I'll know from her reaction when I get there if it's over.'

'And you said she's gone to Kerry?'

'One of the islands off. It's called Colton – it has amphibian footprints from 385 million years ago. One of my friends did a research paper on them.'

He hoped, compared to Corfu, the island sounded the better option. He was going anyway, but the less aggravation he got, the better.

'How long?'

'A few weeks. I'll be back in time to register for college. I've already put my option choices up online.'

'You'll bring your mobile with you?'

'Sure thing, Mum, but the signal might be crap.'

'When do you plan on going?'

'There's a train leaving Connolly station shortly. It's real cheap on account of it being a late booking, and there's a boat Aoife told me about. I can catch it at the other end.'

'Sounds like you have it all organised.'

'You keep telling me I need to get better at that stuff.'

She gave him a look that said, half-heartedly, she agreed. Even if she had her reservations, it didn't matter now. He was going. At some point, even she knew, she had to untie the apron strings.

Spring Valley Village, Texas

IT HAD BEEN A LONG THIRTY-SIX HOURS FOR LEE Fisher, before he stopped at the less than classy Sunset Motel for what should have been eight hours' sleep, but in motels and strange beds he invariably ended up thinking rather than sleeping.

The following morning, he fired his backpack into the boot of the hired black Cherokee jeep, and took the interstate, driving through Alabama, Mississippi and New Orleans, before finally arriving at the outskirts of Spring Valley, ten minutes away from his brother's house, by late afternoon. Seventeen hundred miles equated to a lot of thinking, and the Mason case was clawing at his brain the same way something caught in your tooth could bother the hell out of you, the constant irritant that told you it wasn't going anywhere.

The temperature guide on the dashboard said ninety degrees outside, heat not uncommon for the early days of September. On the floor in front of the passenger seat were the two books he had brought with him for recreational reading – George Orwell's *Animal Farm* and a 1930s English detective novel called *The Mad Hatter Mystery* by John Dickson Carr. He had read both books before, but he liked the familiar, and a few days' annual vacation at his brother's place needed other forms of escapism.

Before he left, there had been another development in the Mason case: a laptop they hadn't seized the first time around on account of it being locked away in the storeroom of the boutique below. Someone needed more space, and the locked unit had been forced open. It was only then that the manager remembered Mason asking him if he could keep it there. Mason had had the only key and, considering the contents, that was no surprise. It hadn't taken them long to find the wiped files and images of children. They weren't the worst he had ever seen, but they indicated a penchant of sorts, and these things were usually lifetime tastes rather than random interest.

The images had made him think about his brother's two sons, Joshua and Matthew, aged ten and eleven, but for all the wrong reasons. John, his brother, had taken the happy-family route, unlike him, but then again, they'd always done things differently. According to John, it wasn't that they were unalike, it was simply that they chose different ways to do the same things.

The jeep screeched to a stop, a large brown hog staring at him. No doubt, Lee thought, an escapee from a local farm. The hog didn't look like he was in any hurry, taking up the centre of the road. Lee leaned further back in the driver's seat and, instead of losing it, began to think about that *Mad Hatter* detective story. It was the second in the Dr Fell mysteries, with lots of questionable ingredients, stolen hats, crossbow bolts and missing manuscripts. The plotting was masterly, with an air of humour, a good example, too, of the 'onion' technique – peeling away at things until you got to the core. As the hog eyeballed him, he thought about his nephews again, and what he would do if anyone ever harmed either of them. He'd rip out their insides and chop them into pieces, not unlike how Mason's body had ended up. Just then the hog turned, as if sensing menace, and walked off the road with the same slow vigour that Lee figured had got him there in the first place.

He had five days' vacation ahead of him, but something told him, in much the same way as he liked to read the same books over and over again, that the investigation would never be far from his mind. There was a lot about the killer that he hadn't worked out, but whoever they were, they had a dark history. No one is born with that kind of killer application. It takes skill, and skill is rarely achieved without experience. Lee had had more than his fair share of encounters with the less than friendly types of this world, so he was good at reading people, spotting a rat or a do-gooder within a hundred-mile radius. Mason's killer had known more than the logistics of the apartment: they had known how to get to Mason. The man had lived alone for years, but something or someone had influenced his decision to give the killer access.

Kate

DESPITE HER EARLIER ENTHUSIASM, NOW THAT she was sitting in her car by the O'Neills' seaside bungalow in Skerries, Kate wished she wasn't there. She had almost convinced herself that a past patient had probably sent the note, but even if they had, that didn't mean it was nothing to worry about. She had called into Charlie's school on the way to the O'Neill house. It was unorthodox, but it settled her mind to see that he was okay. Would it be an overreaction to take him out of the equation for a little while, until she got to the bottom of things? She didn't want to upset him any more than she had to, but it was always better to err on the side of caution. Maybe he could spend a while with Declan. But how long is a while? He couldn't stay away indefinitely.

Ahead of her, at the top of the road, she saw an old woman with grey hair putting one frail foot in front of another. She was dressed in a pair of flat black furry boots and a heavy black coat, and Kate knew, from a photograph Adam had given her, she was looking at Ethel O'Neill. There were family similarities too. She had the same pointed nose and elongated chin as her brother, the chief super. Michael O'Neill had been in his sixties, but seeing his widow, there was no denying that she was a lot older than her late husband. Kate decided to hold back until the woman was inside the house, but as Ethel reached the gate, she hesitated before opening it, as if she was unsure she should continue. Kate waited.

By the time Ethel arrived at the front door, Kate couldn't take her eyes off her, fascinated as she watched her remove what looked like a wristband of red wool, with keys dangling from it, and struggled to get one into the lock.

Stepping out of the car, Kate called, 'Mrs O'Neill?' She waved, and walked towards her. Ethel blinked a number of times in quick succession, as if she was trying to work out why this stranger was calling her.

'I'm Kate. We spoke on the phone.'

'Did we?'

'Yes, you said I could come round.'

Ethel gave her another blank look.

Kate continued, 'I have some questions for you about your husband.'

'Michael? Do you know Michael?'

The widow might be more than mildly forgetful, Kate thought. Dementia was a more likely diagnosis. Kate took a step forward, offering to take the key. 'Here, let me help you with that. These locks can be tricky.'

'Yes, they can be ...'

'Kate, my name is Kate.'

Ethel reminded her of her late mother. One moment she wouldn't recognise Kate, and the next she would. As Kate turned the key in the lock, Ethel stared at her front garden. 'I need to get a boy in to cut the grass. Michael used to do it.'

'It must be hard for you.'

'Yes, it is ... I try not to think about it too much. Now that the funeral is over, I suppose I'll have to get on with things.'

Shit, Kate thought. How would she react if she was in Ethel's position and she had to face all of these questions so near to her husband's death? 'Ethel, I'm really very sorry, and if you'd prefer to do this another time, that would be fine.'

'I'm all right. Michael did enough thinking for both of us.' A hint of bitterness in her words.

Inside, the house was cold. Either there was no heating system or Ethel had forgotten to switch it on. Looking around, Kate saw a bag of unopened logs by a burner in the sitting room. 'Shall I light the stove, Ethel?'

'Oh, yes, do. I'll get us some tea.'

Ethel departed to the kitchen with her heavy coat and boots still on. While she waited, Kate took in her surroundings – the flowery wallpaper, the dark curtains, a cabinet bursting with china, ornaments scattered on side tables, shelves of books in every available wall space, the embroidered headrests on the sofa and armchairs, and the newspapers piled waist-high under the window.

She listened to Ethel move about in the kitchen, cups clattering against one another, and a kettle that seemed to take for ever to boil. Kate noticed other things too, after she'd lit the stove: a dinner plate and a cup of cold tea at the far side of the sofa. Judging by the hardened stains on the plate, it had been there for a while. There was a shopping bag with groceries behind the sitting-room door. When Kate looked at the contents, she saw the milk and eggs in the bag were out of date. All the tell-tale signs were there. If she could see them, then the late Michael O'Neill had noticed them, too. Would a loving husband, in his full faculties, leave his wife with dementia to fend for herself? Ethel, Kate thought, must have been having one of her good days for Adam and the others not to realise how bad she was. She had seen her own mother trick others, learning ways to compensate: letting others finish your sentences, or doing things like Ethel did, tying your front-door key around your wrist in case you forgot where you'd left it.

Kate looked around the room again. The walls were missing the usual photographs of children's communions, confirmations or weddings. Then she remembered that Adam had told her the couple were childless, and as she was thinking that, she spotted a charcoal sketch of a teenage boy. It had prime position on the china cabinet to the left of the stove. Kate walked over, picking up the frame and turning it around to see if there was a date or something else on the other side. She was still holding it when Ethel returned, carrying a tea tray laid with daisy napkins, a small white jug, a sugar bowl and a large yellow teapot but no cups.

'Handsome, isn't he?' Ethel said.

'Yes, he is.' But Kate's words were hesitant, mainly because she had worked out why the sketch interested her.

'He's dead now, like Michael.'

'I'm sorry to hear that.'

Ethel put the tray on a low table, staring at it as if she was trying to work out what was missing.

Kate stood up. 'I'll get some cups.'

'Oh, yes, thank you ...' And there it was again, the look on her face as if she was trying to remember Kate's name.

'Kate. Kate Pearson. We spoke on the phone.'

'What a lovely name.'

It didn't take Kate long to find the cups in the kitchen, but once there, she saw even more clues. Cupboards filled with tins and jars of the same things, unopened mail, out-of-date bread and more cartons of eggs.

When she returned to the sitting room, Ethel had taken off her coat. It now rested on the back of her chair. Kate handed the picture frame to her, asking, 'Why don't you tell me what happened to him?'

'It was a long time ago. I'm afraid my memory isn't what it used to be.'

'That's okay. Take your time.'

Kate hadn't expected tears but the image obviously affected Ethel. 'It broke both our hearts. I was older than Michael, you see. We tried to have children, but we couldn't. I left it too late to get married, too late to have a child, too late to do a lot of things ...'

'What about the boy in the frame?'

'We fostered him. No one knew who his father was, not even his mother.' Disgust coming into her face. 'She was a strange one, neglected the boy, and the authorities got wind of it.' She sounded as if she was telling Kate an enormous secret. 'They started calling around, checking on them, until they finally took him away. That's when we got him.' She smiled.

'He obviously meant a great deal to you.'

'Oh, yes. He was tough, though, and bitter too.' A reluctant laugh. 'He certainly didn't want to live with us.'

'What happened to him?' Kate asked, even though she already knew the answer.

Another blank stare, then Ethel asked, 'My handbag ... where did I leave my handbag?'

'You left it in the hall. Hold on, I'll get it for you.'

When Kate returned with it, Ethel turned the handbag upside-down, emptying most of the contents onto her lap, then pulling out a torn and battered envelope with an address on the front, handing it to Kate. 'It was when we lived here.'

Kate stared at the address. The house was only minutes away from where she used to live. It made sense now. She had known from the start that the sketch was of Kevin. She hadn't remembered Ethel or Michael O'Neill, but then again, they had only lived near her for a brief time.

'That house was too big for two people. Michael wouldn't hear about us fostering again, not after what happened.'

Kate knew exactly what had happened, and the similarities between his death and that of the late Michael O'Neill weren't lost on her. Had it crossed Ethel's mind that they had both died in the same way? Could Michael have lived with the guilt all these years, and decided to take his own life, leaving the world in the same manner as their foster son?

'Did you mention Kevin to the police, Ethel?'

'Yes. No. I'm not sure. I think I did.'

'Did you mention that he died the same way as Michael?'

'I don't want to talk about that.'

'It could be important.'

'I said I don't want to talk about it. Michael is gone, and that's the end of it.'

Kate knew better than to push it, and even if Ethel hadn't mentioned Kevin to the police, she knew, through their background checks, that they would have discovered it by now. Adam should have mentioned it to her, especially as he must have connected it with that old story.

'Ethel, do you understand about the missing money?'

'Our life savings lost.' Her tone angry.

'Have you any idea who Michael could have given the money to?'

She didn't answer.

Kate tried again: 'Was Michael under any kind of financial pressure?'

'The police think he was being blackmailed, you know.'

'And what do you think?'

'I don't think he would have …'

'Would have what?'

'Do that thing they're saying he did.'

'Being blackmailed, you mean?'

She nodded. 'He wouldn't have got involved with anything like that.'

'And the meetings he used to go to, Ethel, do you know anything about those?'

'No. I don't know anything about any meetings. Michael wouldn't have allowed himself to be blackmailed,' she said, with indignation. 'I just know it.'

'So, you moved after Kevin's death?'

'That house was bad luck. Some developer bought it, and the one next door.'

'I used to live nearby.'

'Did you, my dear? Maybe I know your family.'

'Off Merton Avenue, number thirty-seven Springfield Road.'

'Oh, you're that Pearson girl.'

Kate had no memory of ever being referred to as 'that Pearson girl', but the manner in which the words were delivered wasn't positive.

'Yes,' she was suddenly nervous, 'that's me.'

Ethel remembered the tea tray, and began pouring hot water into both cups.

'Oh dear, I must have forgotten the …'

'I'll get the tea bags.' Kate flew into the kitchen, frantically searching for a caddy. She went back to the sitting room and put the teabags into the pot. 'Ethel, you were talking about the Pearson girl – me.'

'You went missing.'

'You remember that?'

'Of course I do!' As if insulted by Kate's last question. 'The whole neighbourhood was out looking for you.'

'How long was I gone?'

'I'm not sure. It was a long time ago.'

'I only remember bits of it.' Kate realised she was confiding in a near stranger, but continued all the same. 'I think the shock of what happened might have blocked out parts of my memory.'

Ethel didn't respond, and Kate feared another blank session.

'Ethel, can you tell me what you know?'

'About?'

'About me going missing.'

'You went missing? I didn't realise.'

'I'm the Pearson girl, Ethel.' Kate told herself to remain calm. 'Sorry, you were telling me about the Pearson girl going missing.'

'Oh, yes. Did you know her?'

'Yes, I knew her.'

'The Pearson girl,' Ethel repeated the words, as if to remind herself of what she was trying to remember. 'There were some people they thought had done it. There were awful rumours.'

'What kind of rumours?' Kate didn't want to rush her, but she felt she was getting close to something. She couldn't afford to let it slip. 'Ethel, what do you remember?'

'I don't know. The girl was found. That was the main thing, thank goodness.'

'You said there were rumours? What kind of rumours?'

'Sorry, dear. I can't remember them now. You could talk to one of the neighbours.'

Kate had avoided doing exactly that for some time. In part, it was because she wanted to get the memories back without outside influence, and her parents had always made light of what had happened to her, or seemed to. The general consensus was that it was best not to talk about it. Unsavoury things were brushed under the carpet. Neither, if Ethel was correct, had Kate ever contemplated that she might have been missing for any more than a very brief period. Kate asked her next question without thinking, almost as if one part of her brain was working ahead of another.

'Did you and Michael know a Malcolm Madden? He would have been in his mid-twenties back then.'

'I don't think so. I can't be sure. The name sounds familiar, but …'

Kate's disappointment must have been obvious, because Ethel tried to comfort her: 'I can see this is troubling you, my dear.'

'Yes, I guess it is. Not remembering something can be frustrating.'

'I understand that.' And then her face lit up. 'You could try Michael's notebooks. He used to write in them all the time.'

'Do you have them?'

'Not here. They're in the lock-up.'

'Where's that?'

'Did you see my handbag, dear?'

'It's beside you. You have some of the contents on your lap.'

'So I do.' She started to root through the array of bits and bobs. 'Oh dear,' she said, 'I can't find it.'

'What are you looking for, Ethel?'

'There's a card with the address on it. It must be somewhere.'

Kate lifted the empty handbag. 'Do you mind if I check inside?'

'Work away, my dear. Those pockets can hide things on you.'

Kate searched through each of the inner sections, finding a small white card with a key in one of the zipped pouches. 'Is this it, Ethel, the address and key of the lock-up?'

'I think so. Michael put lots of our old stuff in there.'

'Ethel, did you mention the notebooks or the lock-up to the police?'

'No, I don't think so. Do you think you'd be able to find it? I can come with you, if you like.' Her tone was more upbeat. 'I need to get some milk and eggs.'

Special Detective Unit, Harcourt Street

ADAM LOOKED OUT AT THE HUB OF ACTIVITY beyond the glass panels of his office. He wasn't happy about keeping information from Kate. Although the techies hadn't found anything on the newspaper clipping, it hadn't stopped him digging further. The cryptic note had come too close to the opening of the investigation for his liking. With Malcolm Madden connected to O'Neill, he'd decided to carry out some house-to-house enquiries with Kate's old neighbours. Tongues always got looser over time, and the information he was given came from two separate sources.

The term 'closed circle' or 'private grouping' came up, and with the images Lee Fisher had told him about on Mason's computer, it certainly raised more questions than answers. According to both sources, Kate's father, Tom Mason and Michael O'Neill had been part of this elusive grouping. All were dead, although Kate's father had died from natural causes more than ten years earlier. The statements didn't prove there was anything unsavoury going on. The men moved in the same social circles. They knew each other, and they would possibly have had a lot of other things in common. But if they knew each other, had Malcolm Madden known O'Neill for longer than he was saying, even though he was younger than the others?

Kate had spoken to Adam a great deal about her father. He knew the man could be cold, and in Kate's early years he had been capable of bouts of aggression. Adam hadn't pushed her on it, but he believed her determination to help others in vulnerable

106

situations stemmed from her father's anger, and her mother's inability to protect her. According to Kate, she and her father had made peace with each other well before he died, but there had still been a disconnection, and after his death, Kate's concentration had been firmly on her mother, especially after she'd developed rapid dementia.

It was too early to be making any hard allegations about paedophilia, but the thought had crossed his mind. He had worked with such groupings before, and part of their success was the veil of secrecy and trust that often made the core difficult to penetrate. He wasn't ready to go to the PIU, the Paedophile Investigation Unit. For that he'd need more than references to elusive groupings.

His rank as a senior investigation officer meant he had access to the higher levels of the police database, PULSE, but in the PIU, the names of previous victims and suspects, even those spanning back twenty or thirty years, were stringently protected.

Kate

KATE WASN'T SURE THAT BRINGING ETHEL O'NEILL with her had been such a good idea, but there was no denying, she wanted to know what was in those notebooks.

Driving to the lock-up, she kept thinking about the possibility of her being missing for longer than she had originally thought. Ethel had said the whole neighbourhood was out looking. She had mentioned rumours. If Kate had been missing for hours on end, what had happened in the intervening period? In her memory, she had been followed by someone, a man. He had grabbed her from behind at knife point, but she had gotten away almost immediately. If she had been missing for longer, what did that mean? Why had she obliterated it from her mind? It might have been shock, but surely her parents would have known there was more to it: they had always treated it as a minor incident, one best forgotten. Had she done that? Forgotten it because they said so? It was possible. Anything was possible. She had tried Adam on the phone several times, but on each occasion, it had gone to voicemail. She didn't want to talk to anyone else, and she didn't want to wait either. For all she knew, the police had already been to the lock-up. Still, as a precaution, she decided to use the protective gloves and footwear from the boot. Being stupid once was forgivable, but twice was sloppy.

Opening the back of her hatchback, she called to Ethel, 'I won't be long. Wait here, and then we can go and get the milk and eggs.'

'Take your time, my dear. I'm very tired. I'm not sleeping well these days.'

'Why don't you take a nap?' She moved around to the passenger door. 'Here, I'll lower the seat back for you.'

Leaving an old woman, especially one with Ethel's condition, alone in a strange car, wasn't a sensible idea, but when she saw Ethel close her eyes, she felt somewhat relieved. Should she lock the doors? If she did, and Ethel woke up, the locked doors might frighten her. She'd have to take a chance. As she looked up, she saw a young man at the top of the lane. He was dressed in a dark tracksuit with the hood up, covering his face. He stalled, looked towards her, then moved on. She was suspicious of everyone these days. She waited until she was sure he was gone before approaching the garage. She counted ten garages in total.

Access was through a side door, with the main door locked with a metal padlock. There were no windows, so once inside, Kate fumbled around for a light switch. Something smelt, and when she put her gloved hand to her nostrils, she knew what it was immediately: stale urine. When the light bulb flashed on, it caused spots to form in front of her eyes and for the first time, she realised how nervous she was. She retched at the rancid smell, but even so, as she had done earlier in the O'Neill house, she took in her surroundings.

The space was full of boxes of various shapes and sizes, and more books, only this time, they were mainly hardcover editions. She opened one of the books, then a second and another, noting they were all first editions. Michael was a collector. On a low box to her right, she saw four large leather albums. Picking up the first, she couldn't be sure that the smell of excrement she detected was human. Closing her mouth tightly, to stop her stomach heaving, she found stamps inside the album, detailed to the side with the date, origin and their element of rarity.

Her eyes were then drawn to four black metal boxes on top of one another. Walking towards them, she slowed down, hearing footsteps pass by outside. She hoped Ethel was still asleep. When it went quiet again, she continued, opening each box to find smaller ones inside, with coins from different parts of the world. Again they were marked with individual details, a rectangular white sticker on the bottom of every box. The late Michael O'Neill, she thought, was organised, consistent and, most likely, patient.

When adults become collectors, their collections can become an extension of their identity – a sort of attempt at immortality, living on even though the person doesn't. What else did they tell her about the late Michael O'Neill? Was his desire to own and collect rare items a form of control? Could it be indicative of anxiety around personal relationships? His position as a teacher was important too. Adam had said he used to lecture on social policy: was his authoritarian role a mask for something else?

When the side door of the lock-up squeaked open, Kate jumped, turning quickly to see who was behind her. If Ethel noticed the shock on Kate's face, she didn't comment: she looked lost, standing there, not saying a word, taking in her surroundings. She paid no heed to the putrid smell, finally asking, 'Did you find the notebooks, my dear?'

'Not yet.'

'I didn't realise Michael had so much stuff.' Ethel peered around the lock-up. 'They could be in that tea chest over there. I remember it, I think.'

'Why don't you go back to the car, Ethel? It's a mess in here.'

'We need to get the milk and eggs.'

'I know that.'

Kate escorted her out into the lane, watching while Ethel walked to the car and sat back inside. This wasn't going to be easy, she thought, but she was committed now.

Inside again, she stared at the tea chest, then took in the contents of the frames hanging on the left-hand garage wall. The only wall without urine stains. At first, she thought they were another type of collection. The frames nearest to her contained species of butterflies, but there were other insects, too, stuffed rodents and what looked like framed strands of hair.

Kate thought about the violation of the place. Had Michael O'Neill done it? Was he under duress? Or was someone else responsible? She took a step closer to the frames containing the hair. There was no way of knowing if they were animal or human.

When she flipped the lid of the tea chest open, it was full to the brim of large hardback notebooks. Like the other collections, each had been clearly marked, this time with a specific year, dating from 1980 to 1988. If 1980 was the year O'Neill had started teaching, strange, she thought, that the notebooks ended in 1988. He had continued teaching for a long time after that. She wondered why he had made the career switch. Surely lecturing was more lucrative than primary school teaching. 1988 was also, coincidentally, the year of her attack, and the year Kevin had died. Maybe Michael had stopped filling them in after the boy's death.

Doubling back to check on Ethel, she was relieved to see her fast asleep in the car. With little time to waste, she went back to the tea chest, but as she did so, almost instinctively, she began to go over things in her mind, pulling together all the bits she could remember. She had been attacked from behind after separating from her friends, looking for a stray ball. When he'd grabbed her, and she screamed, she'd felt as if her screams were coming from somewhere distant. He had held a knife to her throat, and thinking this, she raised her hand to her neck, getting the smell of urine once more. Why remember some parts and not others?

Despite there being no heating on in the lock-up, her body felt warm. Her chest was hot too, with red blotches, confirming her nervousness. It was only then that she heard someone else approach the lock-up door. There was more than one person. She listened to the low voices, holding her breath, trying to work out what she would say if anyone stepped inside. Paranoia set in – could someone have followed her again? She knew she was being daft, but she couldn't shake the notion that she was the one under some kind of microscope, rather than the other way around.

When the low voices stopped, she listened to the wind whizzing underneath the door and let out a sigh of relief. Whoever it was had moved on. This time, she thought about all the things she couldn't remember, asking again how long she had been missing. How had she managed to find her way home? What had his face looked like? She flicked open the first record book from 1980, four years after she was born. Reading page after page, she noted that Michael O'Neill recorded details of the school day, community events, items of local interest, like the passing away of the parish priest or the opening of a new club. None of it was of any major consequence, but detailed nonetheless.

She went to 1981, and found more of the same. Why was she waiting? Why didn't she simply open 1988 and be done with it? Stop running, she told herself. She pulled out the notebook with '1988' on the front, closed the lid of the chest and placed the notebook on it. Other memories were flying through her mind. There was that feeling of utter panic, a sense that she was alone with the man, somewhere far away from the people who could help her. Think hard, she told herself, but it was as if she was searching her brain in the same desperate way that Ethel couldn't remember things. Damn it, think.

She stared at the notebook. Her last memory was of being dragged through trees. Her feet had hurt, and she had lost her shoes. She hadn't remembered that bit before. Her white ankle socks had become wet and mucky, and her underarms were sore from where he had held her, his fists tight around her chest, the knife still in his hand. All of this was new. She thought about the smell of alcohol on his breath, something that had never left her, but what about his hands? They were strong, the fingers chunky – she could see them now, another fragment of memory. Was he wearing a ring? She couldn't be sure. She held the notebook, still hesitant.

'Open the damn book,' she said out loud. 'Stop running.' She opened the pages one by one, and it didn't take long to reach the date she was looking for. She read the early contents quickly, mainly around the school day. At the end of the page, she found it – 'Local Girl Goes Missing'. Underneath, her name and other details: 'Kate Pearson, aged 12, a student of St Mary's School for Girls'. Under that, there was another note, giving details of a local search party being set up: 'So, the community was definitely involved.'

Something banged against the lock-up door, two loud cracks. She looked up, turning fast towards the side entrance, thinking it was Ethel again, but no one entered. It might have been the door contracting, she thought, but she couldn't shake her anxiety, looking all around her. You're alone, she told herself. She went back to where she had stopped reading. The entry went on to explain that the local community had searched all evening, but the schoolgirl, Kate Pearson, hadn't turned up. It was true, then. She couldn't have been missing for only a couple of hours, as her parents had told her. But if not a couple of hours, how long had it been? Hours, days, longer? The following entry covered the next school day. Speed-reading the opening content, she found nothing of significance, but on turning the page, she knew she was getting closer to something, closer than she had ever been.

She stared at the next two pages for what felt like for ever, realising quickly that the following page didn't correlate with the previous one. Pages had been cut out. She stretched out the fold in the notebook, seeing the neatly severed remains of sheets tight to the spine – the same edge as on the newspaper clipping.

Flicking through the rest of the notebook, she checked to see if other pages had been removed, but none had been tampered with, as far as she could tell. It was only the pages after the day she had disappeared. She checked again, doubting herself, telling herself to take it slowly this time.

It was only when she looked at the back of the notebook for a second time that she saw the plastic pocket on the inside cover: in it, a folded page of a newspaper. She opened it. The article had a photograph of her and Adam leaving the Circuit Court in 2012. It was during the William Cronly trial, the man responsible for the murder of two twelve-year-old schoolgirls that year. Both she and Adam looked sombre, trying to avoid the cameras as they walked down the steps of the court.

Kate couldn't believe what she was looking at. Why had Michael O'Neill an article about her and Adam at the trial? Cronly was still serving out his prison sentence. Did someone want her to find the clipping, perhaps for the same reason they had sent the note to the apartment? Her visit to the lock-up had been random, dependent on Ethel's unreliable memory, yet something about it felt orchestrated.

She thought about Malcolm. There was an age gap of at least fifteen years between him and O'Neill, but now that the connection with Kevin was clear, she knew Michael O'Neill and Malcolm must have been neighbours at one point. They could have known each other back then. She needed to talk to Adam. She swallowed hard. Time was running out. She couldn't risk leaving Ethel on her own any longer. On leaving the lock-up, she fired the protective gloves and footwear into a nearby skip.

Ethel awoke as soon as Kate opened the car door. She hoped she didn't smell too bad, but she also knew she had to bring the conversation back to the lock-up and its contents.

'Ethel, the notebooks?'

'Notebooks? Oh, yes, I remember now. Did you find them?'

'They were in the tea chest, as you said.'

'There's so much stuff in there. I knew Michael was a hoarder but, heavens ...'

'Do you remember when the things were stored in the garage? Was it when you moved house?'

'I think so. It was so long ago. Some friends of Michael's helped him move it all.' Her eyes lit up with delight, as if she had won a prize by remembering such a tiny thing.

'Who helped?'

She looked confused again. 'I can't ...'

'Were they neighbours?'

'I'm not sure. They might have been.'

'Please, Ethel, it's important.'

She bit her bottom lip. 'Valentine. There was a man called Valentine.'

'Valentine Pearson?'

'Yes, that's right. Did you know him?'

'For a time.'

'There was another man too.'

'Who, Ethel?'

'I can't ... I don't ... It's there, the name, but I can't catch it.'

Kate wanted to scream, but with Ethel becoming increasingly upset, pushing it wasn't going to help. Turning the ignition key, she said, 'Don't worry, Ethel. Let's go and get the milk and eggs.'

'I think the name started with M.'

Malcolm Madden, Kate thought. His name started with M, but then again, so did a great many others. Was she creating links that might or might not exist, and what about Adam, why hadn't he mentioned Kevin being O'Neill's foster son? Why had he held this information back from her?

The Game Changer

IT WASN'T LONG BEFORE KATE AND ETHEL'S VISIT TO the lock-up was reported to the Game Changer. Success meant anticipating a variety of moves and potential counter-moves, and having eyes and ears in any number of places was always useful. The group member who reported the incident believed Ethel O'Neill could be troublesome.

CENTRE OF LIGHTNESS
20 Steps to Self-enlightenment Programme

Confidential Record: 122

Ethel O'Neill is in denial, clinging to the notion that her husband was a good man, in the same way that desperate people believe in some form of salvation, a reward beyond this life. Why? They're not prepared to face the consequences of another answer.

Michael O'Neill didn't like being reminded of his sins — a man uncomfortable with the truth. If you get away with something for long enough, you come to believe you have invested a great deal in it. All those lies and cover-ups and near misses, and people who could have ratted on you, but didn't, feed into the belief that you have managed to bury the truth.

The Game Changer had to convince him that what he needed most in life was forgiveness. It was an easy pill to swallow, a sugar-coated alternative when punishment didn't look nearly as attractive. It helped him to part with his money, and once that was done, forgiveness was

---

denied. Humiliation played a role too: being forced to urinate and soil the walls of the lock-up eradicated the last of his pride. His death was always on the cards, and if fragile Ethel decides to complicate things, she too will be crushed.

(Page 1 of 1)

Kate

KATE HAD BARELY AN HOUR BEFORE SHE COLLECTED Charlie from school, but she wasn't prepared to wait any longer to ask Adam why he had been selective with the information he had given her on the O'Neill investigation. Walking through Harcourt Street station, she was greeted by the odd nod and cheerful wave from people she'd worked with in the past. Only those within the Special Detective Unit would have known she was taking time out, making it easier for her to reach Adam's office without too many questions being asked.

Ever since she'd dropped Ethel off, things had kept churning in her mind, and her uncertainty around the length of time she had been missing all those years ago had taken on a whole new lease of life. She felt as if an enormous chasm had opened, and she had no idea how deep it was, or how far she would fall before she reached something solid. What had felt like vague, unanswered questions, coupled with slight memory loss, had been magnified to something far more ominous by her parents' lack of truthfulness, and with that came more questions.

Right now, the only person who could give her answers was Adam. A group of male detectives were huddled together outside his door. She knew a couple of them, but she wasn't in the mood for polite conversation, shuffling her way through, barely acknowledging anyone. Tapping on the door, she turned the handle and walked in without waiting to be asked.

'Kate.' Surprise showed on Adam's face. 'Is something wrong?

'Why didn't you tell me about O'Neill's foster son?' She slammed the door behind her.

'Calm down,' he said.

'Well, why didn't you?' she asked again, louder.

He moved to her side of the desk, leaning against it, facing her. 'Kate, let's keep the volume down, shall we?'

'All right, but I want answers.'

'For a start, you're not part of the investigation team.'

'That didn't stop you asking me questions, seeking my opinion ...'

'Is it wrong that I value your views?'

'No, but you could have told me about Kevin.'

'Look, when we found out O'Neill's foster son had died in a similar manner, it added weight to O'Neill's death being suicide – a kind of copycat death, the guy reflecting a form of solidarity or regret for what had happened before.'

'No argument there.'

'But the boy's death happened a long time ago.'

'So?'

'I already guessed it was the guy you mentioned but, frankly, Kate, that was it. End of story.'

'Rubbish.'

'What do you want from me?'

'The truth would help.'

'Okay, fine.' He folded his arms. 'I knew you were upset over the note.'

'What has that to do with anything?'

'And then with the possible connection to Madden. When the link to the boy's death was made, I didn't ...'

'You didn't what?'

'I didn't want you jumping to conclusions.'

'What kind of conclusions? You're not back to that crap about me not being myself?'

'When you got that note, almost immediately it was like you wanted to connect it to what happened to you all those years ago.'

'That doesn't mean I was wrong.'

'No, it doesn't, but with Kevin's death happening the same year, I was afraid you'd put two and two together and come up with—'

'With what? Some sort of conspiracy theory?'

'Yeah, something like that.'

She sat down on the chair, keeping her voice calm. 'You knew I was going to talk to Ethel O'Neill. You should have briefed me.'

'I know that.'

'So why didn't you?'

'In this instance, I thought that the more open you were going in, the better.'

'I don't agree.'

'Look, it was a long shot that you'd get anything out of Ethel. I told you that from the get-go.'

'Something stinks here.'

'What stinks is that you're used to being in the driver's seat.'

'That's harsh.'

'What happened to you wanting to take time out to be with Charlie?'

'You're changing the subject.'

'Can't a guy make a point?'

'I want to be assigned to the case.'

'Impossible.'

'Why? It wouldn't be the end of the world if I came back early, even if only to concentrate on this particular investigation.'

'It's not going to happen, Kate. Accept it.'

'It can happen if you make it happen.'

'It wouldn't be wise for anyone involved.'

'Why not?'

'Because you're personally involved, that's why not.'

'And you're not?'

'That's different. I was assigned to the case before any connection was made. Listen, Kate,' his tone softening, 'you're doing the right thing taking time out. Even I can see the difference it's making to you and Charlie.'

'Bullshit. Let's leave my parenting skills out of this.'

They both turned as the office door opened.

'Everything okay, boss?' It was one of the detectives Kate had worked with before.

'Yes, fine, Fitzsimons.' Adam sounded snappy. 'I won't be much longer.'

With the door closed, Kate walked over to the window. Adam followed her, putting his hands on her shoulders. 'Don't be angry, Kate. You know how these things work.'

She shrugged him away. 'I read O'Neill's notebooks.' She sounded calm but stern, not turning to face him.

'What notebooks?'

'He kept records of his school years – at least, those from 1980 to 1988.' She emphasised 1988 so that he was aware of the significance.

'I didn't know anything about any notebooks. Where were they? At the school? At his house? We searched that place from top to bottom.'

She turned to face him. 'Ethel told me about them.'

'She didn't say anything—'

'Rapid dementia. Remember, I had plenty of experience of it with my mother.'

'Where did you find them, the notebooks?'

'A lock-up garage off Buckingham Street in Rathmines. They've had it since their move in 'eighty-eight.'

'You should have phoned me straight away. You shouldn't have gone in unsupervised.'

'I tried to call you but your phone rang out.'

'And you didn't think to leave a message or talk to anyone else?'

'I didn't want to talk to anyone else. Anyway, I wasn't alone. I was with Ethel.'

'You still should have waited.'

'It might have been nothing.'

'Who's talking bullshit now?' It was his turn to pace the room. 'Did you at least wear protective gear?'

'I had gloves and shoes in the car.'

'That's something, but— Jesus, Kate, can't you see? It's why being involved isn't a good idea. This is too close to you.'

'I don't believe Michael O'Neill killed himself, not with his wife being the way she is. It goes contrary to his profile. He wouldn't have left her to fend for herself.'

'You can't be sure what thoughts went through his mind.'

'I know that, Adam, but …'

'But what?'

'O'Neill had an entry about me in the notebooks, about my disappearance. But that's not all. The place was soiled with urine and possibly human excrement.'

'Hold on. Are you saying someone broke in?'

'I don't know, but what I do know is that for a short while the O'Neills lived in the same neighbourhood as me, with their foster son, and not everything is as it should be.'

'I realise that.'

'There were missing pages and entries in the notebooks.'

'What do you mean?'

'The pages after the note about my disappearance had been cut out and …' She paused, as if still trying to work out how it was all connected.

'And what?'

'They were cut out using the same type of scissors as the note delivered to the apartment.'

When he didn't answer immediately, she continued: 'You'll need to take your time in the lock-up. Michael O'Neill was quite a collector, or someone else was. He had any number of collections, books, stamps, even insects.'

Adam looked as if he was trying to digest the information she had given him. Finally, he said, 'The lock-up must have been rented. The team checked all O'Neill's assets. There were a number of official items held at his solicitor's office and at the bank, but nothing referred to a garage off Buckingham Street.'

'The notes confirmed I was missing overnight …' She wondered if she should tell him about Ethel O'Neill mentioning her father's name, and him helping them with the move. Could she trust what Ethel had said? The name could have been triggered by their earlier conversation about her disappearance. Instead, she said, 'Adam, you can't keep me out of this.'

'I'm more determined than ever to do exactly that.'

'I know I should have got clearance about the garage before going in.'

'Too right you should have, but it's not only that.' He was angry now. 'There are too many things linking you directly or indirectly to this.'

She moved closer to him. 'Assign me to the case. If an absolute link is established, I'll pull back. I promise.'

'You've already given me the link. You've connected the clipping sent to the apartment to the pages from the notebooks, and entries about you.'

'It's a common enough style of scissors.'

'Stop backpedalling, Kate. If you thought it was nothing you wouldn't be jumping up and down in my office asking to be assigned to the case.'

'Fine. If I can't be assigned to the investigation, can I at least have access to the individual case files?'

'No can do. The chief super would have a heart attack.'

'Adam, I can't do what I do best unless I have the necessary information to work with.'

'I realise that, but remember, you're not on the case. You don't need to work on anything.'

'You want to shut me out.'

'Stop being melodramatic.'

'If I can't work with you, I'll have to work without you.'

'Kate, if you start marching around *unofficially* in this investigation, it will only mean trouble, and there's going to be shit to pay about you going to that lock-up garage alone.'

'That's your final take, is it?'

'Yes.'

'Then there's no point in me wasting my time here.'

Walking towards the door with her back to him, she said, 'Tell your guys when they're looking in O'Neill's lock-up to pay particular attention to the framed collection, especially the hair samples.'

'Hair?'

'Yes – hair.' She turned to face him again, holding the handle of the door behind her.

'Kate, we'll need a full statement from you, sooner rather than later. I know you have to collect Charlie but arrange a minder for him and get yourself back here. I'll ask one of the new guys to take it from you. It'll be easier that way.'

'I'm always willing to co-operate with the police.' A note of sarcasm in her words.

'Now you're being childish.'

'Adam, I have one last question for you.'

'What's that?'

'William Cronly. Is he still locked up?'

'Yes, as far as I know he is. Why?'

'Someone with access to the O'Neills' garage and the notebooks has a special interest in us.' She knew she was thwarting him, but she didn't care.

'Why do you say that?'

'At the back of the 1988 notebook, you'll find a page from a newspaper with a picture of us walking out of the Circuit Court during the Cronly trial.'

'What do you think it means?'

'I've no idea.'

'Kate, quit messing. If you have a theory, spit it out.'

'Okay, then. I think whoever left it there is playing games.'

'Like the evidence left at the Mason crime scene?'

'Perhaps, but I'm not going to stop trying to find out, whether I'm part of this investigation or not.'

'Kate …'

She put up a hand to stop him. 'Don't waste your breath. You've already told me what you think.'

'I'll need to be kept in the loop.'

'You mean I've to tell you my every move?'

'I mean exactly that.' Fitzsimons knocked on the glass panel. Adam raised his hand, spreading his fingers, telling him, another five minutes. 'Kate, however this unfolds, I can't have you playing renegade cop.'

'You can't stop me looking into my past.'

'No, I guess I can't, but if anything else turns up, like that garage, promise me you'll make contact before you do anything.'

'What about you? If you discover information, and it involves me, will you tell me?'

'I'll do what I can.'

'I see,' she replied, pulling the door behind her.

Special Detective Unit, Harcourt Street

ADAM O'CONNOR WASN'T KEEN ON BEING IN THE dog-house after his conversation with Kate. He had told her a limited version of the truth, but even before their argument, this had gone way beyond personal for her.

Opening his office door, he roared at Fitzsimons, 'We have a temporary change of plan. Get yourself in here.'

'What's up, boss?'

'We need to get a warrant for a lock-up garage off Buckingham Street. It was either rented or owned by the O'Neills. I want to know which. If it isn't theirs, I want to know who owns it. Talk to the neighbours around Buckingham Street. See if they can give us anything. I'll put a trace through to Dublin City Council and the Land Registry, but something tells me this isn't going to be straightforward. I know those lock-ups. They're usually let or sublet all over the place.'

'Who'll sign off on the warrant request?'

'I'll ask the chief super, but have Judge Keegan on standby. There's been enough time wasted on this one, and it feels like someone else is ahead of us.'

'Do you know what's in the garage?'

'According to Kate, it's something of a treasure trove. We'll need the tech guys too. And include someone with an in-depth knowledge of hair fibres.'

'Will do.'

'And get that guy Ferguson involved. He studied insects, didn't he? What do you call it?'

126

'Entomology.'

'Fitzsimons, I'm impressed.'

Adam knew his phone call to the chief super wasn't going to be an easy one. He would be furious about Kate taking matters into her own hands and going into the lock-up without clearance. The sooner Adam worked out how all of this fitted together, the better it would be for everyone. Before he made the call, his mobile phone rang. Seeing it was Marion, Addy's mother, he picked it up. 'What's up?'

'It's Addy.'

'What about him?'

'He's going away for a few weeks.'

'Where to?'

'Kerry. He'll be there with Aoife.'

'A holiday?'

'Sort of – a bit like a back-to-nature kind of thing, but he'll be home before college starts.'

'I rang him a few times, he never phoned me back. Is he there?'

'No, sorry, Adam, he's already gone.'

'Okay – thanks for letting me know.' Even though he had no right to be annoyed, he still felt it.

Hanging up, he dialled the chief super's number, knowing he would get an earful about Kate's escapade. If it led to a breakthrough in the investigation, moods might improve, but somehow he doubted it. In the few months since Kate had taken a step back, in the chief super's eyes she had gone from Dr Kate Pearson to *your girlfriend*, and thinking about Kate again, Adam also knew that somehow he would have to try to get her back onside.

Addy

ADDY WAS GLAD TO BE WEARING HIS HEAVY PARKA
when he felt the sharp Atlantic breeze as he stepped into the boat
for the island crossing. Although the sun was still shining, in the
distance he could see a blanket of cloud hovering over land, giving
the small island an eerie, almost mystical appearance.

Apart from the local fisherman guiding the boat, the only other
company he had was a woman with a baby. He had helped her to
load her stuff, a large suitcase, a buggy, and a baby travel bag. She
looked nervous, so for the first while, other than small pleasantries,
he hadn't said very much.

'My friends call me, Addy,' he finally blurted out, fighting to be
heard above the roar of the wind.

She nodded at him.

'I guess we're both going to the same place.' Another attempt at
conversation.

'I'm Sarah,' she said, leaning over to shake his hand, 'and this is
Lily.'

'You have her wrapped up well.' He hoped he sounded friendly,
even though something about the woman and her baby seemed odd.
She was younger than his mother, and very different: she looked
like a bit of a hippie, wearing little or no makeup, her long dark hair
was tied in a side plait.

'It won't be long now,' hollered the fisherman, not looking at
either of them as the seagulls clattered overhead. As it turned out,
Addy hadn't needed to pay for the boat trip. The fisherman told him
someone on the island had already looked after it. He hadn't pushed
it. The guy didn't give the impression he was the chatty type.

Looking at Sarah again, with the baby blanket dropped down a little, Addy got his first proper view of Lily, realising for the first time what had spiked his curiosity. The child hadn't cried or moved since they'd made their way on to the boat. Seeing the face, he knew immediately that it was a doll, and instantly felt embarrassed for the woman. He hoped she hadn't noticed his reaction. A part of him felt sorry for her. Another part thought, what the hell? If pretending the doll was a baby made her happy, what harm was she doing? People fool themselves with worse things. It was only when she asked him if he knew Saka that his body stiffened.

'No, I've never met him. And you?'

'Yes. He's been very good to me, as have many others from the Centre of Lightness.' She gazed into the distance, then added, 'They've all been very kind about Lily too.'

Addy didn't answer. Instead, he looked down at the sea, now grey under the dark clouds. He pulled the zipper of his jacket up tight to his chin, hearing the sound of the Atlantic splashing against the side of the boat, tasting salt water in his mouth, his cheeks frozen.

Closer to the island, high waves replaced the calmer waters with a rush of whiteness as the boat chopped towards land. One wave superseded another. Addy didn't particularly mind the rolling of the boat, or being soaked by the spray, or the cold Atlantic wind biting hard. He didn't even mind the woman fretting about the baby doll, or the fisherman seeming to refuse to catch his eye: for some crazy reason, all of it felt like a kind of adventure.

When the boat pulled into the shore, the wind was stronger again, and after he'd put on his backpack, seeing that Sarah was struggling, he picked up her suitcase and the buggy. 'Are you all right?' he yelled.

'Yes, yes, I'm fine.'

She looked around her as Addy watched the boat they had come in pull away. His earlier sense of adventure had been replaced with apprehension and he wondered what he was letting himself in for.

Together, they climbed the steep pathway from the shoreline to higher ground. According to the fisherman, it would lead them to a view of the commune house. Addy thought about how the three of them must look: a kind of crazy mismatched family fired together – a fortyish woman, a baby doll and him. Thinking about his friends back in Dublin, he felt oddly older and, in a strange way, responsible for this near stranger, a woman who seemed to be making her way to some kind of Promised Land.

Spring Valley Village, Texas

LEE TOOK A SWIG OF BEER, ONLY HALF LISTENING to his brother. The night was a balmy sixty-seven degrees, and the brothers had decided to have their drinks outside on the porch while John's wife, Margaret, put the boys to bed.

They could hear night crickets, their familiar chirping sound feeding into the relaxing air, and an alternative to the din of Manhattan, with its constant crowds and sirens.

'You seem distant, Lee,' John finally said, copping on to the fact that his brother was no longer following the conversation.

'Do I? Sorry.'

'Yeah. Ever since you got that phone call an hour ago.'

'Force of habit, I suppose.'

'Didn't you tell them you were on vacation?'

'I told them, all right, but some things can't wait.'

'They'd wait if you were dead.'

'Cheerful.'

'Just saying it as it is.'

Lee took another swig of his beer, his lack of response acting as agreement that John was right. The call had certainly been an interesting one, another wacky addition to the Tom Mason investigation.

'Can I ask you a question, Lee?' John leaned forward on his chair.

'Sure.'

'Why do you like to read those detective novels?'

Lee picked up his battered copy of *The Mad Hatter Mystery*. 'What? This?'

'Yeah.'

'I suppose because I like puzzles.'

131

'But you've read that one loads of times. I've seen you with it before.'

'No matter how many times I read it, I always find something I missed the previous times.'

'And that's important?'

'To me it is.'

'What about all the other books in the world?'

'It's good to know your limitations, John. If I lived to be ten thousand, I wouldn't get to read all the books out there. So, I work out which ones are important for me, and I concentrate on them.'

'Was that phone call from the precinct?'

'It was.' He stretched out his legs. 'An investigation is a bit like a book, bro. The more time you spend with it, the more rewards you get.'

'A bit like a marriage, too.'

Lee smiled. 'Not quite, but I reckon nearly as time-consuming.'

John stood up. 'Shall I get us a couple more beers?'

'Sure.'

When John went inside, Lee thought about all the statements they had taken on the Mason case. None had given the investigation team a whole lot to go on, and it had taken them a while to track down Mason's sister, Emily Burke. She was now living in Montana, and Jimmy Maynard, his partner, had been right to ring through the details of the interview to him. Jimmy and Lee worked well together. They were both capable of keeping their cards close to their chest, while always ensuring their partner was kept in the loop. Jimmy hadn't mentioned anything to Emily Burke about the questionable images they had found on her brother's computer, but he had pushed her for information about her brother's life prior to his time in Manhattan. The political stuff they already knew, but Tom Mason being part of some intellectual study group in the eighties had spiked Jimmy's interest, especially as the sister seemed to have a strong aversion to telling him too many concrete details about it.

Kate

WALKING OUT OF ADAM'S OFFICE, KATE WAS CLOSE to tears. It wasn't only the angry words that fuelled her upset, but that they had argued, really argued. It had felt like a repeat of Declan and her, all over again. The type of argument had changed, but she was still part of it. Adam had been right about one thing: she was too close to all of this. Outside factors were forcing her to face up to things she might not be ready for. If it hadn't been for that note, she wouldn't be so apprehensive, not just about her own safety, but about Charlie's too. She wasn't the first person to get a harassment note. If any regular person had received one, they would have completed an official police report, and that would have been the end of it, unless things took a darker turn. Nonetheless, the uncertainty felt risky, nor was she sure what her next step would be, or how she would be able to unravel things outside the investigation team. One thing she was certain of, though: irrespective of Adam's instructions, she would do whatever it took to get answers, and to make sure Charlie was safe.

Passing the myriad faces in Harcourt Street, her mind jumped in different directions. She was going to be outside the loop, operating alone, and she would have to find ways to compensate for that. She hadn't mentioned to Adam Ethel's reference to her father, and part of her knew why. She wasn't sure yet how to deal with that either. Malcolm was right. Her father had been an enigma, a man of secrets, and the trouble with secrets was that sometimes when things are hidden, once unearthed they can change everything. If she was turning her past life into some kind of investigation, a certain vulnerability and fear came with it, and a sense that something from long ago wasn't right, even if she wasn't sure what it was.

When Ethel had mentioned her father's name, she hadn't simply felt another pull back to childhood: it had been like a calling card, sucking her in. Almost without warning, in the corridors of Harcourt Street police station, another memory returned. It wasn't of the day of her attack, but days, perhaps weeks, before.

Her father had been in one of his dark moods. His silence hung everywhere, filling the air with rage. She had gone to her bedroom to stay out of his way. Voices from outside had brought her to the window. She'd recognised Kevin, looking cool in his black T-shirt and jeans. He wasn't alone. That man and the girl were with him again. The man was older, and the girl was probably the same age as Kate. They were laughing at something the man had said, but Kate kept staring at Kevin, not paying much attention to the other two. There was a look in his eyes that she hadn't understood at first, but then she'd realised what it was because she was feeling the same thing: fear. When she heard her father move around downstairs, slamming doors, her anxiety intensified. Then her mind skipped again, from that day to another afternoon, when she had bumped into Kevin on the way home from school. She was wearing her school duffel coat, her hair tied back neatly in a ponytail. At the time, because of her bad eyesight, she had worn horn-rimmed spectacles. Instinctively, her adult self touched her nose, thinking about all the times she'd had to push her glasses up after they had slipped down. Even when the glasses were gone, she'd move the imaginary ones up her nose, getting a form of solace from an action no longer required. Kevin had asked her to sit on the canal wall. She was excited and nervous that he wanted to spend time with her, even though she hated the way she looked, and wished she was older, prettier, less like a nerd. Thinking back, she couldn't remember what they had talked about, but she remembered being with him, and that he had been kind.

With more people passing her in the corridor, Kate stepped to the side, leaning against the wall, bringing her mind back to her last memory. At the time, her head had been full of silly notions, a mix of pre-adolescence and early pangs of attraction. Her twelve-year-old self had idolised the teenager. She even remembered walking by his house, hoping he would come out to say hello, imagining what it would be like when the two of them were older, and she wouldn't be an ugly duckling. He would fall in love with her. She had imagined the two of them talking about that day, the one when she'd spotted him from the window, when there was something about the man and the girl that had frightened him. What had he been afraid of?

No matter how hard she tried, nothing more would come, and when Kate stepped outside into the fresh air, she realised something else about that memory. She wasn't sure whether it was an instinct, or whether her subconscious mind was playing tricks on her, but something told her that finding out who that man and girl had been was going to be important.

The Game Changer

A VISIT TO THE ISLAND WAS REQUIRED, BUT A reflection on Kate's progress was also necessary. Kate liked to meddle, and an inquisitive mind needed to be tied in knots. People would soon doubt her judgement, and she'd become further entrenched and isolated, her obsession a form of weapon that could be used against her. Kate was a *maximiser*, and one with very high standards. A maximiser goes out of their way to make the right decisions, and because of this they're plagued with endless questions. It's Kate's desire to maximise that fuels her constant journey as a seeker. She makes a decision, but continues looking. She falls in love, but still questions. The more effort someone puts into reaching the right choice, the higher their expectations are, and the harder it is for those expectations to be fulfilled. Ultimately, dissatisfaction increases, and they reach a kind self-fulfilling prophecy.

People were like stacks of cards: the older they got, the more levels they built. Apply the right pressure, and they are easily reduced to a four-year-old child, with all the fears and uncertainties that irk them most.

The island visit would happen soon enough. The group members were all individuals with potential benefits for the Game Changer. A mix of nationalities, who by and large were also people with money. Those who had reached leadership status would manage fine for the next few days. By the time anyone started digging up graves, or anything else on the island, the Game Changer would be long gone.

Placing the laptop on the old desk, in what used to be Kate's parents' bedroom, the Game Changer began another report, pondering on how useful it was to have members of the police force as part of the group. It was an organisation in which trust was paramount, officers putting their lives in danger every day. Each member needed to know that their group was strong, and although made up of many individuals, they saw themselves as a single entity. Within this, a certain level of blindness was inevitable, and this form of blindness could be easily manipulated.

CENTRE OF LIGHTNESS
20 Steps to Self-enlightenment Programme

OBSERVATIONAL TARGET: Kate Pearson

Kate will continue to experience isolation and confusion. Elements of her past will force her to ask questions about herself and what she believes. This will ultimately lead to despair. She might lose all sense of who she is, whom she can trust, and an overwhelming feeling of hopelessness will ensue.

Hopelessness brings a form of emotional freedom, the knowledge that nothing a person can do will change anything. Human beings complicate their lives, while death on the other hand is simple. There is a relief in that too, for some, but there will be no relief for Kate. As a maximiser, she is also a fighter.

September 1988
Twelve-year-old Kate picked up a near-dead female blackbird. The bird's beady eyes elicited a form of empathy from her. Her father, Valentine Pearson, dumped it in a bin. The bird formed part of the Game Changer's collection. After the Game Changer scooped it out, a line with a pen was drawn down its chest, starting at the throat. The knife brought the slow illicit sound of skin being torn, before removing it in its entirety, the same way someone might take off a coat.

(Page 1 of 2)

CENTRE OF LIGHTNESS
20 Steps to Self-enlightenment Programme

Kate would know that some psychopaths enjoyed collecting body parts. The Game Changer over time has examined many segments of the human body, as well as those of animals, and other forms.

Initial studies concentrated on insects, with an appreciation for watching them when they were trapped, especially their futile attempts at escape before a slow, resolute death.

The eyes of Kate's dead blackbird underwent optical nerve examination. The ophthalmic, maxillary and mandibular branches leave the skull through three separate foramina, with the ophthalmic nerve carrying sensory information from the scalp to the forehead, the upper eyelid, the conjunctiva and the cornea of the eye.

Overview:
During the next phase, Kate will come down from her ivory tower, and when she does, she will have no idea that the Game Changer is waiting for her, or how much the Game Changer intends for her to suffer.

(Page 2 of 2)

Special Detective Unit, Harcourt Street

AS ADAM WAITED FOR THE SEARCH WARRANT FOR the O'Neill garage, he began trawling through media footage from the eighties, examining cases of convicted paedophiles. As yet, he hadn't found anything remotely connected to Michael O'Neill, Valentine Pearson, Tom Mason or Malcolm Madden. It was early days, though. These things took time. If there was something to be found, he needed a lucky break, enough for PIU and the Domestic Violence Unit to play ball. It was standard to make enquiries via both departments, as history dictated the two often overlapped.

With the longer timeframe for Kate's disappearance now in the mix, based on what she had found in O'Neill's notebooks, Adam was prompted to check if a missing-person report had been filed in 1988. If she had been missing for an hour or so, there would be nothing, but with the disappearance being longer, he wasn't surprised that a file existed. Although there wasn't anything too unusual in the statements taken at the time, some parts were interesting.

Kate had separated from her friends. Her parents had become concerned when she hadn't returned by six o'clock. According to her mother, they contacted the parents of each of her girlfriends, assuming Kate had gone to a friend's house. It didn't take long to establish that she hadn't, and that it was at least four hours since any of her friends had seen her. The alert was sent via Rathmines police station, and a search by locals had ensued. By morning, with no sign of Kate, the worst was feared, but then at ten past one that afternoon, Kate had arrived home. She claimed she couldn't remember what had happened to her, other than something about being grabbed from behind. Her mother's statement was one of relief that her daughter had returned home safe and sound. Her father's was more official and reserved, stating that both he and his wife were relieved to have Kate back, and what had probably been an attention-seeking stunt on his daughter's behalf had ended without anyone being hurt. It wasn't surprising that no more was made of it. A missing person, even if it was a child, wouldn't have warranted a criminal investigation. Once Kate had returned home safely, that would have been the end of it. Also, it seemed that Kate's limited memory of the events was overshadowed by her father's view about it being an attention-seeking exercise, and the police investigation was closed.

Depending on how they got on in the O'Neill garage, and considering how Kate had lost it with him, he would have to tread carefully. He also knew that keeping her in the dark might prove to be a decision he would regret. She wouldn't stop digging, even if her close association to the case made her the worst candidate for reaching clear and logical conclusions. Nevertheless, she could also be the key. A lot depended on how she handled this emotionally and, from her angry outbursts in his office, he had his concerns that her normally rational thought processes would win out.

When the all-clear came through from Fitzsimons on the warrant, Adam thought about what Kate had said about the newspaper cutting of the Cronly case in the back of the notebook. It was certainly a curveball. Why was it in O'Neill's garage, and why at the back of the 1988 notebook? Kate was certainly right about one thing: this case felt as if someone was playing games with them.

Addy

ONCE ADDY AND SARAH REACHED HIGHER GROUND, they could see the main commune building, with a series of linked whitewashed cottages. Aoife must have been watching out for him because, within minutes of reaching the upper level, he saw her leave the main building, waving to them. She was with another guy. Don't jump to conclusions, he told himself, but when they got closer, even though it had been only a short while since he'd seen her, she looked different.

She seemed older, more conservative, with her flat shoes, black trousers and white blouse, like something his grandmother would have worn, buttoned up to the neck. Her hair was different too, flying loose around her face, as if she was some wild woman of the islands. It unsettled him, but he didn't say anything.

When Addy reached out to hug her, she put her hand out instead, shaking his before she did the same with Sarah, as if they were polite acquaintances, not boyfriend and girlfriend. Then she introduced Stephen, who, with his short blond hair and clean-shaven face, looked to Addy like one of those holier-than-thou nut-jobs, who knocked on your door wanting to convert you to the good life. Addy took an immediate dislike to him, especially when he rested his hand on Sarah's shoulder.

Walking towards the commune house, Addy kept in line with Aoife, and even though there was a good distance between Sarah and Stephen further up the footpath, he kept his voice low: 'I'm not going to have to change my designer wardrobe, am I?' he asked, half joking.

'No,' Aoife replied. 'You'll be different.'

'How do you mean different?'

'You're one of the helpers.'

'So?'

'You can wear whatever you want.'

'And you can't?'

'Of course I can, but my choice of clothing is part of the programme.'

'You look like something out of a convent.'

'I don't care. What matters is how I feel inside.'

'I preferred you the way you were.'

She stopped walking. 'Addy, I don't expect you to get it, but I have my reasons.'

'Try me.'

'The clothing is a statement. It frees me from the social pressures of how other people think I should look.'

'Like attractive, sexy?'

'Yes, something like that,' she said coldly. She continued walking.

'Look, Aoife, I want to understand. Honest, I do.'

'Do you?'

'Yes.'

'Addy, I'm not altogether sure why you came here.'

'You asked me to come, remember?'

'I did, I know, but a lot has changed very fast.'

'Like what?'

Again she stopped walking, and so did he. 'The way I used to dress wasn't about self-expression. That's part of the lies they feed you, and the more you think that stuff is important, the more you'll strive for something unattainable. You don't need twenty pairs of shoes, you need one. It's commercial brainwashing, nothing more.'

'And dressing like my granny is what exactly?'

'It's my choice, and part of my progression in the group programme.'

'But as a helper I don't need progression – is that it? What does that make me? A group leper?'

'Why are you so angry, Addy? I never led you to believe you'd be anything other than a helper. Your contribution will be valued.'

He decided to change tactics, add a bit of humour. She always liked his jokes. 'I hope this helper lark doesn't require the sharing of blood or anything, because it's a long swim home.'

'Will you stop being so immature? And remember, leaving is your choice. No one will keep you here if you don't want to stay.'

It was then that Stephen turned back to them, asking Aoife if everything was okay. For the first time, Addy heard the guy's strong American accent.

'Fine,' she called back, then faced Addy. 'While you're here, you need to realise that everyone who is part of the programme believes in it. Your lack of respect will only get you into trouble.'

He was tempted to ask what kind of trouble, but then a large bell rang out from the tower at the front of the commune buildings.

'Hurry up,' shouted Stephen, as if he was the person in charge. 'If we don't get a move on, we'll miss the next group meeting.'

Inside, Aoife and Stephen went towards the meeting hall, and Addy and Sarah were led in the opposite direction along a series of long, linked corridors, by a female member. The woman looked about the same age as Addy's mother, but twice the size, with eyes that appeared as if they were about to pop out of her head. Halfway along the corridor, they stopped: Sarah and her doll were directed into a room to the right. Addy heard something about setting up the camera and a recorder, but then the door closed behind them.

Waiting in the corridor, he pulled out his mobile phone. 'Damn, no bloody signal.' When the female member returned, she instructed him to follow her. Her tone didn't encourage conversation. Close to the end of the linked corridors, she stopped, and he did too.

'This section,' the woman said, 'is where the helpers stay.' She opened a door to a room the size of a prison cell. Inside, there was a single cast-iron bed with a white cover, a wooden desk and chair, and a small window with iron bars. The furniture looked like it belonged in a Amish house. There was a matching chest of drawers for his clothes, and a single lightbulb without a shade in the centre of the ceiling.

As if she was reading his mind, she said, 'You will be sharing bathroom facilities with the other helpers. Most of them are male. Jason and Owen are Irish, Christopher and Alexander are American, Asan is from Dubai, and Karl is German.'

'A regular United Nations.'

'Sorry?'

He remembered Aoife's warning about him not making fun of the members or the programme, so he said. 'Ah, nothing – forget I said anything.'

The female member didn't seem perturbed so she continued where she had left off. 'There is a roster on the bathroom door. If you don't put your name on it, you won't get a bath. Any questions?'

'What's with the bars on the windows?'

'This end of the buildings gets the worst of the island breeze. During a storm, we use the shutters, and we need the bars to keep them intact.'

'Is there a separate toilet?' he asked.

She didn't answer him, at least not for a few seconds, and although he wasn't sure at first, he soon grasped that she was sizing him up, giving him the full body check. His neck felt hot, and even though he told himself not to be daft. It was then that he noticed her staring at his neck, and it must have been really red, because she gave a wry smile. He looked away. She took a step closer, and he jumped back with more force than he'd intended.

'Follow me,' she said. 'There is no need to be embarrassed – we're all friends here.'

He glanced down at the lock on the door, noticing there wasn't a key on either side.

Again, she knew exactly what he was thinking. 'We don't believe in locked doors here. We're a community.'

Following the woman up the corridor, he saw Sarah come out of the room she had gone into earlier. She was some distance away, but he could see that she was hunched over, and thought she was crying. He waved, but she turned her back on him, holding the doll closer to her chest, as if it might be in some kind of danger.

When Addy and his guide reached a wooden pine door with 'Helpers' Toilet' painted on it in white, the woman said, 'If you report to the entrance of the commune house in an hour, I will let you know your duties.'

Kate

KATE KNEW CHARLIE WOULDN'T BE HAPPY ABOUT going straight from school to Sophie's house. It wasn't that he didn't like Sophie. She had been the family child-minder for at least three years, but with Kate taking time out, Sophie was now minding another child – Thomas, aged four. To Charlie, the age gap of three years was like an eternity, and no matter how Kate packaged it, he didn't like it.

She got the police statement out of the way first, knowing, despite the argument with Adam, that it was the right thing to do. Her next call was going to be with Malcolm, and instead of phoning ahead, she decided to go directly to his office. It wasn't that she thought Malcolm was behind the note, but she felt that he was another person who wasn't being straight with her. His secretary was friendly when she arrived, but unimpressed when Kate insisted on seeing him, even though he had a busy schedule.

'He won't mind,' she reassured the woman, and within moments, Malcolm was standing at his open office door.

'Come in, Kate. Always good to see you.'

She didn't reply, but followed him into the room.

'Sit down, Kate. You look concerned. What's the matter?'

'I'm not completely sure.'

'Oh?'

She stared at him, the man she'd known since childhood, the one who'd called so often to the house as a young college student that he'd seemed part of their family. He looked far more sophisticated now – tall, lean, his straight black hair cut tight, his skin tanned, impeccably dressed. For an instant, Kate tried to see him as he used to be, an untidy, enthusiastic twenty-something, who ate like he'd never see food again. Finally, she said, 'I understand DI O'Connor has spoken to you about the O'Neill investigation.'

'Why, yes, Kate, he has. Is that an issue for you?'

'You know that we're …'

'In a relationship?' he replied, finishing her sentence.

'Yes, we are, but that isn't why I'm here.'

'No?'

'My visit isn't about him. It's about Michael O'Neill.'

'Michael?'

'I understand you two knew each other.'

'Yes, we did.'

'Did you know each other in 1988?' She maintained eye contact, watching for any small alterations in expression.

'I understand why that year is important to you.'

'Did you know him then, or didn't you?'

'I had my reasons, Kate, for not giving the police the exact date of our first acquaintance.'

'And what were they?'

'I wanted to protect you.'

'What from?'

'Are you sure you want to hear this?'

'Considering I don't know what you're going to say, no, I'm not sure, but I still want an answer.'

'Okay, then.' He let out a sigh. 'I was an ex-student of Michael O'Neill's, from his time as a lecturer. It was through Michael that I originally met your father. They were part of a group of academics who met on a regular basis in the late eighties.'

'So?'

'It was made up of men, mostly the same age as your father and Michael – early to late forties. I understand there was a selection committee who voted on membership approval.'

'You were in your twenties then?'

'That's right, and far too young to be taken seriously, or to be part of any of their meetings.'

'So they were all academics, professionals?'

'Yes.'

'Where did they meet?'

'Various places, but it was rarely at the members' homes.'

'I'm assuming they met to discuss the issues of the day, or something like that.'

'That's how it was viewed.'

'You sound as if you might have another opinion.'

'The group may have gone beyond the original scope.'

'I don't follow you.'

'Your father's area was literature, others had different skill sets. It's important that you realise, Kate, it was a different time back then.'

'Yes, indeed, but you haven't explained how they went beyond the original scope of the group.'

'You've heard of Jean Piaget?'

'You're talking about the Swiss developmental psychologist?'

'Yes. Piaget was known for his epistemological studies with children. His theory of cognitive development and epistemological view, linked together, are referred to as genetic epistemology.'

'What has that to do with my father and this grouping?'

'I'm getting to it. Piaget died in 1980, but his studies were of interest to the group. As with many other intellectuals at the time, they were concerned about the education system in Ireland, which was primarily controlled by religious orders. Piaget placed great importance on the education of children, declaring that it is only through education that societies can be saved from possible collapse.'

'Okay, I follow you so far.'

'I'll cut to the chase, Kate. The goal of genetic epistemology is to link the validity of knowledge to the model of construction, showing how the knowledge is gained, thereby affecting its validity. It also examines how people develop cognitively from birth through the four primary stages, sensorimotor up to age two, pre-operational from age two up to seven, concrete operational, aged seven up to eleven, and formal operational from eleven years onwards.'

'Yes, but—'

'Let me finish.' He sighed, as if the next part of what he was about to say was difficult for him. 'The group of academics that your father and Michael and, indeed, Tom Mason were associated with decided to conduct their own experiments. And before you ask, no, I don't think there is any connection to Michael O'Neill's suicide.'

'The police think differently.'

'Well, I'm not privy to that. You've asked me what I know and I'm telling you.'

'Okay,' she said, although everything felt very far from okay. 'Are you saying they conducted some kind of education experiment on children?'

'From what I can gather, and again, I emphasise I was on the periphery, it was deemed inappropriate to examine very young children, but a decision was made to look at boys and girls aged ten to fifteen. This age grouping would incorporate both the concrete operational phase and the formal phase leading into adulthood.'

'I'm assuming, Malcolm, this was done with parental permission.'

'As I said, Kate, it was a different time.'

'That's all very well, but we're talking about children.'

'Look, I'm not here to defend their decision, I'm merely trying to be upfront with you.'

'You also said they went beyond the scope of the original brief.'

'There were rumours.'

'What kind of rumours, Malcolm?'

'It was probably no more than idle gossip. Normally, I don't condone this type of silly nonsense.'

'Humour me.'

'It was feared that some members may not have been as upstanding as they should have been.'

'Like who?'

'Michael O'Neill for one. It was thought he had a weakness for young boys, although there was never anything official on his record, at least not to my knowledge. I doubt he would have been able to continue teaching as long as he did, if any dirt had stuck.'

'What about my father? What was said about him? And before you try to mollycoddle your reply, if you're worried about my feelings, don't be. I'm only interested in the truth.' Kate knew she was sounding more confident than she felt. A huge part of her wanted the floor to open up so she could bury herself and hide. She had no idea how she would react if Malcolm said anything bad about her father.

'Kate, are you sure you're okay? You've gone a sickly colour.'

'I'm fine. I want the truth, nothing more.'

'The truth is a precious commodity, Kate, and not always easy to determine, especially after the passing of time.'

'Still, you must remember what was said.'

'Dirt sticks, I know that.' He paused. 'There was something about a woman who made some wild accusations.'

'What kind of accusations?'

'It came to nothing in the end, but these things are complicated. Your father was a man of strong opinions, and he would have stacked up a number of enemies along the way.'

'You're saying people made up lies about him to damage him?'

'It happens. We like to think the world is a fair place, but it isn't always.'

'Do you know the name of the person who made the allegations?'

'I had an idea at the time, and if my guess was correct, she was a very sick woman, and by that, I mean she was mentally unstable. She died a number of years ago.'

'What did my father do to her that she'd say something like that?'

'Kate, if it's okay with you, I'd prefer to stick to what I know, rather than some kind of wild conjecture.'

'I still don't understand. Why didn't you tell all this to DI O'Connor? Why did you think you were protecting me?'

'It was probably stupid, but I didn't want all this nastiness to come out and affect you in any negative way. I know things are difficult for you right now. Plus, I had a fondness for your father.

If it wasn't for him, I wouldn't be the man I am today. I didn't want any of that old nonsense rising to the surface, especially when it wasn't relevant.'

'You need to let the police decide what's relevant.'

'I know, you're right, Kate. As I said, it was stupid of me. I'll rectify the situation as soon as we finish here.'

'I'm glad to hear it.'

'Kate, are you sure you're fine? You really don't look well.'

'Don't I?'

'What is it? Have you been having more memory recalls?'

'I don't remember telling you about that.' Her head felt woozy.

'Don't you? It was the other day, when we were talking about your journal writing, you were saying it was bringing some strange stuff up, things that made you fearful.'

'I remember now.' She wanted to throw up.

'You do understand, Kate, that despite the mind being infinitely resourceful, it's still capable of making mistakes. The more your recollections are encouraged, and kept within the safety of the internal cognitive processes, the better the outcome. Outside influences, especially those that cannot be fully relied upon, are best avoided.' He frowned. 'You don't think I had anything to do with Michael O'Neill's death, do you?'

'That's not my call.' She needed to hold things together, because right now, everything seemed to be unravelling. Again sounding more confident than she felt, she said, 'I strongly advise you to tell the police everything you know. After that, we'll have to see where it all leads.'

'I respect your wishes, Kate. You're the one in the driving seat.' He was calm, non-adversarial, and also, she thought, somewhat cold.

'I'm not comfortable that you lied about Michael O'Neill.'

'And I'm not comfortable that you doubt me.'

'That part can't be helped – at least, not until I get my head around all this. I realise you were trying to protect me and my father's memory, but it was a wrong judgement call.'

'And you've never made a mistake?'

'I didn't say that. I've made plenty, but even so ...'

'I care about you, Kate, a great deal.'

'Then you won't mind me asking you another question?'

'Anything.'

'Did you know O'Neill's foster son?'

'Vaguely – his death caused a reaction at the time.'

'Was it connected to my father? Or any of the others from this elite grouping?'

'Not that I know of,' he replied, although his tone suggested otherwise.

'My father told me it was an accident.'

'As I said, it was a long time ago.'

'One more question.'

'Yes?'

'Have you always known I was missing for longer than I originally believed? By that I mean over twenty-four hours.'

'Yes, Kate, I did.'

'And you chose not to tell me?'

'Maybe I let my professional opinion get in the way of honesty.'

'I'm not your patient. I don't understand.'

'I wanted you to work it out for yourself. I hoped your journal writing would fill in some of the gaps for you. Your own professional training will tell you it was the right thing for me to do. If the answer came from your mind, without my influence or interference, it would have greater validity.'

'How long was I missing for?'

'About twenty-four hours, no more than that.'

'What explanation was given for my disappearance?'

'You mean from your father?'

'Yes.'

'There had been talk of your parents splitting up. He put it down to childhood anxiety, attention-seeking.'

'I never heard anything about that. There were arguments, sure, but nothing about them separating.'

'For what it's worth, I don't believe it was an attention-seeking stunt. I think your father wanted to put the whole thing behind him, wrap it up nice and neat and encourage it to go away. You know what he was like.'

'Actually, Malcolm, I'm not sure I do.'

'He didn't like things that didn't fit neatly into boxes, and anything personal like that, well, to be honest, it probably made him feel exposed, especially considering what we discussed earlier.'

'You certainly seem to have got past the enigma phase of your relationship with my father.'

'I looked up to him, Kate. I won't deny that.'

'That must have been nice for you.' She sounded clipped.

'And, as I've said, I've always had your best interests at heart.' He stood up, walking over to her. 'Look, I know this is hard, and you might think it strange me suggesting this, but if you ever need to get away, to take a break from your normal routine, I have a place I go to. It helps me to recharge my batteries.'

'I'll think about that, but thanks.' She stood up to leave.

'One last thing, Kate,' he said.

'Yes?'

'If I think of anything else connected to your past, would you prefer me to share it with you, or not?'

'I want you to tell me everything.'

'As always, Kate, I support your wishes.'

'And don't forget to contact DI O'Connor. You need to tell him everything you know, irrespective of whether you believe it to be relevant or not.'

'I will, and … Kate?'

'Yes?'

'I want you to take care of yourself. You've always been very good at helping others, but you must remember, sometimes you need to concentrate on yourself, be more selfish.'

'I'll bear that in mind.'

Stephen

I DON'T LIKE AOIFE'S FRIEND, ADDY. I DON'T LIKE the way he talks so fast, or how he seems to think he's funny. While I was with that woman and her stupid doll, I heard most of their conversation. It's not that I don't trust Aoife. I don't trust him.

I looked back at one point and he had a stupid smile on his face. I thought about ripping it apart, attacking it with a knife. I thought about the size of the blade I would use – something small enough to stab him in the eye. I would go for the right eye first. I imagined him jerking back, blood spouting out all over the place.

I'd like it if he tried to attack me. It would fuel my rage. I would blind him in the first eye in seconds, and now I can see his head firing all around the place.

I saw the way Aoife looked at him when the bell rang out. It told me he had let her down. She knows he doesn't belong here, the same way I do. If I attacked his eyes, I could use a screwdriver or a sharp nail. I could hide that in the palm of my hand. Take the bastard by surprise. 'What the fuck?' he might say. I'll give him what the fuck. I'll give him a hell of a lot more.

The woman, Sarah, wanted to know what part of the United States I came from. I told her from outside Salt Late City. 'Like, where the Mormons live?' she asked, the same way every other stupid non-American does.

'Yes,' I said, just to shut her up. She wanted to know if I was religious. I wanted to say, No, but then I started thinking about my mother screeching at me. The way she'd hit me with that Bible of hers, disgust spilling out all over me, all over my body, telling me I was a stupid sinner, until the day I couldn't take it no longer and I showed her once and for all.

She wasn't preaching after I dragged her by the rope. I tied it to the rear of the pickup truck, zooming around at speed, creating dust clouds over her fat, wrinkled body, until she looked like a grey heap ready for dumping in the ground. I imagined the insects eating her, moment by moment, hour by hour, day by day. They'd have a feast, a fat feast. I visualised them getting fat on her, rolling on their backs, full-bellied. They always started with the orifices: the eyes are usually the first to be eaten, leaving two dark crevices. I imagined that too. Which was why, before I left for the island, I dug out her grave. I wanted to see what was left of her. She was nothing but a pile of bones, but then I saw the worms wriggling through the muck, looking slick and juicy, like they had her inside of them, bulging, slimy, crawling, and I knew she was everywhere, under the foundation of the house, in the barn, hiding in the underbelly of the pickup truck. I felt her fat filth all over me again, so I drove and drove, wanting the worms to fall away. I bought new clothes. I had a shower in a motel. I kept on going, until the worms couldn't get me no more, until I reached the island, and safety.

'No,' I told the woman with the stupid doll. 'I'm not religious.'

'And you like it here on the island?' she asked.

'I love it.'

'You've lovely teeth,' she said.

I didn't answer her, because the other two had caught up with us, and the guy was standing so close to me, I knew I could rip out his eyes with my fingers.

When we got to the commune house, the new visitors took it all in, the same way as I did when I first arrived – the whitewashed houses with their black slate roofs and tall chimney stacks. The first house is where the bell tower is, where we have most of our meetings in the main hall. The whole commune is now open, no locks on the doors, except for the rooms below ground, and the infirmary. Only the seniors and the medical staff can go there. The houses used to belong to islanders, but they all emigrated. Then an entrepreneur renovated the place as holiday homes, with a café, like a mini-hotel. It didn't work out, and now they belong to us.

At the meeting, I made myself forget about that fool, Addy. I couldn't allow him to be a distraction, so I settled my breathing, realising everyone was waiting. The group gathered in close, side by side, holding each other by the hand, forming a circle of unity and commitment. I looked at Aoife. I saw that she'd forgotten about him too. He isn't one of us. I've become close to Aoife so quickly. I've dreamed about the two of us being together, properly together. Dreams are the start of everything for me. If I dream it, then it will happen. I dream about killing before I do it. The first time was a girl called Rosie. She had auburn hair. She had rosy cheeks too. I like it when a name fits the face. I hadn't planned on taking her or anything, but then I saw her mother leaving her in the car, going into that convenience store. Rosie was ten, and when I opened the door and said, 'Hello, Princess,' even though she didn't smile, she didn't create a fuss either. After I took her, I remembered the bad dream I'd had a couple of nights before. How a girl was annoying me with her crying, going on about stuff, repeating words that messed with my head. I had to shut her up, and in the dream, she was dead, and soon, too, so was Rosie.

Being on the island has taught me to love myself again. It has taught me that I'm not a monster. Saka, Jessica and the others have helped me so much. When I looked over at Aoife, I was glad it was my turn to speak today. I want Aoife to understand how I've suffered.

I saw her in the shower the other night. There's a small peep-hole between two of the cubicles. I saw her get out of her clothes, shake out her hair, and stand in her white panties before pulling them down. I thought about touching her, and I got aroused. I'm getting aroused thinking about it now.

At the meeting, I say to everyone, 'My mother told me I was a monster.' Everybody waits, because no one ever rushes you here.

You're not allowed to interrupt when the chosen member is talking. 'But she was wrong,' I say, my voice loud and clear. 'I'm not a monster. I'm a good man.'

They repeat my words, every one of them, including Aoife, chanting, 'You are not a monster. You are a good man.' They say it over and over and over, and the more they say it, the more I believe it. I am not a monster. I am a good man. I am now on step fifteen of the twenty steps. I am close to reaching my destiny, fulfilling my path, and being completely free. It's all I ever wanted in life, recognition of who I am, and I can feel the surge of strength growing inside of me, waiting to rise, like the phoenix from the blackened ashes.

Kate

EVER SINCE HER CONVERSATION WITH MALCOLM, Kate had felt unsettled. She sensed something changing inside her, but she wasn't sure what it was. There was so much about her younger years that had brought her sorrow. It wasn't only her father's temper, or how, at times, she was such an introspective child. It was more than that. Somehow, she'd always felt that if she was going to survive in this world, she'd be doing it on her own. She felt the same way now – isolated, increasingly introspective, as if all the answers were inside her. She couldn't get her father out of her mind. What if Malcolm had told her something truly awful today? Despite all his failings, deep down, until now, she had believed her father to be a complicated but basically good person. What if even her fragile notions of him were blown apart? Would she hate him? Would all the good bits, the parts that told her he cared for her, be shattered?

The note had complicated things too. Perhaps it was random. Perhaps it was a one-off, a sick joke, feeding into her paranoia, but the timing, with so many other things happening, couldn't have been worse. One way or another, she would have to decide on what course of action to take in relation to Charlie, even though, with everything else, not having him close to her would break her heart. When she picked him up from Sophie's, she did her best to hide her anxiety, but all of that changed when they reached the front steps of the apartment building.

Normally she would have dismissed a dead bird on the steps as nothing, a fluke, an accident, but when she saw the raven, something told her it was far from that. Charlie was full of curiosity about it, but all she could think of was what the bird represented, the perceived magic of the Raven, supposedly giving courage to enter the darkness of the void, the place of all that is not yet in form. Was it another message? Was she losing it? Becoming completely paranoid?

By the time Adam arrived home, she felt more vulnerable than after their argument earlier on.

'Okay, Kate, I'll say it first,' he said, entering the kitchen.

'Say what?' She didn't look up, continuing to chop carrots, as if that was the most important thing in the world.

'I'm sorry about being sharp earlier on.'

'Don't worry about it.'

'Are you okay?'

'Everybody seems to be asking me that today.' She fired the carrots into a pot of water.

'Can we start over?' He took a bottle of Sauvignon Blanc out of the fridge, and two glasses from the cupboard, placing them on the kitchen counter.

She watched him open the bottle, but didn't say anything. When he handed her a glass, she reluctantly took a sip, then asked, 'Did you check up on the O'Neill lock-up?'

'Yes, we did.'

She could tell he wasn't happy that she was talking about the investigation again. 'And?'

'And what?'

'Did you find out who owned it, for a start?' Her voice was sharper.

'Yes.'

'Adam, just tell me.'

'Kate, we've already had this conversation.'

'I know.' She softened her tone. 'I'm not asking you to tell me everything about the investigation, but after all, it was me who found the garage in the first place.'

'I know you did.'

'So cut me some slack.'

'For what it's worth, it's owned by a company called Holmes & Co.'

'What do they do?'

'Not a lot. The articles of association are as broad as they come. The company was bought off the shelf. The only information we have is the registration address, which belongs to an accountancy firm in town. One of the guys is checking it out.'

'Was there anything else?'

Adam took another sip of his wine, as if contemplating whether or not he should answer her. Finally, he said, 'Kate, we didn't find any notebooks in the garage.'

'That's impossible.'

'Nor did we find any hair samples.'

'I don't believe you.' Unable to hide her shock.

'The other collections were there, all right, and the lads combed the place. I even drafted in a specialist in the area of hair fibres.'

'Someone must have taken them. You're making it sound as if I made it all up, or imagined it.'

'I'm not saying that.'

'I must have been followed. That's the only logical explanation.'

'The way I see it, Kate, is that there are two possible explanations.'

'Why do I get the feeling I'm not going to like either of them?'

'Explanation one, by not ringing in the information about the garage, you inadvertently gave someone else the time to remove valuable evidence.'

'And explanation two?'

'Don't take this the wrong way.'

'Don't take what the wrong way?'

'You could have been mistaken.'

'You're being ridiculous. I saw them with my own eyes. I read the notes. I looked at the newspaper cutting.'

'That wasn't there either.'

'Adam, this is nonsense.'

'I also spoke to Dr Madden.'

'I told him to contact you.'

'Well, he's not on the top of my popularity list.'

'He told you about the rumours around my father and the so-called studies?'

'Yes, he did, although I'd heard the rumours already.'

'What do you mean? How long have you known?'

He drank more of his wine, not answering her.

'You decided not to tell me? That was it, wasn't it?'

'Keep it down, Kate. Where's Charlie?'

'He's in bed.'

'Shit, I didn't realise the time.'

'You're not realising a lot of things.'

'Look, I wanted to tell you but—'

'So why didn't you?'

'You were so damn argumentative today.'

'So tell me now.'

'I pulled the missing-person file on you from 1988. And, as Dr Madden confirmed, you were missing longer than you originally thought.'

Kate visualised the dead raven they had found on the steps of the apartment building. Her missing gaps in memory felt like the void the bird represented. 'So why didn't you tell me about the rumours?'

'It was difficult. I don't know, maybe I was trying to protect you.'

'You too?'

'What do you mean?'

'It doesn't matter.' She put her hands up to her face.

'Kate, you're not making this easy.'

'You're the one telling me I imagined seeing things in the garage.'

'I didn't say that. I said there were two possible explanations and, depending on how you want to look at it, at best you were mistaken, at worst you messed things up.'

'Why would I be mistaken?'

'Dr Madden gave us a full statement.'

'I know. You already told me that.'

'Off the record, he told me he was worried about you.'

'And you believed him?'

'I'm worried about you too.'

'Jesus, I can't believe what I'm hearing. Ask Ethel O'Neill. She was in the garage – only for a few seconds, but she was there. She must have seen some of the stuff.'

'She doesn't remember going to the garage. The notebooks didn't register with her either.'

'She has Alzheimer's, for Christ's sake.'

'Kate, listen to me.'

'Do you believe me, or don't you?'

He didn't say anything for a second. 'I want to believe you.'

'What about the note? You saw that yourself.'

'We don't know that it has anything to do with this.'

'But someone sent it. Someone wants to mess with my head.'

'Kate …'

'There was a dead bird on the apartment steps today.'

'And?'

'It was a raven.'

'Kate, you're not making sense.'

'Think about this for a second,' her voice agitated, 'what if someone did follow me to the garage and took the items, what then?'

'I don't know … but there is something else I need to talk to you about.'

'What?'

'Malcolm Madden's statement gave me extra clout with PIU.'

'What? The Paedophile Investigation Unit? But those allegations were pure hearsay.'

'I know, but with Malcolm confirming O'Neill was part of that group in the eighties, and the uncertainty around his death, it was enough to warrant reasonable suspicion.'

'My father was part of that group too.'

'I know that.'

'What did you find out?' lowering her voice to barely a whisper.

'Listen, Kate, I know this is tough on you. It's a lot to take in.'

Leaning against the wall in the kitchen, almost as if she was in a trance, she said, 'After my conversation with Malcolm, I remembered something else.'

'What?'

'At first, I couldn't work out my age, but I must have been around six. I was standing in the kitchen at our old house. It was dark, and I think it was the middle of the night. I was wearing a purple nightdress. My father was there. Neither of us said anything to each other, but I felt uncomfortable, as if something I didn't understand was happening.'

'That doesn't mean anything, Kate. You've said yourself a million times that disjointed memory cannot be relied on. Maybe you were frightened because it was the middle of the night – perhaps your father had scolded you or something. There could be any number of reasons why you would have felt uncomfortable. It doesn't mean your father was a ...'

'Say it, Adam, say what you're thinking.'

'I'm not thinking anything, and for what it's worth, I found nothing with the PIU.'

'But you said a minute ago that you had something you needed to talk to me about.'

'Okay, but let's sit down inside.'

'I'm fine here.'

'Are you sure?'

'I'm sure.'

He let out a sigh. 'When you run checks with PIU, it's customary to check with another department.'

'Which one?'

'Domestic Violence. It's standard to source data from both bodies.'

'And?'

'Something came up about your mother.'

'What?'

'There's no easy way to say this.'

Kate wanted to block out his voice, to be a child again, so she could run away, or hide under the blankets in bed, until everything was all right, until all the bad thoughts disappeared.

'Just tell me,' she finally said.

'Your father hit your mother. It happened more than once. Kate, she was a victim of domestic violence.'

'She can't have been. It's not true. I would have known. I would have remembered.' She closed her eyes, as if trying to concentrate, to take it all in.

'You would have been very young.'

'But even so.'

'You said yourself that there are parts of your childhood you can't remember.'

'But most of that is normal. It's the same for lots of people, but this, Adam, how could I not know something like this?'

She heard him say, 'People are good at keeping secrets ...'

He continued talking, but she had already stopped listening, retreating to a part of her memory, her mother's subservience, the tension at home, the fear, anger, dread, but there was something else. What was it? Was it to do with her father? Was he part of something more sinister than she could have imagined?

'Kate, what's wrong?'

'I don't know,' she replied, her voice shaking, sounding uncertain.

'Some of this must come as a shock.'

'That's the thing, Adam, it doesn't. None of it does.'

The Game Changer

O'NEILL'S NOTEBOOKS, ALONG WITH THE HAIR samples, were piled high on the table. It was good timing getting to the garage before the search warrant had been approved. Kate's plastic gloves and booties were no longer in the skip either. They had been retrieved for the Game Changer, who held them close, isolating the smell of rubber and waste from Kate's scent, the same way a tracker dog would inhale in preparation for their prey.

CENTRE OF LIGHTNESS
20 Steps to Self-enlightenment Programme

People think fear is created by others, or something outside themselves, but most of the fear people conjure up comes from within. The missing pages from the notebook gave Kate more to think about than if they had been there. Imagination is a powerful tool.

Lisa is now ready for the island. It will do her the world of good. Her camers can be too demanding. She hasn't been in touch with her family in years. They don't understand her, making it easy for Lisa to exchange one emotional prison, at the beck and call of her camers, for another: life on the island.

Lisa doesn't do complications. She is a straight-for-the-marker kind of girl. There are 5,000 euros left in her bank account, but her sexual appeal is on a par with the money she has shared. Her skills will be an asset on the island. Sex is a common denominator. It, too, locks people in.

Members stay for lots of reasons. Sex is one of them. Not everyone is capable of developing multiple relationships, but many will confuse sex with emotional payback.

(Page 1 of 1)

Sarah

THE FIRST EVENING ON THE ISLAND HAD FELT strange. A strangeness that Sarah suspected came from within. She had always felt different from others, and for the first time in a long time, she didn't care to apologise for it, or to pretend that she was the kind of person who worried about stupid things like a perfect house or any of that stuff so-called *normal* people cared about.

'Everyone wanted me to accept a dead daughter,' she whispered angrily under her breath. 'How could that be normal?' Nobody had said it to her outright, but that was what they meant. They said Lily was in a good place now, or time was a great healer, or that Lily would be for ever in their prayers. They thought Sarah could get up in the morning and continue to do ordinary things as if nothing had changed – that she could drink coffee, or make lunch, listen to the news, watch television, read a book, or go out to meet friends, that she should ignore it, get over it, move on.

'I only went back to work to fill the days with something other than sadness,' she had told the camera earlier. It wasn't because she wanted to forget Lily, or to deny her. She was searching, and she understood that now. She was lost, but on the island she would put that old world behind her. Saka and the others were her world now. They accepted her wholeheartedly for who she was, and she was happy that she was part of the circle of trust, and that she didn't have to pretend any more. The group was the only family she and Lily needed.

She held her baby in her arms, and there was comfort and release in not having to be around John any more, witnessing his daily torture, criticising them both.

Another change was coming over her. Her emotions were churning, like the waves crashing against the shore, but she told herself her past vulnerabilities were turning into strengths. She cradled Lily, listening to the island breeze, unforgiving and relentless, like a crazed god who didn't want to settle until his wishes were granted.

She thought about John's anger again: if the wounds hadn't been so deep, the rage wouldn't have been so strong. She would contact him soon, and tell him that they were both happy. Part of her already knew she was never going back. When Lily began to suckle, she repeated the words out loud, 'I am never going back. I am never going back. I am never going back.'

She had sworn the oath of secrecy on arrival, and she knew she would gain strength from the union of members. If she was called upon, she would not falter.

'We're safe now, my darling,' she told Lily. Before she'd left for the island, she had taken out enough money to cover them for at least a year. She wanted to be generous. Saka had told her that some people couldn't afford the same level of contribution, members like Aoife or Stephen. They had no income or savings. Why shouldn't they have the same opportunities as her? And Saka had said she could stay as long as she liked.

John would have been furious as soon as he discovered how much money she had taken. He'd have ranted and raved and let his anger out, but in the end, he would realise that it was rightfully hers.

She took two tablets from the bedside locker, the ones given to her to help her relax. The water felt cold as she swallowed them. Soon her eyelids were heavy and the tension remaining in her limbs had eased. Cuddling Lily, she heard her say, 'Mama,' for the very first time.

Kate

THE NIGHT LED INTO THE EARLY HOURS OF THE
morning, and Kate was tossing and turning in the bed, having
the same dream as before, only this time someone was trying to
suffocate her. It started with her memory of the attack from
childhood, then she would see her father hovering, watching her
without saying a word, before her mother appeared. She could only
barely make her out. It was as if she was coming in and out of focus,
then Kate would hear the loud voices, and her mother whispering,
'The children, the children.' After that, she would feel as if she was
falling into an abyss, tumbling into missing hours, and a darkness
full of vulnerability, before the presence would arrive, and she
was aware that there was someone other than her and Adam in the
room. They would stand on the right side of the bed, and she would
sense them getting closer, moving to the other side, where she slept.
When they stood directly over her, they pressed down with what
felt like a large pillow. And she couldn't breathe, and would force
herself to wake up, discovering none of it was real. The last time she
had woken up, Adam was gone.

After breakfast, she thought about phoning Declan and asking
him to mind Charlie for a while, but perhaps Adam was right.
Maybe she was overreacting. The note was upsetting but, other
than her paranoia, there hadn't been anything else to justify such a
drastic move.

When she had dropped Charlie safely at school, she made up her
mind what she would do next. It had been years since she had gone
to the place where it had all begun. She had knowingly avoided
stepping back into that world, but now it felt like the right thing to

do. She knew there wasn't any logical reason for that, but logic and emotion didn't always go hand in hand.

Walking towards the car, she felt the autumn sun on her face. She had the distinct feeling that somehow she was travelling back in time. Her mind felt absorbed. It was as if she was driving to her destination on autopilot. Instinctively, she went over the fragments of information she could be sure of and, almost as if time was playing tricks on her, she reached the mountain road sooner than she expected. She parked the car nearly a kilometre away. The road was deserted, other than the odd passing vehicle. Ten minutes later, she stepped in from the main road and searched for the opening she had discovered years before.

It was overgrown and practically hidden by the surrounding woodlands, unless you knew what you were looking for. She imagined lovers using it as a secret sanctuary, or children, on discovering the opening at the end of the pathway, treating it like a hideaway. As she walked in deeper, closer to the centre, she took in everything around her, the sights, the smells, the sounds. With the overhang of the trees blocking the sun, and the sharp breeze whirling in different directions, the space felt several degrees colder than it was outside. She could hear her footsteps and felt like an intruder within the orchestra of woodland sounds, the place almost bewitching, seductive, until she felt like that twelve-year-old girl again.

In a few more steps she would be at the centre, where the light could push through, the exact place she had gone searching for that missing ball. Standing in the opening, her adult self realised that, coming out from the darkness of the trees and the undergrowth, she would have become clearly visible to anyone watching her from the woodlands. There were any number of vantage points within the trees, any number of places her attacker could have hidden. He would have been able to bide his time, making sure her friends were far enough away, ensuring they couldn't help her. They couldn't have heard any sounds she made, those silent screams she remembered, the ones that sounded as if they belonged to someone else.

Kate stopped in the centre, concentrating on the roar of the wind, which was gaining strength, causing the loud creaking of branches on the taller trees. She tried to break down the different sounds, gaining a fuller concept of the terrain surrounding her. She heard twigs breaking underfoot. Was someone else in the woods? If they were, they might be close. She knew the area could play tricks with sound, the wind and streams pulling conversations and other noises from miles away, misplacing them, making faraway things seem closer than they were, but then she heard the sound again. She glanced around her, trying to work out which direction the noise had come from. It was impossible. Calm down, she told herself.

Taking a couple of steps forward, she heard the crunch of her own feet on the forest floor, then stopped again. Could her footsteps be echoing? As a child, she wouldn't have thought about any potential danger. She would have focused on the task in hand, simply following the ball. Leaning down, as she would have done all those years before, she mentally and physically retraced her steps, searching in the darkness of the lower woodland for an imaginary ball that she would never find.

After a few moments, she sat up on her hunkers, looking all around her again, realising that she had limited visibility. She couldn't see behind her. Even if she turned her upper body as far to the left or the right as she could, there was still a blind spot. He must have been observing her, contemplating his next move.

Was that why she felt someone was watching her now? Was her mind playing tricks on her yet again? Telling her she was no longer alone? Standing up, she hesitated before turning, part of her feeling more like the twelve-year-old girl than her adult self. What would she see if she turned? Would he be standing waiting for her? Would he say, *I remember you, Kate*?

Her body moved in slow motion. It was like some elements of what she was feeling were in the present, while others were firmly rooted in the past.

The terrain didn't change as she turned. It was as if it was mocking her, taunting her to find the subtle differences that could give answers. The sights, sounds, smells and wind chill remained the same; the only things looking back at her were the trees, tall and dense and capable of hiding secrets. Slowly her eyes moved towards the sky. It was clear and blue. Then, with an innate mixture of anxiety and concentration, she looked down again, searching through the lower foliage of the spruce trees, past the thick bark and into the dark undergrowth, before finally focusing on a brown mound, minuscule in the distance.

With each step she took towards it, the mound grew larger and clearer, until she stared into the beady eyes of a dead female blackbird. She picked it up, thinking of the dead raven on the steps of the apartment building the day before. The raven had been dead for some time, but the blackbird was still warm, its neck severed, the blood spilling between Kate's fingers, the brown foliage covered with muck. She turned it over, seeing that both wings had been torn from their sockets, each hanging limp. The wounds couldn't have been made by a woodland animal. The cut to the neck was too clean. It had been slit by a blade, the torn wings pulled back in an almost identical fashion.

A number of thoughts merged in her mind. Someone had done this to the bird. They wanted her to know they had made it suffer. And that someone was still watching her.

Chloë

MAMMY SAYS I SHOULD LOVE THE ISLAND. SHE SAYS it's beautiful.

I like the wind because it blows in different directions, and sometimes if I run fast enough, I can work out the exact spot where it goes from right to left.

I miss my school friends, and my other friends from where we used to live. Most of the people here are big people. Some are friendly, but I don't like everyone. Mammy says it's not good to dislike the people here. Now I don't tell her about the people I don't like, not now.

I miss Daddy too. He said he loved me more than the whole world, but he is in the whole world, and I am here. A woman with a baby doll has come to the island. She thinks it's a real baby, which is silly. I asked her could I play with it, and she said I was too young. I wanted to ask her why she thought the doll was real, but I didn't. Mammy used to say it was good to ask questions, but she doesn't say that now.

I like the water here too. I really like the waves. They can be ginormous, and when I'm by the water, the sound of the waves and seagulls blocks out loads of stuff. I miss my bedroom, and our street, and buses, and escalators in shopping centres, and birthday parties. I had one friend here. His name was Donal. He liked the wind too. He was a bit older than me, he was ten.

A few weeks ago, when we were messing in the water, he told me he could swim home if he wanted to. I told him that was stupid, but he didn't listen. He started swimming straight out. 'Look, Chloë,' he shouted, 'I can swim to the sun.' The sun was orange, and halfway down in the water. He waved to me a few times, and I think I told him to come back in, but I can't be sure. His head kept getting smaller and smaller. When it was really tiny, it went in and out of the water, disappearing and reappearing. Then I couldn't see his arms any more, even though a few minutes before, he was waving them like mad. The sea ate him – gobbled him up whole. That's what I told everyone. They didn't say anything bad when I told them that the water had eaten Donal, but they looked at me all serious and I wanted to cry. I didn't. I wish Donal was still here, but he's gone, like the escalators and all the other stuff.

I found Mammy spaced out this morning. I knew she was spaced out because Donal's mammy used to be spaced out too, and that was what he used to call it. Her eyes were all funny, and she did everything really slow. Donal's mammy isn't spaced out any more. She does a thing called meditation. Humming and closing her eyes and raising her arms up to the sky with her legs crossed. I don't know why she isn't spaced out any more and Mammy is. I asked Jessica why Mammy can't do meditation instead of taking medicine, and she said everyone was different, and she needed her pills to get better. I don't think Jessica is a doctor. If Mammy dies, I'll never get home. Mammy uses a wheelchair now when she leaves the room. She doesn't leave the room much, except for the meetings, or if she needs to talk to the camera. Sometimes Jessica lets me ride on the back of the wheelchair. Sometimes I slip, and my foot gets caught in the wheels, and I scream. Mammy doesn't say anything, and Jessica keeps on pushing.

A new boy arrived with the woman called Sarah. He's much older than Donal. I think he's nice. He threw my Frisbee up so high it took ages to come back down. My neck hurt looking up at it in the sky. I nearly toppled over and he laughed. His laugh reminded me of Daddy's. It sounded like a donkey. Mammy used to say Daddy laughed like an idiot, especially when he was curled up in a ball on the floor. She wasn't really giving out about him. She was only messing. When I jumped on Daddy's back, he would laugh more, and Mammy would say there were two of us in it, a right pair. I miss Daddy laughing too. I miss Mammy saying stuff like that. I hope the boy stays for a while. He says he's here on holidays, but other people said that, and they're still here.

Saka calls me one of his island children. He says he knows the sea ate Donal, and that makes me feel better because he believes me. There are other children here too, but Saka says I am more special than any of the others. He says that when he whispers in my ears it's the sea talking to me, not him. I don't know how he knows that, but everyone says he knows lots of stuff.

Saka says that I don't have to go to the meetings if I don't want to, so I don't. Some of the children go anyway. He says I'll know when I'm ready, even though I don't know what I need to be ready for. When I asked Jessica, she told me, 'It's about becoming grown-up,' and if I'm a good girl, I won't have to wait too long.

Sometimes I like to hide behind the big rock down at the water's edge. The big rock is where Donal and I used to play. We called it that after we measured all the other rocks. We didn't have a ruler, so he used my body instead. Donal had a purple marker, and I stood beside each rock while he measured me against it with one eye squinting closed, drawing an imaginary line from the top of the rock to me. When we worked out the biggest one, it got the name Big Rock. Sometimes, when the tide comes in, you can't see all of it, but that doesn't mean it isn't there, or that it isn't Big Rock any more.

Daddy used to say, 'Your eyes don't see everything.' Now I know what he meant. Mammy used to say, 'You need eyes in the back of your head,' but I haven't worked that out yet.

My granny died before we came to the island. Mammy said it was because she was sick. I got upset because I get sick sometimes and I didn't want to die. Mammy told me not to worry, that really Granny died because of her age. I wish she had said that in the first place. Then she said Granny was in Heaven, but she doesn't say that any more. All she says is that Granny is gone. Because I am six that means I'm not old at all. I'll live longer than anyone else on the island, and then I'll be on my own, without people or escalators or Daddy or anything except the waves and the sea and the wind. I like the wind the best. It didn't eat Donal.

Spring Valley Village, Texas

HIS FIRST NIGHT IN SPRING VALLEY, AND LEE HAD slept better than he had done for a long time. He hadn't set the alarm, because he didn't need to. John had left early for a basketball game with the two boys, so Margaret in the kitchen was his only company. He liked Margaret. She wasn't the kind of woman who intruded on your personal space, unless you happened to invite her in.

'Coffee?' she asked, as he sat down on one of the high stools at the kitchen counter.

'I'm not used to a woman spoiling me, Margaret, but sure, why not?'

'Black, one sugar?'

'I can see why my brother fell for your charms.'

'Good memory, that's all. Mind if I join you?'

'It's your kitchen.'

She stretched her arms over her head, and he took in her curved shape, thinking of a whole different set of reasons why John had been drawn to this woman.

'Well,' she said, 'it's always good to have you with us, even if it's only for a few days.'

'The demands of being a New York detective,' he laughed, 'you can never get too far away from it.' Picking up the cup, he took a mouthful of coffee, then raised the cup to her, as if in salute, saying, 'Just as well I love it.'

'What is it about it that you love?'

'You mean besides catching the bad guys?'

'Besides that.'

'In one way or another, Margaret, I think I always wanted to be in the force. John will tell you, even as a kid, I fancied myself as a bit of a hero. That was before, of course.'

'Before what?'

'Before I realised how muddy the waters could be. Unfortunately, there's a lot of grey in my line of work.'

'I don't doubt it.'

'People are complicated.'

'I don't doubt that either.'

Margaret topped up her coffee cup, allowing a long, easy silence to settle between them, until Lee said, 'I like my personal space too. I like living alone. It suits me.'

'Do you ever think about Marjorie?'

'Sometimes.'

'I can't believe how long she's been gone.'

'Neither can I, but the past is always part of the present, in one way or another.'

He didn't mind her bringing up Marjorie. In fact, that was one of the reasons he liked visiting. If Marjorie had lived, she would be the same age as Margaret. They had been in the same year in high school.

'Any regrets, Lee?'

'Yeah, lots of them.'

'Which one stands out?'

'It's not like you to pry.'

'John's worried about you.'

'He shouldn't be.'

'He thinks you need a good woman in your life.'

'I had a good woman.'

'But …'

'No buts, end of story. Marjorie was here, now she's gone, and there isn't a darn thing anyone can do about it.'

'I guess not.'

He looked at her, not saying anything for a few moments. She didn't rush him.

'My main regret, Margaret, is that I didn't make contact with Marjorie before she died.'

'You didn't know she was dying.'

'I knew I loved her, and we were miles apart.'

'All relationships go through bad times. You weren't to know she wouldn't get better.'

'I know that, but still. You asked me my big regret, and now you have it.'

'Has it changed you, Lee?'

'Yeah.' He took another gulp from the coffee cup. 'Now, if something is crawling at my insides, I don't let it go. I stick at it until, one way or another, it's resolved. Life's too short to leave important questions unanswered.'

'Which is why you're such a good detective.'

'I guess things have a habit of coming full circle, eventually.'

Kate

ALL THE WAY HOME, KATE FELT RATTLED. WALKING back down the mountain road, she kept turning around to see if anyone was following her, checking the signal on her phone in case she needed to get help. When she saw her car up ahead, her anxiety didn't lessen, and after pressing the key fob to open it, she locked the doors as soon as she was inside. She looked ahead, seeing an empty road, nervously turning around, double-checking that the back seat was empty. That she was alone.

Leaning down, she pulled a facial wipe from her handbag. The blood from the dead bird had dried on her hands. Sitting in the car, she noticed there were specks on her jeans too. After cleaning her fingers, she wiped what she could off her jeans, then looked around her again. If someone had followed her, and was watching her now, they were doing a good job of hiding. She pulled her seatbelt down with such force that it got stuck halfway, and she wanted to scream but managed to extend it and snap it into place. She turned the key in the ignition. The engine cut out. She tried again, but it did the same. Stop panicking, she told herself, or you'll flood the darn thing. Counting to ten, she turned the key for the third time. Thankfully, the engine ticked over.

As she travelled down the mountain, she told herself she was safe, that she was overreacting, and the further she drove, the less her heart raced. On reaching the apartment building, she parked the car and ran up the steps, still feeling anxious and threatened. Even when she shut the main door, she spent more time than normal checking the communal hallway, breathing heavily. Turning the key in her apartment door, her hands were shaking. Once inside, she slammed the door behind her. It was then that she saw the letter on the floor.

The Game Changer

LOOKING AT THE FRONT DOOR OF KATE'S APARTMENT
building, the Game Changer visualised her inside, imagining what
she would do once she found that another note had been delivered.
She'd seemed nervous getting out of the car. It was obvious she
sensed the Game Changer was following her, and she was becoming
increasingly rattled.

Kate needed to think more about death. People argue all the time
about it or, rather, the form death will take. Some people want it to
happen fast. They say things like they don't want to suffer, thinking
they might be able to choose. Others prefer surprise, or they want to
be prepared, to have time to say goodbye. Even the death of animals
can wind people up. Many enjoy meat created by the slow bleed,
a method preferred by those of Islamic inclination. There will be
argument and counter-argument about the cruelty involved. Many
say that speed reduces pain and advocate more mainstream methods.

The Game Changer watched a pig slaughter once. There was a
lot of noise. Pig squeals are particularly piercing to the ear. The pigs
walked into a pen as if they were about to be given a meal, but they
soon sensed that death was hovering. Each one got an electrode with
two pads placed behind their ears, a charge administered to stun
them. Not all of the animals were knocked out effectively. Some
were still conscious, even when they were hanging upside down. A
large incision was made to bleed them, the location of the incision,
and the precision of the blade, determining how quickly the pig
would die, as the blood dripped into the buckets below. One way
or another, the animal died. Arguments about how much suffering
was involved can only be resolved by those who suffered the death.
That is, if animals could talk, and dead animals at that. With Kate,

it will be a slow bleed. She will cross paths with Stephen first. His dreams dictate his actions, and dreams are more easily manipulated than reality.

CENTRE OF LIGHTNESS
20 Steps to Self-enlightenment Programme

Confidential Record: 136B

Most people enter deep sleep several times a night.

The first analysis of sleep stages was completed in the 1930s, when scientists began to do overnight EEG recordings.

Deep sleep is the time of near-complete disengagement from the environment. Many physiological processes occur during this time.

REM, or deep sleep, is the dumping ground for unresolved issues, things that won't go away, things that are bothersome.

Stephen has many things like this in his life, things that will never leave him.

Kate will infiltrate his deep dream state, as she did the Game Changer's.

NB Even in death, she may not disappear, not completely.

(Kate will need to leave the apartment soon. She will have to collect Charlie from school. Like the pigs in the slaughter house smelling death, she may already be expecting the worst.)

(Page 1 of 1)

Kate

INSTEAD OF PICKING UP THE NOTE, KATE WALKED into the bedroom and took a pair of protective gloves, along with an evidence bag, from Adam's locker. She returned to the hall, bagging the note before reading it. This time it was on plain white paper, and the message, although short, had been typed.

Her breathing was still heavy, but a rage was building inside her, a rage that wanted to know who the hell was sending the notes and why.

She read it quickly, jumping over the words, knowing she would reread them again and again. Before she had read it a second time, her mobile phone rang. Adam. Answering it, although she had washed her hands, she saw some hardened speckles engrained in her skin, tiny flecks she must have missed in her panic.

'I'll have to phone you back,' she said, not giving him the opportunity to say anything more. Rushing to the bathroom, she thought about the bird, her eagerness to get away from it, and how afterwards, when she arrived back at the apartment, even before she saw the note, she hadn't felt safe. It was after that that the anger had come, and now, scrubbing off the remaining blood, it was as if that action might take away the fear.

She turned the hot tap on full throttle, the water almost boiling, and continued to scrub her hands with soap, checking and rechecking that all the blood was gone. When she turned off the tap and examined her hands, her palms and fingertips were bright red, raw and shrivelled from the heat.

Ringing Adam's number, she told herself to calm down. When he answered, all she said was, 'I've got another note.'

'Is it the same as before?'

'No.' Her words were coming out faster. 'As soon as I realised it was hand-delivered, I put protective gloves on. I got an evidence bag from the bedroom.'

'Good.'

'This time, it was typed.'

'Read it out loud.'

'Okay.' But as she sat down, the image of the dead blackbird came back to her. She felt like vomiting. 'Hold on a second, Adam. I don't feel well.'

'Take your time. I'm not going anywhere.'

'The note is short,' she added. Her hands were shaking. 'It says, "I hope you liked my present. Did the bird bring back fond memories? I'm keeping an eye on you, but then again, you know that already. It's good to be close, Kate, isn't it? I'll be in touch again real soon."'

'What bird? Is it the dead raven?'

'No, it was earlier today. I decided to go to the spot where I had originally gone missing.'

'And?'

'I thought someone was watching me. At first, I put it down to my heightened stress level, but then ...'

'What?'

'I was about to leave the woods when I saw it, a dead blackbird. I wasn't sure what it was at first, so I stepped closer, and when I picked it up, the bird was still warm. Someone had slit its throat, and had pulled back both wings. It felt like a message. Then when I got back here and saw the note, I knew, even before I read it, that the two were linked. Whoever was watching me must have doubled back here after I'd found the bird. My car wouldn't start, at least, not at first. It would have delayed me a few minutes, but maybe that was enough.'

'Calm down, Kate. Think. Have you any idea who could have sent it? What's the relevance of the bird?'

For a few seconds she didn't say anything, but then she remembered. 'Jesus,' she said. 'It can't be that.'

'What?'

'It happened when I was a child.' She paused. 'I found a near-dead blackbird at the side of the road. It was a female, the same as the one I picked up today. I hoped it would survive, but it didn't. My father buried it. I remember crying. I thought my father could fix everything. That he could make the bird better, but he couldn't. I guess it was the first time I really thought about death.'

'Who else have you told about it?'

'No one ... I may have said it to Malcolm, but I can't be sure.'

'I'm going to pull that guy in again. He's tied into this somehow.'

'What do you think the note means?'

'At the very least it's intimidation, although at face value, there's nothing particularly threatening about it.'

'Whoever it is, they want to rattle me.'

'I know that. Let's hope the tech guys can pull something concrete from this one.'

'Something tells me they won't.'

The Game Changer

There are reasons why each of us do the things we do. Psychopaths are no different. Put 3,000 people in a room: 30–35 of them will be absolute psychopaths. A much larger number will demonstrate psychopathic traits.

The top five things that identify a psychopath are:

1. Lack of remorse.
2. Nothing is ever their fault.
3. Switching charm on and off, like a light.
4. Being completely and utterly self-focused, rarely, if ever, doing anything that isn't beneficial to them.
5. They are game players – they like playing tricks, telling lies.

Many psychopaths are found in banking. Surgeons, lawyers, sales and media people are close contenders, but finance offers a great attraction. Why? The same reason paedophiles are found in schools: that is where the children are.

(Page 1 of 2)

CENTRE OF LIGHTNESS
20 Steps to Self-enlightenment Programme

Confidential Record: 143 – cont.

The Game Changer is prepared to kill and to destroy others merely to achieve power – a versatile parasitic predator. If they choose to kill you, or to destroy you, or both, you will be the last person to see it coming.

The human mind is delicate. You need to be patient with it. Some will put up a harder fight but, ultimately, they will all arrive at the same fate. On the island, most have sworn the oath of secrecy. The oath is seen as a form of protection, and one of the key cornerstones of the 20 Steps to Self-enlightenment: without group fortification, weaker members may perish, and no one believes they want that.

(Page 2 of 2)

Kate

AFTER TALKING TO ADAM, KATE KNEW, IF SHE WAS going to manage this, panic and anxiety weren't her friends. Adam was sending over a courier to pick up the note, so before he or she arrived, she copied the wording into one of her journals.

With at least an hour to go before she had to pick up Charlie from school, she decided to record aspects of Michael O'Neill's death, and how, if at all, she fitted into the picture.

Pressing the record button, she began: 'Michael O'Neill's death can be interpreted in two ways, either as a suicide or as a death staged to look like one. If the death was caused by someone else, what do the crime-scene factors tell us? First, it is likely that there was a relationship between the killer and the victim. The exact details of the relationship are still unclear. However, to carry out this act successfully, assuming it was murder, the killer would have had to be familiar with the routine of the deceased. Access to the house would also have been a requirement. With no forced entry, the most likely means of access was via permission of the victim.'

She paused, thinking about the large sums of money withdrawn. She pressed the record button again. 'Assuming the cash withdrawals are connected to the victim's death, the perpetrator of the crime and the beneficiary of the funds are possibly one and the same. The missing money has prompted a suspicion of blackmail, which is backed up in a number of ways. First, the victim's profile indicates financial prudence and sensibility. Second, all of the money was withdrawn in cash, in amounts of five thousand euros, totalling the O'Neills' life savings. Third, the victim displayed signs of stress in the weeks preceding his death, despite his mood improving in the

187

later stages. Fourth, the victim was retired, and although investment couldn't be ruled out, no records of this have been found. To date, the police have been unable to locate the missing funds.

'Another disturbing aspect of Michael O'Neill's death is the planting of DNA at a crime scene in New York. The victim, Tom Mason, was killed in May of this year.'

Kate stopped the recording again, and considered what Malcolm Madden had said about her father, and the two dead men, Michael O'Neill and Tom Mason, all being part of the elite group. At best, it would seem they used questionable means to study cognitive processes among minors. She leaned back in the chair, making a mental note to ask Adam if the Manhattan detective, Lee Fisher, had information about this so-called academic circle. Two dead men, she thought, of similar age, one of whom had obviously been murdered. Money unaccounted for, the planting of DNA, historical rumours about her father, a closed and suspect grouping, Kevin's death, which had had similarities to O'Neill's, the degradation of the garage and the missing items. Someone had been there after Kate and Ethel O'Neill had left, removing the notebooks, the hair samples and the reference to the Cronly murder case – death, secrecy, money, rumour, and a lot of question marks. Adam and Malcolm had both alluded to her inadvertently slotting things together, things that might or might not be connected. Were the notes part of all this? Whether they were or not, someone had sent them, and someone had killed that bird.

She looked up at the mind maps on the wall, including the ones she had recently created. 'Michael O'Neill, DEAD. Subset A: cause of death – carbon monoxide poisoning. Subset B: treated as suspicious – suicide/foul play. Subset C: large amount of money missing. Subset B1: suspected blackmail.' She added another strand: 'Kevin, foster son, similar MO, death 1988.' Taking a red marker from her desk, she stood up, circling '1988', then creating another subset: 'VICTIM: Michael O'Neill. Previous accusations of paedophilia.' Then, reluctantly, she created another subset, this time with her father's name in it: Valentine Pearson. It was a different time, Malcolm had said. It was common knowledge that reported sex-abuse cases were handled badly in the eighties.

She went to the subset marked 'Known Associates', looking particularly at Malcolm Madden, making another link outwards, writing, 'LIED to the police.' Her gut told her to believe him, but the mind map told her to doubt. With the red marker, she underlined each element where potentially the investigation mind maps and her memory mind maps held common factors: O'Neill; his foster son, Kevin; entries about Kate in the teacher's notebooks, Malcolm; 1988. She created a subset under the title 'Commonality'. She noted similar-type scissors used in both the newspaper-clipping note and the pages removed from O'Neill's notebook.

Before adding more details to the mind maps, she thought again about the newspaper article she'd found in the back of the 1988 notebook, the one about her and Adam and the Cronly trial. That had to be intentional. Was someone trying to create a mystery where none existed? She added another subset, this time including the Cronly murder investigation. Both victims were female, both pre-adolescent, the same age as Kate was when she was abducted. If someone was playing games, what did they want?

She pressed the record button. 'Missing newspaper clipping found at the lock-up garage rented by the O'Neills, related to the Cronly trial. It depicted DI O'Connor and myself. Possible reasons why? Michael O'Neill, or someone else with access to the garage, maintained an interest in me, DI O'Connor, the murder trial, or all three. Content of article was general information about the prospective length of trial, overview of victims, the witnesses called that day, including myself and DI O'Connor.' She hadn't a copy of the article, but she could easily find it on the Internet. One line in it kept repeating itself in her mind. It was about the age of the victims. Going back to the mind maps, Kate made a list of items noted in the news report, underlining the age of the victims, twelve, in red, then doing the same with her mind map.

All of a sudden, the air in the room felt sparse. She stepped back, taking in the mind maps in front of her. One range had the late Michael O'Neill at the centre, the other had herself. From the short distance, another thought crossed her mind. What if neither of them was at the centre? What if she had been looking at this all wrong? What if both were merely part of a bigger picture? And if the centre was different, what was it?

Sarah

SARAH HADN'T THOUGHT SHE LOOKED ON SEX AS A taboo. Since Lily's birth, she and John hadn't had sex. He'd made numerous approaches but had accepted her rebuttals. She'd told him she wasn't ready. And then how could she think about sex with the loss of their daughter? Soon he'd stopped asking altogether, and not long after that, they hadn't always slept in the same bed. The double bed they used to share felt large, cold and closer to the world Sarah knew she was creating for herself. She missed his warmth, missed knowing someone was there beside her.

Now, on the island, everything seemed brighter. She didn't crave darkness and despair any more. Since coming here, she realised her life was no longer about having John in it. Over the last few days, she had even found it difficult to remember his face. At other times, she would wonder if he existed at all. Had she imagined him? Made him up? But she could hear his voice inside her head, telling her he wanted her to come home. She wasn't going to do that. She was told she could send a letter, and someone would bring it to the mainland. The mobile signal was bad. It was impossible to make a call. She had tried a couple of times, and failed.

She heard a word repeating in her head. The word was *taboo*. It felt out of context. Another girl, called Amanda, was partnered with her that day. She was nice, if not particularly good-looking. She wore heavy glasses, and when she took them off, her eyes looked smaller, like tiny beads. Sarah felt bad about being so shallow and scolded herself. She tried to make a bigger effort to listen to what Amanda had to say.

The medication meant her concentration kept drifting, and she found herself doing more looking than listening. Sarah figured Amanda had been talking for a very long time. She must have stopped paying attention ages ago. Amanda was talking about relationships, saying how ever since she'd come to the island, she was less hung up about them. She was telling Sarah that love was for sharing. Sarah nodded. It hadn't crossed Sarah's mind to seek out relationships. Being a mother was all-consuming, but she had heard the other women talk.

They said the medication had helped them to loosen up; they were less highly strung and intimidated. She didn't pay much attention to them. They had their lives and she had hers. She knew that was wrong of her because things were different on the island. Everyone was family. Everyone cared. During her last session in front of the camera, she realised she was still clinging to old habits, and no one can move forward by carrying on the same as before.

Sarah had stopped listening to Amanda again, although she hadn't seemed to notice. Amanda was talking about sex, and when she repeated the word *taboo*, it jolted Sarah out of her thoughts.

Amanda looked down at Lily, asking if Sarah ever thought about having another baby, a brother or a sister for her little girl. 'What would be so bad,' she continued, 'about giving Lily a sister or a brother?'

Sarah didn't know the answer to that, but it was okay, because Amanda filled the silence by talking even more. Sarah nodded every now and again to keep looking interested. The medication made things like that easier, and part of her didn't mind that her brain was slowing down. It was a relief at times to be free of those constant aching questions.

She stared at Amanda, and she noticed that Amanda's voice was separating from her face. They were cutting out shapes from old newspaper. Amanda was cutting out diamond shapes that were linked together. Sarah was cutting out shapes to make paper boats. She remembered making them when she was younger. Her mother would bring her to the park, and they would float them in the pond.

Amanda was talking about Japan now. How it used to be customary to give young people what they called a pillow book. Sarah raised her eyebrows, unsure how they'd got on to the subject of Japan. Amanda didn't notice, telling her that the pillow books were small volumes of coloured woodblock prints showing the details of sexual intercourse.

'A picture paints a thousand words,' she said, as if it wasn't a cliché. Sarah tried to remember other clichés, but she couldn't. Not one. Her mind was stuck.

'The pillow book,' Amanda said, 'saved the parents the embarrassment of explaining intimate sexual details.'

Sarah nodded again.

'Now things are different,' Amanda continued. 'People can find out anything they want from any number of sources. Sex is no longer a taboo.'

Sarah registered the word. Amanda must like it because she kept saying it. Sarah repeated the word inside her head, *taboo, taboo, taboo, boo, boo, boo*, and she started to laugh, and Amanda asked her why she was laughing, and for no good reason, Sarah said, '*Boo*,' out loud, and then she said it again, and it sounded like the funniest thing she had ever heard, so she laughed some more, and Amanda laughed too, and after a few minutes, Sarah apologised for laughing, saying she didn't know why she had.

'That's okay,' said Amanda. 'It's good to laugh.' Then she told Sarah that sex shouldn't be repressed. Having relations with multiple partners, Amanda said, was nothing more than a freedom of expression, a celebration of life, of enjoyment. 'Don't you agree, Sarah?'

Sarah said, 'Yes,' because she didn't know what else to say, but she must have looked a little shell-shocked and unsure, because she could see that Amanda wasn't happy with her reaction. Then Amanda's face softened, as if she thought Sarah might be a bit slow, or like a child, someone who couldn't grasp a full understanding of something.

'Sex is a natural thing,' Amanda said. 'I love it now.'

'Didn't you love it before?' Sarah asked.

'Not really, but it's different on the island.'

'So much is different here.'

'I prefer older men,' Amanda whispered. 'They appreciate you more.'

Sarah wondered if she would view John as an older man. He wasn't much older than Sarah, but he looked it. She could hear the wind whistling outside.

She could see Amanda's mouth opening and closing, but she couldn't hear what she was saying. It was as if someone had turned the volume down. Sarah imagined John in their house. She could see him moving about, getting out of bed, going to the bathroom, brushing his teeth. He always got up before seven, even on the weekend. She tried to remember what day it was, but it was useless. She visualised John going downstairs in his dressing gown, after he'd had his shower. Then he would put the kettle on, lifting the small blind at the sink to let in the light. The kettle would be full from the night before. He would set the table for one because he was on his own now. Sarah wondered how that would make him feel. She could hear the imaginary click of the knife he would use to butter his toast, and the spoon he would use to stir one teaspoon of sugar into his tea. When he was ready, he would put the radio on, and read the newspaper he had collected on his way home from work the previous day. By seven thirty, he would be done. Then he would clear everything into the dishwasher. He would check that it was stacked properly to get the best economic value. He would fold his newspaper and bring it into the sitting room, dropping it on the coffee table, then walk back upstairs to get dressed.

Sometimes he stopped at the top of the stairs. A couple of seconds would pass before she might hear his feet move again. After he was dressed, he'd go downstairs, back into the hall, pick up his bundle of keys and open the front door.

'Are you listening, Sarah?' Amanda asked.

Sarah didn't answer. She looked down at the newspaper cuttings instead. One of the paper boats was lying sideways, so she turned her head in the same direction. 'I would like to paint them,' she said, 'the boats. I would like to give them some colour.'

'That sounds nice,' Amanda replied. 'Did you ever paint proper pictures?'

Sarah didn't know what proper pictures were. She never had known. John wanted paintings to look like replicas. He'd say stupid things, like 'Isn't that great? It's like an actual photograph.'

'I used to paint,' Sarah said then, 'but that was a long time ago.'

'There are plenty of artists here.' Amanda sounded excited. 'You'd like Arnold, or even Leo, or both.' Then she giggled, like some silly adolescent. Sarah kept listening as Amanda told her again that she had embraced her new sexuality. The words *taboo, taboo, taboo, boo, boo, boo*, were going off inside Sarah's head, but this time she resisted the urge to say anything.

'What about your sexual fantasies and desires?' Amanda asked.

Sarah thought about her question, then said, 'That was a long time ago, before Lily was born.'

Amanda looked down at Lily, asking Sarah which step she was on. Sarah knew they weren't supposed to talk about steps to each other. It was part of the oath of secrecy. Everyone's journey was different, and it didn't do to undermine someone else's progress. Amanda must have sensed she had said something wrong, so instead of looking at Sarah or Lily, she returned to her paper diamonds, picking them up in her hand. 'Aren't they nice?' she asked. 'All the same size, joined together neatly in a row.'

'Like us,' Sarah said, and it must have been a good thing to say, because Amanda laughed again.

Sarah's mind drifted, but she could still hear Amanda talking about her desires and fantasies, and telling her that hers would come back. That she was still a young woman.

Sarah heard Lily crying. It was near feeding time, and she

preferred to feed Lily alone, in the comfort of their room. She told Amanda she had to go.

'Next time,' Amanda said, 'ask one of the other women to mind Lily, and I can introduce you to Arnold and Leo.'

Sarah stared at her blankly, finding it hard to breathe. She needed to get away. She began to retreat, walking backwards, not looking where she was going, hoping she was walking in the right direction, clutching Lily in her arms.

Amanda followed her, and for some reason, Sarah felt as if her feet were stuck to the floor. They wouldn't move. Amanda reached out and rubbed the back of her hand down the side of Sarah's face. The hand was warm and gentle, but then Sarah got scared, thinking Amanda was going to drop it to her breast, but instead she said, 'It's okay, Sarah. You must take it one step at a time.'

Kate

KATE HAD SPENT THE WHOLE NIGHT IN CHARLIE'S bedroom, like a hen watching over her eggs. Working with the mind maps the previous evening hadn't given her any new answers, but it had focused her thoughts.

She purposely didn't wake Charlie for school. She had no intention of letting him out of her sight until she was able to work something out with Declan.

The techies hadn't managed to get anything forensically off the letter or the envelope, but she had decided to reduce her contact with Malcolm, just in case.

As she waited for Adam to come out of the shower, her earlier resolve, fuelled partly by rage, partly, determination seemed to be fading fast. If she was honest with herself, whatever hold she felt she had on things kept swaying in her effort to take everything in. No matter how much she pushed herself, she couldn't remember ever seeing her father physically abuse her mother, but that didn't mean it hadn't happened. She was often asleep by the time he got home. They lived in an old Victorian house, with thick walls, and her bedroom was the furthest away from the sitting room downstairs. It explained why her mother never stood up for herself, or questioned her father in any real way. Kate didn't need her mother to be alive to know that his rages could be terrifying. There was never any doubt in Kate's mind that if she pushed him he would hit out. If she asked Adam for the reports from the Domestic Violence Unit, he would probably agree to let her read them, but she wasn't ready for that, not yet.

'Are you going to be okay?' he asked, coming out of the shower.

'I think so, but I'm not leaving Charlie here. He's been through enough.'

'What do you mean?'

'I'm going to pull him from school, at least until we know there's nothing to worry about. I can talk to Declan later on, and see if he can take some time out. He works from home most of the time, and right now, Birmingham feels a lot safer than this apartment.'

'Kate, I won't let anyone hurt you or Charlie.'

'I know that,' but even as she answered him, a part of her knew that he couldn't guarantee anything.

'I'm going to see if I can get some surveillance arranged.'

'On what grounds? Two anonymous notes and a heap of questions nobody knows the answers to?'

'Leave it with me, but you're right about Charlie. There's no point in taking any chances.' He moved closer to her. 'Do you want me to stay here with you? I can, you know.'

'I'm tempted to say yes, but you're better off trying to get to the bottom of things.'

'Promise me you'll hold off leaving the apartment until I work out something by way of security.'

'I promise.'

When Adam left, she decided to make the phone call to Declan. She had left Charlie's bedroom door ajar, wanting to keep an eye on him. He was sound asleep. She punched in Declan's direct number.

'Is everything okay?' he asked immediately. 'Is Charlie okay?'

'Yes, he's fine, but something's come up.'

'What?'

'It could be nothing.'

'I don't like the sound of this.'

'No, honestly, this is simply a precaution, nothing more.' She paused, wondering how best to put the next part. 'I've been getting notes, two to be precise. I don't know who is sending them, but they both came to the apartment and—'

'What kind of notes?'

'They're probably some idiot's idea of a joke, but I don't like that they're coming here, and I thought it would be a good idea if Charlie went to you for a while, until I can get a handle on who's sending the notes and why.'

'Kate, are you sure this is simply a precaution? Are the notes threatening?'

'Not in themselves. They're more intimidating than anything else.'

'You sound awful.'

'Well, I feel pretty awful.' Her stomach was churning. She needed to get a handle on this stress. 'I know I'm not giving you much notice, but I don't want to take any chances.'

He didn't say anything for few seconds, as if he was contemplating what she had said. 'You're right,' he said eventually. 'Best not to take any risks.'

'Thanks.'

'You don't need to thank me. I'm his father.'

'I know that.'

'Hold on. Let me check the next flight.'

She saw Charlie stir in the bed.

'Kate, are you still there?'

'Yes.'

'There's one leaving at midday, so with a bit of luck I can be with you early afternoon.'

'What about work?'

'I can reschedule. I'll bring Charlie to see my folks first, then get a flight back tomorrow morning.'

'He'd like that.'

'What about school?'

'Leave that with me. They won't be happy, but it can't be helped.'

'Kate?'

'Yeah?'

'You really do sound worn down.'

'Do I?'

'You never change, you know that.'

'What do you mean?'

'There's always something pulling you in different directions.'

'You're wrong, Declan, I can change. Everyone can change.'

∞

Charlie was excited about his dad calling, but even so, he didn't like the sudden change of plan. What would his teacher say? He didn't want to miss school. What about the school concert? Was it to do with Adam? Did they have a fight? Why couldn't she come too? Did Dad not want her to go?

One question after another, all of which she attempted to answer, reassuring him that it wasn't anything to do with him, Adam or his dad.

Sitting at the breakfast table, with a full bowl of cornflakes and an undrunk glass of orange juice in front of him, he asked, 'What is it, then?'

Ask a direct question, Kate thought, and you usually get a direct answer. She knew she couldn't tell him everything, but she had to tell him something. Pulling her chair closer, she kept her voice low and calm. 'Charlie, do you remember a time a couple of years back when that man took the two of us away in a car?'

'You said he was in prison, that he wouldn't be able to hurt us any more.'

'He is. I said that because it's true.'

'What, then?'

She wished there was an easier way to explain things: frightening him was the last thing she wanted to do.

'You enjoy being with Dad, don't you?'

'Yeah.'

'And you also know that because of what happened Mum is always extra, extra careful?'

'You don't want anything bad to happen to me.'

'That's right.' She ran her fingers through his hair. 'You're so clever.' She was smiling. 'So the thing is, Charlie, something has come up that might be absolutely nothing.'

'Like a bad dream that isn't real?'

'A bit like that, only it isn't even a dream, just a couple of things that I need to sort out.'

'What kind of things?'

'That doesn't matter. The only thing that matters is that I want to make sure you're okay.'

'I hate it when you do that,' his bottom lip was quivering, 'when you hide stuff.' He pushed away the cornflakes, spilling the milk on the table.

'I don't hide stuff from you.'

'You do.'

'I know it's hard, honey.'

'I hate you.'

'Don't say that, Charlie.'

He looked down at his cereal bowl, saying nothing.

'Can I promise you something, Charlie?'

'I don't care.'

'You know you don't mean that. I'm going to promise you that you won't be away for long, and that you and your dad will have a great time. That even though I know you're not happy about this now, I'm not doing it for any reason other than I love you. I'll ring you every day, and I'm going to get this sorted out real fast.' She took his hands in hers. 'You do believe me, Charlie, don't you?'

'I guess.'

'I love you so much.'

'You promise it won't be for long?'

'Promise, cross my heart and hope to die.'

'And you'll call me every single day.'

'Twice a day.'

'Okay, then.'

They packed his case together, once Kate had made the call to the school. And true to his word, by early afternoon, she heard Declan's two sharp rings in quick succession on the intercom.

'You made good time.'

'Jesus, Kate, you look so bloody pale.'

'It was a long night.'

'Dad! Dad!' Charlie ran into his arms.

He lifted the boy high in the air, swinging him around.

'Thanks again, Declan,' she said, holding back the tears. Despite her brave talk with Charlie, she hated the idea of being separated from her son.

'No need for thanks. You know me, I love being with this crazy chap.'

Kate watched Declan turn their son upside down, all his questions temporarily forgotten, as she felt like a good mother and an awful mother at the one time.

Part Two

Addy

IT WAS TWO WEEKS SINCE ADDY HAD ARRIVED ON the island, and lots of things had surprised him. One was how little he had seen of Aoife, especially in the last few days. She was progressing well within the programme, she had told him. The higher she went, and the more steps she managed to accomplish, the more reflection sessions were necessary, alone and with other members.

He had also noticed how often that arsehole Stephen seemed to be hovering around her. When Aoife was there, Stephen behaved as if he was supportive and kind-hearted, but Addy saw a different side of him. Even if Aoife wasn't prepared to believe what he told her about the bastard, it didn't make him any less of an arsehole. Stephen was one of the leaders, and as such, respect was inherent in any relationship he had with other members. Leaders didn't do chores. They were there to support others emotionally. Some members worked, but the helpers did most of it. They all had different reasons for being there. Jason and Owen were a bit like him: they needed time away from home; the two Americans, Christopher and Alexander, turned out to be brothers, and they were planning on checking their Irish family roots in the spring. Asan was the quietest of all, but he was a good worker, and Karl did most of the mediation between them and the leaders, which suited Addy just fine.

He had thought a few times about going home, but he wasn't prepared to admit failure. Even though there was a lot about the whole commune thing that he didn't like, the routine of life on the island, in some ways, felt like an escape, while the isolation and the harsh Atlantic climate were growing on him. He enjoyed the physical work, caring for the vegetable patches, which now required the planting of garlic, onion and leek, before the hard winter set in. He learned about late cabbages, kale and sprouts, and he also noticed that his body was becoming fitter and leaner. Instead of finding it hard to sleep at night, as he used to at home, by ten o'clock he willingly collapsed into bed.

He had learned to be a better listener. He listened as members spoke about finding themselves, creating a new beginning, almost like a rebirth. They felt the commune offered them sanctuary, a place to reflect, to stay true to their individuality, which the world beyond the island didn't support.

Many said they regretted allowing themselves to be indoctrinated by mixed messages from outside, and that their minds had been manipulated for the gain of others, successful businessmen, bankers, corrupt governments. A lot of what they said made sense, which was partly why it was almost too easy to accept all the other bits. The utter devotion for the leader, Saka, for example, and the way members who were considered *delicate* spent so much time in their rooms. He knew there was an infirmary for anyone seriously ill, which was out of bounds to the likes of him. He had seen Sarah with the baby doll a few times. She'd seemed totally out of it. He'd noticed other things too. Members would turn up for chores, then wouldn't appear again. When he asked about them, he was told they were doing the work of the commune elsewhere. He assumed they had gone back to the mainland, but it all led to a transient existence where, more often than not, although he was in a place filled with people, he found himself spending more and more time alone.

Even though there was a lot of talk about the 20 Steps to Self-enlightenment Programme no one shared the steps with him. Most of what he knew, he had already learned from Aoife before he came. He'd heard talk about an oath of secrecy, when others thought he wasn't within earshot, and a pathway to defined individuality, to embracing yourself, not the person others wanted you to be.

It was a strange sort of freedom, he thought, coming to an island to escape. Yet, it was creeping in on him too. Just as his skin was changing colour from working outdoors, his muscles felt firmer, and the complications he had left behind – his mother being overprotective and Adam bulldozing his way into his life – no longer hijacked all his thoughts.

Before Adam was around, he'd imagined his father as someone completely different from the guy he'd come to know. The awkwardness of their silences, when neither of them could think of anything to say to each another, felt similar to the divide of the Atlantic between the island and home in Dublin.

He had yet to meet Saka. An audience with him wouldn't be granted if he wasn't a member. This had irked him more at the beginning than it did now. He had no intention of entering any programme, but some battles weren't worth it. If idiots like Stephen got a kick from being in authority, well, sod them. But it was the arsehole going on about helpers not being able to attend meetings that finally made up his mind: whether he was invited to one or not, he was going to find out what happened at them. With Saka and his assistant, Jessica, on the mainland, Addy decided to make a move.

The closest he had managed to get to the main meeting room was the hall area. The double doors were guarded, so he decided to join the meeting the only way he could, knowing that getting in through the main doors was impossible. It was while he was messing around with Chloë a few days earlier that he'd found the external drain shaft, the one located at the back of the meeting room. She hadn't paid any attention to it, but the sounds had drawn him in. He'd heard the testing of microphones, and the checking of speakers. He hadn't recognised any of the voices, but if he managed to get to the back of the building unseen, he'd be able to listen in.

Lying flat on the grass, he heard everyone converging. A final toll of the bell initiated the proceedings and the first, only, voice was female. He couldn't be sure, but he thought it belonged to Chloë's mother. She usually kept herself to herself, but he had heard her call to Chloë a couple of times.

'Welcome to today's meeting,' she said. 'I feel privileged to stand before you, my friends and new family. The words spoken here today are not easy words. They come from a troubled place, a place many of us know well.'

Addy leaned in closer to the drain, and when he did, he noticed a narrow air vent in the wall. Through it, he could see part of the female speaker. She reached for a book behind her, and although he couldn't see her upper body, he knew she was standing in front of a lectern.

'The extract I read today, like all extracts from the *Book of Enlightenment*, is unlike any of the doctrinarian-type messages that our old minds were exposed to before coming here. The steps to enlightenment give us hope, and it is this hope that will make us stronger and capable of withstanding pain.'

There was complete silence in the hall, except for the words and movements of the speaker. Addy already knew that members weren't allowed to interrupt each other, especially if they were revealing part of their journey. Obviously, the speaker was being treated the same. He felt his heart hammering in his chest, and despite not wanting to take his eyes away, every few seconds, he glanced behind him to make sure he was alone.

The speaker picked up where she'd left off: 'Thousands of years ago, the earth was filled with reptiles, earthbound creatures crawling along the ground, unable to free themselves from the restrictions of their physical form. Many soon realised it wasn't about becoming better at crawling, it was about transcending the concept of themselves as life forms. Some grew feathers and wings and turned into birds, defying the force of gravity that had held them. They didn't become better at walking and crawling, they found a new way, a better way.

'I spoke earlier about pain. It is a difficult path we follow. Not everyone understands our enlightenment or fulfilment, but it has been that way since the start of time. We do not preach religion, but we can reflect on the past in order to understand the present and the future. Two thousand years ago, a carpenter, a prostitute and twelve other outcasts started a group that challenged the values of their time, believing their leader, the carpenter, was the son of God, that he had the power to walk on water and even rise from the dead. Their beliefs were scorned and criticised, and tension became inevitable between them and the old ways of Judaism. They spoke of kingdoms – kingdoms the Romans didn't want.' The speaker paused, giving everyone time to grasp the message. 'The Romans already had a kingdom, you see, which they controlled.

'And so the founders of Christianity were mocked, and crushed, and suffered enormous pain, yet they survived. They became accepted as mainstream, and soon they became the new way. To doubt Christianity was to defy all that was right and good about creation. You may ask why Saka wants me to tell you this. The reason is simple. If you are a dissenting voice, someone who is looking for a new and better way, you will be scorned. You will be criticised and mocked. You may even be rejected by those you love. Many are still trapped, like the reptiles crawling in the dirt. The message today is clear. Whenever you hear such abuse or criticism, you must hold steady, knowing that closed minds cannot see or understand the things that we can see.

'Many of us talk about success – success in becoming the people we strive to be. The 20 Steps to Self-enlightenment Programme sets goals for each of us. Do not confuse goals with wishing or daydreaming. Goal-setting is the strongest force for self-motivation. You were born to shape a destiny for yourself. Grasp that challenge, be fulfilled within it, and never fool yourself into thinking you can truly succeed as an individual by accident or luck. Real success depends on your potential to develop, to follow the steps on the programme. If you can do that, you'll get closer to your desires. The simplest definition of success is the realisation of worthwhile, pre-determined, personal goals. We are all here together, but each of our journeys will be different.

'I want you to hold each other by the hand, look into the faces of your new family, see what they can see, and together, like the birds, we too will grow wings and transcend the locks and chains that the world has imposed on us. We will be united, like the waves in the ocean, each one of us part of an overall pattern, a strong and worthy member of something far bigger than us, which will help us in our preparation for what lies ahead.'

Addy couldn't take his eyes off the tiny air vent, as the congregation stood up, holding hands, then hugged each other in silence. It was clear that the words spoken had come from the speaker's heart. And although he couldn't envisage himself growing wings, he could see how easy it would be to swallow all this stuff. He couldn't see any faces, but there was no mistaking the sense of community. Every man and woman in there, with their common bond and their self-enlightenment, would walk out of that hall feeling elevated, special.

He was so engrossed in his thoughts he didn't realise he had an audience. Leaning up on his elbows, having heard something move behind him, he turned his head.

When he saw the fury on Stephen's face, he knew that saying anything in his defence would be pointless. Stephen wasn't alone. He held Chloë's hand. They looked like some sort of weird couple. Their blank stares freaked him out, but then he saw the curling up of Stephen's lips, a smile partly suppressed, an expression of future pleasure coming into his eyes, and Addy knew the guy had been biding his time. He'd been waiting for this moment, and whatever plans he had for Addy, there was going to be nothing nice about them.

Kate

IT SEEMED TO KATE THAT EVER SINCE CHARLIE HAD left with Declan a couple of weeks earlier, everything had come to a standstill, including the investigation. Adam had managed to get limited surveillance organised, and even though it was good to see the squad car passing by, she still felt like a prisoner inside her own home.

When her mobile phone rang, she picked it up. It was Adam.

'How are you feeling?' he asked.

'I'm okay. This virus seems to be coming and going.'

'It's stress, Kate. Why don't you see a doctor?'

'If it doesn't pass in the next few days, I will.'

'You're losing weight too.'

'Stop worrying about me. I'm fine.'

'If you say so.'

'I'm missing Charlie.'

'I know.'

'He can't be kept out of school indefinitely.'

'Listen, Kate.' He paused. 'Something's come up.'

'What?'

Almost reading her mind, he said reassuringly, 'It's nothing to do with you personally, only …'

'Only what?'

'It's to do with the investigation, but I'm hesitant about getting you involved.'

'Whatever it is, it can't make me feel any worse.'

'Lee Fisher's back from leave. They've managed to have a more in-depth interview with Mason's sister, pushing her on this group thing.'

'Fisher's confirmed Mason's involvement in the Dublin grouping?'

'Yeah.'

'It could be the common denominator?'

'Perhaps. We're both trying to track down other members. They may not all be in Ireland, but that's not why I phoned you.'

'Oh?'

'I'm looking for your advice. We might have linked O'Neill's death to two missing-person cases – well, not exactly missing.'

'I'm not getting you.'

'Technically, they're no longer classified as missing, but they were at one point. Look, Kate, I probably shouldn't have called. Maybe this is a bad idea.'

'No, go on. You said you think they're connected to O'Neill's death – why do you think that?'

'Okay – if you're sure?'

'I'm sure.'

'The number of people reported missing in Ireland annually is around three thousand.'

'But most are found?'

'Thankfully, yes, and the couple of dozen who aren't are generally people who don't want to be found – adults who want to get away, rebellious teenagers, that kind of thing. Most have probably gone to another jurisdiction.'

'So how are these missing-person cases connected to O'Neill?'

'They *may* be connected, we don't have anything conclusive, but something has come up with similar cash withdrawals.'

'Really?'

'We set up a team to trawl through PULSE, looking for anything that involved large sums of money going missing. Most of it was fraud stuff, a few cases of reported blackmail, extortion, et cetera, none of it was similar to O'Neill, with the exception of two missing-person cases: Amanda Doyle and Robert Cotter. They had no connection with each other, but both withdrew large sums of money in cash from their bank accounts before they made contact with home, one by way of a telephone call and the other with a letter.'

'And that's why they're no longer considered missing persons?'

'Precisely, but neither of them told their family where they were, only that they needed time to themselves, and that the money they'd withdrawn was in part to help them form a new life. If contact was going to be made, it would be from them.'

'As you said yourself, Adam, many people simply want to start afresh.'

'I know, but the cash withdrawals were in the same quantities as those made by O'Neill.'

'That's strange. What did the families say about their mental health before they left?'

'Again, there was a similarity to the O'Neill report. Both were low in themselves at one point, possibly clinically depressed, but their spirits rose shortly before their departure.'

'O'Neill's departure was death, Adam. The money wasn't any use to him dead. Someone else had to be a beneficiary there.'

'I know that, but with these two cases, we're talking in excess of a hundred thousand euros. That's a lot of money. But that's not all. This is where it gets weird, Kate. Apparently, they were both on some kind of self-help programme, not with a doctor but some kind of organisation.'

'What else did their families say?'

'They both mentioned the word "enlightenment". It could be a coincidence of course.'

'Have you found anything on the potential organisation involved?'

'Not yet.'

'What about O'Neill? Anything to indicate he was connected to something like this?'

'No. The only connection is the large cash withdrawals, and those unexplained meetings.'

'It's thin, Adam. The connection with the Manhattan murder is stronger.'

'Maybe, but I'm not ruling anything out.'

'Remind me what was written in blood on that mirror in Mason's apartment.'

'It said, "He saw the light."'

'Hmm, it could be linked, and certainly enlightenment can come at a high price, especially if it involves a darker element.'

'You mean some kind of cult, a mad religious following?'

'They're not all based around religion.'

'If it's a scam, Kate, so far there's nothing obvious appearing on the radar.'

'Notoriety doesn't always surround these groups but, as you said, this may not be connected.'

'Kate?'

'Yeah?'

'Work aside, I'm worried about you. Ever since I told you about your mother making those reports, I know it's been tough on you.'

'It's not your fault.'

'For what it's worth, your mother never pressed formal charges.'

'She lived in fear, far more than I realised. I've been thinking about it a lot. I remember in my late teens, my father changed.'

'How did he change?'

'He became less hostile, broken in a way.'

'Any idea why?'

'No, but he did say something to me a few years before he died. It was partly the reason we grew closer in my twenties. I can't remember what had happened beforehand, but I think he discovered something, or heard really bad news, because he went to his room and didn't appear for days. When he came out, he asked me would I sit down with him for a while. That was when he said it.'

'What did he say?'

'He said he was sorry. You have to understand, Adam, he wasn't a man who apologised, ever.'

'Did he tell you what he was sorry for?'

'He said he was sorry for being so angry when I was younger, sorry he hadn't been a better father, sorry for all his mistakes. Then he told me he loved me, and that as every day passed, he loved me more.'

'They're important words to hear.'

'I know. At the time, they meant everything to me.'

'And now?'

'Now, there are a lot of unanswered questions, and I worry that the mistakes he apologised for aren't ones I can forgive.'

'One day at a time, Kate.'

'I know that too.'

'Any word from that Malcolm guy today?'

'Not yet. I'm not answering his calls.'

'You told me he was like a surrogate father to you at one point.'

'I guess I haven't had a lot of luck when it comes to father figures.'

'You're not exactly hanging out with the father of the year, considering my track record.' He laughed, but she knew, deep down, part of him was hurt by his own self-criticism.

'Adam.'

'Yeah?'

'Addy will come around, you'll see, and thanks.'

'For what?'

'Asking for my advice. It's good to know you still believe in me.'

'I always have, Kate, but when it gets personal, it also gets tricky.'

She was about to hang up when she thought of something else. 'Adam, I never asked, did you find any evidence of a forced break-in at the O'Neill lock-up?'

'No.'

'It was strange that the place was soiled, wasn't it?'

'There are a lot of strange things about this case. The guy must have been under a lot of distress to behave so out of character.'

'The urine and excrement were tracked back to him?'

'They were.'

'If the same person is responsible for O'Neill's death and Mason's, then in its own wacky way, we could be back to the killer leaving some kind of message. It was Mason's finger and blood that were used to write that message on the mirror.'

'If that's the case, the big question is why?'

'It could be arrogance, Adam, their way of saying, "Come and find me."'

As she hung up, it was like her investigative and analytical brain had slipped back into action. Going into the study, she picked up her recorder, thinking about the two missing-person cases of Amanda Doyle and Robert Cotter. She had told Adam that the connection was thin, but even so, it couldn't be ignored. She pressed down the record button on her voice recorder. 'To date, the police have been unable to locate the missing funds that belonged to Michael O'Neill. Two recently reported missing-person cases, those of Robert Cotter and Amanda Doyle, also had cash withdrawals linked to their disappearance. At this point, the police have not yet been able to establish a concrete link. Nor can they be sure that other unreported cases exist. In both cases, Amanda Doyle and Robert Cotter made contact with their families, possibly to reduce concern and to limit questions being asked.'

Kate stopped the recorder, walking around the room, thinking about the possibility of unreported cases. It didn't take her long to begin again. 'In the case of missing persons, if a person isn't in a relationship, and is living alone, their disappearance can go unnoticed for some time. Phone calls to an employer or a message to a close friend may be sufficient to ensure their departure and, perhaps, unreported financial withdrawals go unnoticed. The cash-withdrawal elements of all three cases, Michael O'Neill, Robert Cotter and Amanda Doyle, link them tentatively, with the missing-person reports on Cotter and Doyle mentioning each being on some kind of enlightenment programme. So far, the police have not been able to identify the organisation involved, or whether it is involved in extortionist methods and/or cult-like associations.'

Kate glanced at her mind maps on the wall. 'There are three principal characteristics surrounding the definition of a cult. One is a guru-type figure, or leader, someone who over time seeks worship rather than following the founding group's principles. Another is reform-like characteristics, a systematic method of indoctrination being applied, usually done with a high emphasis on confessional-type sessions. A third characteristic is exploitation, which comes from above, via the guru/leader, or high-ranking people close to him or her. This exploitation can be economic, sexual or both.'

She stopped the tape. All of a sudden she felt cold. Maybe Adam was right: maybe she should see a doctor. She went over to the study window. It was barely open a couple of inches, but the breeze was strong so she shut it. Looking down at the small table beneath, it was the first time she noticed things had been moved.

The Game Changer

THE GAME CHANGER ENJOYED SITTING IN THE DARK. The camera was disconnected but a small audio recording device was close at hand. Pressing the record button, the low, steady voice sounded powerful, godly, and almost visceral within the confines of the darkened room. It was good to be in Kate's old bedroom, with her notebook and pen resting on the windowsill.

'Confidential Note 152. It will be fascinating to see who dies first.' A smile came to the Game Changer's face. 'Some members will put up a fight, or attempt an escape, but a great many will go willingly, believing they have been given the greatest gift of all. Not one of them is of any importance. The Game Changer hates them all. They are fools, with more money than sense, or young idealists, like Aoife, protected her whole damn life. Even Stephen is only part of the game because, like the Game Changer, he seeks power too. He would crush anyone without hesitation, pathetic mother-hater and child-killer that he is. They're all pawns, nothing more. The Game Changer is the one in control. The manipulation of others is of limited value. The real power lies in governing life and death. The seclusion of the island is psychologically and logistically paramount. Being removed from outside influences fosters an emphasis on a specific subject matter.'

The Game Changer stood up. 'The boy, Addy, is trouble, but irrelevant. His importance was simply to keep Aoife sweet. Of course, she doesn't offer money. She offers something far greater. Stephen doesn't like the boy. He would kill him in a second, if asked.'

Walking over to the windowsill, the Game Changer picked up the notebook and pen, then pressed the record button again.

'Kate will know a lot more by now, but she will not be able to connect all the pieces. She has probably surmised that the bird was killed for her benefit. Weeks have passed, but it will still play on her mind. The longer she is restricted to that apartment, the more her mood swings will increase. One moment, she will think she is doing well, the next, she will crumple. When she does, she will remember the warmth slipping away from its body, death, not life, becoming the bird's reality. It will be her reality too. Most people ignore the prospect of dying. They fool themselves into thinking it isn't absolute, that the one thing they can be sure of won't happen to them, at least not yet. An elusive event, something they don't need to be reminded of, even though each time they look at their watches, mobile phones, clocks, TV programmes, another moment of their life is over, bringing them closer to the black hole, the one without a get-out clause, but still, they continue to behave as if they can delude, delay and ignore it.

'Ethel O'Neill is like the blackbird, easily slaughtered. Kate is still trying to work out the *why*. The cause and effect aren't clear. She sees the ripples, but she cannot see the core from which they flow.'

The Game Changer contemplated the next visit to the island, knowing the latest. The next speech would be an important one. The wording, as always, was critical.

'All beliefs serve as self-limiting devices. Others may call you crazy, but the madness is theirs, not yours. In Plato's cave, the cave people lived with their backs to the light. It shone in behind them. All they could see were their own shapes in shadows, allowing the shadows to become their only reality. Each day, the cave people watched the shadows move, believing that was life. Their whole existence, awareness, was defined by their limited vision, not realising it was the light and their movement that created the shadow world. The cave people couldn't see beyond the constraints of their beliefs. They saw the shadows as the only possible form of existence, making it impossible to see anything else. One day, a man turned and walked out of the cave. When he returned, he told his old friends there was a wonderful world behind them. All they had to do was turn around. The cave people told him he was mad. What did he mean by another world? The only thing that was real was the shadows.

'If you are trapped in one reality, it is impossible for you to see another. Not everyone can be the man who turned around and walked out of the cave into the light.'

The Game Changer thought about Michael O'Neill's collection of butterflies, then pressed the record button again.

'When a caterpillar turns into a butterfly, the other caterpillars, instead of admiring it, only see difference. They will want the butterfly to turn back, but it can't.

'Confidential note 152A. All of it is an illusion. This happens when people swap one reality for another. Members think that by following the steps in the programme, they have escaped the misconceptions of their past. They believe they can now see things that other delusional people, those they have left behind, cannot see. It is the biggest trick of all, their certainty, and having escaped one lie, they cannot see that they are now living another. They have simply exchanged prisons. They misinterpret their new life as freedom, when it is nothing more than a different illusion of it.'

Addy

ADDY SAT IN THE DARK, HIS KNEES TUCKED INTO HIS chest, his arms wrapped tight around them. A spider crept along the ground, fast and furious. He watched it disappear into the muddied wall, wondering about his own escape, and why he had been so stupid. Staring at the iron grille above the door, the one that locked him in, he listened to noises coming from above – footsteps, muffled voices, the odd thud or whimper, making his mind up that as soon as he got out of there, he would get off the island – even if part of him still hoped to sort things out between him and Aoife.

He had known Stephen had been testing him, hoping he would crack, talking about his *incarceration* being a reward for his idle curiosity and blatantly breaking the rules. He knew the bastard hated him, but it was Chloë's face that kept coming to him now. Stephen had told her to go back to her mother, and she had looked so lost, like she thought she'd failed somehow.

When the bastard pushed him down the steps, Addy thought he was going into some kind of underground storage area. He had given Stephen a few digs, and even though the guy had got the better of him, there was something tempting about doing real harm to him.

When he realised where he was, his first thought was that this sicko was going to do him in. There was a certain look in the guy's eyes, as if a mask had been taken down, and it had made Addy want to lunge at him again, which he did. He'd gotten Addy in a headlock then, and trying to break free had only given the bastard more satisfaction. 'I could slit your throat in a second,' he'd said, 'I could pull your eyes out and blind you.'

Addy didn't reply, and then he saw that Stephen had taken a small knife out of his pocket and was turning it, like it was an extension of his hand. That was when he started going on about the history of the place. How the original buildings didn't have proper foundations. At first, Addy couldn't work out where any of it was going, but he kept his eyes on the knife, ready to protect himself if he had to. The guy went on and on about how the cells were originally built for murderers and thieves sent to the island to die, how the prisoners had no means of escape, and how the guards had had their own favourite type of punishment, burning body parts, smashing bones or pouring water down a prisoner's throat, as if the man was drowning over and over again, until eventually he lost his mind. Stephen could have been making the whole thing up to scare him, but Addy had been freaked out by the sound of Stephen's voice, a kind of menace within it, as if he was under some kind of spell.

All the time Stephen was talking, Addy had taken in as much about his surroundings as he could. The room they were in was smaller than his quarters above, and there were no windows to allow in daylight. There were a couple of vents feeding into some kind of pipe system, but the only door other than the one they had walked through led to a small cubicle, with a washbasin and toilet.

Addy let the bastard talk, wondering what Stephen was going to do with that knife. When he finally left without using it, and Addy was alone in the cell-like room, he didn't feel quite as much bravado as he had earlier on, listening to the group meeting and, as Stephen had said, breaking the rules. Once he was on his own, the initial relief was followed by questions. What if the bastard left him there? Who would ask questions? Who would even know where he was? Would Aoife ask? He checked his pockets for his mobile phone. He didn't have it. Maybe it had dropped out in the struggle, or maybe he'd left it in his room. It wouldn't help either way. The signal would be worse below ground. If he'd had his phone though, at least he could have looked at his photographs, the ones of him and Aoife. It would have been some sort of link to normality. She had sent him a selfie a couple of months back, one of her alone in her bedroom. She looked gorgeous in it. What if Stephen had his phone? There was a password, but maybe he could bypass it – maybe Aoife would tell him what the code was. He thumped and kicked the walls then, knowing he had to think of some way to get out of there, and fast.

Kate

KATE STOOD AT THE WINDOW, HER HANDS MOVING around the objects on the table below. She had a set way of laying out the items: pens and pencils in the circular container to the right, her small notebooks piled neatly on top of one another to the left, and a photograph of Charlie, in a heart-shaped silver frame, beside them. Adam seldom came into the study, he knew it was her work area, but someone had switched things around. The breeze was strong from the window, but it couldn't have moved them, not like that. A couple of things were missing too. A notebook and pen set, with a pattern of exotic birds, a present from Adam. They had joked about it. He had told her she should keep it by the bed, in case she woke up some morning with a life-changing idea. Could someone have been in the apartment? She hadn't been out in days. She put her hand down on the table again, her fingers scrolling down the pile of notebooks looking for the one with the birds on it, even though she knew it wasn't there.

She felt cold again, shivering. Feeling faint, she sat on her study chair, the one that had belonged to her father. She lowered her head to her knees as the room began to spin, but no matter how she tried to get the image out of her head, all she could see was the dead blackbird, its throat slit, warm blood seeping through her fingers. The bird had been killed for her, but it had suffered too: its wings had been torn from their sockets and the dead eyes had stared up at her, saying, this is your fault, this happened because of you. 'Who are you?' she said out loud. 'What do you want?'

Almost as if her mind was trying to fill in the gaps, she heard the words, 'I want you, Kate.'

The first note had said something close to that. It had said, 'I remember you Kate.' If they remembered her, she must have known them, or did she? What if it was somebody who was obsessed with her? But they knew about the dead blackbird, and that had been years ago. 'Who are you?' she cried, raising her head.

Assuming it was the same person who had sent the notes, could they have gained access to the apartment? Malcolm had been there, but that was ages ago, and he hadn't left the living room. The sender of the notes had got past the keypad lock. They could have been in the corridor any number of times. What if she had been careless? What if Adam or she hadn't shut the door properly? Unless you pulled it after you, the door closed slowly, enough time for someone who was watching, hiding, to gain access. She looked at the key in the study door. She always kept it in the same place, but it wouldn't have been hard to find, not if you had time on your hands.

She needed to get to the bathroom: her stomach was doing cartwheels. She had to calm down, get her head straight. Maybe she had put the pen and notebook somewhere else. Her mind had been all over the place lately. Within seconds, she was throwing up, and then the shivers came back. She couldn't stop herself shaking. Then she heard her mother's voice: 'Get into bed, Kate. You're not well.'

She felt exhausted. Perhaps she should lie down, get some sleep. The bed felt warm. She pulled the duvet over her head, the way she used to do as a child, and for the first time in years, more than anything she wanted her mother beside her, telling her everything would be okay, that she wasn't to worry. Without warning, the tears came, and with them a form of relief. Finally, wih the warmth coming back into her body, she closed her eyes and slept.

312a Atlantic Avenue, Brooklyn, New York

IT WAS CLOSE TO MIDNIGHT BY THE TIME LEE LEFT his ninth-floor apartment for his nightly walk. Warm days and cool nights made October one of his favourite months, the crisp fall air refreshing after the higher temperatures of Spring Valley.

Since he'd returned to the city, Marjorie had never been far from his mind. Whenever he took time off, it happened that way, almost as if she was waiting for his mind to slow down so that she could creep back in. He didn't mind remembering and, looking up at the night sky, he figured it usually came back to the same thing: he hadn't expected her to die so soon, or so abruptly.

He had imagined their relationship reaching the point of no return, both of them lacking the will to go on, but it had never come to that. Despite going their separate ways, they had never got over one another. When she died, he felt cheated that the last stage of their relationship had been taken from them – it clawed at him even now. He missed her, and he'd meant what he'd said to Margaret. His biggest regret was that he couldn't turn back the clock and make sure he was with her at the end. It wasn't ego. It wasn't because he wanted to know if she'd needed him there before she died. That was part of it, but not all. He had missed their final dance, the last bit of their life they could have shared, and there wasn't a goddam thing he could do about it. Death does that. It finishes everything.

Slowing down to light his cigarette, he wrapped the palm of his hand around the small flame, blocking out the breeze. It cooled his skin, like a lover's enticement, gentle and provocative, tingling and almost ghostlike, as his thoughts shifted to the investigation.

The Mason case was bothering him for any number of reasons. Detective O'Connor had drawn up a list of names, all male, involved in the 1980s grouping, and Lee had extracted as many as he could from Mason's sister, Emily Burke. Some of the men on the list were already dead, and outside of Mason and O'Neill, their deaths were due to natural causes, and beyond suspicion. Of the few from the list that they had been able to track down, none was keen to elaborate on the group to any large degree, saying it had been active over a quarter of a century earlier. Many of them had been on the fringes, and if anything sinister was going down, they appeared unaware of it. He agreed with O'Connor on one aspect, though: if the Manhattan and Dublin deaths were related to the 1980s research studies, there had to be a reason why Mason and O'Neill had been targeted when others on the list hadn't. Either the killer had only limited details about the identities involved or their emphasis had shifted.

Kate

IT WAS DARK BY THE TIME KATE WOKE. SHE LOOKED at her mobile phone – 7 p.m. She had slept for over four hours. She never slept during the day, and then everything came tumbling back: feeling unwell, throwing up, and wondering if someone had been in the apartment, the missing notebook and pen, the dead bird, and the notes, then her mother's soothing voice. Crawling out of the bed, she took off her clothes, discarding them on the floor, still lacking energy, and wondering if she would feel any better after a shower.

The water was piping hot and felt good on her skin. If she stood there long enough, could she wash away all that was troubling her? *Concentrate*, she told herself. *Remember how much better you felt when you were talking to Adam, discussing the missing-person case. Keep busy.*

She switched off the shower, wrapped herself in a towel and left the bathroom. As if to ease her thoughts, she noticed the squad car passing the living-room window. *Work, Kate. It's what you do best.*

She played back the tape recording from that morning. Something still bothered her about the missing-person cases. If they were connected to the Mason and O'Neill deaths, the potential cult association might have other sinister connotations.

What if this enlightenment group had some tie-in with the original group in the eighties? Both O'Neill and Mason had been members, as had her father, and all three were now dead. She stared out of the window, thinking about her father again. Even though there were a great many unanswered questions about him, she had no doubt that records would have been kept of the meetings that took place. Could they still exist and, if so, where would they be?

She picked up her phone to call Adam. He was late, which also meant he was busy, and she was half expecting it to go to voicemail when he answered.

'I didn't expect you to pick up,' she said, 'I was going to leave a message.'

'Are you okay, Kate? You sound tired.'

'I've just slept for four hours.' She remembered the missing pen and the notebook. 'Adam, did you move that notebook and pen you gave me? It was in the study, but I can't find it.'

'Not guilty.'

'I had this mad notion that someone had taken it, but it must be around here somewhere …'

'Kate, I don't mean to rush you, but I'm up to my neck in it here.'

'Sure. Sorry. My mind keeps drifting these days. I wanted to ask you something.'

'Shoot.'

'I know I'm not part of the investigative team, but can you tell me everything you know about the two missing-person cases?'

'Why?'

'I'm not sure yet. Do you have the files?'

'I have them right here.'

'Will you read them to me?'

'What – now?'

'Yes.'

'Kate, this is irregular.'

'Please – even the cover sheet.'

'Okay.' She heard paper rustling. Then he began: 'Robert Cotter, fifty-four years old, was reported missing on the sixth of April 2015. The missing-person report was filed by his wife, Michelle, stating that her husband had left home without any explanation or correspondence. There had been no domestic issues, according to his wife, and although all three of their children were grown-up, and they were no longer living at home, Michelle didn't believe her husband would have left without an explanation to them. Robert

Cotter's details were circulated via the PULSE database, and posted publicly online via the Trace Missing Persons site. The last sighting of Robert Cotter was at Bridgemount Road, Stillorgan, at approximately 1 p.m. on the seventh of April. He was described as five foot six, heavy build, grey-black hair, balding at the top. He was wearing light blue jeans, a navy Aran jumper, white shirt, a short blue rain jacket, and black work boots. When he failed to return home after forty-eight hours, his wife, concerned about her husband's whereabouts, contacted friends and family. She also did a complete search of their home. It was while looking through the house that Michelle Cotter found her husband's wallet and ATM cards. On the thirteenth of April, seven days after her husband had been reported missing, he phoned her. The number identification on her mobile phone came up as withheld, but she recognised his voice immediately. He told his wife that he needed time away to work things out. When she asked him what these things were, he stated it was nothing to do with her, and that he loved her very much. All he needed was time. It was during the phone call that he explained he had withdrawn substantial amounts of cash from their joint bank accounts, and that he didn't need his ATM cards any longer. He repeated that he loved her, and the children. If they loved him, he said, they would understand. His mobile phone was pinged, and the call was traced to outside Adare village in Limerick. No further sightings have been made since the last one reported in Dublin. He has made no further contact with his family. The money was withdrawn in amounts of five thousand euros, and totalled forty thousand. Prior to his disappearance, Robert Cotter was described by his wife as being a little down, but he had seemed very happy shortly before he left. He also spoke to her about being on a self-discovery journey, seeking what he had called enlightenment.'

'Amanda Doyle? What does her cover report say?'

'Hold on a second, Kate.' He put the phone down and she heard more rustling. 'Right, here it is. Do you want me to read that word for word as well?'

'Yes.'

'Okay. Amanda Doyle, thirty-eight years old, was reported missing on the twenty-first of April 2015, from her home in Scotts Lane, Greystones. Amanda is described as being five foot four, average build, with short blonde hair, fair complexion, and wears glasses. She was last seen on the day of her disappearance, wearing tight black jeans, a black leather jacket and a distinctive pink cotton scarf. Amanda was single and unemployed. Until her disappearance, she lived with her father, a widower. When Amanda failed to return home on the twentieth of April, her father became increasingly concerned and, in the missing-person report, stated that his daughter was reliable and always contacted home when she was away. He confirmed that their relationship had become more distant since the death of his wife, Amanda's mother, six months earlier, and that they had had numerous arguments. Amanda had withdrawn her entire inheritance (received after the death of her mother) from her post-office account – sixty-two thousand euros. Her father said Amanda often suffered mood swings, one minute being very down, the next more upbeat. She had become something of a recluse prior to her departure, listening to what her father described as self-help type recordings, mainly in her bedroom. Amanda had a pay-as-you-go mobile phone, and the last time it was used was prior to her disappearance. Details were circulated via the PULSE database and the online site, Trace Missing Persons. Seventeen days after the missing person's report was filed, Dermot Doyle received a letter from his daughter with a postmark from Courtown in Wexford.'

'Do you have the letter there? Can you read it?'

'I suppose, but I'll want some answers at the end of all this, Kate.'

'Sure, and I know you're tight on time.'

'Right, here it is.' He cleared his throat.

'Dear Dad,
Please do not worry about me. I'm in a good place and I'm happy.
I hope you are not too lonely. I'll come home as soon as I can, but
I do not want you to fret. I know we have had our disagreements,
and I understand now that it's because you miss Mum, too.
I'll try to write again as soon as I can.
Your loving daughter,
Amanda'

'What else is in the files, Adam?'

'Statements from their friends and family, most repeating what's in the cover report. Both cases have more references to some kind of self-enlightenment journey. The wording in each is slightly different, but as I said before, there's a correlation between the unaccounted-for large sums of money and the O'Neill case.'

'And as soon as Robert and Amanda made contact with their respective families, despite the missing money and the lack of information about their whereabouts, their disappearance was seen as a choice they'd made.'

'It's your turn, Kate. What are you thinking?'

'I have another question for you.' She sat up further on the couch, feeling a lot better than she had felt earlier on.

'Go on.'

'What did Robert Cotter work at?'

'He was a plumber. The company he worked for closed, and he started up his own business. Why do you ask?'

'How long ago?'

'I hate it when you answer one question with another.'

'Just answer me.'

'It was about a year ago. He was doing well, according to his wife.'

'But something substantial had changed in his life.'

'What are you getting at, Kate?'

'Amanda had lost her mother. Robert left his old job and started a new business. Michael O'Neill retired from teaching.'

'But O'Neill didn't say anything about being on a self-enlightenment journey.'

'Maybe not, or not that we know of. The point is both Robert and Amanda were at a psychological junction sometimes referred to as "in between".'

'Meaning?'

'They were in between different emotional and structured patterns in their lives, making them more ...'

'More what?'

'Susceptible.'

'Susceptible to what?'

'Pretty much anything. It's like their antennae were on high alert, and potentially, they could have been looking for new answers, seeking a different life pattern.'

'So?'

'The missing money is important, especially if there is an influencer, a common denominator that may or may not have affected their behaviour.'

'You're talking cult again.'

'Yes, I guess I am.'

'What makes someone join one of those nutcase groups?'

'You don't have to be mentally ill to be drawn into one, if that's what you think.'

'Go on.'

'Nobody sets out to join a *cult* – people join a new religion, or they look to a cause. From the inside, the group can appear noble, inspirational, but then a line is crossed, and the group changes.'

'From a regular group to a cult?'

'That's right.'

'How does that happen? People aren't stupid.'

'No, Adam, they're not. That is why cult leaders often use good intentions to draw people in. Once people feel part of something, they are then more vulnerable to further mind-altering points of view. To an extent, we've all been manipulated to believe certain things, whether through advertising campaigns, media, key peer groups, or any other channel of information we deem worthy of being absorbed into.'

'But surely a wacky cult is different.'

'Not really. By and large, when people hear arguments that support their current ideals, the new information reinforces an accepted viewpoint. When there are dissenting voices, their minds turn away, shutting out the contradictory messages.'

'So, what turns a group with good intentions into a cult?'

'The group's leader. Most fulfil at least eight of the nine characteristics of narcissism.'

'Okay, I'm listening.'

It felt good to have her mind focused. 'I thought you were in a hurry.'

'I am, but this could be important.'

'Okay, here it goes. The malignant narcissist has a desire to bring people down, in the same way that they feel they may have been brought down in the past. Many cult leaders have early experiences of abandonment, neglect and disappointment with parental and authority figures.'

'And the nine characteristics of narcissism are?'

'A grandiose or exaggerated sense of self-importance, an obsession with fantasies of extraordinary power and success, a belief that they are special and unique, only understood by others of their own elevated standing, of which, I might add, there are usually very few, if any. Also, they will have an intense need for admiration, along with a delusional sense of entitlement. He or she will feel that rules and normal standards don't apply to them. Because of this, they will exploit others without remorse or guilt, alongside an absence of empathy. The latter is an almost universal trait with all narcissists. They're so caught up in their own grandiose ideals that they pay no real attention to others in any genuine way. In the courting or initiation stages, they will fake empathy. They also have a tendency to be envious, choosing their targets carefully.

The targets may be people they are jealous of, someone with more money or power than them, or even someone who had a better start in life, perceived success, attractiveness, anything that warrants the narcissist's attention. They will also have an extremely arrogant attitude, and will be judgemental and dismissive of others.'

'Going with this cult idea for a second, let's say, Kate, someone starts to smell a rat, and things aren't what they initially thought they would be. It's no longer the good-intentioned group they joined. What happens then?'

'Because of the charismatic nature of the leader, most won't see the cracks until very late. Some may question, but because they're cemented in a belief that the cult or grouping was originally a good thing, and probably something they've invested an enormous amount of emotional and perhaps financial resources in, they will resist the belief that the group is more bad than good. They will look only for answers to reinforce all the positive elements. Walking away when you've invested so much isn't easy, even if you see the cracks.'

'The dissenters, what happens to them?'

'Dissenting voices will be seen as a form of disobedience and punished.'

'How?'

'It depends. They might be ostracised by the group, although if it's a location-based cult, other punishments could be applied.'

'Like?'

'Solitary confinement for one.'

'Prison?'

'Yeah – the group becomes like a family. The exclusion is used to discourage the member from challenging the group's belief, but there have been other examples of coercion, the use of sedatives, mind-altering drugs or, even worse, death.'

'And people stand by and let this kind of thing happen?'

'As I said, many don't see the cracks, or if they do, they'll be in part-denial. Other ploys are used to assist the mind manipulation.

Confessional-type environments are commonplace. By confessing so-called sins or weaknesses to the group or to an individual within it, the cult gains emotional power over the person. They see the cult, their forgiveness and acceptance, as an extension of their core values, making it more difficult to break down the walls of misguided belief.'

'I see. At least, I think I see.'

'The cult or group is usually steered by a manipulative, charismatic and narcissistically driven individual, wanting to build their own sense of power and glory. It's all a mask, or a series of masks, used to block out dissension and, for the most part, convince others that the choices they have made are their own.'

'What drives these cult leaders? What's the bottom line?'

'Power, money, sex – all three motivations can be present.'

'Fuelled by one person managing to get a hell of a lot of others to do what they want?'

'Yes.'

'I find that hard to believe. I mean, in today's world, information is at everyone's fingertips.'

'Many believe we're living in a more narcissistic age.'

'It all sounds a bit fanatical to me.'

'One man's cult is another man's religion or belief. Even in certain communes where child abuse takes place, the members of the cult don't see themselves as criminals. They see themselves as followers of God or some other ideology.'

'Crazy.'

'Adam, one last thing, can you read Amanda Doyle's letter again? There was something odd about it.'

'What?'

'I'm not sure. I want to write it down word for word.' She walked into the study, picked up a pen from the small table under the window and opened one of the notebooks, suddenly feeling unsettled again that items had been moved. 'Adam, are you still there?'

'I'm here.'

'Have you noticed anything being moved in the apartment?'

'No, why?'

'I'm not sure. It's like the pen and notebook I can't find. The things on the small table under the window in the study look like someone moved them.'

'Are you sure?'

'Not one hundred per cent. The window was open and there was a strong breeze.' She paused. 'I might be mistaken.'

'You sound tired again, Kate. Will you make that appointment with the doctor?'

'It's too late now. They'd be gone, and I'm fine, honest.'

'So, do you want me to read Amanda Doyle's letter again?'

The letter – she'd forgotten. There was something odd about it.

'Kate, are you still there?'

'Yes, sorry. Read it out and I'll write it down.'

When he had done so, she stared at her own handwriting. What was it about the wording that was odd? Could it be possible? She'd have to check the second note again, to be sure.

'Kate …'

'Adam, there are similarities.'

'Similarities to what?'

'The note sent to the apartment.' She looked up at the transcribed words on the page she had pinned to the wall, pulling it down, underlining certain words from both. 'The writer of the note and the letter elides particular words and not others. *I'm, I'll,* and *It's* are used in each, and some of the words that are not elided are similar – *I hope you liked, I hope you are not lonely,* and *I have, we have.*'

'I'm not getting you, Kate.'

'People use elisions all the time, but there is a cross pattern here. In neither message does the writer elide *I have* or *we have* to *I've* or *we've*, and then there's the repeat of the phrase, "I hope", yet the elided words remain constant. Adam, I'm not a script expert, but I do know certain things about it.'

'Like what?'

'We all have a unique way of writing, and while two or three people can share a couple of individual characteristics, sharing numerous ones is less likely. It's not simply the form of script used. It's the terminology, the shortcuts, the common phrases. All kinds of similarities and differences can be examined, but the bottom line is, I think there's a chance that both the notes and Amanda Doyle's letter were created by the same person.'

'That's a long shot.'

'I know it is, but even so.'

'But Amanda's father recognised his daughter's handwriting. You can't think she's behind this?'

'I'm not saying that. What I'm saying is, that irrespective of who wrote the note, the person who created the content could be the same.'

'So someone forced her to write it?'

'Or helped her, and dictated it that way.'

'Kate?'

'What?'

'This thing keeps coming back to the one person.'

'Who?'

'You.'

Sarah

SARAH HEARD LILY CRYING, BUT WHEN SHE GOT OUT of bed, the crying stopped. The room felt as if it was without sound, except for a drumming noise inside her head. Maybe it was the extra medication. They told her she had become unsettled, that the new tablets would help her to relax.

She looked at Lily in the cot: she was sound asleep, but Sarah worried that she might have sensed her unease. Babies are intuitive. They pick up on changes of mood, any anxiety or stress.

Sarah had been fine yesterday, until Amanda brought her to meet those two men. She didn't want to meet them, but she was trying to be nice. Lily was asleep in her cot, and that girl Chloë, and her mother, said they would call her immediately if the baby woke up. Amanda had been so insistent, telling her they were only going across the hall, and that Lily would be fine, and that she needed to meet more of the others, so they could all become closer as a family.

When she saw Amanda flick her short blonde hair provocatively, initially Sarah hadn't thought too much about it, not until the two men smiled and walked over to be closer to her. She had stood there and watched them, as if she was some kind of ghost allowed to be in another person's story. Then the men started to fondle Amanda, one from the front, and the other from behind.

'Come over here, Sarah,' Amanda had said. 'It'll be fun.'

She stepped closer, but she was unsure. It was then that Amanda took her by the hand, pulling her into their inner circle. There were hands and lips moving everywhere. When one of them stroked her nipples, her breasts hardened, and all she could think of was Lily, and how her breasts were for her baby, not for them. She let out a gasp, and they must have thought it was a gasp of pleasure because they began to get undressed, smiling at her, like she was part of some game. She pulled back, but for some reason, all of a sudden, she couldn't move. Then she watched one of them take Amanda from behind, slapping her naked thighs, telling her he knew she liked being called a naughty girl. That was when the other man approached Sarah again, only this time she didn't let out a gasp, she screamed and screamed and screamed. She screamed until she couldn't scream any more. She couldn't remember how she'd got back to her room, but she recalled Amanda's last words to her. Amanda had told her she wasn't ready, that it was too soon, but she made it sound as if Sarah was a failure, and maybe she was. Looking down at Lily, she thought about Amanda's words again. Maybe a failure was all she had ever been.

Kate

ANOTHER DAY, AND TO KATE IT FELT LIKE A REPEAT of what had gone before. This siege mentality couldn't go on indefinitely. Adam had promised he'd call as soon as he heard back from the handwriting specialist, and she had already phoned Charlie twice. Because of the notes and everything else, on Adam's advice she had curbed her time at Ocean House temporarily to zero, and with each passing day, she was getting more frustrated. Malcolm hadn't phoned for two days, finally getting the message that she wasn't going to answer, and so far, if nothing else, the dizzy spells had stopped.

She couldn't risk going for a run, and the only other thing capable of reducing her stress level was work. The mind maps on the study wall felt like a myriad of questions silently roaring at her.

Picking up her mobile, she thought about phoning Adam, then thought again. If he had information for her, he'd call. If the specialist linked the notes she had received and the letter, what would that mean?

She had made a series of notes after discussing narcissism and cult factors with Adam the previous day, and flipping open the notepad, she went to a new page and wrote – PRISONER IN MY OWN HOME, in block letters. The words stared back at her in much the same way as the mind maps looked down on her, questioning.

Peering at the word 'prisoner', she thought of the cognitive studies done by the so-called academic grouping her father had been associated with. In the eighties, she knew, a number of experiments had been carried out in the US around the behaviour of individuals within a group or a controlled dynamic. In one study, experimental volunteers were divided into two fictitious groups, prisoners and guards, before being placed in a pretend prison. Although there was nothing to divide either grouping, their members chosen from similar social and intellectual backgrounds, in less than a week the study had had to be stopped. The fake guards were harassing and abusing the fake prisoners, and those suffering harassment were showing severe signs of emotional meltdown. Experimentally, none of it was real. The prisoners, although dressed to look like prisoners, had not broken the law. The fake guards, dressed in prison guard uniforms, had never trained as prison officers.

The study examined why people who were not real prison officers, placed in a pretend prison, had abused people who were not real prisoners. Was it simply the uniform they wore or the contained nature of their environment? The answer was both, but it was far more than that. In another experiment, participants knowingly delivered a lethal dose of electrical current to others because the person in authority, the man wearing the white coat, had told them to. Later on, the participants had learned the whole thing had been staged. Nobody really got an electric shock. Although controversial, the study revealed a great deal about human behaviour. Take a person out of their normal routine, give them a new set of rules or guidelines, even those planted subliminally by people they perceive to be in authority, or deem worthy of respect, and their behaviour will alter, and not always for the better.

She flipped over another page, and again wrote in block letters, first 'YOU' and then 'WHY'. What was the motivation? Why was she a target? Stuck in the apartment, she was trapped. Had that been the plan? It seemed as if her life had become like quicksand, wanting to swallow her. She had spent enough time helping others through difficulties to know that once you start falling, gaping emotional holes appear. People can spend a lifetime trying to avoid things, but eventually they catch up with them. What felt strange wasn't so much that it was happening to her but that someone else was pulling the strings.

She opened the top drawer of her desk, and picked up her journal, deciding to concentrate on the good parts of her life. Charlie was a big part of it, and so, too, was Adam. They hadn't made love in more than a week, and last night he had whispered in her ear that he missed her. She had missed him too. They had kissed long and hard, and then, like the previous day, she had burst into tears for no reason. Maybe she was pre-menstrual, or maybe, she thought, she was going out of her mind.

When the phone rang, she jumped, and it took her a couple of seconds to regain her composure. It was Adam.

'Any news from the specialist?'

'Not yet, Kate, but something's happened.'

'What?'

'There's no easy way of saying this.'

'What? It's not Charlie, is it?' She heard panic in her voice.

'Ethel O'Neill is dead.'

'What? She can't be.'

'It looks like an accident, a suspected hit-and-run. I'll have more information later on, but in the meantime, be careful.'

'You don't think …'

'Be careful, Kate, that's all I'm saying.'

Sarah

SARAH AWOKE TO THE WIND HOWLING AROUND HER. Someone had closed the shutters in her room. She stood up, but as soon as she did, her head felt woozy. She staggered across the room, holding onto the wall for support, thinking that if she could reach her medication on the small table she would feel better. She must have forgotten to take her tablets. Her eyes hurt. When she put out her hand to get the pills, she missed the table completely, crashing against it instead. Everything on it, including the pill bottles, rolled around at her feet.

She could tell something had smashed. Her legs went then, and she slipped down the wall. The closer she got to the floor, the more shards of glass she saw. She was glad Lily was safe in her cot. If she had been able to walk, she could have cut herself. Sarah knew she needed to do something to make things right, but she wasn't sure what it was. She knew there was something she should be remembering, but her mind was stuck.

The glass on the floor kept changing shape and colour. It turned red, and Sarah realised her feet were bleeding, even though she didn't feel any pain. When she bent down to the glass to try to pick up the pieces, her head went funny again. The floor was a mess. There was something she was supposed to do with her tablets. She hadn't taken them – that was why she was unwell. She could see two more pill bottles on the floor, but she couldn't remember which tablets she was due to take.

It was difficult to unscrew the bottle with the green tablets in it, and she kept dropping it. Her fingers were covered with blood too. She banged the bottle on the floor, but it didn't work. It wouldn't open, so she leaned down beside it, and somehow the top came off. She poured the tablets into her hands. They looked like coloured sweets, a mix of green and red, and when she pulled her hand closer to her face, she put a load of them into her mouth. She needed water to swallow them. She knew she had a bottle of water somewhere in the room, so she tried to stand up, but she must have moved too fast, because her body started to sway again, and the room was spinning in the other direction, as if it kept changing its mind. She saw the bottle by the bed. If only she could get to it, she could swallow the tablets and everything would be okay. Holding onto the wall, she steadied herself, but it was useless: everything was moving with her, and then she was down on the floor again, dragging herself towards the water bottle.

She could hear Lily crying. She couldn't help her. She couldn't move, and closing her eyes, the darkness swirled around inside her head. She remembered the water. She needed to get water. As if it was a miracle, she realised she was holding the bottle. She twisted the cap until finally it turned. She swallowed as much as she could, getting more of the tablets down. Lily was screaming. She could hear John too. He was in the room with her. He seemed taller, darker, and he was looking down at her, telling her she needed to get up. She needed to do something important. His voice wouldn't stop, and Lily was screaming louder. Somehow Sarah crawled across the floor. She saw the tablets, lots of them, rolling around between the shards of glass in front of her. She was supposed to take her tablets. They would help her to get better. She needed to stop the room moving, so she grabbed as many tablets as she could. She put a load of them in her mouth, and some went down her throat, but then she couldn't breathe. The tablets were caught halfway down. The bottle of water was on the red floor, lying sideways, half full and half empty. All she had to do was pick up the bottle, but it rolled away from her. She crawled after it, feeling more glass shards cut into her. She didn't care. She needed to swallow the water. She felt the chill of the water streaming down her neck and chest. Some of it must have gone in, because the tablets weren't stuck any more. She laid her head on the floor. John was gone because, no matter how hard she tried, she couldn't see or hear him. Lily was gone too, and then the room went silent, except for the buzzing inside her head, before everything went black.

Kate

KATE WASN'T SURE HOW SHE FELT. IT SEEMED unbelievable that Ethel was dead. Something about her, other than the dementia, had reminded Kate of her mother. Ethel and her mother had been too quiet for this world.

Kate flicked around the television stations, more for something to do than anything else, catching part of a news report on missing schoolboy Peter Kirwan. It was the twenty-eighth anniversary of his disappearance, and looking at an old black and white photograph of him, aged fourteen, she thought of Kevin, and how he'd died, and how now his foster parents were also dead. If Ethel's death hadn't been an accident, was it connected? On autopilot, she walked towards the study door, but when she leaned down to take the key from under the plant pot, it wasn't there. She looked up at the door, seeing the key in the keyhole.

Once inside the room, her past looked back at her from the mind maps all over the wall, and as her eyes moved across the various headings and subheadings, she wondered if someone was purposely trying to draw her into something. Were they trying to create smokescreens that would cause her to look the other way, or the opposite? Keep an open mind, she told herself. Facts don't lie. She looked at the note she had written beside Malcolm Madden's name. 'HE LIED' jumped out at her. Underneath Ethel O'Neill's name, she wrote 'DEAD – hit & run', and immediately thought about the possibility of more victims. If this was all interlinked, any number of motives could be at play – revenge, money, power – and there was every chance that others might have to pay a large price, including her.

She looked at Charlie's happy face in the silver photo frame, and she thought about herself as a child, and how she used to like her own company. In fact, she had sought it out.

Staring at the mind maps again, she decided the best approach was to separate herself from them, to treat Kate Pearson as a separate entity, someone who was either at the centre or periphery of an investigation. She pressed the red button on her recorder.

'Kate Pearson is the only child of Valentine and Gabrielle Pearson. The family were respected members of the community. They lived at thirty-seven Springfield Road, Rathmines. Valentine Pearson was a professor of literature at Trinity College, and was also an active member of various local bodies prior to his retirement in 2004, a year before he died. Both parents are now deceased.' She stopped the recorder, thinking about the physical-abuse reports, before pressing the record button again. 'On the outside, the family appeared normal, but there were elements of emotional and physical abuse due to the dark moods of the father, Valentine. His wife Gabrielle reported the abuse to the police on a number of occasions, but she never pressed charges. In 1988, their daughter, Kate, at the age of twelve, went missing. The girl had been with friends near Ticknock when she got separated from the main group. A local search party was organised, but she remained unaccounted-for overnight. On her return home the following day, she appearing unharmed, but she had gaps in memory. The disappearance was put down as an attention-seeking stunt, and no further investigations were made. In the same year, another juvenile from the immediate locality, Kevin O'Neill, aged fourteen, died of carbon-monoxide poisoning. Kevin was fostered by Ethel and Michael O'Neill.' Kate switched off the recorder – making a note to ask Adam about Kevin's surname. He had been with the O'Neills only a short time, so he had probably maintained his birth name.

Thinking about her late mother, Kate was hesitant about starting the recording again, wondering, if her mother was still alive, what she would tell her. She had certainly kept her secrets. Kate hadn't witnessed the abuse, but she knew her father was capable of it. Why had he changed in her teens? Why had he become a quieter, less aggressive man? People don't change overnight, not unless something huge happens. Maybe her mother had found out something about him, which gave her the upper hand. Kate had made peace with him a couple of years before he died, but no matter how many apologies her father had made, she'd known there would always be distance between them. She had put it down to not forgiving him for his moods, but what if there was more to it? Then that sentence hit her. The one she couldn't get out of her head a few of weeks before: *The things you can't remember are the very things your mind wants you to forget.*

She pressed record again, clearing her throat. 'Kate had some clear and distinct memories of what happened to her prior to and at the initial point of her abduction/attack. She recalled glimpsing a man from the corner of her eye, before being grabbed from behind. Her attacker held an army knife to her throat. She remembered the smell of alcohol on his breath, and being dragged through trees. In recent memory recalls, other pieces have slotted into place. Her feet had hurt, she had lost her shoes, and her white ankle socks had become wet and muddy. Her underarms were sore from her attacker dragging her. Kate described his hands as strong, his fingers chunky.' She looked up at the mind maps on the wall, pulling more information from them, and pressed record again. 'In Kate's initial recall of the incident, she escaped her attacker, and remembered seeing two men standing close to a clearing in the woodland. She believed it was because of them that she escaped, assuming her attacker thought it was too risky to take her with the men being so close.'

Kate had never paid the two men much attention before. They were strangers, who had unwittingly been the reason for her escape. But what if they weren't strangers? And what about that extended timeframe? Malcolm knew about it, and so had her parents, others too, but everyone had been happy for her to believe otherwise. Why?

Was it to protect her, or was it to stop her finding out information that others didn't want her to know?

Walking over to the main mind map, she created another link, with the two male witnesses in it. She thought about the rumours surrounding Michael O'Neill, Tom Mason and her father. It was only then that she remembered the news report about the schoolboy Peter Kirwan. He had gone missing in Dublin in 1987. There was a year-long gap, but that wasn't much. Could that case be connected? She drew another circle with the boy's name in the centre.

Like a great many other people in Ireland, Kate was familiar with the case. The police had launched a large-scale search of the area surrounding Peter's home and school, with many local volunteers offering their assistance. But the only discovery made was the red and blue scarf the boy had been wearing the day he disappeared, found by the father of one of his classmates when helping to search the park close to his home. A forensic examination of the item revealed no useful evidence. The police conducted extensive interviews, and then turned to a clairvoyant in a desperate effort to learn any information that could lead to Peter's whereabouts. Though many sightings had been reported over the years, no one had succeeded in finding out what had become of the boy.

She pressed record. 'The late Valentine Pearson, Michael O'Neill and Tom Mason were members of an elite grouping believed to have carried out experimental studies of young boys and girls. It is also believed that they did so without parental permission, and the exact nature of the group is currently unclear; however, all members were male, with similar age profiles and academic backgrounds. At the time of Kate Pearson's disappearance, as in the Peter Kirwan case, which happened a year earlier, there were rumours and theories as to why. Nothing concrete to support these rumours has been found, but DI O'Connor, of Harcourt Street Special Detective Unit, is working with the PIU on a general review of historical cases of paedophilia, as well as collaborating with Lee Fisher from NYPD 7th Precinct, Lower East Side, Manhattan, who is heading up the

Tom Mason murder investigation. DNA found at the scene matches that of the late Michael O'Neill, although he had never been in the city. Ethel O'Neill, his widow, is now deceased. She died as a result of a reported hit-and-run, which may, or may not, be linked to the current investigation.'

No matter how Kate turned things around, parts of her past and the investigation kept crossing. She pressed record again. 'The suspected blackmail theory behind the death of Michael O'Neill has been linked to two missing-person cases, those of Amanda Doyle and Robert Cotter. All three parties withdrew large sums of money prior to their death or disappearance. All withdrawals were made in cash, in multiples of five thousand euros, and all of the money is unaccounted for. Both Amanda Doyle and Robert Cotter made contact with their families, officially taking themselves off the missing-persons register, despite their whereabouts being unknown. There is evidence suggesting that Amanda Doyle and Robert Cotter were on some kind of self-discovery or -enlightenment path. Combined with the large sums of money withdrawn, and all links to family and friends severed, their disappearance is consistent with cult-type influences.'

Kate's final recording covered the transcripts of the letter sent by Amanda Doyle, and the wording of both notes, specifically the second, currently with a script specialist.

She leaned back in her father's chair. There were three possible scenarios. First, her close personal involvement with the case could be compromising her analysis. Second, someone was intentionally creating links that might or might not be real or substantial. Third, all or some of the strands were definitively linked, and if they were, not only would she potentially be in danger but the suspicious deaths and disappearances could also be indicative of murder on a much wider scale.

Addy

THE FIRST NIGHT ADDY SPENT IN THE SMALL ROOM, all sorts of crazy thoughts went through his mind. What if he was the only one down there? How long would this ridiculous incarceration last? Why had Aoife not come looking for him? Why had he gone to the island in the first place? Was it really about Aoife, or because he needed to get away? His mind kept going back to his life as it had been before. He hadn't realised how unhappy he was. Even when his anger wanted to bubble over against Adam, trying to come to terms with a father being able to live a life without his son, all Addy had ever wanted was to know who his father was and for him to be part of his life. He had spent his whole life filling in gaps, making up all sorts of possibilities as to why his father wasn't there. The reality hadn't measured up, and a huge part of Addy's existence had shifted gear. He had fought hard against it. He didn't want Adam to be the missing link. He had created his own missing links of the kind of man his mystery father would be, and they didn't match up to Adam.

The days that followed were no better. Three times daily, members came with food, but no one spoke to him. It was like a seal of silence. To them, he supposed, he was there to reflect, to gain some sort of personal growth. During the day, he thought about Aoife, and every time he heard a sound, he would think it was her, only to be disappointed. If Stephen had told her he had gone home, she would have believed him, but what would be the point in that? As soon as he saw her, he could tell her the truth. That was when the crazy ideas had started to take hold. Other people had supposedly left the island, but what if they hadn't? Supposing he never got out of there? Even if his mother made contact, she could be told the same thing: he had left. Who would be any the wiser? Neither did Addy know why Stephen hadn't returned, but he guessed it wasn't because he didn't want to. Maybe he'd been sent to the mainland. That would explain his absence, especially if Saka or Jessica had wanted him to do something. He liked looking good in their eyes.

He had nightmares about the prisoners sent to the island, their torture, screaming for mercy from their abusers, and each time he imagined the abuser's face, it belonged to Stephen.

He had woken up an hour ago and couldn't go back to sleep. He put his hands to his face, squashing his fists tight into his eyes, seeing stars and doing it again, pressing harder, as if the pain could ease things. He listened to the gurgling of the water in the pipes, the creaking of floorboards above him, the sound of the wind outside, until he thought he heard something different.

Instantly he panicked. What if it was Stephen? What if this was it? What if all that he feared was actually going to happen?

He saw a gleam of light flickering through the slits in the grille above the door. Moving closer, he braced himself, determined that if anyone opened the door, he would try to bring them down, no matter what. But the door didn't open. Instead he heard a light tap, then a second.

'Who is it?' he asked, keeping his voice low. Whoever it was had tapped lightly for a reason. When no one answered, he said, 'Is that you, Aoife?' Still no reply. 'Chloë?'

The light moved, and he thought, What if they leave without saying anything? He moved as close to the door as he could and said, a little louder this time, 'Chloë, if it's you, speak to me. It's Addy. You know I won't harm you.'

He saw the light move again, then a piece of paper was passed under the door. He grabbed it, holding it up to the light in the grille, and read, 'THEY THINK I DROWNED – MY NAME IS DONAL.'

Addy tried to think fast. He didn't know anyone called Donal, but the name was familiar. The words were written in purple marker, and the writing looked childish, the last few words squashed together, as if the writer had run out of space.

Again, he whispered through the door, 'My name is Addy.'

'I know your name.'

He sounded young, maybe even as young as Chloë. For the first time in ages, Addy thought about Kate's son, Charlie, and how crazy it would be for him to be standing outside a door of a locked room, writing notes to a stranger. 'Donal, I need you to listen to me. Can you find the key to open the door?'

'I have to go. I'll be back tomorrow.'

'No, no, don't go,' Addy pleaded. 'We can help each other. I can help you. You want me to help you, don't you?'

'I heard you the other day, talking about Chloë to Stephen, wanting to know if she was okay.'

Addy sensed a gleam of hope. 'Do you know Chloë?'

'She used to be my friend.' Disappointment in his voice.

'Why isn't she your friend any more?'

'It doesn't matter.'

'Donal, look, don't go. We can help each other.'

The light moved away from the door, and Addy clenched his fists in frustration. Something told him if he yelled after the boy, it would make more trouble for both of them.

He paced the room, then eventually got back into the bed, curling up under the blankets, telling himself that the boy had said he would be back, and despite all the adults above him looking for self-enlightenment, Donal might be his only hope.

Jesus, he thought, how had he gone from being a guy studying an arts degree at college to this? His life was a fuck-up. He had jumped at the first chance he'd had to get away, following Aoife, not only because he cared about her, but because he had nowhere else to go. He was no better than some of the guys he hung around with, directionless in one way or another, going with the flow. How pathetic was that? How pathetic was he?

Earlier that day, Addy had tried again to engage with the members who delivered the food trays, but it was the same as before: no verbal contact. It was like they were struck dumb, with a stupid look on their faces, as if they knew stuff that he didn't know, the kind of look his mother gave him when she was pissed off with him.

He thought again about the boy. Why did people think he'd drowned? Why was he sneaking around late at night? He didn't even know what the boy looked like. All he knew was that he was a friend of Chloë's and pretending to be dead.

Again he thought if he didn't get out of there he would be considered a missing person. Not all missing persons find their way home, and for some, there was a very good reason for that. He told himself to get a grip, to stop losing the plot. That's what Stephen wanted, for him to be having a freak-out. If he got out of there, would he be able to convince Aoife to go home? Why had he stayed, knowing she didn't want him? All that crap about enjoying the physical work, liking the ruggedness of the island, it was a load of rubbish: he just didn't want to go home and face the fact that there was nothing there for him. The island, for all its odd stuff, had given him a sense of independence, away from his mother and the friends he'd known since bloody playschool.

Getting out of bed, he kicked the wall again, and didn't feel much better afterwards. Despite the screwed-up mentality around the place, he had liked the way people talked to him, as if he was a man, not a boy.

Some bloody man he'd turned out to be. He thought again about all the stuff he had made up about his missing father, and how in a million years, Adam would never have fitted the bill.

The Game Changer

Confidential Record: 161

There are always loose ends, sloppy bits that require clearing up, especially where people are concerned, despite humanity being predominantly predictable.

The fund now stands at two million euros, with more soon to follow. All attempts at interference will be squashed. From the outside in, it is hard to unravel the maze, but from the inside out, the Game Changer can see clearly defined pathways.

The members in the police force have confirmed surveillance is still in place for Kate. They also believe Ethel's death has upped the stakes, but no one is any closer to finding out anything of substance. They share this information unaware of how the Game Changer fits into it all.

Kate Pearson has become an important part of the process. There are times when the Game Changer is torn. Implementing two ambitious plans simultaneously carries risks, but the Game Changer is up to the challenge.

(Page 1 of 1)

Kate

WHEN ADAM ARRIVED HOME, HE LOOKED exhausted. Kate waited until he sat on the couch beside her to say, 'It seems like you've had a rough day too.'

'Not as bad as the chief super.'

'How's he taking it?'

'How do you think? First his brother-in-law, and now his sister.'

'It's awful.'

'For what it's worth, Kate, she died instantly. Judging by the force applied to the body, whoever hit her was doing some speed.'

'Any witnesses?'

'No. It happened down a minor road. It took a while to ID her. She hadn't any identification on her, no handbag, nothing other than a woollen wristband with keys.'

'Is there any word on the notes and Amanda Doyle's letter?'

'I'll probably have it in the morning.'

'Not what I wanted to hear. I'd hoped you would know more by now.'

'There's something else you might not want to hear.'

'What?'

He moved closer to her and softened his tone: 'I've been exploring reported paedophile cases from the eighties. Something's been rattling me about that whole cognitive study for a while – too many middle-aged men for one thing.'

'I'm listening.'

'One of the guys in PIU knew I was doing some general checks, and he approached me about why. I told him about the cognitive studies, the dates, the location, the profiles of the guys involved, and he was able to arrange limited access to a particular PIU file.'

'Which one?'

'I haven't got the name, that's confidential, but I did read it.'

'And?'

'The statements were taken from a woman who only recently came forward, describing her repeated abuse in the late eighties. As I said, I have no names, just part-access.'

'What do you mean, "part"?'

'PIU operates differently from the other divisions. I'd need to have something solid before I could demand names. Unless I can prove something criminal is conclusively linked to their data, everything is by their guidelines. Neither do I have all the transcripts, at least, not yet, and some of what I have has been blocked out, although I've read enough to be talking to you now.'

'Adam, what is it?'

'I think you should read the woman's statement. There are similarities to what happened to you.'

'What kind of similarities?'

'She was abducted in broad daylight, and she was the same age as you at the time of your attack. The general location matches too. Also, the person who took her grabbed her from behind. They held an army knife to her throat.'

'That doesn't necessarily mean …'

'No, it doesn't, but I still think you should read the file.'

'Everything seems to be happening at the one time. And being cooped up here in the apartment day and night, without Charlie, is driving me crazy.'

'I'll bring you in in the morning. Let's take stock after that.'

'Okay.'

'There's one other thing.'

'What?'

'We've managed to get more information on Holmes & Co., the company that owned the lock-up on Buckingham Street.'

'Okay.'

'The accountancy firm who set the company up is the same one used by Malcolm Madden. Naturally, I looked deeper.'

'Go on.'

'Madden and some others recently transferred ownership of a number of properties, including the lock-up garage, into Holmes & Co. About twenty properties in total, all rented out, mostly on long-term leases. The change of ownership was purely technical. In real terms the same people owned the properties.'

'So why set up Holmes & Co?'

'Some of the investors were looking to opt out early. They decided that, once the interested parties were bought out, it would be prudent to set the holdings up under company status.'

'Why use the name Holmes?'

'It's the name of one of the principal investors.'

'So, it could all be legit?'

'It could be. I rang Madden, wanting to know why he hadn't shared the information about renting the garage to Michael O'Neill.'

'What did he say?'

'Not a lot. He wasn't impressed at the late hour. He said he hadn't realised it was information we wanted. It was a rental arrangement, and once the rent was paid, it was purely business.'

'You think he's drip-feeding you information?'

'I do.'

∞

Sitting in Adam's office, Kate felt as if she was watching everything in slow motion. Adam opening the file, checking the content, looking up at her reassuringly, removing some of the pages, then turning the set of papers face down in front of her on the desk.

She stared at them for a couple of seconds. 'Can I read them on my own?'

'If you want,' he moved to her side of the desk, 'but before you do, you realise none of this may be connected to you.'

'I do.'

He leaned down to kiss her, not caring who was watching from outside. His kiss was gentle, loving.

'I'm okay,' she reassured him. 'I just need time to take it all in.'

'I'll be right outside.'

Kate waited until the door was closed before she began to read. She already knew from Adam that the statement had been written by a woman, but the opening lines were something she could have written herself. It explained how the girl thought someone had been watching her. The man had waited until she was on her own, grabbing her at knife point. The description of his hands and the smell of alcohol on his breath were identical to her story, and as Kate turned to the second page, it was as if someone else was walking over her memories. It felt like a warning. That all the bits she had forgotten might soon be revealed, only this time through the voice of another.

The next part of the statement dealt with a description of the location the woman had been taken to. Like Kate, she had had a short memory loss, a lapse in time that she was unable to fill. According to the statement, she believed the man had drugged her, placing a cloth with something pungent over her mouth. She had assumed afterwards it was chloroform or some other form of sedative. The more Kate read on, the less aware she became of her surroundings, or that someone could barge in at any minute. As the words unfolded on the page, her mind went to a place that felt raw; somewhere she had to go alone, the very core of her.

The woman described a prefab structure she was brought to, with grey walls and aluminium windows, three windows in total, all the same size. The front door was heavy, a fire door, with multiple locks. At first, the only noises she heard came from outside – cars and other vehicles going by at speed. They seemed to be a distance away, the traffic sounding like a constant low hum. Every now and again, she would hear a dog barking. When she came to, she had no idea where she was. She was in a strange bed. There was a steel bucket in the corner, and despite not wanting to, she used it to urinate. She remembered screaming a number of times, but nobody heard her. The windows were locked, and even though she was alone for a very long time, she also knew that eventually someone would come.

Reading on, Kate could see herself in that room, remembering how she had felt someone would find her, and in that same instant, she wondered if the woman had felt the same. All of a sudden, it was like she had gone back in time, the statement unlocking a pathway in her mind. She remembered making promises to God that if she got out of there, she would help others, do all sorts of stuff that twelve-year-old girls promise. She remembered worrying that her mother would forget about her. That she would get on with her life without Kate. There was something else, a kind of sick feeling at the base of her stomach, telling her bad things were about to happen. She heard the traffic driving by in the distance too, the same as the woman remembered, and looking straight ahead of her, Kate visualised the windows and the heavy grey door, the multiple locks, her desperation to get home, and how the night had brought darkness, and with that more fear.

She stood up and walked across the room to get water from the dispenser in Adam's office, gulping it down, remembering how thirsty she had been all those years ago. The condensation had built up on the windows, and she had licked them to take away the dryness. Sitting down again, it was as if she was re-entering some kind of time tunnel, but the next part of the statement felt different: the words, correctly or incorrectly, didn't feel as if they belonged to Kate but, rather, to the other girl.

It was dark when the door finally opened. I couldn't be sure if it was the same man who had attacked me, because I had not heard his voice, but when the door opened, it wasn't one man but two. They both wore black balaclavas over their heads. One of them had crocked teeth and smelt of nicotine. Neither of them spoke to me. I screamed, telling them

I wanted to go home, pleading, and even though they did not laugh out loud, I could tell by their eyes that they didn't care, looking at each other, and then looking at me. The man with the horrible teeth held me down. He slapped my face a few times, called me a sexy little thing. He sounded posh, not that that mattered, and I'm sure I must have fought back because then he tied my hands to the bed, and said, 'That will teach you, you little whore,' and before I could do anything, the other man was on top of me, ripping open my top, pulling off my training bra. I felt his hairy legs on me. I screamed when he pushed inside of me. The pain was awful. I have never felt anything like it before. I must have blacked out, because the next time I opened my eyes, the other man had taken his place. It's the end for me, I thought. I'm going to die. The next thing I remember, the man had his hand over my mouth. He kept pushing, saying, 'Lovely princess, pretty princess,' and making horrible noises, grunting with each push. He was heavy. I thought he would crush me. He punched me, even when he was inside of me, grabbing my arms, squeezing them. I'll never escape I thought. He'll break me, I thought. He's going to break me, I thought. I'll never forget that feeling. He kept pushing and squeezing, and making all those horrible sounds. Then he dropped like a large bear on top of me. I couldn't breathe. The blackness came back. I can't remember what happened next. I must have been out of it, because when I opened my eyes, it was daylight and I wasn't tied to the bed any more. My body didn't feel as if it belonged to me. I found it hard to move, and I didn't want to look at what they had done to me. I was not wearing any pants, and I was sore all over. I thought if I sat up I might crack, but I did it anyway, and I saw my swollen legs. I smelt too. There was sticky stuff, dried semen, in streams down my legs. The bed was bloodied, and I knew the blood was mine. The same way I knew they would be back.

Kate sat upright in the chair, rigid, living the girl's horror in her mind. She looked at the statement reference at the top right (S1 of 3). Adam had said there were more statements. She placed the pages on the desk, as if she was distancing herself from them, as if the physical gesture of moving them further away would give her the opportunity to come back to the here and now, and get her away from that locked room. She had relived everything the girl had written, right from the description of the abduction, the room she was taken to, and what had followed. Parts of it belonged to her memory too, the knife at the throat, the smell of alcohol and now more. She remembered the room and the sounds from outside, the constant stream of traffic, the fear, the desire to escape and knowing she couldn't, the intermittent sound of a lone dog barking, all part of her recent dreams. But the sexual attack, that recollection, felt like the other girl's alone. Kate knew she could have blocked it out, but she had connected to those other details so surely part of that would have come back too if it had happened to her.

Hearing the door to Adam's office open, she jumped.

'Sorry,' he said. 'I didn't mean to startle you.'

She didn't reply.

'You've read it, then?'

'It's one of three statements.' Her voice was steady, although her mind was turning over.

'I'll try to get the rest. They might have felt there was enough to work on. As I said last night, they're not inclined to share information unless a definite link is made.'

'We live in a horrible world,' she muttered.

'I know. If I could get those bastards, I don't know what I'd do to them, especially … if that girl had been you.' He let his words hang in the air.

When she didn't reply, he said, 'You wanted to know Kevin's surname? It was Baxter, his mother's name. She died of an overdose a couple of months after his death.'

'Adam, I want you to ask the PIU something.'

'What?'

'Ask them what the girl saw when she looked out of the window.'

'Why?'

'I don't know. If the man who took that girl is the same man who attacked me, I think I was in that room. I remember the windows and the door, and the sounds. I also remember what I saw when I looked out.'

'You could have ... what do you call it? Superimposed her memory on yours.'

She thought about what he had said. It was possible, she knew, but all of it had felt so real, like something she needed to grasp. It was as if all the things she thought she understood, the pieces that made up her life, her decisions, her drive, were now redundant. It had been reduced to that room, where she was a scared young girl, where she had had no control, and even though she hadn't understood, she'd known something bad would happen. Was she in denial? Could she have got to this point in her life and not realised she was a victim? How could that be possible?

'Kate?' Adam was holding a cup of water in front of her. 'Drink this.'

She tasted the water, had a couple of sips.

'Kate, take your time, but tell me what you saw when you looked out of that window.'

Her words came out slowly, as if she was telling herself at the same time. 'I saw a patch of recently dug-up soil.' What did that mean? Why did she remember that? 'I ...'

'Keep going, Kate.'

'And some low hedge. In some places, the hedge was broken.' She swallowed more water. Why was that important? Because you felt trapped – everything was important.

'What else?'

'Beyond that, there was a path. It was made of sand.' She looked up at Adam. 'It sloped upwards. It was as if the Portakabin was at a lower ground level.'

'You're doing great, Kate.'

'Am I? I don't feel great. I feel ...'

'It's okay.'

'No, Adam, it's not okay. None of this is okay.'

'I know that.'

'Can I have a copy of the statement?'

'I'll do my best.'

'Does the PIU know the location of the cabin?' Her mind was still reeling.

'No, but considering the sounds the girl heard …'

'The sounds we both heard.'

'Sorry, the sounds you both heard. The place is probably off a motorway, but which motorway and where it is is anyone's guess.'

'The maze keeps expanding.'

'We'll keep digging, Kate, and we'll find answers.'

'How can you be so sure?'

'Because I cannot accept the alternative.'

312a Atlantic Avenue, Brooklyn, New York

LEE TOOK A LARGE CARTON OF JUICE OUT OF THE fridge, his mind not yet ready to close down for the evening. They had received new information on the Mason murder. Emily Burke, the victim's sister, had had a call of conscience. By itself, it didn't mean a whole lot, except to add credence to the questionable nature of the Dublin grouping. She described her late brother as a weak man, saying that even though the group was set up with good intentions, it wasn't long before the scope went beyond intellectual conversation and cognitive studies. Emily had admitted to Lee's colleague that, while she had been visiting her brother the previous year, he had gotten very drunk one evening. Tom Mason had confessed to things that, otherwise, he might not have. The grouping, according to him, had decided to evaluate a wider base sample. They wanted their evaluation to have more diversity, thus ensuring their educational development theories had a better scientific basis. They had started looking at children from lower socioeconomic groupings. These children, Emily told Lee, were vulnerable, not only because of their age but because, in some cases, the lack of parental or family support made crossing the line less risky. They had hired a thug called Willy Stapleton to trap a couple of children. Willy had addiction problems, and needed the extra money, so he was easily convinced. Mason admitted the situation had got out of hand, with one thing leading to another. He hadn't expanded beyond this, except to say that a decision was reached to draw a line across the continuation of the study. He had clammed up after that and, anyway, Emily hadn't wanted to know any more.

It was all a long time ago, and both of them had started their new lives in the US.

Lee would speak to DI O'Connor in the morning, but none of it brought them any closer to finding Mason's or, potentially, O'Neill's killer. The widow was now another victim, but even so, what did they have? A lot of questions about a grouping from over twenty-five years earlier, one that had included Mason and O'Neill, a crime scene with DNA leading them to a Dublin suicide victim, and now a fatal hit-and-run. The child pornographic images on Mason's computer, and O'Neill's rumoured weakness for young boys, added a darker element to the eighties group, along with the suicide of the O'Neills' foster son, Kevin Baxter. If Emily's statement did nothing else, it compounded the notion that there could be unknown victims from back then, and victims had been known to reverse roles. He knew O'Connor was looking at statements from a historical case being dealt with by the Irish Paedophile Investigation Unit. He also knew O'Connor's live-in partner, Kate Pearson, was tied into the mix in any number of ways. Her father, Valentine Pearson, had been a member of the grouping, and she had been abducted as a minor, but was released unharmed. Kate had spoken to O'Neill's widow prior to her death. The fact that Kate was receiving anonymous threatening notes might or might not have anything to do with the investigation, but it added to the conjecture, and right now, nothing was sticking.

Swallowing the last of the juice, he fired the empty carton into the recycling bin, pondering the latest line of enquiry, the one supporting extortion of money from the Dublin victim, and a potential tie-in with Irish missing-person cases. This investigation could add up to a lethal cocktail, filled with sexual abuse, revenge, murder, large-scale extortion, and any number of people paying for the sins of the past. The problem, despite the many strands, was that they were no nearer to homing in on the killer. The net kept widening.

Systematically peeling back the investigative onion in his mind, he figured that of those associated with the investigation who were still alive, certain people were constant. One was Kate Pearson, and another the psychologist Malcolm Madden. His wife had given him an alibi for the evening O'Neill had supposedly committed suicide, but she wouldn't be the first spouse to lie for a partner. O'Connor was concerned about the anonymous notes sent to Kate. Lee wondered how well he would conduct an investigation if Marjorie was still alive, and it was her, not Kate Pearson, under threat. At the moment, everything pointed to potential fallout from previous events, but as yet, with the killer unidentified, there was no guarantee that only one killer existed or that any of these various strands were actually connected. If they could get to the bottom of *why*, a great many aspects of the investigation might fall into place – or collapse like a deck of cards.

His trip to Dublin to extract that DNA sample might have to be brought forward. If Kate Pearson was too close to all this, then so was O'Connor. The danger of the Irish detective missing something happening right under his nose wasn't a possibility that Lee was prepared to entertain.

Addy

THE FOLLOWING NIGHT, THE LIGHT IN ADDY'S ROOM changed again. Someone was at the door, but this time, whoever it was had a torch. He watched the light move, filtering through the grille and the slit under the door. He got out of bed, and when he was close to the door, he asked, 'Who's out there?' Nobody answered.

'I know someone's there. I can see your shadow moving.'

'It's me again, Donal.' The boy's voice was barely above a whisper. He sounded frightened.

'Are you okay?' Addy kept his tone soft, not wanting to give the boy any reason to flee.

'I'm sorry about before. There were too many people around upstairs.'

'How are you getting down here?'

'Through the water-pipe chambers, but I have to be careful.'

'Donal, listen to me. I need you to look for a key, something to open the door.'

'You're safer where you are.'

'No, I'm not. I need to get out.'

'If you're missing, they'll come looking for you.'

'I can't stay here.'

'If they wanted you dead, they would have killed you by now.'

'Who would have?' Christ, what did he mean? He reminded himself that he was talking to a kid.

'The leaders – they decide everything.'

He didn't want Donal doing another disappearing act, but he needed to push him.

'Donal, why are you pretending to be dead?'

'If they knew I was alive, they'd kill me too.'

'You're talking about the leaders again?'

'Yes.'

'What makes you so sure?'

'I've seen what they do. I've seen the graves.'

Addy closed his eyes, telling himself to keep cool. All of this could be nonsense, but one way or another he needed to keep Donal talking. 'How many graves?'

'I don't know. Sometimes they use the same one for a couple of people.'

Addy heard the boy's nervousness. 'Donal, are you scared?'

'A bit.'

'I'm scared too. It's not a nice feeling.'

'I told Chloë I was going to swim home, but I was lying to her. I'd seen them the night before. They knew someone was watching them, but they weren't sure it was me. My foot slipped, so I ran, and they ran after me. I didn't know what to do.'

'So what did you do?'

'I told my mother.' He sounded like he was about to burst into tears.

'Donal, are you okay?'

'Yeah.' Now his words came fast: 'I can't be sure she told them. She didn't believe me. She told me I was making it all up, and that lying was wrong. I ran outside and hid, and when I started walking back, I saw some of them look at me, like they knew it was me all along. I thought they'd wait till it was night. That's when they have their secret meetings. The ones only the leaders go to.'

The boy didn't answer.

Addy didn't know how to respond, and the silence felt like a gulf between them. Finally, he said, 'Donal, that doesn't mean your mother doesn't love you.'

'I watch her sometimes.'

Another silence.

'Donal, can I ask you something?'

'What?'

'Does anyone else know you're alive?'

'I don't think so.'

'What age are you?'

'I'm eleven this month. It's October, isn't it?'

'Yeah – I'm nineteen.' Addy still felt uncertain about what to say next, but then Donal began to open up.

'I broke into a cemetery once. My friends dared me, so I did it.'

'Oh?'

'I mean, I didn't want to, but then I remembered my dad was there, so I went to his grave, and I ...'

'What did you do, Donal?'

'It's stupid.'

'Tell me anyway.'

'I dug a small hole with my hands. There were stones on top of the grave, pebbles, and under that, loads of muck. I lay on top of it, on my stomach, with my hand down the hole. I couldn't reach the coffin or nothing, but the clay felt cold and damp. I didn't cry because I knew Dad wouldn't let anything bad happen to me.'

'It must be hard to lose a dad.' As soon as Addy said it, he thought about Adam.

'I had a pet hamster too. I missed him when he died, but I missed Dad more.'

'Donal?'

'Yeah?'

'Are you going to let me out of here? You know where the key is, don't you?'

'I can't.' He sounded scared again.

'Donal?'

'Yeah?'

'I'm worried about Chloë.'

The boy didn't answer.

'She's younger than us, Donal. She might need our help.'

'Other people have done bad things to her.'

'What kind of bad things?'

'I don't want to talk about it.'

'Was it Stephen? Has he harmed her?'

'It's not him. Look, I need to go. I'll be back tomorrow.'

'Donal, stay, I promise I won't ask you about the key again.'

But the torchlight disappeared.

The Game Changer

Kate

BACK AT THE APARTMENT, KATE MADE UP HER MIND that the situation couldn't go on. She had told Adam as much driving back from the station. He wasn't happy about it, but if she didn't start making changes, getting away from those four walls, taking risks, when would she be able to bring Charlie home?

Standing at the large living-room window, she people-watched, seeing a number of teenage girls on their lunch break from the local school, huddled in groups. A couple were on mobile phones, others eating bread rolls out of paper bags. Most were talking, laughing at each other's jokes. A man passed on a bicycle, wearing a sky-blue helmet and canary-coloured wet gear.

Kate's breath fogged the windowpane, and she used her index finger to draw circles linked together, like tiny atoms under a microscope. Something was changing inside her. Although she wasn't sure what it was, she knew there had been a shifting of perspective, and it was more than introspection or a virus. 'You think too much,' her mother used to say. 'Have more fun. Stop dwelling on things.'

Hearing her mother's voice, she thought again about Charlie coming home. Since he had left, other than a missing notebook and pen – which could be anywhere, considering how her mind had been – nothing out of the ordinary had happened, and the notes had stopped. 'Give it a few more days,' she heard her mother saying. 'After that, he can come home.'

Adam had finally got the report back from the script expert. He had examined the note sent to Kate, and the letter from Amanda Doyle. Although the similarities were remarked upon, there wasn't enough to determine they had been created by the same person. It was a possibility, but not an absolute. Perhaps she had overreacted, allowing her fears and imagination to get the better of her. Either way, it didn't matter now. She was going to put an end to this self-determined prison, and if nothing else happened, Charlie would come home, and that would be that.

Having read the statement at Harcourt Street, she didn't feel like doing much of anything, and glancing at the study door, she knew she wasn't ready to start looking at the mind maps again or make any notes. Instead, she went into the bedroom, pulling out the memorabilia drawer, already knowing what she was looking for: an old photograph album she had put together as a child. The album had been a seventh-birthday present, and it had a blue plastic cover with the picture of a chestnut horse on the front.

The first photograph had been taken at Christmas time. She was standing outdoors with a baby doll in her arms, pretending to feed it milk from a plastic bottle. The next one was of her and her mother. They were at a funfair, standing in front of the bumper cars. She had pink candyfloss in her hand. Kate pulled the photograph closer, peering into her mother's face, wondering what thoughts were going through her mind. Was she happy, despite all the anger? Only one of the images included Kate and her father. He always preferred to be behind the camera, rather than in front of it.

The two of them were walking through town, and the man on the bridge, the one who took photographs of people coming from O'Connell Street, had taken it. They'd been to see *Back to the Future* with Michael J. Fox. Kate had been ten at the time. She took the photograph from the sleeve, the plastic making a sound like Sellotape when she pulled it back. Examining the reverse side of the image, she saw '26198/3' written in pencil, probably put there by the photographer as a reference. Underneath, she saw her ten-year-old handwriting. In blue biro she had written, 'Dad and Kate, 1986, O'Connell Street Bridge'. She wore a loose tartan jacket, with a grey T-shirt underneath, and black jeans. If her hair hadn't been in a ponytail, she might have been mistaken for a boy. Beside her, her father wore a long grey overcoat with a cream scarf, and a light grey trilby. Half his face was hidden in shadow, and the half that wasn't looked happy.

She thought about a quote by Chesterton, talking about families: *When we step into the family, by the act of being born, we step into a world which is incalculable, into a world which has its own strange laws, into a world which could do without us, into a world we have not made. In other words, when we step into the family, we step into a fairy-tale.*

To Kate, the term 'fairy-tale' meant the inexplicable. She wondered how anyone could look back and work out what had really happened in their childhood, or fully understand the *why* of things. In the photograph, her father looked like a proud man, someone others could depend on. But she knew, more than anyone, how his mood could change from angry to friendly at the sound of a doorbell ringing. What kind of person could switch like that? Fooling others so well that only those in the inner family circle held their breath in fear of the anger that would still be there after the visitor had gone.

Kate went back into the living room. The clatter of schoolgirls outside had subsided. She needed to do something useful if the day wasn't going to be a total write-off. She thought about the missing-person cases again, telling herself she had to keep her mind occupied. Rather than going into the study, she picked up her mobile phone to record. 'Heading – Cult Groupings with Narcissism.' She cleared her throat. 'One of the standard common denominators is group isolation, taking members to a place where they have limited contact with the outside world. Isolation feeds into the notion that the beliefs and structures of the artificial world of the group are primary. The types of individuals drawn to these groupings can vary. They attract people from different cultures, educational levels, emotional and intellectual ability, and socioeconomic ranges. Most usually have a desire for change, and to find something their current lives are unable to give them.'

She remembered a study she had done on the rise of Flower Power in sixties California. The movement had attracted young people like moths to a flame. Initially, it was all about peace, love and freedom, but over time, especially in San Francisco, a darker element had come into play, and a couple of years into the movement, as busloads of young Americans were arriving, instead of flowers in their hair they needed protection.

The phenomenon of the Manson killings, even now, was testament to that. In Kate's eyes, it was a perfect example of how a social outcast, someone who had spent much of his early life in prison, could change the lives of others dramatically. Charles Manson had never come straight out and said he manipulated those around him. Instead, he was still adamant that what they had done, they had done of their own free will.

The two massacres of Hollywood's elite, the first when the actress Sharon Tate and her friends were brutally butchered, the second the subsequent night at the LaBianca residence, were not drug-induced. The killers had been perfectly lucid and, in most people's eyes, capable of knowing right from wrong. However, even a non-professional study of the lead-up to the killings could identify reasons why an unremarkable social outcast managed to turn young people seeking peace and freedom into vicious killers.

Over time, if you wipe away someone's identity, persuade them to forget everything they have ever learned, you are left with a blank canvas, which someone can manipulate, bit by bit, substituting a particular philosophy or belief for their own. The group gradually becomes more aligned with the leader, and in Manson's case, to such an extent that his followers would have done whatever he told them to do. All of the techniques used by Manson – isolation on that old movie set in the desert, convincing his followers that he was godlike, their guru, getting them to dress as Indians, or cowboys, or other fictional characters on a daily basis, along with drugs for periods when time disappeared – fed into their indoctrination, and loss of individuality.

On the first night of the killing spree, when Manson woke the girls, telling them to do whatever Charles Watkins, the only male killer who accompanied the girls to the Tate residence, told them to, they followed his instructions, carrying out the killings as if they were Manson himself. Psychologically, and in every other way possible, they became Manson, the elevated sense of him. He told his followers that he didn't lie and that he would die for them, asking them if they would die for him. When asked about the killings afterwards, he said, 'I walked with them, but they made their own choices. I told them to leave something, the same way as I would, to make a statement.'

Through manipulation, Manson had led middle-class, disillusioned young people to madness, down a path he had created and from which he had nothing to lose. The social outcast and victim became the powerful game changer, and while others moved on – hippies no longer wearing flowers in their hair – forty-six years later those, including Manson, who had carried out the crimes were still in prison. His followers had done things that, years later, they found impossible to understand. They had followed an anti-social, manipulative man who could become anyone those girls had wanted him to be. The gradual reduction of self, vulnerability, hourly indoctrination, led to an utter belief and obedience, as if to God, so that one day he could say, 'Get up and do what I tell you to do,' and those mind-altering methods had created short moments of evil.

Kate recalled a television interview with Leslie Van Houten, one of the killers. Leslie had been in her forties, and when asked what she had thought would happen that night, she had said, in a gentle tone, barely above a whisper, 'I knew people would die. I knew there would be killing.'

Addy

ADDY'S MIND JUMPED IN ANY NUMBER OF directions. He thought about Donal and all the crazy stuff he had said. He thought about Aoife, too, and how much she had changed. Neither, as he thumped the wall in frustration, could he get out of his mind the idea of Chloë being in danger. He didn't trust Stephen, and although he hadn't met Saka or his sidekick Jessica, he didn't trust them either.

Increasingly desperate, he contemplated the use of physical force to escape. If he attacked one of the members delivering the meals, he might manage to get to the stairs but, more than likely, not a lot further. Being trapped made him feel as though he was wearing a neck brace, especially in the middle of the night when he faced hours of isolation.

The only way he was going to get out of there was if he convinced some of the members that he had changed his ways and wanted to be part of the programme, to become *self-enlightened*. That day, those delivering the food had started talking to him, and it became increasingly obvious that they believed they were helping him; they saw his isolation as a form of therapy.

He asked thought-provoking questions about the programme, telling a couple of them how much his time alone had helped him. How it had taught him to value each moment, saying things like, 'The most important answers are often within us.' At first, he had worried they wouldn't believe him, but then he became more confident, and the more conversations he had, the more he hoped he was bringing them onside. He used information given to him by one member to feed to another. One had gone as far as saying he was now on the right path. All of which, if Addy was patient, would bring him nearer to getting out of there.

One wrong move, though, one stupid statement, and he could jeopardise everything. He put his hands to his unshaven face, then became conscious of his body odour, impossible to get away from. He had changed not only physically but emotionally, as if he had a new outer skin, as if the doubts and questions were making him stronger, more focused. The last thought he had was of Aoife, and how, if he could, he would make one final effort to convince her to drop this madness.

Kate

KATE PHONED ADAM, AND TOLD HIM SHE WAS GOING
for a run. She was apprehensive, but she had to start somewhere.
She hadn't planned to go back to her old home, but thirty minutes
after making the call to him, she stood across the road from the
house she had grown up in.

The earlier rain had eased, and with the sun coming out from the
clouds, the passing traffic made swishing sounds on the wet tarmac
and through the puddles. She stared at the house, as she had a few
weeks earlier, and thought about ringing the bell. Perhaps this time
there would be an answer, and she could walk on the floors she had
once run on as a child.

Unlike the other houses, there wasn't any smoke coming from
the chimney and the windows looked darker. Immediately she
understood why: the heavy curtains were drawn. She told herself
that nobody was at home, yet she crossed the road regardless,
repeating what she had done before, ringing the doorbell and not
expecting an answer. She listened as the bell rang in the hallway,
visualising her mother rushing to the door. Kate put her fingers
to the lock at the top, imagining her father turning his key. Other
memories came back: the three of them together, returning from
the park, their cheeks rosy red with the cold, all wearing coats,
scarves and gloves, huddled on the front step, waiting to get inside
to the warmth. She thought of birthday parties and Christmases,
when her father had taken down the video camera and recorded all
the happy bits, as if they, instead of the dark times, were the long-
standing proof of their lives.

'Can I help you?' a female voice hollered from behind.

Kate turned to see the old woman with the dachshund.

'There's nobody home,' the woman said. 'They've gone away.' This time she was wearing a clear plastic raincoat with the hood up.

'Do you know when they'll be back?' Kate asked.

'It'll be a while. I'm keeping an eye on things for them.' The woman maintained her position at the gate, as if she was some sort of sentry. 'Who's asking?'

'My name's Kate Pearson. I used to live here.'

The woman blinked a few times. 'Oh, yes, I remember you. You're the girl that went missing.'

'That's right,' Kate replied, although she was becoming increasingly uncomfortable with being referred to in that way. 'Do you know where they've gone, or if there's any way I can contact them? I'd like to visit the house for old times' sake.'

'I used to know your mother,' the woman replied, instead of answering Kate's question. 'We played bridge together.'

'Mrs Grant, is that you? I didn't recognise you.'

'Well, none of us is getting any younger.' Her tone said she was insulted by Kate's remark.

'No, no, I didn't mean anything by that. It's just that it's been so long.' Her sentences came out on top of one another. 'Sorry, Mrs Grant.' She smiled, attempting to retrieve the situation. 'I think you look great.'

'I like to exercise. There's no point in letting the body age too fast.'

'Absolutely not.'

'You can call me Pat, seeing as how you're not a child any more.' Clearly she was mellowing.

'Good to meet you again, Pat.' Kate walked towards her.

'I have a key if you want it,' the old woman said, as if it was some kind of tease, then added, 'there's an alarm connected to a security depot, and they need a local key holder. I wouldn't be giving it to anyone, mind, but I guess it wouldn't do any harm for you to have a quick look around, seeing as how I know you.'

'Great.' Kate could hardly believe her luck. 'That's really kind of you.'

Pat Grant rooted in her bag, while the dachshund glared at Kate, but obediently remained in the sitting position. 'They've gone somewhere on the south coast, on holidays.' She held up the gold Yale key, then handed it to Kate. 'They must be mad in this bloody awful weather.'

'Indeed.'

'Don't be long now. I'll be back with Hubert in a quarter of an hour. The wet weather isn't good for his bones, especially if he's out too long. The alarm is inside the door,' then lowering her voice, 'the code is "pass".'

Kate held the key in the palm of her hand. 'I'll be quick. I promise.'

∞

Turning the key in the door, she wasn't sure what she was expecting, but in the hallway her heart quickened, as she punched in the alarm code. It wasn't the idea of being inside someone else's home. It was the acknowledgement that somehow, again, she was stepping back in time. She had last been inside the house eight weeks after her mother's death, to clear away her things. The memorial cards had been sent out, the visits to the solicitor and the bank sorted, and all the other details that followed a person's death completed.

Back then, the house hadn't pulled at her memory strings. Her mother had been in the nursing home for so long that the place didn't feel the same, seeming more like an empty shell of what it used to be. Leaning against the front door, another image jumped into her mind: her mother in her final days, her lower lip dropped in an effort to breathe, her frame shrunken to little more than bone, the veins on her hands protruding, and that vacant stare, the one that looked beyond you.

That afternoon, though, the house felt different, and she could see the place anew, with open doors leading to each of the rooms, every element containing part of who she used to be. The light forced its way from behind the drawn curtains, and she could feel a draught sneak up the hallway from the back of the house as she breathed in her old home again.

The first new owners had been a young couple. Later, she learned they had fallen on hard times, the husband's business collapsing with the end of the Celtic Tiger, and the house was resold. To whom, Kate had no idea.

She switched on the light in the hall, opening the front zip of her rain jacket. There were new furnishings – lamps, carpet, an umbrella stand – and pictures on the wall. It was as if someone had taken a drawing done by another and changed it, putting items where spaces had been blank.

Conscious of time, Kate walked through the house, until she stood outside her parents' bedroom. The doors had remained unchanged, other than a fresh coat of cream paint. Holding the handle, she paused, wondering again what she expected. How many times had she turned that handle in the past? How many times had she stood in that exact spot? She tried to envisage herself as the twelve-year-old who'd thought she knew so much.

Turning the handle with a jerk, she pushed the door forward with such force that it bounced back on itself. She was surprised to find the room empty of furniture, except for her mother's old dressing table and stool. Kate had cleared out most of the stuff to charity shops, and anything that wasn't good enough had gone in a skip. In the haze that followed the funeral, could she have forgotten them? It didn't matter one way or another. Perhaps the new owners had found them and decided to keep them.

Kate took a couple of steps closer, visualising herself as a child, looking in the mirror after she climbed onto the stool, her younger self gazing back at her. She brought her hands to her face, touching her older features, aware that the flow of fresh tears was close. There was something utterly private about this room, which she had never noticed before. Perhaps it was the half-darkness, creating an intimacy, but this was the room where her parents had made love, where, more than likely, she had been conceived. Now both of her parents were gone and, with them, their secrets.

Kate looked at her watch, knowing Pat Grant would be back soon. Reluctant to leave, something guided her to the drawers of the dressing table, which she opened one at a time. They were empty. She sat down, running her hand across the top, feeling the waxed wood beneath her fingertips. It was as if she was physically trying to connect with her mother by touching something that had belonged to her. She raised her hand to the mirror, passing her fingers around the edge, stopping at one of the sides, feeling something behind the glass. She stood up, pulling the dressing table out from the wall. Stuck to the back with Sellotape was a folded newspaper clipping. She removed it carefully. It was old and faded. She placed it on top of the dressing table, pulling back the curtains to allow in light. With it came a chill, and she shivered. In the street below, she saw the spot where she had stood when she was looking in. She opened the paper, conscious that it could fall apart because of its age. She looked at the date – 30 November 1987. The lead article was about the disappearance of Peter Kirwan. At the bottom of the page, there was a photograph with the caption 'Schoolgirl delighted to meet the President', and underneath, she saw her eleven-year-old face, with her name, Kate Pearson, written in bold type. It had been a school visit to Áras an Uachtaráin, and she had completely forgotten about it. She looked again at the article about the missing schoolboy, realising that his name and the date at the top right of the newspaper had been circled in red pen. Who had done that, and why?

Behind her, the bedroom door creaked, closing, and suddenly she needed to be out of that room. Everything she had heard about paedophile rumours, unofficial cognitive testing of children, her father and Malcolm, and all the unanswered questions, came ramming into her mind. Had her father kept the clipping on the pretext it was about her, when all along, there was a very different reason? If he had, why had he circled the boy's name and the date, bringing attention to something he wouldn't want highlighted? And why hide it at the back of her mother's dressing table? Unless it hadn't been her father who'd put it there. What if it had been her mother? Had she known something so terrible that she had kept it as a permanent marker?

Sarah

AT FIRST SARAH WASN'T SURE WHERE SHE WAS. There was a bright light above her head, and as her eyes settled, she realised it was a fluorescent tube. It was blinding. The smells around her reminded her of hospitals. When she tried to move her head, she couldn't. Her mouth was dry, and something was stuck into her right arm. It felt heavy, as if she was weighed down by it. She wasn't alone. There were muffled voices in the room. She recognised one as Jessica's. The sharp light eased. She blinked rapidly, and shapes became clearer. She caught a whiff of disinfectant.

'We thought we'd lost you, Sarah.' The voice sounded strangely cheerful. It was Jessica's.

'Where am I? Where's Lily?' she screeched. 'I can't see her! Where have you taken her?'

'Calm down.' Jessica's voice still upbeat, sickly sweet. 'Lily will be here soon.'

'You don't understand,' Sarah pleaded, trying to force herself into a sitting position. Her body felt like a lead weight. She realised the thing in her arm was an intravenous drip and her flesh was badly bruised. 'I must see Lily,' she roared, 'she's my baby.'

Jessica placed her hands on Sarah's shoulders, easing her back down.

'Where is she?' Sarah hissed, spitting at Jessica.

Instead of being angry, Jessica rubbed Sarah's forehead with her hand. For an instant, Sarah thought she was going to throw up. It was then that she heard the wheels, tiny spinning wheels. She managed to turn her head towards the door. A slim woman in her mid-twenties, attractive, with shoulder-length honey-brown hair, and wearing a white hospital coat, pushed a clear plastic cot with a baby inside it into the room. She knew it was Lily, and her body eased with relief.

'Is she okay?' Sarah asked, hoping they would tell her what she wanted to hear.

She expected the woman in the white coat to answer, but instead, Jessica said, 'Look at her, Sarah. She's perfectly fine. Isn't that right, Dr Redmond?'

'Mother and baby are doing great, but Sarah can call me Lisa.'

'I need to talk to John,' Sarah muttered. 'He'll be worried.'

'Plenty of time for that.' Jessica smiled.

Sarah looked around the room for her mobile phone, but couldn't see it. 'Where's my phone?' she asked, sounding accusing.

'Sarah, it's important that you remain calm. You know the signal is bad here on the island. I'll get one of the members to fetch it for you, shall I?'

'Please. Thank you, Jessica.'

'But first you must look after your baby.'

'Yes, of course,' she replied, looking at Lily, feeling guilty, but even as she was thinking that, she realised her mind was on some kind of slowdown. She saw Dr Redmond, Lisa, increase the flow of liquid from the drip under Jessica's instructions.

'What's that?' she asked.

'Extra fluids,' replied Jessica. 'We need to keep the supply at a high level, now that you've come back to us after your turn.'

Sarah kept staring at Jessica, watching her pick up Lily from the cot, ready to hand her to her.

'What happened?' Sarah asked. 'I remember taking tablets, but after that, I can't remember anything.'

'You took too many, Sarah. It's nothing to worry about now. We'll have you on your feet in no time.' Jessica fixed the blanket around Lily before handing her over. The pain wasn't so bad for Sarah now, but the room was turning, and her vision blurred. She felt as if she was about to drift into sleep, but instead, she tried hard to concentrate.

'My phone,' she mumbled. 'I need to call John. I want him to come here. I want him to come for us.'

It was Jessica's voice she heard next: 'The weather will ease soon,' she said. 'You can call him then, and I'm sure he'll want to come to see you.'

There was an element of doubt implicit in her words.

'It's okay, Sarah,' the doctor said.

Sarah couldn't remember her name. The doctor leaned in closer, lowering her voice to a whisper, as if she was about to tell Sarah a secret, something between only them. 'Sarah, listen to Jessica, the medication has worked wonderfully. We're all very pleased. You're on the mend, but you need to keep healthy, for Lily's sake.'

Sarah blinked in acknowledgement, pulling her body upright again, somehow managing to repeat her earlier words, 'I need to call John,' her voice a crackly whimper. She saw disapproval in their eyes, and then her mind didn't want to think any more. She needed sleep. When the darkness hit, it was a relief, until she heard the doctor speak again, asking Jessica about her.

'You're aware, Lisa, of what we've been told about dissenters? Saka won't be happy that Sarah is harbouring links to her old ways. He will see it as an offence, an affront to the self-enlightenment path.'

'Should we mention it to him?'

'I'll tell him. He can decide what's best. If Saka agrees, we can give her back her phone.'

'Jessica?'

'Yes?'

'That thing we spoke about this morning, about there being no absolute right and wrong?'

'What about it, Lisa?'

'Do you think that extends to life and death?'

'Saka believes many people see death as welcoming. It is ahead of us all.'

Kate

WHEN KATE HEARD THE DOORBELL RING, SHE FROZE.
It must be Pat Grant, but what if it was someone else? She took a
number of tentative steps towards the bedroom door, and as she
did so, the bell rang again, three fast rings, indicating impatience
that it hadn't been answered the first time. She took the stairs a
couple at a time, stopping when she reached the bottom, hearing
Pat Grant's voice calling through the flap of the letterbox. It wasn't
the woman's impatience that had made her pause: it was because
she had remembered something else. Not now, Kate told herself,
opening the front door.

'You took your time.'

'Sorry,' Kate replied, breathless. She composed herself, then
asked, 'Pat, do you know the names of the people who live here?'

The woman eyed her with suspicion.

'Please, Pat. It's important.'

'I can't say I ever met him. It was the woman who gave me the
key.' She still seemed unsure.

'What was her name?' Kate pushed.

'Jessica.' A slight pause. 'Yes, that was it.' Her voice was more
confident. 'I never got a second name. I didn't want to pry.' She
raised her eyebrows, indicating to Kate she had already been in the
house for too long.

Kate repeated the name a couple of times. It meant nothing to her.

Pat Grant stretched out her hand for the key. 'Well,' she said,
stepping back to allow Kate to leave, 'if you're quite finished?'

'Yes, of course.' Kate placed the key in Pat's palm, then punched
the alarm code in to reactivate it, and joined her on the front step.

'Are you all right, my dear? You look like you've been to hell and back.'

'I'm fine,' she replied, although she felt far from it. 'The house brought back memories, nothing more.'

When they reached the gate, Kate said a speedy goodbye to her old neighbour, desperately wanting to get away from the house she had once called home, from the rumour and innuendo about her father, from the agonising memories of her mother's death, and the anger that had been so much part of their lives.

Kate ran and ran, and when she thought she couldn't run any faster, she pushed herself even more, the pain of endurance acting like some form of balance against the thoughts jumping around in her mind. She needed time to think, but she wasn't ready to let anything settle. Instead, it all crisscrossed inside her head, Malcolm and her father, the anonymous notes, the feeling of being watched, followed, the fresh memories from her past, her mother, Charlie, her failed marriage with Declan, Adam, and the one aspect of her past that she couldn't deny: that it was full of secrets and lies. What lay behind them? What had lain behind her father's anger? And why had she never sought answers before? Was she a conspirator in all this? Had she done something wrong?

Finally, she climbed the stone steps to the front door of her apartment building, hearing the familiar beep of the access code being punched in. Stepping in from the cold into the warmth of the hall, her body pumped out more sweat. Once inside the apartment, she checked that everything was as she had left it, lifting up the plant pot to make sure the study-door key was underneath. Going into the living room, her eyes scanned the room for anything out of the ordinary. Walking into the bedroom, she did the same, then sat down on the bed.

It was only when she felt safe, and confident that she was alone, that she could allow herself to drift back to memory. After her father's death, her mother had said, 'That's it, then,' as if he was something to be put behind the two of them. There hadn't been any outward sign of sorrow. Kate had believed her mother was being brave. It was then that she thought of all the other conversations they had had, before her mother's mind had slipped. Strangely, none had been about her father. The conversation Kate had remembered at the bottom of the stairs was one she had pushed to the back of her mind. It had taken place shortly after her father's death. Her mother had phoned her one night out of the blue, asking if she would take her for a drive. Kate hadn't asked where to, knowing that grief operated in strange ways. Instead she waited while her mother put on her heavy coat and fur hat. Kate had told her she looked like a Russian. 'A warm Russian,' her mother had replied, sounding ever practical. Pulling the passenger door closed, and putting on her seatbelt, she said to Kate, 'I want you to drive me to the mountains.'

Kate thought she knew the route her mother meant. As a family, they had often gone for Sunday drives around Glencree, so she started the engine even though it was after eleven o'clock at night. They drove past rows of houses with smoke billowing from the chimneys, city traffic giving way to clearer roads on the outer suburbs, then reaching the mountain road that would lead them to Glencree. Kate decided to pull in at the viewing point with the lights of the city below. 'Don't stop here,' her mother said. 'Keep going towards Killakee.'

There was something about her mother's words that told her to do as she was asked, and to do so without question.

The road had narrowed, and her mother had said, 'Not much further now,' then instructed her to stop near a tumbledown bridge. When Kate pulled in, there was nothing but pitch blackness around them, and when her mother opened the passenger door, Kate had worried she would trip and fall on the mountain road. She had opened the driver's door to follow her, but her mother had told her she was better off alone. Kate hadn't wanted to intrude on her privacy, but she put on the car headlights, hoping her mother wouldn't be long. The last thing either of them needed was a dead car battery and to be stranded on a dark mountain road.

Sitting in the car, Kate watched her mother take a dozen steps towards the bridge, then stop to look down into further darkness and, what seemed to Kate, a steep drop. For a brief few seconds, Kate worried her mother was going to do something stupid, that she might even climb up on the bridge and jump off. Why had she thought that?

When her mother got back into the car, she shut the door, put her seatbelt on and looked straight ahead. She had asked Kate if she thought this was a good place to die, and Kate had wondered about suicidal thoughts again. When Kate didn't answer, her mother broke the silence, saying, 'I know someone buried near here, a young boy.' There was something about the way she'd said it, as if the words were full of regret.

The strangeness of the event, and the relief that her mother wasn't suicidal, had kept the memory in the back of Kate's mind. At the time, she had thought about the various burial grounds nearby, the ones that locals used, empty plots belonging to ancient relatives. She hadn't pushed it but now all she could think of was that newspaper article, and the red circle around the name Peter Kirwan. Was it guilt her mother had felt that night – for a dreadful wrong?

Special Detective Unit, Harcourt Street

ADAM HAD KNOWN THAT THE DNA SAMPLE extracted from Michael O'Neill and shared with their US counterparts on an intelligence basis would need to be verified Stateside. He wasn't surprised to hear that Detective Lee Fisher would be making the trip himself. The senior officer attached to an investigation was often the one who made the journey to pick up the sample. Adam himself had made any number of trips abroad to do the same thing. What he hadn't expected was the timing of the visit. The police in Manhattan were no closer to identifying a suspect than they were in Dublin, so what was the rush to collate evidence for a trial that might or might not take place?

His gut told him there was more to it, and during their telephone and Internet communications, Fisher had seemed circumspect about the many strands developing in the O'Neill case. That circumspection, Adam decided, was behind the timing of the visit, and he wondered whether, if the boot was on the other foot, he would be doing the same thing.

Lee Fisher's flight into Dublin airport would arrive the following morning, and Adam had already committed himself to collecting the detective. Despite the risk of jetlag, Lee had insisted on attending the next brain-storming session at Harcourt Street Special Detective Unit, scheduled for less than an hour after his arrival. Adam admired the detective's determination and vigour – if nothing else, having a US investigator present would add some colour to the proceedings.

He looked at his mobile phone. Three missed calls from Addy's mother, Marion. There was no denying the magnitude of change in his personal life. At times, it had felt like a baptism of fire. Being with Kate was the best decision he had ever made, but he had gone from being a man without responsibilities for anyone other than himself to loving and worrying about Kate, while attempting to have a relationship with a son he'd ignored for years. He needed to be a solid figure in Charlie's life too, and Adam was concerned about how their relationship would develop after Charlie returned to Dublin, having spent time with his real father. He wasn't complaining. This was par for the course, and although Addy wasn't making things easy for him, he also understood that his son's aggression and distance were no more than he deserved. Still, if he was honest, Addy being away had made some things a lot easier.

Knowing he had a number of calls to make around the investigation, he texted Marion instead of calling her, saying it would be another hour before he could be in touch.

Addy

THE CLOSER ADDY GOT TO BELIEVING HE WAS wangling his way out of solitary confinement, the more he thought about what Donal had told him. The boy was obviously frightened. Why else pretend to be dead? Donal thought he had seen bodies being buried but he might been have mistaken: things looked different at night. It was all too ridiculous and extreme, and a child's imagination could conjure up all kinds of stuff. Hadn't he gone a little stir-crazy on a few nights, convincing himself he heard the boy moving around in the pipe chambers? Maybe Donal didn't trust him any more. It was then that Addy remembered something Adam had said to him. It was about people thinking that the truth was an easy thing to work out, but it wasn't. Addy hadn't paid much attention to it, putting it down to Adam playing his new father role, but, still, he did need to work a few truths out.

Start off with the facts, he told himself. Let them lead to balanced conjecture. He began to make a mental list of all the things he could be sure of. If he got that right, it was a good beginning. The clearer a person was about where they wanted to go, the better chance they had of getting there.

Once he was outside, he could consider his next move. His instincts told him to get as far away from the island as he could. His heart told him differently. Even if Donal was wrong, he couldn't shake off what the boy had said about Chloë. Neither could he turn his back on Aoife.

He might have felt like a fraud when he arrived, and a bit of an overgrown kid, but things had changed. If Chloë was in trouble, he would try to help her. He would find Aoife too. He might be his father's son, but he wasn't going to turn his back on those who needed him.

The Game Changer

Kate

KATE OPENED THE BOX OF HER MOTHER'S correspondence in the memorabilia drawer. In it, there were mainly postcards, most from Kate, sent when she was away on holidays, letters from her mother's school-friend who had emigrated to Australia before Kate was born, her mother's Christmas-cake recipe, old photographs, a few lists, a couple of Kate's school reports, birthday cards, all neatly bound by a single white ribbon. None of it gave her any more information than she already had. Had the solicitor said anything to her after her mother died? Was there anything unusual in the will? She couldn't think of anything. What about emails? Maybe if she went back over some old ones from the solicitor, something would click.

She turned on the laptop, waited for her emails to load, and the first thing she saw was a recent one from Ocean House. They had been unable to reschedule an appointment for a client who only ever dealt with Kate. She thought about phoning Adam but, damn it, she needed to get her life back. She fired off a reply. She would make the appointment. It was in less than an hour. What was the harm?

∞

After the session, which had gone well, she started to feel a lot better, and more like her old self. She rang Charlie before she left the office. Their conversation raised her spirits.

Locking the office door, the last person she expected to see was Malcolm Madden, and immediately, her mood changed.

'Kate, it's good to see you.'

Bluff it out, she told herself. 'What brings you here, Malcolm?'

'I was hoping to meet someone.'

'Oh?'

'Yes. They attend meditation sessions here, but there doesn't seem to be anyone there. I haven't heard from you for a while.'

Had he followed her? Was he making this up? 'Things have been tricky.' She tried to keep her voice steady.

'Are you setting a distance between us?'

'How do you mean?'

'I sense things have changed.'

'There's been a lot happening, that's all.'

'Have you had more flashbacks?'

'Some.'

'Do you want to talk about them?'

'Look, Malcolm, I'm sorry. I have to go.' Would he let her? She looked around. There was no one else nearby.

'No problem, Kate. You do whatever you need to do. I might wait here for another while in case my appointment shows up.'

Their eyes locked. 'I'll be in touch,' she finally replied, heading towards the stairs.

'And I'll look forward to it.'

While she was making her way to the car, the heavens opened, bringing a thunderous rain shower. It wasn't long before her clothes were soaked. The rubbery sound of tyres coming to a halt at the traffic lights was amplified, and most of the cars had their headlights on. She was still uneasy about Malcolm. She felt exhausted, too, and it wasn't the first time this sudden exhaustion had come upon her of late. There had been other tell-tale signs too – the vomiting, the sick feeling in the pit of her stomach, especially in the mornings, tenderness in her breasts, her more frequent visits to the bathroom.

Sitting in her car, she locked the doors, putting her hand on her tummy, telling herself it was nothing more than her brain working overtime. She wasn't even late, but then she remembered the one and only risk they had taken. She had awoken well before the alarm clock had gone off, and looked at Adam's broad back in the bed. There was something so right about the two of them being together, and as the morning sun fought to gain access to the room, in an almost dreamlike state, she had reached over and touched him. He turned immediately, responding to her kiss, wrapping his arms around her before his hands travelled, her desire increasing, until not making love wasn't an option. Neither of them spoke, their lovemaking desperate, passionate and needy. He had paused only once, his eyes asking if she wanted him to stop, but she pulled him closer, their heat radiating off one another, his breath short, warm and intense, his hands caressing, their desire furious, all-consuming, almost primal. Afterwards, he told her how much he loved her. She felt the very same way.

Leaning back against the headrest, she knew if there was a new life growing inside her it wasn't something either of them had talked about. The prospect of having another child didn't frighten her. If anything, it was the opposite. She wasn't due her period for a few days. The sickness could still be a virus, or her stress levels. Either way, the prospect evoked emotions she hadn't expected, so it was a few seconds before she registered that her phone was ringing.

'Kate, it's Adam. I couldn't get you at home.'

'Hold on. I'll put you on the hands-free set.'

The car was still parked, but she needed time to pull herself together.

'Is everything okay?' she finally asked.

'Lee Fisher's arriving tomorrow. A visit was always on the cards, but it's earlier than expected.'

'Do you know why?'

'My feeling is he wants to be closer to things as they unfold here. He's asked me to apply more pressure on PIU.'

'I suppose that's not a bad thing.'

'No, Kate, it's not, and it makes sense too, based on new information he has from Tom Mason's sister.'

'What new information?'

'Apparently the victim had had one too many drinks when he spoke to her about the research element of the eighties studies, and how some members had taken the view to expand it to lower socioeconomic groupings. According to Emily Burke, they hired a thug called Willy Stapleton to …' He paused.

'What is it, Adam? What did they hire Willy Stapleton to do?' Her voice shook.

'The guy had an addiction problem. He needed money to feed it, so he would have done whatever it took.' Again, he paused. 'Look, Kate, there's no easy way to say this, and you have to bear in mind it could have been drink talking.'

'Say it anyway.'

'According to Emily Burke, Willy Stapleton entrapped children for the study.'

'Entrapped?'

'He abducted them.'

'That's crazy, Adam.' She thought about her father. Despite his involvement in unorthodox cognitive studies, she couldn't see him being part of anything like that. Then she remembered the old newspaper clipping hidden at the back of her mother's dressing table. 'It couldn't be,' she said out loud.

'I know it's hard to take in.'

'Adam, I need to talk to Malcolm. He must know what went on.'

'I don't want you going near that guy.'

'I met him a few minutes ago.'

'Where?'

'Ocean House.'

'I thought you'd gone for a drive before your run. You didn't say—'

'It doesn't matter. What matters is that I need to find out the truth, irrespective of how bad it is. The not knowing is driving me insane. What if Willy Stapleton was the one who abducted me?'

'There's something else, Kate.'

'What?'

'Stapleton died ten years ago, from cirrhosis of the liver.'

Kate didn't know what to think. At some level she had always thought that one day she would be able to confront her attacker. She had stopped listening to Adam, but then she heard him say, 'Emily Burke told Fisher the study came to an abrupt end when things started to get out of hand. He wants to look at the missing-person cases too.'

'Adam, what if all the strands are linked – the missing persons, the murder in Manhattan, the suspicious deaths of the O'Neills, the events in the eighties, the notes, me?' She looked around her, half expecting to see Malcolm. 'What did PIU tell you about the girl's attackers?'

'She hasn't given names, claiming she never knew who they were, but one of the detectives is suspicious she's holding back. She was taken more than once.'

'What?'

'Her abductors threatened her, saying if she told anyone about what had happened, she'd be killed.'

'But what about her family and friends? Didn't people ask where she'd been? There must have been physical signs too.'

'I guess that depends on the level of parental structures in place. She was taken three times in total.'

'That's like targeted child prostitution.' An image of her own father flashed in front of her. This was beyond anything she'd thought possible.

'The world is a very sick place, Kate.'

'Adam, what if it had been me instead of that girl?'

'It wasn't you. Anyhow, if what Emily Burke said is to be taken at face value, you wouldn't have been targeted. You weren't part of any lower socioeconomic grouping.'

'It could have been mistaken identity. If the girl was taken more than once, maybe my abduction was a mistake. You said Stapleton had drink issues. It's not beyond the bounds of possibility.'

'No, it's not ...'

'And my father, if he was involved, he might have been the reason I got away.'

'Stop there, Kate. As yet, there is nothing to link the woman's statement to Mason or O'Neill.'

'But there are similarities to her abduction and mine. You said so yourself – and, no matter how you can turn this around, letting me return home was a risk. If someone did intervene, someone of influence, someone who was part of the elite grouping, it could have been my father.'

'What do you want me to say, Kate?'

'Nothing. I want you to listen.'

'I am listening.'

'Why do you think my parents didn't tell me the truth? Their denial would have escalated my anxiety over the events, feeding into further memory shutdown. Even now, Adam, I still get edgy if I hear someone walk behind me, if they get too close.'

'I know.'

'Christ, what must that girl have gone through? The lack of support had to have left her feeling completely abandoned. If something ever happened to Charlie, I wouldn't allow any stone to be left unturned. If I had to, I would spend my life finding out the answers.'

'I know that too.'

'So why didn't my parents look for proper answers? They were intelligent people, my father especially – he didn't believe in grey areas. If there was a truth to be found, he would have looked for it. Unless …'

'Unless what, Kate?'

'The truth wasn't something he wanted to hear.'

Addy

ADDY HAD CONTEMPLATED BEING ALLOWED TO leave the room for so long that his body was actually shaking seconds before it happened. Unlike his arrival, when he'd had that fight with Stephen, he took in as much of his surroundings as he could, his eyes darting in different directions. In the corridor, he counted five other rooms. There were keys hanging on a hook on the wall. The walls seemed deep, and when he looked up he saw extra insulation fitted between the rafters, along with streams of fluorescent tubes: the place was without natural light. Before mounting the stone steps to an upper door, he spotted the air vents, behind which, he thought, were the ducts to the plumbing pipes. He thought about Donal, wondering why he hadn't returned.

Upstairs, everything seemed luminous, daylight catching him unawares. The two members accompanying him brought him back to his old room, and all the time, he kept thinking they were going to change their minds and take him back downstairs. He told his body not to shake, and his face to smile, to appear as if this was all okay, because to do anything else would risk everything.

He felt his heart thump in his chest, as he rooted through his backpack, looking for his phone. The battery was dead, but he found the lead in the bottom of the bag. His hands fumbled, plugging it into the phone, his fingers no longer adept at doing the simplest of things. When the green battery light came on, he stared at it, his hands shaking. He needed to get a grip.

Holding the phone with both hands, he waited for instructions to punch in his password. With each number, the phone bleeped, the sound seeming loud, amplified. He went through the images, frantically looking for pictures of home, keeping an eye on the signal bars, just in case. Hearing footsteps approach the door, his instinct was to hide the phone, but then he realised he was no longer under suspicion: he was a member now. The door opened without a knock, and a woman, who introduced herself as Jessica, gave him a weak smile.

'You'll want a shower, an opportunity to freshen up.' It sounded like an instruction rather than a request. He felt dirty beside her, uncomfortable about his appearance, his greasy hair, unshaven face and the stench of body odour.

'Yes,' he answered, needing to clear his throat, his voice croaky. 'A shower would be good.'

'I see you've checked your phone.' She made it sound as if he had done something wrong. 'You'll find everything is as you left it, except yourself. We all need time alone to clear our thoughts.'

When she stepped out into the hallway, she left the door ajar, then returned with towels and soap. 'You can use the shower room at the end of the corridor. Take your time.'

'Thanks.'

'After that, we can set up your first session.'

'Already? I was hoping to get outside for a bit.' He could tell from her face that she wasn't pleased.

'Of course.' She smiled. 'Why not stretch your legs? It will do you good.'

He held her stare.

'I'll leave you to it,' she paused, 'but call into the commune room beforehand, and meet some of the other members. It won't take long.'

'Okay.'

She closed the door, and he waited, counting each of her steps, until he couldn't hear them.

The Game Changer

CENTRE OF LIGHTNESS
20 Steps to Self-enlightenment Programme

Suffocating gases, like carbon dioxide and methane, are not toxic. They are capable of killing, as was the case with Michael O'Neill, but the gases are not poisonous in themselves. They merely act as an alternative to air.

The gases intersperse until their presence diminishes the level of oxygen in the atmosphere. At that point, they become the chosen method of inhalation for the body. Enclosed areas contain approximately 21 per cent oxygen. When you add suffocating gases, oxygen drops proportionately. If oxygen falls below 15 per cent, it leads to lethargy, disorientation, confusion, coma and ultimately death.

Carbon dioxide is preferable to methane because the latter is capable of being detected in the blood. With carbon dioxide, during an autopsy, things are trickier, as it already makes up part of the blood supply. Prior to death, it will rise irrespective of cause, and a medical examiner will have difficulty in determining it as the culprit.

Nevertheless, when multiple loss of life takes place, an invisible cause of death will not avoid the killings being classified as suspicious. Once the dust settles, certain logical assumptions will be drawn, but they won't be able to point any fingers at the Game Changer.

(Page 1 of 1)

Addy

STEPPING OUT OF THE SHOWER, HE EXAMINED HIS shaven face in the mirror. He wasn't sure who was looking back at him. It certainly wasn't the Addy who had come haphazardly to the island. All of a sudden, he was Addy with a plan.

He'd have to contact his mother soon, but that wasn't going to happen without a mobile-phone signal. He also needed to get off the island. The fisherman who'd ferried him over had been paid by someone else, so Addy would have to find out how to arrange a crossing, and also to come up with a good reason for leaving, without too many questions being asked. None of it was going to happen until he talked to Aoife and was sure that Chloë was okay.

Reaching the commune room, he thought about knocking on the door, but then he remembered he was one of them now, so he turned the handle and walked in.

There were nine people in the room, and all of them stared at him simultaneously, but none asked any awkward questions, so he took a couple of tentative steps forward, letting the door close behind him. The room was flooded with daylight from the roof windows. With the walls a brilliant white, he wondered if his eyes were still adjusting from being down below. On the wall opposite the door there was a long cream banner: 'Silence – Physical and Visual Communication Only'.

He wasn't sure what that meant, but before he could work out his next move, a girl he hadn't met before walked over to him. She was about his age, and attractive with shoulder-length brown hair and large blue eyes. She stared at him before putting her arms out straight in front of her, indicating that he should do the same. He followed, as instructed, and watched as she raised her arms to shoulder level, opening her palms, and facing them towards him. Again he did the same thing, their palms joining together, their fingers intertwined, as if they were about to do some kind of weird dance. The others in the room were doing the same thing, all in pairs.

After a couple of seconds, the girl moved her hands to the right, and then to the left, his moving with hers. Everyone followed suit, as if there was only one person in the room instead of ten. When he looked at the girl, there was warmth and kindness in her eyes, but something else, too – a form of blankness. The longer they stared at one another, the more he felt that her eyes could swallow him.

The hand-movement exercises lasted only a few minutes, but to Addy, they seemed to take an eternity, with every change of positioning done in unison, as if they had all assumed one identity.

Then, without explanation, everyone stopped and formed a circle, without touching, but standing side by side. A bald man with glasses lifted a small brass bell and rang it twice. Soon Addy realised they were working on facial expressions. The man held a wide-eyed stare, the others copied, and so did Addy. Then the man made a happy face, smiling, and again, they all did the same. Each time the facial features changed, the group followed, until the man rang the bell again, marking the end of the session, at which they all hugged each other in pairs, then did it collectively as a group, maintaining their silence throughout.

At least that was over with, he told himself, as he made his way back to his room. His phone was now fully charged, and turning to leave the room, he was surprised to see Aoife standing in the hallway waiting for him.

'Aoife!' He rushed to her and hugged her, but her stiffened body told him to back off.

'You look well,' was all she said, as she pulled away from him.

'And you look distant.'

'Do I?'

'What's going on, Aoife?'

'Things have changed, Addy, that's all. I'm a leader now, and I must act accordingly.'

'Meaning what?'

'Meaning I have other responsibilities. You will understand more when you're part of the programme.'

He wanted to tell her the truth, that he had no intention of becoming part of any programme, but the girl standing in front of him wasn't the Aoife he knew, the one he had fallen in love with. She was in there somewhere, and even though he hated admitting it, telling Aoife the truth was too big a risk.

'Aoife.'

'Yes?'

'I was thinking of going back for a while, to talk things out with my mother.'

'You should be careful, Addy. Some people find it hard to understand the steps in the programme. Rejection and criticism are burdens we have to bear.'

'Will you come with me?'

'No. I'm needed here.'

'But I need you. Does that not matter any more?'

'I have to put the group first.'

'Why?'

'They are my family now.'

He wanted to shake her, to shout at her, to grab her and force her home, but even as he was thinking this, he also knew, if he wanted to get Aoife off the island, he'd have to try something different. Only he didn't know what that was, not yet.

'I need to go outside for a while,' he said.

'Perhaps I will see you later.'

He watched her walk away, knowing that the physical distance she was placing between them paled in comparison to her emotional detachment. This whole thing felt all wrong. He had to come up with another plan, but first, he needed to find out about Chloë, and even though, officially, he wasn't a helper now, talking to the guys felt safer than asking questions of the members.

Only Karl and Asan were left. The others had gone back to the mainland. They also told him there was only one more boat crossing planned. Addy asked casually if they were taking it. They weren't. The boat was due to arrive in two days' time. When he mentioned Chloë, neither of them had seen her, which was exactly what he hadn't wanted to hear.

John F. Kennedy Airport, New York

LEE'S DELTA AIRLINES FLIGHT WAS DUE TO LEAVE John F. Kennedy airport at 10.05 p.m.; with a transfer time of seven hours, it would arrive in Dublin at 5.05 a.m. New York time, or 10.05 a.m. Irish time. The terminal building was full of noise, messages coming over the tannoy system about departures or calls for late passengers, people talking, creating a communal hum, trolleys, suitcases on wheels, airport staff on mobile devices, all adding to the din, within a place populated by strangers with little in common other than that most were leaving town.

He checked the departure monitor. The flight was on time. He had no interest in shopping, and even less in engaging anyone in conversation. It would be another thirty minutes before boarding, and he despised waiting around. Putting his earplugs in, he leaned back in one of the black leather seats with aluminium arms and legs in the departure lounge, and let his mind drift to the investigation.

His first appointment was with Detective Adam O'Connor, but he was keen to talk to Kate Pearson, too. The anonymous notes sent to her might be extraneous, but they certainly fired more questions into the mix. If they were tied into this complicated web, could they have been created as camouflage, a tool to take focus away from something else, or as a statement of future intent, or both? The timing was critical too. Why were all these things happening now? Kate's father, Valentine Pearson, was potentially her tie-in to all this, but Malcolm Madden had been a close friend to him. Madden hadn't been in Manhattan at the time of the Mason killing, but that didn't mean he couldn't have orchestrated it. Could Madden be looking to settle old scores, wanting Kate and others to pay for a past wrong? Jealousy, revenge, harbouring a grudge, or any number of motivations could be the root cause. But even if all of this was tied into historical events, some elements of it had to have been dictated by more recent developments.

It was important, he told himself, especially when there was no clear idea of who was pulling the strings, to keep the options open. All of this made sense to at least one person, and right now, that could be almost anyone.

Kate

SOMEHOW KATE MANAGED TO DRIVE BACK TO THE apartment, even though everything felt as if it was closing in on her. She couldn't get Charlie out of her mind either. She needed him back. She needed to know he was close by and okay.

Adam was right: it was better for him to talk to Malcolm than for her to have any more contact. Before she opened the study door, she looked at a photograph of her mother and father on the wall. They were like strangers. It was as if her life, or what she thought was her life, was false, laden with deception.

She picked up her handwritten notes from the previous day and began to record: 'TRAJECTORY OF MOTIVATION BETWEEN EVENTS ALIGNED WITH THE O'NEILL AND MASON INVESTIGATION AND ASSOCIATIVE CULT ELEMENTS. The creation of a cult-type environment is usually initiated by one key figure or leader. This individual is often charismatic, and capable of convincing a great many people to follow a particular cause. Generally, people enter these forms of groupings because they are looking for a new way and, indeed, have good intentions. The negative element is orchestrated by the leader, where narcissism plays a primary role. Many use their grandiose ideas of themselves to overcome deep-rooted emotional flaws, establishing an environment that will feed into their elevated self-belief as a reinforcement of their importance.'

Kate looked up at the mind maps on the wall, wondering if a cult leader existed, and if so, how and why they were tied into everything. She pressed record again. 'The motivations of a cult leader, and those who are prepared to kill, have certain commonalities. Each will feed into a belief of power and control over their potential victim or

313

victims. Each will create an environment where strategic elements are stacked in the killer's or cult leader's favour.'

When her mobile phone rang, Kate jumped. Seeing the call was from Malcolm, she let it go to voicemail. After a few moments, she pulled down some textbooks, specifically around cult development, especially those that included widespread extortion of funds. It wasn't long before she came upon details of the Jonestown case, and began recording again. 'Jim Jones was the American founder of the People's Temple group, which in November 1978 became known for mass suicide by poisoning in their isolated community called Jonestown, located in Guyana. The initial ethos, by which the so-called church was founded, was based on equal treatment of African Americans and many became members. Jones authored a book called *The Letter Killeth*, pointing out what he felt were absurdities, contradictions and atrocities in the Bible. In the summer of 1977, he moved most of the thousand members of the People's Temple to Guyana from San Francisco, after the church was investigated for tax evasion. Jones stated that they were being crucified for their moral stance against injustice, and that they would create an agricultural Utopia in the jungle, away from racism and other negative groupings.

'People who left the group prior to its move to Guyana told the authorities of brutal beatings, murders and a mass-suicide plan, but were not believed. In November 1978, a US Congressman, Leo Ryan, led a fact-finding mission to the Jonestown settlement after allegations by relatives of human-rights abuses. When some members wanted to leave with the Ryan group, it is believed Jones became infuriated with the defectors, and this was the impetus for the final mass suicide: 913 of the remaining inhabitants of Jonestown, 276 of whom were children, died. While some followers obeyed Jones's instruction to commit 'revolutionary suicide' by drinking cyanide-laced grape juice, others died by forced cyanide injection or by shooting. Many of the people involved believed Jonestown, as Jones had promised, would be a paradise. According to subsequent news reports, copious amounts of drugs such as Thorazine, Sodium Pentothal, Demerol and Valium were administered to Jonestown residents. Various forms of punishment were used, including locking people away for extended periods of time, and members who attempted to run away were drugged. The children in the commune addressed Jones as Dad, and money extorted, including social-welfare payments, contributed to Jones's wealth of $26 million until he died on the day of the mass suicide.

'He died from gunshot wounds, and it is still unknown if the death was self-administered or he was murdered. During the suicide, everyone, including the children, was told to line up and was given a small glass of red liquid to drink, a ritual that had been repeated many times in preparation.

'On the day of the mass suicide, Congressman Ryan, along with four journalists, was shot dead when they tried to escape with defectors, and a meeting was subsequently called by Jones. Jones assured his supporters that Guyana soldiers or CIA-sponsored mercenaries would soon emerge from the jungle to kill them. That day, the children were poisoned first, and many believe this was partly why so many adults continued with their own deaths.'

Kate pressed the pause button, again looking up at the mind maps on the wall, seeing the names of Mason, O'Neill, Malcolm and her father. Each had links to the earlier studies in the eighties, a grouping that appeared to have derailed from its loftier aspirations of furthering education by acquiring key knowledge, to something allegedly fuelled by abuse of power, and a darker element. What did she know about Malcolm, other than judgements formed as a child? Did he hold a grudge for not being accepted into the illicit grouping? Had he his own agenda and, if he had, was it to the level of someone like Jim Jones, capable of manipulation for their own ends? He certainly had the training necessary to enact some kind of psychologically fuelled power exercise, but it all felt so far-fetched – except, she reminded herself, extreme narcissists behave differently from everyone else. Their behaviour can be fuelled by actions that others may deem of little consequence, while the narcissist perceives them as huge, especially if the act is seen as a personal affront, demeaning them as individuals, unable to tolerate the belittlement of others.

Kate was about to press the record button, when she heard Adam arrive home. She thought about telling him about the possibility of her being pregnant, but it felt like the wrong time. Instead, when she joined him in the living room, she said, 'I'm going to ask Declan to bring Charlie home.'

'Are you sure that's a good idea?'

'Don't you want him back?'

For a split second, he hesitated. 'Of course I do.'

'What's wrong? I thought you'd be happy with Charlie coming home.'

'I am.'

'You don't sound it.'

'It got me thinking about Addy, that's all. I've had his mother on the phone. She's fretting about him not being in touch.'

'Are you worried?'

'He's a teenager. They're not always reliable.'

'Isn't he with Aoife? You could contact her.'

'I tried both their numbers, with no luck. Marion says Addy warned her that the mobile signal was bad.'

'You could contact the Coplands – Aoife's parents.'

'Marion's done that already. They had a letter from her after Addy arrived, but nothing since.'

'He's due back in college next week, isn't he?'

'That's the plan.'

'I'm sure he'll be in touch.'

'I hope so. Sorry if I sounded a little off about Charlie coming home. I guess I've a lot on my plate right now.'

'We both have.' She put her hand on her tummy, feeling

lightheaded again. 'We can talk more later on.' She closed her eyes, the sudden exhaustion hitting her, like a slap across the face.

'Kate?'

'Hmm ...'

'PIU has released another statement. I want you to read it before Fisher arrives in the morning. I have a copy of it with me.'

The Game Changer

CENTRE OF LIGHTNESS
20 Steps to Self-enlightenment Programme

It requires a cool and clear head to maintain all the strands when the game is coming to an end, and the rewards are so close that you can taste them.

One of the members on the mainland will deliver another note to Kate, and our date with destiny will soon be close at hand.

The next speech to group members will place emphasis on mental illness. Our mixed-up world is doing a fine job of producing mixed-up people, mixed up about religion, sex, society and so much more, including economics, money and greed.

We live in a society where belief in capitalism as freedom is rampant — protecting the right of the free market, giving everyone the opportunity to succeed, with the rich getting richer and the poor poorer. The Game Changer will tell them that those holding the power are able to tilt things towards their own kind. The speech will say human happiness is the key. We are not obliged to be richer, busier, more efficient, productive or progressive. We are not obliged to be any of those things, if they do not make us happy.

Everyone is part of the GAME, whether they like it or not, and ultimately, an individual, or a group of individuals, in a position of power, can decide if someone lives or dies.

(Page 1 of 1)

Addy

THE FIRST PLACE ADDY DECIDED TO LOOK FOR CHLOË was down at the water's edge, and once he reached the shore, the weather turned bitterly cold, with strong gales blowing in different directions. Flocks of seagulls clattered overhead, as if they were laughing at some unshared joke. He kept calling Chloë's name, screaming at the top of his voice, knowing the beach was one of her favourite places, and it was as good a place as any to start.

'Chloë!' he roared, cupping his mouth with his hands. He took in the span of the island, and when he finally reached the large rock she had told him about, he stopped and, again, looked all around him. He could see the long stretch of stony beach, the rugged cliffs above, the wild grasses and the angry sky littered with birds, and all the while, his eyes filled with water from the sharp winds.

The skies darkened even more, and an unexpected blast of hailstones thundered down. Instead of leaving the beach, he held onto the large boulder, as if it was the wheel of a boat caught in a storm. He yelled Chloë's name once more, and no one, other than the birds, answered.

Getting down on his hunkers, he saw the purple line markings on the large boulder, similar in shade to the purple used on Donal's scrawled note.

'Donal!' he bellowed. 'Where the hell are you?' He pulled himself up, the wind causing him to lose balance. 'Chloë! If you can hear me, I'm at the big rock. Donal! Chloë! It's me, Addy!'

When the sun came out from behind the clouds, the hailstones stopped as suddenly as they had begun. Even the sound of the birds lowered, as if the wind was taking a deep breath, allowing a second or two of calm. Addy couldn't be sure, but he thought he saw someone or something move behind him in the hedgerow. It might have been a rabbit or a hare, but something had moved.

'Donal, is that you? I know you're there. Stop playing games and show your face.'

Despite his brave words, his fear increased. He was becoming increasingly anxious as to who was close by, and why they were not showing themselves. Then he saw another movement, and this time he knew he wasn't mistaken, because the person wasn't hiding now. They were standing right in front of him.

Kate

KATE CLOSED HER EYES IN PREPARATION. ADAM wanted her to read the statement, and if he did, there was a reason why. She didn't want to enter that world again. In part, she wanted to put it all behind her, to pretend everything was okay, that things were normal, but wasn't that what she had tried to do all her life? Running away, always coming back to the same thing?

'Are you ready?' he asked.

She didn't answer him, but took the statement out of his hands. 'I'm going to read it in the study.'

'Maybe it's best if you stay here.'

'No, it'll be better if I read it alone.'

'Remember, Kate, don't fall into the trap of superimposing someone else's memories on to yours.'

'I won't,' she replied, even though she knew that was impossible to control.

In the study, before reading the statement, she looked up at the mind maps on the wall one last time, thinking about Peter Kirwan's disappearance, wondering what he had gone through.

Her eyes dropped. The woman's handwriting was neat, contained, with joined-up script that leaned to the right. All the letters were consistent and free-flowing, the visual appearance giving nothing away about the prospective horror of the content to come.

Again her identity was hidden, and this time the statement had gaps, with large sections blacked out. Kate took a deep breath and began.

The second time I was taken, it felt like a repeat nightmare that I would never wake up from. Like before, I must have lost consciousness for a while, and when the door to the Portakabin opened, it was pitch dark outside. I didn't know what time it was. The two men came in, and the taller man locked my hands to the bed with handcuffs, while the other one put a rag in my mouth as a gag. It's never going to stop, I thought. I'll die this time, I'm sure of it.

Kate was finding the process even more harrowing the second time around. But what about what the girl had gone through? All Kate had to endure was words. Opening her eyes, she continued reading. The next part was blacked out, so she skipped down the page.

The men kept talking to each other, like it was okay to do things like that. I wanted to be anywhere other than there. I didn't want my body any more. I wanted to give it to someone else, to not be part of it. The smaller man walked closer to the bed. He had a metal pole in his hand. He banged it off the wall a number of times, and the sound got louder and louder, before he placed it across my chest, and pressed down hard. The other man had a camera and he started taking photographs. The gag was moist in my mouth. I realised the man with the camera had a knife in his pocket. I'm going to die, I thought again. This time I'll be left here. It's the end, but of course it was not.

The next page was blacked out in its entirety, except for sentences at the end.

Afterwards I looked at the knife and the bar on the bed, and the taller man asked if I wanted to keep them as mementos. If I had the knife, I thought, I might be able to save myself next time, so I nodded. He leaned down to open the handcuffs and I imagined pulling the balaclava off, but I knew if I saw his face, I would never get away. It's hard to live, knowing what happened to me but I'm a survivor.

Kate wanted to throw up, but she leaned forward and tried to steady her breathing. She could hear Adam talking in the other room. He sounded animated. A moment later he was standing at the study door.

'Kate, are you okay?'

She looked at the statement, then up at the mind maps again, staring at her father's name, wondering what part, if any, he had played in all this. When she finally spoke, it was as if someone else was talking. 'Adam, I was thinking about what you said, about the girl being taken more than once.'

'What about it?'

'The abduction and the abuse, bringing her to the same place, all of it. Everything about it is organised, orchestrated and points in one direction.'

'And what direction is that?'

'A single abuse victim is unlikely, and they wouldn't necessarily have been gender specific.'

'You're thinking Kevin Baxter?'

'Yes. There could be others. Fear, shame or both may have played a role in them for not coming forward.' The newspaper report on Peter Kirwan flashed before her eyes. 'Adam?'

'Yes?'

'I'm assuming you've looked at the Peter Kirwan case. It was a year earlier, but ...'

'I have, Kate, along with a great many others.'

'And?'

'I met the family liaison officer a short while ago. He's a good man, and twenty-eight years is a long time to know the family but not know what happened to their son.'

'I went back to my old house today.'

'Why?'

'I'm not sure – I guess I wanted to be there again. I met a neighbour, Pat Grant. She had a key belonging to the new owners.'

'I called to your old house too. It was a while back, near the start of the investigation. I decided to do some house-to-house when that first note arrived. I figured it couldn't do any harm.'

'And did you speak to them, the owners?'

'I spoke to a woman, yes. She was the one who initially told me about the rumours. Apparently some of the old neighbours had shared them with her.'

'And did you call to *these* neighbours?'

'I did, and they backed up her statement or, rather, at least one of them did.'

'Adam, I found something in the house.'

'What?'

'A page from an old newspaper. It was from 1987. It was taped to the back of my mother's dressing table. I'd been on a school trip to the Áras that year and managed to get my picture in the paper.'

'So?'

'It also had an article about Peter Kirwan. His name and the date of the newspaper were circled in red – the thirtieth of November 1987, two weeks after he'd gone missing.'

'It could be a coincidence.'

'I thought you didn't believe in them.'

'I don't, Kate, and I promise you, I'll run it by the guys in PIU. Anything to do with that old case, no matter how minor, is valuable.'

'Adam, what if my father was responsible?' she croaked. The room was spinning.

'Kate, don't go cracking up on me, not now. I need your help.'

'What?'

'I got a phone call a few minutes ago from a man called John Sinclair. He's reported his wife missing.'

Addy

THE BOY TILTED HIS HEAD TO THE SIDE, AS IF ADDY was the one who wasn't supposed to be there rather than the other way around.

Addy stared at him. Then he said, 'Why were you hiding like that?'

'I wasn't.'

Addy recognised the voice immediately as Donal's.

'Donal?' he asked, to double-check.

'Keep your voice down.'

'You said you'd come back, but you didn't.' In that split second, Addy wanted to shake him. He took a step nearer, realising he was clenching his fists.

'It was risky. They're getting more careful – watching everything. They could be watching us now.' He glanced around him.

'They?'

'The ones I told you about – the people who buried the bodies.'

Addy loosened his fists.

'I hear you're a member now.'

Addy could tell the boy was nervous, so he softened his tone: 'I had to pretend to be one to get out of there.'

'Why were you calling Chloë?'

'I want to find her.'

'You think I'm going to help you, don't you?'

'Maybe that's why you came out of hiding.'

'I told you, I wasn't hiding. I needed to stop you roaring, that's all.' He kicked the ground.

'I'm not roaring now, and you're still here.'

'If you told them you were a member, you lied.'

'I was pretending.'

'Lying is wrong.'

'You lied to me, Donal. You said you'd come back and you didn't.'

'I couldn't. That was different.'

'For all I know, you lied about everything – burials, secret meetings, something happening to Chloë.'

'I can prove it to you about the burials.'

'How?'

'I can bring you there.'

'Why should I trust you?'

'You don't have a choice.'

'Why don't I?'

'Because time is running out.' He sounded breathless. 'There's a boat coming in a couple of days. I overheard the others talking about it. It might be the last one for months.'

'I know about that.' Addy was calmer. 'You know where Chloë is, don't you?'

'I can't be sure.'

'Donal, don't mess with me.'

'She could be with Saka – in his rooms.'

'You need to take me there.'

'I can't.'

'You have to.' Addy was close enough to grab him, and when he did, Donal arched his back as if to defend himself, his body rigid, then attempted to pull away. He was cowering.

'I'm not going to hurt you, Donal.' Addy guessed this wasn't the first time someone had taken hold of him in an aggressive way. Maybe Chloë wasn't the only child at risk. He loosened his grip, hoping he hadn't pushed things too far.

'I'll take you to Chloë, but first, I'll bring you to the burial ground,' Donal said.

Kate

KATE LISTENED AS ADAM EXPLAINED ABOUT JOHN Sinclair, and the report he had filed in relation to his wife. It was similar to the others. Sarah Sinclair had left a note to say she was going away for a while. Her husband had hoped she would make contact, but when he didn't hear anything from her, he made a number of attempts to get her by phone, with no luck. He decided to let it go for a while. They had been arguing, and he thought she needed time to cool down. It had been their wedding anniversary a couple of days earlier, and even though they'd had their differences, he was sure she would be in touch. When she didn't call, he made more attempts to contact her, but he couldn't get through on her number. After that, he reported it to his local police station. The report went up on PULSE, and one of the other detectives in the unit had picked up on it. Sarah Sinclair, according to her husband, had withdrawn a large amount of money in cash before she left, similar to Amanda Doyle and Robert Cotter.

'What do you think, Kate?'

'I don't know,' she answered, putting her head in her hands, trying to concentrate. She wanted the old Kate back, the one who would have responded in seconds, but the old Kate didn't exist. Then she remembered her earlier notes. 'I was looking at cult behaviours, to see if there was a link with the Mason and O'Neill cases, and the missing-person reports.'

'Did you come up with anything?'

'If there is cohesion between them, it could be related to a form of empowerment.'

'I'm not getting you.'

'I was thinking about Malcolm, and the possibility that he felt ostracised in some way, being kept on the fringes in the past, outside the core grouping. That if a cult exists, it could be a replacement for the group in the eighties, only this time with someone else in control – him. But I don't know – it all sounds too crazy.'

'You mean like a copycat type thing. Recreating another study group, with him in the lead?'

'Maybe – it's a possibility.'

'Fisher has Malcolm on his radar too.'

'Did Sarah's husband say anything else in the report?'

'Yes. Like the others, his wife mentioned some kind of enlightenment programme.'

'So, it definitely ties in.'

'I've arranged to see him in an hour. I want you to come with me.'

∞

John Sinclair's house was in Terenure village, no more than a ten-minute drive from the apartment. When they arrived, it was obvious that he was deeply upset. He led Kate and Adam into the front living room, and all she could think was that she was looking at a broken man.

Adam was the first to speak. 'I know this must be difficult for you, Mr Sinclair, but believe us when we say we have your and your wife's best interests at heart.'

'You can call me John – a simple name for a simple man.'

'John it is, then.' Adam introduced Kate, then picked up where he had left off. 'You reported your wife missing a couple of days ago, when she didn't make contact with you on your wedding anniversary.'

'That's correct. It's an important day for both of us.'

'I understand that.'

'No, you don't.' His voice was harsher than either Kate or Adam had expected. 'It's not only because we got married that day. It's also the day our daughter died. Her name was Lily. She was only a few days old. Sarah found it difficult to accept. It was easier for her to pretend.'

Kate sat forward. 'How do you mean?'

'A few weeks back, she ordered this bloody baby doll from the States.' He put his face into his hands. 'I didn't know what the hell to do when she started going on and on about the doll being Lily.'

'You were angry?' Kate could hear the high emotion in his words.

'Yes, I was. I mean, I tried talking to her, but her head wasn't in the right place for listening. She kept saying I was the enemy, trying to take Lily away from her all over again.'

'What did she mean by "all over again"?' Adam kept his voice non-threatening.

'There were complications with the birth. It was my fault that I didn't get them to the hospital on time.'

'You shouldn't blame yourself,' Kate said, trying to ease things.

'That's easier said than done.' He sounded tight, angry.

No one said anything for a few moments, in an attempt to allow the tension to subside. Finally, Adam flipped the pages in his notebook. 'I understand your wife withdrew a large amount of money.'

'That's right. She said she needed it because she wanted to go away for a while. It was her money. She could do what she wanted with it.'

'Did she ever mention a Michael O'Neill or a Malcolm Madden?'

'Not that I remember.'

'You said she was part of some kind of enlightenment programme.' Adam looked at Kate.

'Yeah, she had CDs she listened to.'

'Do you still have them?' Kate asked.

'No, she took them with her, or else destroyed them.'

'Do you think there was anything odd about them?' Kate's tone was soft, supportive.

'I didn't listen to the bloody things. But I knew they had your man's voice on them.'

'Whose voice?' Adam looked up from his notebook.

'A guy called Saka, but I doubt that's his real name. I mean, what kind of a bloody name is that?'

Adam nodded, then said, 'I think Kate may have a few questions.'

'Ask away – although I can't guarantee I have the right answers.'

'That's okay, John.' Kate sat forward, trying to look more together than she felt. 'Did you notice any personality changes in your wife, either prior to her departure or before she ordered the doll?'

'I don't know. It was like she was a different person. I mean, we had been through a tough time, and we weren't out of the wars, far from it. We found it hard to talk about the past.' He looked away, as if he was trying to find the right words. 'I mean, I found it hard. Sarah wanted to keep revisiting it. I understand that now. I don't think I was the best of husbands.'

'But you said Sarah was like a different person?'

'Sorry, I didn't mean to stray ...'

'It's okay. Take your time.'

'A few months back, when she began going to meetings and such, I don't know, she started treating me like a stranger in my own home. She wasn't the Sarah I knew. She would stay in bed until I left for work in the mornings, avoiding me.'

'Did her sleep patterns change?'

'I don't think she slept much. I'd hear her getting up in the middle of the night to listen to those CDS, walking around the house like a half-dead person.'

'Would you say Sarah looked up to Saka?'

'Yes – I suppose she did.'

'And what about social events, meeting people who would have been important to her – family, close friends, people from work?'

'She didn't want to know about any of that. She went on and on about how everyone was looking at things the wrong way. That we've been brainwashed, that we've stopped thinking for ourselves.'

'So, it wasn't only you she pulled back from?'

'No, I guess not.'

'And what about when she ordered the baby doll? Did she talk to you or anyone else about it beforehand?'

'Not that I know of, although she did talk to that Saka guy. I know that much. When she started bringing the doll to bed with her, treating it like it was Lily, she said Saka told her it was important to be selfish about the things we needed. I mean, Jesus,' he put his face into his hands again, 'I got so frustrated. I didn't know what to do. When she went away, I thought if I gave her some time, she would work it all out, come back home, but she didn't.'

'John, do you need a couple of minutes?' Kate asked.

'No, no. I've waited long enough. Ask whatever you need to ask.'

'What about Sarah's language – the words and phrases she used? Did they change?'

'She talked about stuff like steps in the programme, finding a new way. It felt like she kept repeating the same things over and over, as if the more she said them, the more sense they made to her.'

'It was impossible to break down?'

'It was like she wasn't listening – at least, not to the things I was saying.'

'Would you say her reasoning was somewhat simplistic?'

'I don't understand.'

'Were her thought processes entrenched? Things were either good or bad, very few grey areas?'

'A bit like that. She was certainly singular in her belief that that stupid doll was Lily. I think once that doll arrived it was the end. At that point, she pulled back from work, from everything. It was as if staying in the real world risked Lily – I mean, the doll – being taken from her.'

'Someone found her Achilles heel.' Kate glanced at Adam, thinking about how vulnerable she had felt of late.

'John,' Adam turned another page in his notebook, 'is there anything concrete you can give us about where Sarah might have gone, or who this Saka person might be?'

'No, but she did mention something about an island.'

'Do you know where? Was it abroad or at home?' It was Adam's turn to glance at Kate.

'I don't know.' John Sinclair sounded deflated. 'I asked her about it, but she wouldn't say. I think she regretted telling me even that. It was like she'd let out some big secret, but that Saka guy was part of it. I know that much.'

To Kate, Adam said, 'That island could be anywhere.'

She didn't answer. Instead she turned back to John Sinclair, who had a look of shame on his face. 'John,' she said, 'you've been a great help.'

Adam stood up. 'We'll work on what we have.'

Then John Sinclair said, 'I thought I saw him once.'

'Who? Saka?'

'Yeah, but I can't be sure.'

'What did he look like?'

'Tall, slim. He had a tight haircut. He wore a suit. I only got a quick glance. I couldn't even tell you what age he was, but if I saw him again, I think I'd recognise him.'

They waited until they were in the car to talk. Kate was the first to speak. 'That man looks and sounds broken.'

'You did great in there.' He took her hand in his.

'Did I? I hope so.'

'What do you think about what he said?'

'It certainly sounds like Sarah was embroiled in some cult-like grouping. She displayed a lot of the obvious signs.'

'Like what?'

'Personality change, alteration of sleep patterns, shifts in value system, pulling back from family and social events, a sudden change in language, black and white reasoning, refusing to see grey areas, using unusual jargon – it's all there.'

'What's with the change in sleep patterns?'

'Cults try to alter the sleep behaviour of members, partly to hamper normal, rational thought. Once that's achieved, other methods are applied.'

'Like?'

'Confessional-type sessions aimed at convincing members that the group is their only means of emotional support. Other basic methods are also used, creating a hierarchical or pyramid structure, wearing similar clothing and, as time goes by, cult members are encouraged to see their identity as that of the group, rather than the individual. This can include exercises in reducing the concept of their uniqueness, communal activities, regular meetings, copying each other's physical displays of emotion.'

'Physical displays of emotion? Do you mean like crying together or something?'

'It could include that, or copying facial expressions, hand signals, whatever.'

'I still don't get how people get pulled into this.'

'It's a process, Adam, a gradual, subtle shift, until people are so indoctrinated in what the leader wants them to believe that they can no longer envisage an alternative, or they have committed so much by then that they're emotionally unable to back away.'

'So, other than a potentially fictitious name, and an island, we have damn all.'

'The island makes sense. It creates the necessary isolation.'

'I'll get the team to talk to the relatives and friends of Amanda Doyle and Robert Cotter again, see if the name Saka, or the island location, rings any bells.'

'Adam, I've something to tell you.'

'What?'

'Let's leave it until we get back to the apartment.'

Addy

ADDY EYEBALLED THE BOY, TRYING TO WORK OUT IF there would be any shift in his resolve. To him, it made sense to find Chloë first, but there was something about Donal's vulnerability that got to him. Maybe it was the boy being on his own for so long, without any parental support, or maybe, in part, he saw himself in the kid, putting up a brave exterior while inside it was different.

'All right,' he said, 'we'll go to the burial place first.'

'And then?'

'If half of what you're saying is true, after we find Chloë, we're going to get the hell off this island.'

The boy smiled at him.

'What?' Addy asked.

'We're like Crusaders or Robinson Crusoe.'

Despite all the oddity, Addy wanted to laugh. It wasn't so long ago that he had seen the world as some kind of fictional adventure, a world in which he was the hero, and he had a fictional father, who was a wise man, who brought him from being a young boy to a warrior. But Addy didn't laugh because the real world was a different place. In the real world, fathers abandoned their sons, then tried to be friends with them when all the growing up was done.

'Listen, Donal, you might enjoy playing Robinson Crusoe, but I don't.'

'What about the others?' the boy asked, nervous and serious again.

'What about them?'

'They might be in danger too.'

'Let's just go to this place. We've wasted enough time.'

'He's going to kill them, you know.'

'Who is?'

'Saka.'

'He told you that, did he?'

Donal took a step forward, whispering, like they were conspirators, 'He doesn't come right out and say it, but that's what he means.'

Kate

NEITHER KATE NOR ADAM SPOKE MUCH ON THE WAY back to the apartment, and she was constantly closing her eyes, going in and out of sleep. As he parked the car, she woke up with a jolt. He didn't rush her, but waited until she got her bearings. It was only then that she remembered she hadn't seen the squad car for a while.

'Is the surveillance still in place?'

'I was going to tell you when we got upstairs. It's been pulled back. You know how it is, Kate. After a certain period, it's standard.'

'Let's get inside.' Even without taking a pregnancy test, her body was telling her too many things for it to be anything else and she was determined, irrespective of how upsetting things had been, that she was going to put a positive slant on the news. But, entering the apartment, everything changed. The last thing either of them expected was another note, but there it was, and this time the envelope had her name on it.

'Don't pick it up, Kate.'

'I won't.'

Adam went into the bedroom, pulled out a set of protective gloves and two separate evidence bags. He placed the envelope in one of the bags, and having pulled the note out with his gloved hands, placed it in the other.

The note was short:

Kate – I do not like the way things are upsetting you. It's exactly the same as your mother's death. Everything was too little, too late, wasn't it?

'What does it mean?' Adam asked.

'I need to sit down.'

336

'It's okay. Take your time.' He put his arms around her. 'Tell me in your own words whenever you can.'

'The day my mother died, Adam, she took a bad turn. The nursing home moved her to the hospital for further tests. I went up to see her, and I stayed with her for most of the morning. Obviously I knew she wasn't well, but she'd been that way before. I never thought it would happen, not that day.'

'Go on, Kate, I'm listening.'

'I had to pick up Charlie, you see. I told her I'd be back. I didn't realise – I thought it was nothing more than another turn. The doctors had been so upbeat. I didn't see the harm in going away for a couple of hours. She had fallen asleep. I didn't know ...'

'What, Kate? What didn't you know?'

'I didn't know she would die.' She broke down.

Adam pulled her closer.

'The hospital phoned me, but it was too late,' tears streaming down her face, 'my mother was already dead, and she was on her own. I wasn't there. I let her down. I was all she had, and I wasn't there.'

'It wasn't your fault.'

'That's exactly what I said to John Sinclair, that it wasn't his fault about their daughter dying, but those words don't mean anything, not when it's someone you love.'

'Kate, I know this is difficult, but do you have any idea why someone is sending you these notes?'

'No, but I know what it feels like.'

'What?'

'That whoever it is has been watching me for a very long time.' Standing up, she walked to the study door, taking the key from under the plant pot to unlock it.

He followed her and, for the first time, saw the mind maps on the wall. 'Jesus Christ, Kate. What's all this?'

'I've been trying to put the pieces together.' She took a step closer to the mind map with her name at the centre. 'Whoever he is, there's one thing for sure. He can't let go.'

'What makes you so sure it's a "he"?'

Addy

WHEN ADDY AND DONAL REACHED THE CLIFFS, another cluster of dark clouds gathered overhead. It would be dark soon. Below them, the Atlantic waves crashed against the shore. The temperature had dropped at least another two degrees, and with heavy clouds in front of the moon, it would be pitch black once the sun had gone. Despite everything that had happened, Addy couldn't help but be blown away by the sheer beauty and ruggedness of the place, isolated in the Atlantic, a separate world, out on its own.

The seagulls overhead swooped and squawked, sometimes shadowing them, but always following. He worried they would act as some form of beacon, bringing unnecessary attention, but there was nothing he could do about the dynamics of the natural world. 'Donal,' he called, above the wind, when they reached flatter terrain, 'where do you sleep? How have you survived out here?'

'I've a hideout. There's a boathouse on the other side of the island,' he pointed west, 'I found it when I swam back, after pretending to drown. I have to be careful – they've searched it a few times. I can't leave my stuff there.' His face was serious again. 'I have to wrap up any food I have, and my blanket, and hide them when I leave.'

The boy was proud of himself, and Addy didn't blame him.

With the sun lower in the sky, the sinking amber glow blinded them. Donal put his hand over his eyes to block out the glare. 'Were you scared when you were locked in that room?' he asked Addy.

'Yeah. At times.'

'Sometimes in the boathouse I get scared.'

Addy thought about Charlie, probably doing his homework or playing football or something else a million miles from there.

'You did great, Donal,' he said, thinking for a split second about hugging him, but opting for high fives instead. The small gesture lifted Donal's mood, and Addy laughed when the boy said, 'It's like an adventure, isn't it?'

'You could say that.'

Then Donal asked, 'You do believe me, about the bodies?'

'Let's get there first.'

'Okay.'

'How much longer?'

'Ten minutes, maybe less.'

On the higher ground, they could see the commune buildings and the old church in the distance.

'What's that?' Donal asked, pointing to the commune.

Addy followed his line of vision, and saw black smoke billowing sideways from the helpers' quarters.

Kate

KATE THOUGHT ABOUT ADAM'S LAST QUESTION. There was no reason to assume the sender of the notes was male, but she had. All of a sudden, telling him about the pregnancy felt wrong, and in a way, she was relieved when his work mobile rang.

'I have to go back in. That was Fitzsimons. I asked him to dig deeper into the property portfolio Madden's involved with.' He held up the bagged envelope and note. 'Plus I need to get someone to look at these.'

'They'll be like the others.'

'Don't give up, Kate.'

'I'm not giving up. I'm being realistic.'

'I'll see about getting that full surveillance back in place.'

'The note isn't strong enough. There's nothing threatening about it.'

He took a step closer to her. 'When I get back, let's open a bottle of wine and relax. Neither of us is very good at knowing when to draw the line about putting pressure on ourselves.'

'That sounds like a plan,' she said, even though she knew he would be drinking the wine alone.

'Stay put for now, will you?'

'Sure. Adam?'

'Yeah?'

'I want to transcribe the note before you go.'

'But you know what it says.'

'Humour me.'

He waited while she copied it on to a sheet of paper, then pinned it on the study wall.

'Kate ...'

'You don't have to say it. I'm not going anywhere. I'll stay here until you get back, but I'm not the first person in the world to receive harassment notes.'

'Promise me you won't leave the apartment until I get things sorted.'

'I promise.'

∞

When Adam left, the apartment felt like a monster that was trying to chew her up. Were the notes designed to make her feel that way? Could they be a decoy? One way or another, whoever had sent them had a vested interest in unnerving her. If it was Malcolm, it would explain a lot. Even though they hadn't been in touch for years, he knew more about her than most. Had she shared with him how upset she was at not being there when her mother died? If the sender had been monitoring her for a number of years, there must be something about their shared past that was eluding her.

What if, as Adam had suggested, the sender of the notes was female? She always felt that the centre of the mind maps belonged to someone other than herself. O'Neill, Malcolm, her father, even Mason were all options, but the creator of the notes, irrespective of gender, was a candidate, too. Despite seeing her father's name stare back at her, and all the dark things she'd contemplated he might have been capable of, was she making the classic error of denial? It was impossible to think of him as a child abuser.

She created another map with the PIU victim in the centre, then another, this time writing the name 'Saka'. Could the identity of the sender be in front of her? The abuse victim was now a grown woman. Why had she come forward only recently? Kate knew there could be any number of reasons, but as she was thinking this, she reread the copy of the latest note.

'What are you seeing, Kate,' she said aloud, 'that you can't put your finger on?'

Special Detective Unit, Harcourt Street

ADAM WASN'T HAPPY ABOUT LEAVING KATE ALONE, but he had his own reasons for asking Fitzsimons to get additional information on the portfolio of properties. He was angry that he hadn't made the connection before, but now that his suspicions were raised, if he was correct, the new information would implicate Malcolm Madden even more.

Scanning down the various addresses, it didn't take him long to find the range of properties listed as sites 5–14, all located in the lower Rathmines area, each with a unique folio number. Fitzsimons had done as Adam had requested, and beside the folio references, the individual house numbers and street addresses were now transcribed. Seeing Kate's old house on the list didn't prove anything, other than that it was yet another prime investment site, but comparing his house-to-house notes against the full list, particularly the two witness statements, confirming rumours about Kate's father, he found what he was looking for. Both statements alluding to the rumours had come from two of the portfolio properties, one being Kate's old home. He'd be talking to Malcolm Madden again. The question was whether or not he would wait until Fisher arrived. He'd also get Fitzsimons to find out whatever he could on the two individuals who had given him the information.

Adam had already allocated four members of his team to the task of re-interviewing Amanda Doyle's and Robert Cotter's family and friends. He had also dropped off the note with Forensics. There wouldn't be anything back on it for a few hours, or possibly not until the next morning.

The team had been re-interviewing the family and friends for a couple of hours but, so far, nothing fresh was coming in. Something had to break soon.

It was too late to phone Madden's office, and his private number went to voicemail. On the second attempt he left a message. Tomorrow morning, if he had to, he would sit outside the guy's house and stalk him. Within twenty minutes, Madden's PA phoned back, saying Madden would see him at his home at noon the following day.

'There will be two of us,' he told the girl. 'I'll be accompanied by Detective Lee Fisher of the NYPD.'

That, Adam thought, should give the smarmy bastard something to think about.

Someone – or a number of people – was holding back information. It was late, and he didn't like the idea of leaving Kate alone in the apartment any longer. Tomorrow would have to take care of itself. Right now, someone needed him more than his job did.

Addy

WATCHING THE BLACK SMOKE AND FLAMES POURING from the buildings, Addy pulled out his mobile phone, already knowing he wouldn't get a signal.

'I didn't know you had a phone,' Donal said, sounding disappointed that Addy hadn't mentioned it.

'There's no coverage.'

'You should have told me.'

'Donal, we're going to have to go back. They might need our help.'

'It could be a trap. There are bars on the windows at that end. They're probably all dead by now.'

Addy wanted to tell him to stop being so bloody melodramatic, but what was the point? If anything, it confirmed his suspicions that Donal was inclined to think in a fantastical way, being barely an eleven-year-old. 'It's almost dark,' was all he said in reply. They didn't have any torches, and even though the mobile phone was useless, Addy couldn't risk running down the battery using it for light. 'Which is closer,' he asked, 'the commune or your hideout?'

They both heard the commune bell ring out.

'That's the special code, Addy.'

'What code? Is it a warning about the fire?'

'It could be, but they also use it for the drill.'

'What drill?'

'When Saka thinks it's time.'

'Time for what?'

'He calls it the eternity bell.'

Kate

KATE DIDN'T TURN ON THE LIGHTS. THE SEMI-
darkness seemed to calm her thoughts.

When the doorbell rang, she wasn't sure what to do. Everything
felt like a threat now. In the hall, she pressed the intercom, asking,
'Who is it?' Nobody answered. She tried again. Still no response.
Rushing to the living-room window, she looked out on to the front
steps, hoping to catch a glimpse of whoever had been at the door,
again feeling like a prisoner in her own home.

She hadn't realised how late it was. The streetlights were already
on. When she pressed her face to the glass, the only person she saw
was a male cyclist, the same man who had cycled past the apartment
before. As the window fogged, she told herself someone could have
rung the intercom by accident, but when she heard the key turn in
the front door, panic set in.

How someone had managed to get inside the communal hallway
didn't matter, or how they had got hold of a key. The only thing
that mattered was that they were close. She was glad she hadn't
turned on the lights. The darkness would give her time. She had to
think fast. They would be inside in the next couple of seconds.

Her legs felt wobbly, her head hot and sweaty, and as multiple
thoughts rammed through her mind at the same time, she put most
of her bodily reaction down to fear, until her eyes began to black
out, and her limbs turned to jelly, and she collapsed in a heap on the
floor.

The Game Changer

CENTRE OF LIGHTNESS
20 Steps to Self-enlightenment Programme

The fire didn't take long to get going, or to control. Shock is an effective tool. The group will solidify through fear and an aspiration of protection. They will mourn those who perished, but they will look forward.

The need for guidance and for things to make sense will be swelled, with an increased commitment to finding a better way, and a deeper desire to leave the constraints of earthly life behind.

Time is now required for reflection. After that, the death speech will be shared. They understand what the bell means. They have been warned that some day all of this could happen. The next time they hear the bell, it will add more fear, and desperation. They will wonder if the final moments are close by, the ones they have been told to prepare for, the ones they believe we will share together.

Saka will be taken care of, too. He was never more than a front man, a name to hide behind, a fool of an idealist that the Game Changer picked up along the way, and a whimsical individual at that. He has played the role of sympathetic leader, and will now be nothing more than a convenient get-out clause. Like everyone else, he was fed the information the Game Changer wanted him to know. His demise will be the concluding message: if you love Saka, you must follow him.

(Page 1 of 1)

Kate

WHEN KATE WOKE, IT WAS EARLY MORNING. SHE looked around her, composed at first, realising she was at home, then remembered her fear from the previous night and her blackout. She heard movements in the kitchen. She told herself it was Adam, that it must have been a bad dream. Looking down at her body, she realised she was in her pyjamas. She couldn't remember getting into bed. Had someone undressed her? What time was it? Reaching out for her mobile phone, she saw it was coming close to nine o'clock. Adam always left for work before eight. Whoever was outside was putting on the radio. The volume was loud. If it was Adam, he wouldn't have it on that high. Would he?

Her legs felt like lead as she tried to get out of the bed, then her head did that thing again, and the room began to spin. She was going to be sick. Running into the bathroom, she pulled up the toilet seat, going down on her hunkers to throw up. Whoever was in the kitchen, would they have heard her? She ran the cold tap at a trickle, putting the hand towel under it. It felt cool against her forehead. She started to feel better. It was then that she heard the footsteps. The bedroom door opened. She leaned back against the wall, as far from the door as she could, even though she knew it was pointless.

It was only when she saw his face, realising with relief that it was Adam, that she allowed her body to give up and she collapsed on to the floor.

'Jesus, Kate,' she heard him say, 'what's wrong with you?'

The next time she came to, she was back in bed. Adam was standing over it. When she realised she was awake, he told her that

Sophie, Charlie's childminder, would be there in a few minutes, and that he had called the doctor. It would be a couple of hours before he arrived, but in the meantime, she was to keep taking as much fluid as she could.

'I'm fine,' she said. 'I don't need a doctor. It will pass.' She hadn't the energy to say any more.

Then she heard him say he needed to pick up Lee Fisher from the airport. He would check in on her later. That she wasn't to fret. That everything would be okay. All she had to do was get some rest, and he repeated, 'Keep taking fluids.' Her head felt heavy on the pillow. She closed her eyes again, and then she heard Sophie's voice. She was talking to Adam. After that, she heard the apartment door close. It will pass, she told herself. Get some rest, and everything will be okay.

Addy

THE NIGHT IN THE BOATHOUSE, OR HIDEOUT, AS Donal liked to call it, gave Addy plenty of time to mull things over. The so-called burial ground would have to wait, and whether Donal liked it or not, they were going back to the commune. Addy needed him to get around the place via the pipe chambers. He had been missing for far too long for others not to ask awkward questions. If something bad was going down, Chloë and Aoife were the priorities – it was that simple.

When Donal woke, he didn't argue about going back, and Addy wondered if he had spent a pensive night too. For the first time, he really thought about how the boy must feel, knowing his mother was in the commune but that he couldn't be around her. Beside that, Addy's issues about Adam paled into insignificance.

In the daylight, it didn't take them long to retrace their steps, but by the time they reached the commune buildings, the fire had long gone out. They kept their distance, but they were close enough to see some of the senior members by the burned-out quarters talking to each other.

'We need to hear what they're saying,' Addy whispered to Donal.

'What are you going to do?'

'Get closer.'

'It's not safe.'

'We can't stay here,' Addy said, almost as if he was thinking out loud. 'I need to find out what's happened, and you're going to help me.'

'I'm scared.'

'Donal, don't worry, it'll be okay.'

'You don't know that.'

'Listen, if something bad is about to happen, we need to find your mother too.'

'She doesn't care about me, not any more.'

Addy wasn't sure what to say next, so he said nothing, as they watched the members walk away from the burned-out shell. He sensed this was their chance.

'Donal,' he whispered, 'tell me again about that bell ringing last night. What exactly does it mean?'

'It can mean different things, but the main one is the calling.'

'Calling?'

'It's a sort of dying.'

'You can't have a sort of dying.'

'People die, but then they come back to life.'

Addy remembered the speech he had eavesdropped on in the main hall, the one about changing form. 'Do you mean like a resurrection?'

'I don't know, but yeah. Sometimes they talk all messed up. I don't know what they mean.'

'Donal, I have a friend in there. Her name is Aoife, and we have to find Chloë too. We need to make sure they're okay, so we have to go inside.'

Addy looked at the commune building, thinking about the day he had arrived, travelling over with Sarah on the boat. 'Donal?'

'Yeah?'

'Do you know a woman called Sarah? She isn't well. She thinks a doll is her baby.'

'I know her.'

There was something about the way Donal answered that made Addy suspicious. 'Are you holding something back?'

'That woman.'

'What about her?'

'She's with Chloë.'

'What do you mean?'

'They're both in the infirmary.'

'Why didn't you say so before? Why didn't you say you knew where Chloë was?'

'I thought if you knew where she was, you'd leave me, and I'd be on my own again.'

'Donal, you're going to show me the way into the pipe chambers. Do you hear me?'

'I know where you can get a phone signal too.'

Addy wanted to throttle him, and the boy must have seen it in his face because he started to plead: 'I would have told you, Addy, honest, I swear.'

'Why didn't you?'

'I didn't know you had a phone. Not until I saw you take it out last night. There's only one place you can get a signal.'

'Where?'

'At the old church – it's the nearest point to the mainland, and if you climb into the spire, you can get the signal there.'

Addy tried to keep his voice calm. 'Donal, we're going to go into the pipe chambers together to work out what the hell is going on. Then we're going to find Chloë and anyone else who needs our help. Do you hear me?'

'I hear you.'

Kate

BY TEN O'CLOCK, WHEN ADAM WAS DUE TO MEET LEE Fisher at the airport, Kate's morning sickness had passed. She told Sophie to contact the doctor and cancel the call-out. She said she would be fine, and that she could manage on her own now that she felt better. She opened the fridge to find that Sophie had stocked it up. When Kate thought about the previous day, she realised she had barely eaten since breakfast, and most of that hadn't stayed down. She needed to take better care of herself: she had another life to consider.

Her head still hurt, but she did as Adam told her and kept drinking, then showered and dressed. As she made her way into the study, Sophie was about to leave and she gave Kate a dubious look but, thankfully, she didn't say anything. Kate wasn't sure she had the energy to argue.

The questions from the previous day were still going around in her head, and once inside the study, she looked at the transcript of the latest note. Then her eyes fell to the copy of the witness statement on her desk. Remembering the similarities between Amanda Doyle's letter and the previous notes, she picked up the statement, pondering on the elided word 'it's'. By itself, it was of no relevance, being a common shortcut, but the longer she looked at the wording, the more convinced she became. If she was right, her earlier suspicions would be well founded, even if the questions of 'who' and 'why' remained unanswered.

When her phone rang, and she saw a blocked number, she thought about ignoring it, but instead, she pressed the answer button, relieved to hear Aoife's voice at the other end.

'Aoife, are you okay? No one has heard from you or Addy in ages.'

'Addy's okay, but I'm …'

'You're what, Aoife? You don't sound too good.'

'I've been finding some things difficult.'

Kate thought about the girl's previous problems, and her eating disorder. 'Is everything all right?'

'I don't want to talk over the phone.'

'Is Addy with you?'

'No. I need to see you, Kate. I need to talk to you face to face.'

Kate could hear the desperation in Aoife's voice, and she recognised the shakiness from their earlier sessions. 'Tell me where you are and I'll meet you. Are you at home?'

'No. I can't go there. Can I meet you somewhere else?'

'Sure. Hold on. I'll get a pen and you can give me the address.'

'Can you be there in an hour?'

'Yes.' She had no idea if Adam had managed to get the full surveillance back in place, but the location wasn't far, and Aoife sounded desperate.

She hung up and dialled him.

'Kate, I'm at the airport. Fisher's flight has been delayed. How are you feeling?'

'Better, a lot better.'

'Has the doctor arrived?'

'No, and he won't be coming. Sophie cancelled the call-out for me.'

'Kate, something isn't right. You've been so unwell. There has to be a reason for it.'

Telling him over the phone wasn't going to work, so instead she said, 'Aoife just called.'

'Aoife? Did she mention Addy?'

'She said he's fine, but she wants to meet me.'

'That surveillance will be back in place this afternoon.'

'I've already agreed to see her in an hour. It's not far.'

'Kate, you shouldn't even be out of bed.'

'I'll be careful, and I'll see what I can find out about Addy too.

I can't put my life on hold because someone is sending harassment notes.'

'I don't know, Kate.'

'I'll ring you when I get back. I'll be fine.'

'As soon as Fisher arrives, we'll be going to see Malcolm Madden, but call me whenever. I'll pick up.'

'Adam, there's something else I need to tell you.'

'What?'

'I might have made another connection. Do you remember the similarities between the notes and Amanda Doyle's letter?'

'What about them?'

'The PIU statements have similar variances.'

'The report from the script expert wasn't conclusive.'

'I know that, but it doesn't mean I was wrong. Amanda Doyle's letter was too short for a full analysis, but the statements are longer.'

'I don't know, Kate. You can't think she made all that stuff up?'

'I'm not sure what to think any more.'

'I'll put a call through to PIU and push them in whatever way I can. In the meantime, I'll get the statements looked at by that expert. If we find something solid, PIU will have to give us a name, protection of identities or not.'

Adam

ADAM HADN'T HAD ANY PRECONCEIVED NOTIONS about what Lee Fisher would look like, but when he saw the tall, dark detective, wearing a scuffed leather jacket and jeans, his hair tied back in a bun, with a tight beard shielding his rugged face, he felt awkward in his shirt, trousers and smart jacket, holding a white sheet of paper with Lee's name on it.

'Do you want to drop off your bag?' he asked, when Lee was closer.

'No, Adam, I'm cool. I travel light. It makes getting away a whole lot easier.'

He guessed Lee was joking, but he hadn't the full measure of the guy yet.

'We have a scheduled visit with Malcolm Madden before the next brain-storming session. Are you up to it?'

'Sounds good to me.'

In the car, Adam took Lee up to speed, including Kate's theory about the missing-person reports, John Sinclair's statement, and how the cult theory could be a runner. He also spoke about the possibility of the cult being tied into the 1980s studies, as a means of empowerment, if Madden or someone else narcissistically driven had sought a shift of power.

'We'll need to push him on the tenants of the two properties in Rathmines,' Adam said, turning to make sure Lee was still listening, as the detective had remained silent for so long. Lee kept looking straight ahead of him. The last thing Adam mentioned was the PIU statements, their possible link to the notes and Amanda Doyle's letter.

'So,' Lee said, having waited for Adam to finish, 'if Madden is part of all this, is Kate saying he's looking to be the one in control?'

'Possibly.'

'I like Kate's theory, but the way I see it is that we have a whole load of information but motivation is still thin on the ground.'

'Let's hope Madden's in a talkative mood.'

'He'll talk. We'll make sure he does.'

When Malcolm Madden opened the door, Adam didn't bother with any introductions. He had already given the information about Lee Fisher to the PA, so he wasn't going to waste time on formalities.

Malcolm Madden looked composed, as if two detectives coming to his door was the most normal thing in the world. He led them down a long corridor to the back of the house, opening a door to a home office.

Lee let Adam take the lead. 'You've been less than generous with your information about your property portfolio, Malcolm.'

'I don't agree, Detective Inspector O'Connor. I think I've been extremely transparent.'

'One of the properties is Kate Pearson's old home.'

'So?'

'Another of the properties is close to it.'

'I'm not following your drift.'

'Let me give you some guidance then.' Adam sat forward in the chair. 'I've done some recent house-to-house calls and I happened to meet the occupiers of both.'

'I still don't understand.'

'It was interesting that the two people to spread accusations against Kate's father, and others associated with that academic grouping, were people renting from Holmes & Co.'

'I can't be held responsible for what particular tenants say.'

'Not unless you're feeding them the information.'

'I'm not feeding anyone information, as you call it.'

'Do you know the tenants?' Lee asked, crossing his long legs, and scratching his forehead.

'I know one of them well, and the other was introduced to me recently, but I don't think that's any of your business.'

'Detective Inspector O'Connor here and I don't agree.'

'Is this a formal interview?'

'Would you prefer to go down to the station?' Adam asked.

'No. It's fine here. How's Kate doing?'

Adam didn't like him bringing up Kate. It was as if he was trying to turn this into some kind of social conversation, but he also figured it might be a good way of reeling him in. 'We hope we can depend on your co-operation in all this.'

'I'm always willing to help.'

'So tell us what you know about the tenants.' Adam flipped open his notebook. 'We already have the names, Malcolm, a Jessica Fraser and a Clarence Webb. What we don't know is how, other than being tenants of Holmes & Co, they're connected to you.'

For the first time since their arrival, the man's polished and calm exterior seemed to slip, his face suddenly tired. 'If Kate wasn't part of all this, I wouldn't be giving you the time of day. I hold my client relationships in high regard. Any information I receive as part of ongoing therapy must be protected.'

'Are you saying one or both of these tenants is a client?'

'Jessica came to me for help, and similarly, like Kate, our connection goes back a long way.'

Adam thought about Kate's earlier theory, linking the PIU statements to the anonymous notes. Did Malcolm Madden's relationship with this woman go back as far as the abuse allegations? Could there be a joint agenda going on here?

'Jessica Fraser?'

'She goes by that name now, yes, but it wasn't always Fraser. She changed it by deed poll.'

'Why? What was it?'

'It was after her brother died. She wanted a fresh start.'

'You still haven't told me her original name.'

'Baxter.'

'As in Kevin Baxter, O'Neill's foster son?' Adam didn't attempt to hide his surprise, glancing at Lee Fisher, who was sitting upright in his chair for the first time.

'That's correct.'

'Jesus Christ! Why didn't you think to tell us before?'

'Partly because of client privilege, but also because the woman was fragile. It was all very delicate. I hadn't a problem helping her. I mean …' He paused, standing up, turning his back on both men.

'You mean what?' Lee pushed.

'There were high emotions at play.'

'What kind of high emotions?' Adam asked.

He kept his back to the two detectives before saying, 'Decades of guilt.'

Kate

THE TWENTY-FOUR-HOUR CHEMIST IN HAROLD'S Cross was on the way to her meeting with Aoife. She rang Charlie before she went inside. It felt good hearing his voice. If her suspicions were right, his life was going to be a whole lot different very soon, with a younger brother or sister in tow.

It was strange and exciting picking up the pregnancy-test kit. The girl behind the counter looked at her in that knowing way, which made her feel even more positive about the prospective news. That evening, if she was correct, she would tell Adam. Even if it wasn't something either of them had planned, a new life was a miracle, and that's precisely what she told herself as she went into the ladies' toilet at the Trinity Hotel, unwilling to wait any longer to know for certain.

She watched the kit test area go from white to pink, confirming it was working correctly. In a few seconds, it would either show a plus sign for positive or a minus for negative. When the plus appeared, she didn't know whether to laugh or cry. With everything else going on around her, somehow this young life had been created inside her.

Wrapping the kit in tissue, she put it away in her bag. She would show Adam later, a small but concrete proof of their life changing.

Walking out on to the street, despite the cold, she was glad she had left the car in the hotel car park. Aoife had wanted to meet outdoors, and both of them knew the secondary school well. It was a handy landmark even if it was down a couple of twists and turns. The walk would do her good, she told herself, and the sooner she got exercising, the better.

Crossing the road, she headed for the school gates, happier than she had been in days. No one was around. It was too early for the midday break. She visualised Charlie going to the school when he was older, and a smile came to her face as she thought about him having a younger brother or sister with him – a real family, two siblings, not the lone-child existence she lived.

When a car pulled out from a parked position, the sound of the engine roaring caused her to do a quick double-take.

It moved too fast for her to get out of the way, but before the bang, she saw the flash of the young man's face behind the wheel. Then there was nothing.

Adam

ADAM STOOD UP, MOVING A FEW STEPS CLOSER TO
Malcolm Madden. 'What do you mean by decades of guilt?'

Malcolm turned to face him. 'I had my suspicions about certain
things that went on back then. You know about the academic study
that was set up?'

'Yes.'

'It was Valentine's idea. He always wanted to be the main man.'

'You sound a bit resentful about that.'

'Detective, in every grouping someone wants to be the star.
Valentine was full of his own importance, which was why a lot of
things happened that he didn't know about. Arrogance is weakness,
not strength.'

'You're talking about the paedophile allegations?'

'I couldn't be sure of any of it. At least, that's what I told myself.
Some members of the group had ideas beyond Valentine's lofty
aspirations. Certain members, like Michael O'Neill and Tom
Mason, were weak.'

'By weak, you mean they were interested in more than the
children's educational development?'

'Precisely.'

'And how does this tie into Jessica?'

'Michael abused her brother, Tom Mason abused her – he and
another man called Andrew Foster.'

Lee turned to Adam. 'Foster was on the list from Emily Burke.
He died twenty years ago from a brain tumour.' He asked Malcolm,
'When exactly did Jessica come to you?'

'A few months ago – coincidentally, around the same time Kate and I started meeting more frequently. I remembered the brother more than her. I knew something wasn't right between him and Michael, but …'

'Keep going, Malcolm.' Adam stepped back to allow him to sit down.

'I didn't want to push things at the time, or even later. '

'You're still saying you weren't part of the group?'

'Valentine thought I looked up to him, and I did for a while, but he treated me like a fool, someone to be around when it suited him to get things done … things he didn't want to look after himself. He didn't believe I had enough life experience to be part of the study. It's ridiculous when I think about it now. All his high and mighty ideals and I knew more about what was going on than he did. Sometimes not being at the core can make people more inclined to let things slip. That and personal observations, even if I hadn't got the relevant life experience Valentine preferred.'

'You still bear a grudge, don't you?' Lee asked.

'On the contrary, I'm beyond that now, which is why it was important for me to help Jessica in any way I could. I should have done more at the time, but I wasn't the worst.'

Adam pulled his chair closer to the desk and propped his elbows on it. 'Emily Burke said the group was brought to an abrupt ending. Was that on Valentine's instructions?'

'Yes, but not before a lot of damage had been done.'

'How was Jessica abused?' Adam asked, thinking of the statements from PIU.

'She was taken a number of times. Mason and Foster got a drunk called Stapleton to do their dirty work for them. It was all so easy. The girl was marginalised, and the mother was a disaster. It was because of Kevin that she first drew their attention. At the time of the abuse, she was still with the mother, but she had visited her brother a few times, enough, as I said, to be noticed by the others.'

Damn it, Adam thought. Fitzsimons had mentioned a sister, but because of the change of name, the connection had slipped through the cracks. 'She went to PIU about it, didn't she?' he asked.

'She did. It took her a while, but she said she had finally made up her mind to go to the police.'

'And she had her suspicions about Michael O'Neill and her brother?'

'Yes.'

'What about Mason?' Lee interjected. 'Did she know he was one of her abusers?'

'Yes. I told her everything as I remembered it.'

'So why did she hold the names back from the police?' Adam was still perplexed.

'An abuse victim needs time. They were tentative steps for her. It took guts to do what she did after all this time.'

'Why come to you? If what you're saying is true, and you were indirectly associated with those involved, it doesn't make any sense.'

'A lot of it doesn't. All I knew was that I wasn't going to turn my back on her again.'

'What do you mean?'

'Despite what you think of me, Detective Inspector O'Connor, I'm not a bad man. I knew a lot about what had happened to her – indeed, far more than I wanted to know – but I did nothing at the time. It's not often that you get a second chance to help someone.'

Adam eyed the psychologist up and down, conscious of Lee doing the same. Then Lee said exactly what was on Adam's mind: 'She's used you.'

'I don't agree.'

'How does Kate fit into all this?' Adam asked, barely able to stop himself punching the guy.

'She doesn't. Jessica wanted a fresh start, a helping hand, that's all.'

'Are you saying you didn't discuss Kate?'

'She may have come up in conversation, but not in any significant way.'

'Why let her rent Kate's old house?'

'She didn't look to stay there, if that's what you mean.'

'I'll hold my judgement on that.' Adam looked at Lee.

'The property had been empty for some time. Thinking about it now, I do see where you're coming from, but ...' Malcolm paused for a moment to gather his thoughts. 'I think I've said far too much already.'

'I don't agree.' Adam was no longer able to keep his anger from his voice. 'Kate's been getting harassment notes.'

'She didn't mention them to me.'

'Let's just say she had trust issues.'

Lee glanced at Adam before asking, 'Malcolm, when you heard about Mason, and then subsequently about O'Neill's death, did you not think Jessica could be involved?'

'If Michael decided to take his own life, there wasn't anything any of us could do about it.'

'What about Mason?'

'Jessica wouldn't have been capable of that.'

'And the other tenant, Clarence Webb?'

'What about him?'

'How was he connected to Jessica?'

'I only met him once. He was waiting for Jessica after one of our meetings. She said he was helping her too, with meditation and finding a more positive outlook on life.'

'You like to play God, Malcolm, don't you?' Lee pushed, unwilling to let him off the hook.

'I don't know what you mean.'

'She used you. She used your elevated sense of importance, along with whatever guilt you've been carrying around for the last quarter of a century.'

'I disagree, and again, I want to reiterate, I didn't know anything about any notes being sent to Kate or anything else.'

'Malcolm,' Adam said, his voice more controlled now, 'withholding information is a criminal offence.'

'I realise that, which is why I've told you all this.'

'Why are you being so generous now when you didn't mention any of this before?'

'I haven't been able to contact Jessica for a few days. She's not answering her phone. She and Clarence have gone or, at least, there's no answer at either property. I'm worried about her.'

'Pardon my lack of empathy, Malcolm, but I'm with Lee on this one. She's conned you.'

'Believe what you like.'

'And what about Kate's father? What exactly did you tell Jessica about him?'

When Adam's mobile phone rang out, he raised his hand, indicating to hold the conversation.

'Are you Adam O'Connor?' a woman asked at the other end of the line.

'Yes, who is this?'

'I'm phoning from St James's Hospital. Do you know a Kate Pearson?'

'I do. Is she okay? Is something wrong?'

Addy

ADDY SENT DONAL AHEAD OF HIM AS THEY manoeuvred their way along the pipe chambers. The copper pipes feeding the water supply to the commune buildings were housed in a series of cylinder-shaped stone chambers, all of which were interlinked, and there was barely enough room to squeeze past the pipes, making their progress slow. He had turned off his mobile phone to conserve the battery and was glad he had. It took them two hours to reach the exit shaft near the infirmary. On their way there, they saw numerous members huddled in hallways, or outside meeting rooms. It was impossible to hear what they were saying, but their faces were tense and absorbed. Even without knowing what was being talked about, Addy was convinced that something was happening. There was a change in mood, nothing surer.

The infirmary was off the main corridor, a modern extension in an otherwise elongated rectangular set of buildings, and it was after midday by the time they reached the shaft they were looking for. By then the corridors were a lot quieter.

'It's weird,' Donal said, as Addy followed him down from the shaft opening.

'What is?'

'There are usually others here, members with special passes, but it's deserted.'

Addy opened the first of four doors. The room and bed were empty. When he opened the second, he saw Sarah. She was asleep with a drip connected to her arm.

'Do you know what's wrong with her, Donal?' he whispered.

'I heard one of the doctors talking.'

'And?'

'She took too many pills.'

'An overdose?'

'I guess. They're doping her now. They did that to my mother too.'

'What?'

'It's part of how they do things.'

'I don't get you.'

'To make them think differently. But it's not working with her.' He pointed to Sarah. 'That's why she's still on the drip. It gets the drugs into her system faster.'

Addy thought of their trip over on the boat, how protective she had been with that doll. She had seemed happy, but kind of scared at the same time.

'Are you all right, Addy?' Donal asked.

'Yeah.' He stepped into the room. Donal followed him. Sarah made mumbling noises, as if talking in her sleep.

'How do they get the drugs to the island?'

'By boat.'

'They must buy them online to get that much stuff. They have to have other people ordering the drugs.'

The boy shrugged his shoulders.

Addy stood by Sarah's side, and saw the cot with the doll in it. Someone had smashed the doll's face, and pulled the legs and arms out of their sockets. Who would do something like that? He turned its face away from Sarah, covering the plastic body with a blanket.

'What did you do that for?' Donal asked.

'I don't want her to get upset. I have to wake her.'

'You can't. You don't know what she'll do.'

'I have to take that risk.' But he hesitated, knowing Donal had a point. If he woke Sarah, even if she didn't scream the place down, she was clearly too weak to go anywhere, and they still needed to find Chloë. He wasn't sure what to do next, but then he realised Donal was waiting on his lead, so he finally said, 'Sarah, it's Addy.'

At first, she didn't respond, but then her eyes blinked open and closed, and although she didn't speak straight away, she looked at him warmly, as if he was an old friend. 'Is that you, John? Have you come for me?'

'It's Addy. Remember? The boy on the boat?'

'I want my John.' Her voice was croaky. 'I need him to come here.'

'It's all right, Sarah,' Addy replied, even though he knew it wasn't.

Donal gave him a dig in the ribs, and he turned sharply. 'What?'

The boy pointed to the locker with the mobile phone, and Addy immediately twigged what he meant. With his hands, he signalled to Donal to fetch it, and the boy swiftly moved to the other side of the bed.

Holding the phone, Donal kept his voice low when he said, 'It's been turned off.'

'Sarah,' Addy whispered, close to her ear, 'can you remember the code for your phone?'

She nodded.

'If you tell me, we can phone John.'

'I tried to find his number,' again her voice was croaky, 'but I couldn't.' Her face went tense, and for a moment Addy thought she was about to become hysterical, but she said, 'My fingers kept messing up.'

'I understand, Sarah, but the code?' Addy knew it was a long shot. If the woman wasn't able to find a number in the phone, how was she going to remember a code?

'All zeros,' she said, her voice so low that Addy could barely make it out.

'Did you say zeros, Sarah?'

She nodded again, and Addy looked at Donal. 'Put in four zeros.'

The boy did as he was told, then smiled. 'It has 50 per cent battery.'

'Good. Now switch it off because we'll need it.'

Sarah closed her eyes.

'Sarah,' Addy whispered again, 'I'm not sure if you can hear me, but we need to find someone else. I promise you we'll be back.'

∞

In the last room, they found Chloë. This time it was Donal who stood closest to the bed. He leaned over, his face near her mouth, checking her breathing. 'She's still alive,' he said, excited.

'Shush! Not so loud.'

'I was worried she wouldn't be.'

'What do you mean?'

'She's been here for too long. They only give you a certain amount of time. Then if the drugs and the one-to-one sessions with Jessica don't work, the person disappears.'

Addy didn't need any more things spelled out for him. They had to get help. Otherwise how would they get Sarah and Chloë out of there? He thought about Aoife. Would she help them? Could he trust her?

Think, Addy, think. Use the resources you have. They had two mobile phones and some battery strength on both. It might be enough. Donal said they'd get a signal at the old church, once they went up high enough in the spire. It all felt too crazy, but if someone on the island was operating a blocker system, the church on higher ground, close to the mainland, and away from the commune buildings, would be outside its influence. He had to take a chance. He tugged Donal's arm, and the boy turned away from Chloë.

'Listen, Donal, if you don't want to leave her, I can find my own way to the old church.'

'Can we not take her with us?'

'She's too weak to go anywhere, and so is Sarah. Neither of them could make a trip on a boat, even if we could get them away. We need to get the help to come to us.'

'I'll stay with her.'

'Promise me, Donal, if you hear anyone coming, you'll get back into that shaft as quick as you can, even if it means leaving Chloë behind.'

Addy saw he was fighting back tears, but he nodded. 'In a little while, get back into that shaft. See if you can find out anything about what's going on. It'll take me a couple of hours, going back the way we came, to get to the church, but we don't have any other choice.'

Again the boy nodded, and again, Addy thought about Charlie and a life that seemed a million miles away.

Adam

ADAM FOUND IT DIFFICULT TO THINK STRAIGHT ON the way to the hospital. They said Kate wasn't in danger, but there were complications. He had tried to get answers, but all he was told was that the consultant would talk to him when he arrived.

Almost on autopilot, he phoned Fitzsimons. 'Listen, I have a problem. Kate's been taken into hospital. I don't have any details yet, but I need you to get a few things organised.'

'Sure, boss, fire away.'

'That detective from Manhattan, Lee Fisher, he's on his way into Harcourt Street by taxi.'

'Okay.'

'I want the two of you to work together. Keep digging on Clarence Webb, and change the search from Jessica Fraser to Jessica Baxter.'

'Baxter?'

'She's Kevin Baxter's sister.'

'Shit.'

'Exactly. I want to know what she's been doing up until now, any previous offences, anything at all out of the ordinary, but there must be something on him too.'

'Okay.'

'Also, get on to that forensic writing specialist. I need to know if he's completed his analysis of the notes sent to Kate and the copy transcript from PIU. Apply any pressure that you can, and let the chief super know. Tell him there may be a link between O'Neill's death and the woman's statement. If he can get PIU talking, we might have enough to move this further.'

'Anything else?'

'Yeah. I had to cut short my visit to Malcolm Madden. He's supposed to be on his way to Harcourt Street to give a formal statement. Take the statement with Fisher, and push Madden any way you can, specifically around Valentine Pearson, Kate's late father. Turn the bastard upside down if you have to.'

With that, he hung up, remembering Kate had been due to meet Aoife earlier that day. He tried both Addy's and Aoife's numbers, but he got the usual 'out of coverage' reply. The last number he dialled was the Coplands'. Aoife's mother answered. After the usual pleasantries, he asked to talk to Aoife. When he heard she wasn't at home, he decided it could mean only one thing. She hadn't told her parents she was back.

Driving into the car park at St James's Hospital, he looked like a man possessed. First things first, he told himself. He needed to be sure that Kate was okay, and for now, everyone and everything else had to wait.

The Game Changer

Convincing Aoife to make that phone call to Kate wasn't difficult. The lie she was told is irrelevant too. What matters is that she did it. It was the reason the Game Changer chose her in the first place. Kate has never been able to refuse a lame duck.

Now she is exactly where the Game Changer wants her to be. Stephen did well, but allowing someone else to kill Kate was never on the cards. It seems she will lose the baby too – how utterly tragic.

Kate has always been the precious and sheltered one. Valentine Pearson used to be the Game Changer, but not any more. The irreverence with which he treated others, while protecting his one and only princess, must be atoned for, and when Kate is no more, this Game Changer will be gone, sipping café macchiato in warmer climates, with plenty of other people's money in the bank.

Everyone makes promises to themselves over time. The promises are like map points. The map points changed when the Game Changer caught up with Malcolm Madden. Everything became clearer, and the interest in Kate intensified from curiosity to the ultimate prize, worth far more than money could offer.

The death of the two remaining helpers in the fire caused unease, but death is death, and there is nothing that brings the do-gooders and inspiration seekers together like human loss.

(Page 1 of 1)

373

Kate

DAYLIGHT WAS CREEPING IN AROUND THE WINDOW blinds, and as Kate came in and out of sleep, everything in the room was out of focus. She could hear the 'bleep, bleep' of the monitors behind her, her body too sore to move. What had she been dreaming about?

Distant sounds, car horns, motorbikes, barely audible, came in from outside, everything seeming muffled or cast away to another time and space. She could remember only part of her dream. She had been in that room again, the one in the Portakabin. She could hear a dog barking. She was cold, and more frightened than she had ever been. Then the dream skipped. She saw her father's face. It wasn't angry, it was reassuring, telling her everything would be okay. Where was her mother? Why wasn't she in the dream? Then, she was back in her old bedroom, and Kevin was outside the window. He was with that man and the girl. She wanted the girl to turn around, but no matter how much she wanted it, the girl wouldn't turn.

There was something else. When she looked down at the girl's hands, she was holding a bird, a jackdaw with an ugly mottled beak and closed eyelids. Kate felt something heavy in her hands. She was holding the jackdaw now. It kept getting heavier and heavier, as if she was carrying a baby, not a bird.

The bird was dead, and in the dream, she was trying to tell Adam about the baby, but all the time she felt weighed down, and the heaviness of the dead jackdaw became onerous, like a stone boulder. Her hands wanted to let go, but she couldn't.

Her dream skipped again. She was in front of the secondary

school. The one Charlie would go to when he was older. He was there with his little sister. They were holding hands. He looked so protective of her. He loved his little sister so much. Somebody was calling her name. They were saying it over and over. The voice was familiar, caring.

'Kate,' the voice said, 'can you hear me? It's Adam.'

Special Detective Unit, Harcourt Street

AS LEE ENTERED HARCOURT STREET STATION, HE thought of 7th Precinct on the Lower East Side, where he spent most of his working life. The precinct wasn't unlike many others within the NYPD, unremarkable apart from the investigations they handled, with the best part of ten homicides a month. From the array of whiteboards within the Special Detective Unit, the number of investigations wasn't quite so high, but the place had more in common with a New York precinct than it was different.

Passing through the public section at the front of the building, he noticed a young girl sitting alone, staring at her mobile phone. She glanced at him, and he nodded, but her glare said, Back off. Not everyone is friendly here. He thought about Adam O'Connor, and his hurried departure to see Kate Pearson. He wanted to reverse roles. He wanted it to be him visiting Marjorie, but she was dead, and as he entered the incident room, and took in the photographs of Ethel and Michael O'Neill's bodies from various angles on the incident-room boards, sentiment, he knew, had no place there.

He was keen to get his teeth into Malcolm Madden again, and Fitzsimons had set up Interview Room 9A, which he mentioned was a favourite with O'Connor. Lee felt as if he was slipping into the detective's shoes, but he was comfortable there, even if there were a few thousand miles between Dublin and Manhattan.

Malcolm Madden took a seat opposite him, a small square wooden table between them. Fitzsimons stood to the side, leaning against the wall. The well-groomed psychologist seemed taller in the interview room, but less at ease, which was exactly where Fisher wanted him.

'Malcolm, you were telling us about your re-acquaintance with Jessica Baxter.'

'She was a client and a friend.'

'So you say.'

'I say it because it's true.'

'You're a believer in truth, are you, Malcolm?'

He didn't respond.

'You told us earlier that you harboured guilt about events from the past, namely the abuse of Jessica Baxter and her brother.'

'Yes, but I believe there may have been others too. I can't be sure.'

'And your relationship with Kate's father was complicated? You felt he didn't appreciate your gifts?' Rattle the cage, he thought.

'He appreciated enough to ask me to do his dirty work for him.'

'Was he involved in the abuse?'

'No. He wasn't like O'Neill, or some of the others, but he wasn't without sin.'

'Are you religious?'

'No. What I mean is Valentine often lived up to his romantic name.'

'I don't get you.'

Malcolm let out a long sigh.

Lee allowed the silence to hover for a while, then said, 'Come on, Malcolm. There's no client-privilege argument here.'

'It all happened a long time ago.'

'So I gather.'

'Valentine had a reputation.'

'For what?'

'He was a complicated man. As I said earlier, he liked to be at the centre of things.'

'And?'

'He was also prone to bouts of anger.'

'Beating up his wife? Is that what you mean?'

'I used to look up to him as a mentor. At the beginning he helped me a great deal.'

'Financially?'

'Yes, when I was studying, and in the early days of my practice.'

'So, you owed him?'

'You could say that.'

'And you would have helped him if he'd found himself in some kind of trouble?'

'Yes.'

'And did he find himself in some kind of trouble?'

'More than once.'

'How?' Lee raised his eyebrows.

'He had an eye for the ladies. It fed into his need to be at the centre of things, admired.'

'I sense you're holding something back, Malcolm.'

'He wanted me to give someone money for him.'

'Are we talking blackmail?'

'Not quite, but close.'

'When was this?'

'1988.'

'Which would have been around the time of those so-called experimental studies being stopped?'

'Yes.'

'So, the blackmail and the experiments are connected?'

'It wasn't anything to do with that – not directly.'

Adam

SITTING BY KATE'S HOSPITAL BED ADAM THOUGHT she might have heard him, after he'd said her name the last time: her eyelids had fluttered, but then nothing.

The consultant, Professor Bradshaw, had already told him about the baby. It was early days, he said, but there was no doubt that the survival of the foetus had been compromised by the accident. It would be touch and go for a while. The collision had fractured Kate's ribs, which had punctured one of her lungs. This had caused internal bleeding. If the damage had been any lower down, the foetus wouldn't have had a chance. The consultant was optimistic that Kate would regain consciousness; it was a question of time. They had carried out a computerised axial tomography scan of the brain, and it had come up clear. The brain, he told Adam, like the rest of the human body, had a way of knowing what was best for its survival. Right now, it was telling Kate it needed rest.

Adam had made contact with Declan. He and Charlie were getting the next flight over. It felt weird, telling your partner's ex-husband about something like this. There was no training manual for such things. Part of him was relieved that Declan would be there. It meant he could keep up to speed with the investigation, and where Kate fitted into it. Another part of him didn't want Declan to be at her bedside, especially if Kate regained consciousness while Adam was away. At least he had been able to arrange for a continual police presence outside her door.

Slouching in the armchair, he knew Fisher and Fitzsimons were still interviewing Malcolm Madden, but he needed to think about the information Fitzsimons had been able to feed through to him.

PIU had confirmed Jessica Fraser, *née* Baxter, was the abuse victim who had supplied the statements to the unit. Her past, and that of her brother, hadn't been happy. Their mother, Sharon, had been diagnosed with bipolar disorder, characterised by episodes of mania and depression, fifteen years before her death. During her manic phases, she would break away from reality, ignoring her children. Those with the condition, like Sharon, used alcohol or mood-adjusting drugs during the manic phases to slow things down, and afterwards to lift them when the depression came. During the mania, their self-esteem was inflated to the point of grandiosity. Typical behaviour included obsessive spending sprees, doing things to the extreme, and exhibiting unusual sexual behaviour.

Some of this had come to light when they had looked at the connection to Kevin's suspicious death. Adam already knew that the boy's mother had died shortly after her son. He didn't yet know how Jessica fitted in. The feedback from the writing analysis would take more time, but if Jessica had sent the anonymous notes, he needed to know why. Surely both she and Kate had been victims. Could it be payback for Kate, who had not suffered the same fate, or was there more to it? Jessica Baxter had gone from one foster home to another, but she could hardly blame Kate for that.

Clarence Webb had an equally depressing past. He and Jessica had first crossed paths in their late teens, when they were fostered by the same family. He had a number of minor convictions, but nothing recent. Apparently that part of what Madden had said was true. Webb was involved with setting up a meditative group at one point, but it had fizzled out a number of months before. From what Fitzsimons could gather, Webb wasn't the brightest spark.

Adam thought about Kate, how much he cared for her, and the two of them having a child together. He had made a mess of it the first time around with Addy, running away from his responsibilities and deservedly paying the price. There had still been no contact from Addy or Aoife. Marion was going up the walls. If he could have got hold of his son at that moment, he'd have given him an almighty talking-to. He gazed at Kate, wondering what she would do in his place.

He stretched out in the chair, knowing it would be another hour before Declan and Charlie arrived. He listened as a hospital trolley passed the door, the wheels spinning. It was then that he heard a low voice call his name. At first, he thought he had imagined it, until the voice called again, and he knew Kate was awake.

Addy

ADRENALIN PUSHED ADDY FORWARD. HE WAS thinking about Chloë and Sarah, how weak they both were. He thought about Aoife, and Donal too, and how the boy placed so much faith in him. When he finally got out on to solid ground, his first mission was to get to the church. Something told him that now every second counted.

Before reaching the church grounds, he saw the boat pull into the shore, carrying more supplies. Even from a distance, he recognised Stephen. His return meant trouble. He hoped Donal had done as he'd told him, and that he was safe, even though nothing and nowhere on the island felt safe.

At the entrance to the church grounds, he saw numerous old gravestones. They looked like twisted rocks being swallowed by the earth. The front door was blocked by wooden planks, but Donal had said that the bottom ones were loose. All he had to do was pull them back and push the door in.

The interior was smaller than he'd expected, with rotten wooden pews. The smell of damp hit his nostrils. He saw cracks in the whitewashed wall, some laden with moss, and parts of the plasterwork had broken off in large chunks, leaving gaping holes, like decaying skin. The wooden beams in the ceiling looked suspect too, as if at any moment one might fall. At the top end of the church, there was an altar with a table made of black marble. When he got closer, he saw it was covered with slime and muck. He jumped backwards as something furry scurried past his ankles. He thought it was a rat, but it was a fox escaping through a hole underneath the church wall.

Donal had told him to go as high in the spire as he could, and even before he started the climb, his heart was pounding. Near the top, his hands were shaking. He took out his mobile phone. The battery was about to die, but he needed to call Adam. His father would know what to do. The phone bleeped: only four per cent of battery left. Shit, he thought, but he could see two signal bars. A series of text messages came in, first from his mother, then Adam, and then his mother again. He didn't bother reading any of them. Instead he pressed the dial button, listening as it rang out, once, twice, three times. 'Come on! Bloody answer!' But the call kept ringing, finally going to voicemail. Two seconds later, the phone was dead, and it was only then he realised something or someone was moving around outside. Could he have been followed? He had to be careful. Remain calm. He couldn't fuck up now.

Listening again, he heard the wind whizzing around the church spire. Maybe he'd been mistaken. He swallowed hard, counting to ten, wanting to make sure the coast was clear before he punched the four zeros into Sarah's phone. It took him a while to find her contacts. He scrolled to favourites, looking for anyone called John, worrying that there might be more than one, but breathing a sigh of relief when he found the number he needed. Before phoning, he heard footsteps, the crunch of twigs underfoot, and people mumbling. Shit. He couldn't stop now, even if the others were close by. He dialled the number, knowing he was running out of time.

'Hello,' a man's voice answered.

'Are you Sarah's husband?' Addy kept his voice low.

'Who is this?'

'You don't know me, but I know Sarah.' The words fumbled out as fast as he could say them. 'You have to listen to me. Her life is in danger. Things are not right here. There was a fire. Sarah and some others have been drugged. You need to get help. Something is going to happen, something big.' He drew a breath and, for the first time, acknowledged what had been in his head all along: 'People could die.'

'Who is this?' John Sinclair sounded suspicious, fearful.

'Addy, my name's Addy. You have to phone my father, Adam O'Connor, tell him what I've told you.'

'The detective?'

The footsteps were getting closer. Addy didn't have much longer.

'Tell him people are in danger. There's a cult here on the island, led by a guy called Saka.'

'Where are you?' John Sinclair yelled down the phone, registering the name, Saka, the name he had come to hate.

'The island's called Colton, off the south-west coast.'

Addy heard the church door being kicked in. 'They're about to take me. Tell my dad, there's children here and we're running out of time.'

Special Detective Unit, Harcourt Street

LEE HAD NO IDEA WHAT MALCOLM MADDEN WOULD tell them next, but he had been long enough in the game to read body language. The man's mood had changed since he'd arrived. Initially he had been cagey about answering questions, but now it seemed to bring him some kind of relief to get the information off his chest.

'I knew the moment I saw Jessica who she was. The family resemblance was extraordinary.'

'What do you mean by the family resemblance?'

'To Valentine and then, by extension, to Kate.'

'You're saying Jessica was related to Kate and Valentine Pearson?'

'Yes. That's why the money passed hands. Sharon Baxter claimed Valentine was Jessica's father. He didn't believe her. He'd slept with her, all right, during one of her normal phases.'

'Normal phases?'

'She suffered from bipolar disorder.'

Fitzsimons nodded at Lee, confirming what he'd told O'Connor.

Malcolm kept talking: 'Valentine didn't know that at the time. To be honest, I don't think it was even a fling, more like a one-night stand. She wasn't of the same social standing as him, but very attractive. There was no denying that.'

'Valentine thought the mother was lying?'

'Yes. He was in denial, wanting to believe his version of the truth. He could have insisted on a paternity test, but he didn't.'

'And this happened in 1988?'

'Yes.'

'When Jessica was a minor?'

'Correct.'

'Why wait so long to pay the money? Why didn't it happen directly after the girl's birth, or even before?'

'I don't know.'

Lee's mind was doing somersaults, even though, outwardly, no one would have guessed. 'Malcolm, can I share something with you?'

'What?'

'Kate had a theory about you.'

'What kind of theory?'

'She thought that your having been marginalised from the group all those years ago had in some way undermined you.'

'I can't say I was happy about it.'

'What do you know about cults?'

'Cults?'

'I'm not in the habit of repeating myself, Malcolm. You heard me the first time. What kind of people form them?'

'Usually they have narcissistic qualities. A desire for power, money and other rewards is high within this personality type, and manipulation of others becomes a means of feeding their low self-worth.'

'Do you have low self-worth?'

'No.'

'Does Jessica Baxter?'

'Yes, but I hardly think … I mean, she was a victim in all this.'

'A victim, who, as a girl, you knew was being abused.'

'I've already told you my views. It was wrong of me, but I wasn't the worst.'

'What about Valentine?'

'What about him?'

'Did he know Jessica was abused by his educationally minded pals?'

The Game Changer

CENTRE OF LIGHTNESS
20 Steps to Self-enlightenment Programme

The shock and uncertainty in the intervening hours since the fire has left members looking for guidance. Leave people out on a limb for long enough, and they'll be drawn to those with answers.

Stephen is back. He will deliver the death speech. The Game Changer is required elsewhere.

At some point, people will want to attribute blame, and the finger will be pointed at Saka. Poor, stupid Clarence: he loved getting a new name, such grandiose ideals.

The senior members will supervise the initial suicide watch. After that, dissenters will be separated from the group and corralled into the main hall for further guidance. Sufficient quantities of carbon monoxide will be administered when the doors are locked, and others, including Stephen, will ensure that Saka's instructions are carried out to the letter. The final deaths will be those in the infirmary, quickly followed by the senior members and leaders, who will be the last of the self-administered suicides. They will remain until the very end, a reward for having reached the twentieth step.

I hate them all, every last one of them. None of them has suffered like me. None of them could ever dream of understanding, or coming close to, my power.

Power is a strange thing. The less power other people have, the more you possess. The final death speech will be simple.

(Page 1 of 3)

387

CENTRE OF LIGHTNESS
20 Steps to Self-enlightenment Programme

DEATH SPEECH

The pivotal moment of transition is close at hand. Saka understands his family like a loving father. We started this journey looking for enlightenment, seeking truth. We have gained strength together, individually and as a group, despite and because of what we have suffered.

Others have doubted us, but we see beyond their ignorance and bias. There may still be doubters among you, too, those who are not ready to transcend, but believe this: this truth is our destiny.

The fire was the sign Saka was waiting for. Self-realisation forms our new consciousness. It isn't a flash of insight, or a concept that comes from books or the words of wise men. Self-realisation is not inside your head, a muscular component of your mind. It goes further than that and we have to go further than that to find it.

We have dismissed so many lies, which others have tried to impose on us. Spiritual awakening is bigger than any of their illusions. Anything that isn't about that, you must discard.

Infinity and infinite truth are near. Your moments of blackest despair will soon be gone. You will no longer wear the lenses of other people's stupidity.

(Page 2 of 3)

CENTRE OF LIGHTNESS
20 Steps to Self-enlightenment Programme

You see things as they really are and that life as we know it has no meaning. The truth is in the destruction of that life.

Your freedom is an existence beyond the shackles of earthly bonds. Like the insects that crawled along the ground, and who ultimately grew wings, take your new form.

As your leader, when you hear this, I will already have gone on this adventure. If you love me, you too will follow.

Life is self-limiting. I wait for you now. Our shared and greater reality can no longer be denied.

SAKA

Final Notes
The instructions given to Stephen and the others are clear. After the reading of the speech in the main hall, there will be a period of adjustment, and an opportunity to visit Saka in death. This will be followed by communal reflection, before the division of people into two groupings. Those who wish to join Saka in death, and those who need more time to choose. Logistics are in place to ensure a swift and effective enactment.

(Page 3 of 3)

Kate

'ADAM, IS THE BABY OKAY?' KATE'S VOICE WAS BARELY above a whisper.

He took her hand in his, kissing it. 'It's early days, Kate, but so far so good. The consultant says you need plenty of rest.'

Kate closed her eyes, a mix of relief and anxiety flooding in. 'Adam, what if something happens? What if it doesn't work out? What if …'

'It will work out. If that baby is as determined as the woman I'm looking at, everything will be fine.'

She attempted a smile. 'And, how do you feel about it?'

'Kate, I love you. I love you more than anything. If I'm being honest, I'm nervous about being a father again, but part of me already loves that baby as much as I love you. I only hope I can be a better dad this time around.'

'What if it's a girl? I dreamed it was a girl.'

'Then myself and Charlie will have a battle on our hands.' He kissed her forehead. 'Are you in a lot of pain?'

'My chest hurts, and it's hard to breathe.' She paused, closing her eyes again. 'I remember seeing a car coming out from the side, but I can't remember anything after that.'

'We haven't any details on the car yet, other than a witness hearing it pull away at speed, then seeing you at the side of the road. The consultant thinks you travelled some distance. It's a miracle …'

'I didn't get to see Aoife.' She panicked. 'I was early for our appointment – maybe she came afterwards and thinks I didn't turn up.'

'I don't know what's up with Aoife. I rang her parents. They haven't seen her.'

'What about Addy?'

'Stop worrying about that pair. Declan's on his way here with Charlie.'

'But—'

'There was no point in telling him not to come. I certainly wouldn't have listened if our roles were reversed. And there's twenty-four-hour security on the door. Declan won't let Charlie out of his sight.'

'Okay, I guess.'

'When they get here, I may have to slip out for a while. There are a few loose ends I need to look into.'

'What kind of loose ends?'

'The woman who gave the statements to PIU is Kevin Baxter's sister.'

Kate scrunched her forehead, trying to take in the information. 'I don't understand.'

'Fisher and I interviewed Madden earlier. He's in Harcourt Street as we speak. I'm expecting a call at any moment but, according to Madden, she made contact with him fairly recently. He says he was trying to help her but ...'

'What?'

'Kate, I really don't think I should be worrying you with any of this.'

'You'll worry me more if you don't tell me.'

'She's been renting your old house from Holmes & Co. There's another guy connected as well, a Clarence Webb. They were the ones I got the information from during the house-to-house.'

'Where is she now? Kevin Baxter's sister?'

'Her name's Jessica. We don't know where she is.'

Kate remembered the name Pat Grant had given her. She put her hand up to her head.

'Kate, are you all right?'

'Was Jessica fostered, like Kevin?'

'Yes. Their mother wasn't well. She suffered from bipolar.'

'When was it diagnosed?'

'Before Jessica was born.' He leaned closer to her. 'Listen, Kate, I want you to stop thinking about all that now. The priority is you and the baby.'

'I know.' She swallowed hard.

'And try not to talk so much.'

'Adam, why did she want to live in my old house?'

'That's enough, Kate. Stop trying to find answers. Trust me, I'll get to the bottom of this.' He kissed her on the lips, gently, lovingly.

'Adam, I remember something else. I saw a young man's face behind the steering wheel. I'm not sure I'd be able to describe him. It all happened so fast.'

'Don't worry about that either, not now.'

'Are you sure?'

'Of course I'm sure.'

His mobile rang. 'Hold on a second,' he said, 'it's Harcourt Street. I need to take this.'

Addy

ADDY HAD NOWHERE TO HIDE. THE CHURCH WAS small. They would find him in seconds, and if he had Sarah's phone on him, that would mean trouble too. It wasn't going to take a lot more for that door to open, especially with the number of kicks being applied. He climbed down from the spire, jumping the last bit when he was near the bottom. He hurt his ankle, but managed to push the phone into the hole the fox had scurried through.

'What are you up to?' Stephen shouted, as the door crashed to the ground. His joy at catching Addy unawares was all too clear. He had two other male members with him.

'Nothing.'

'Finding religious inspiration?'

'You could say that.' Addy tried to sound calm, even though he knew Stephen wasn't buying it.

Stephen moved closer, and Addy flinched when he saw him pull out a knife and twirl it in his hand, like before, as if he was trying to decide what to do next.

'I saw you sneak in here.' Stephen sniggered, placing the blade underneath Addy's chin.

'I'm one of you now,' Addy answered.

'Is that right?' Stephen twisted the blade, drawing blood. 'We'll see about that, won't we, men?'

The two other members grabbed his arms, and Addy knew there was no escape. He wasn't sure if John Sinclair had believed him, but at least he had made the call. Now his choice was simple. Either put up a fight and lose, or hope that somehow, if he got back to the commune buildings, Donal could help him.

Adam

ADAM LISTENED AS FISHER RECITED THE information Malcolm Madden had given him. None of it was good news, and Valentine Pearson's role was far murkier than Kate would be able to cope with right now. According to Malcolm, as far as Kate's abduction was concerned, it was a classic case of mistaken identity, exactly as Kate had suspected. Her disappearance had caused the cracks to appear, and Valentine had finally got wise to what had been going on, shutting down the grouping. He wasn't responsible *per se*, but he was certainly guilty of not notifying the authorities. Neither had he dug any deeper at the time to find out the identity of the victims. In Malcolm Madden's opinion, somehow or other, a number of years later Valentine had found out the truth, and although he couldn't be completely sure, Malcolm suspected that he had discovered something else, perhaps a more serious wrongdoing, worse possibly than even the abuse. From then on, Valentine had been a broken man. His arrogance, his angry outbursts, the infidelity had all stopped.

Adam remembered what Kate had told him about the night her father had taken her aside and apologised to her. Maybe he had just found out. By then Jessica would have been a grown woman. Not that it excused anything, but it explained why he had changed so dramatically.

'Is Malcolm still at Harcourt Street?' Adam asked.

'For now, although the only thing we can get him on is obstructing justice by holding back information.'

'Keep squeezing him. Someone has to do time for what happened back then, and right now, he's our only live candidate.'

'I've checked the airlines. We've found a match for Jessica Fraser on a flight to New York, two days before Tom Mason's killing. She was alone.'

'Lee, did Malcolm say how much Jessica knew about what went down?'

'She knew a lot, and my guess is that Malcolm did his fair share of filling in the blanks. He saw her as the victim in all this, and he was her knight in shining armour.'

'Hardly shining?'

'I suppose that's subjective. From what I can tell, he still thinks he's one of the good guys. Adam, what are you thinking?'

'That after Mason and O'Neill were killed, depending on what she discovered from Malcolm, there could have been a shift of emphasis.'

Adam looked at Kate. She was still asleep, but he took the rest of the call outside.

'Lee, are you still there?'

'Yeah.'

'It makes sense that as soon as she found out Valentine Pearson could be her father she turned her attention to Kate. She may have been watching her for years, because of Valentine's connection with the group, or maybe somehow she found out that Kate had been luckier than her and got away. But a number of things are slotting into place.'

'I don't think Malcolm Madden realised he was putting Kate in danger. Jessica had him wrapped around her little finger.'

'Is Fitzsimons there?'

'He's beside me.'

'Ask him to get on to that script specialist. I'm pretty sure the sender of the notes to Kate is Jessica Baxter, but we need him to look at Amanda Doyle's letter again. That, potentially, is a bomb waiting to go off. For all we know, that other guy, Clarence Webb, could be the Saka character.'

'Like a front man, a fall-guy for Jessica?'

'Yeah. What did Malcolm say when you asked him about cults? Did he think Jessica was capable of it?'

'He said no, but he was blind-sided, Adam, only he doesn't want to admit it yet.'

'It all feels too crazy.'

'I've known prisoners to be murdered because they snore in their sleep. Nothing surprises me any more.'

'We'll need a photo of Jessica Baxter.'

'Fitzsimons is organising that now, and I'll keep the pressure on Malcolm Madden.'

'Okay.'

'Are you going to tell Kate any of this?'

'She has enough worrying her without me adding more to the list. Look, Lee, I have to go. The chief super is phoning me.'

It was only as he hung up that he noticed the missed calls from Addy and an unknown number. They must have come through when he'd had his phone on silent.

He answered the chief super, listening as he told him about John Sinclair's phone call. A series of miniature explosions went off in his head. It hadn't crossed his mind that Addy could be connected to any of this, but he'd soon joined the pieces together, and when he had, he knew he must move fast. That phone call had also put Aoife's meeting with Kate in a different light. It could be part of all this. Ethel O'Neill had been killed by a hit-and-run, which meant what had happened to Kate might not have been an accident. He had no time to waste on the script analysis. His gut told him Kate had been right all along, which meant that a great many other things were wrong. The chief super had made contact with the police commissioner: a full marine and air operation was already in place. He didn't want to leave Kate, but there wasn't a damn thing he could do about it.

'What's wrong?' Kate asked, when he came back into the room.

'Kate, I have to go, but I don't want you to worry. I've had a chat with Matthews outside, and I'll be back as soon as I can.'

'But—'

'Rest now. I'll phone you later. I've told Matthews not to let anyone in other than hospital staff, Declan or Charlie. They should be here in the next few minutes.'

∞

On his way to pick up John Sinclair, Adam dealt with one call after another. It was a risk having Sinclair involved, but the chief super was right: he might be able to ID Saka. He rang Fitzsimons too. 'Is there any word on that image of Jessica Baxter?'

'We should have it from Justice in the next half an hour.'

'When it comes in, get a copy over to Matthews, and keep working with Fisher.'

The last call he made was to Declan, telling him how Kate was doing. In less than an hour, the air and sea response units would be in place, and after that, who knew when he would get back?

Addy

STEPHEN HELD THE KNIFE AT HIS SIDE ON THE WAY back to the commune buildings, constantly turning it in his hand. Addy didn't take his eyes off him for a second. He could tell that Stephen was on some kind of high, and even though few words were spoken, the bits of conversation Addy heard told him they were excited about something, and Stephen was going to be an important part of it.

When he finally pushed him into the room below ground, two things came into his mind at once. First, Donal: he hoped they hadn't found him; and, second, that somehow he would be able to get Addy out of there.

The look on Stephen's face as he pulled the door closed, locking it behind him, told Addy he would be back. He was a psycho, nothing surer. At some point, the bastard intended using that knife on him. He wouldn't forget about Addy. It was only a question of time.

∞

For what seemed an eternity, he listened for any sound other than the pipes gurgling in their chambers. If Donal had managed it before, he should be able to manage it again.

When he heard movement outside the door, at first he thought Stephen had come back, but then he heard Donal's voice. 'Addy?'

'Donal, get me out of here.'

He heard the key turn in the lock, and when Donal opened the door, he could have hugged the boy.

'Addy, something terrible is about to happen.'

'It's okay, Donal. Calm down. I got a message through to Sarah's husband, but I can't be sure he'll send help.'

'Addy, I did what you told me. I got back in the shaft. There was another big meeting. I heard some of the speech. Stephen gave it. It didn't sound good.'

'Donal, think carefully. Tell me what you heard.'

'It was about how they were going to find truth and enlightenment and all that other stuff, but this time it was different.'

'Why?'

'Stephen said their time had come.'

'What did he mean?'

'I don't know, but Saka's dead.'

'He can't be!'

'He is, and Stephen says they need to follow him. I heard Stephen talk to some of the seniors too.'

'And?'

'They're all going to see Saka, and then they're going to do it.'

'Donal, slow down. Tell me word for word.'

'They're going to divide the members into groups. Then everyone who wants to follow Saka will go to the other side. That's what he said, and the journey will be painless.'

'Shit.'

'That's not all, Addy. He said that if you don't want to follow Saka, there will be a gathering in the main hall this evening.'

'Do you know why?'

'No.'

'Donal, if Saka is dead, why isn't Jessica in charge? She's the next in line, isn't she?'

'I don't know. I didn't see her. What do you think we should do?'

'Give me a second.'

'The boat has gone. It left ages ago.'

'Listen, Donal, we need to go back to the old church. Sarah's phone's still there. We have to try again.'

Kate

WITH ADAM GONE, KATE COULDN'T SETTLE. HER chest felt tight, and even though she knew the baby was still hanging on in there, she had to ask herself how any of this could be a good start in life.

Despite the soreness of her ribcage, the one thing, other than the baby, she remained focused on was Charlie. When he and Declan arrived, she thought her heart would burst. She couldn't hold back tears of happiness.

'Don't cry, Mum.'

'Oh, Charlie, I've missed you so much.'

'Dad said you were knocked down by a car.'

'Don't worry about that. I'm fine. A few days in hospital and I'll be as right as rain.'

Declan bent to kiss her forehead. 'I see you have your own special company sitting outside the door.'

'It's just a precaution. Adam insisted.'

'He's probably right.'

'Mum, are you sure you're okay?' Charlie asked, sitting on the armchair that Adam had not long since vacated.

'There's nothing to worry about.'

'Where's Adam now?' Declan asked.

'I think he had to go back to Harcourt Street. Something's happening with the investigation.'

'You two are well matched.'

'Maybe we are,' Kate replied, but the last thing she needed was friction with Declan. 'Have you two had any breakfast?'

'We got something on the plane.'

'That's good.'

'According to the nurse, we can stay for fifteen minutes at a time and then we have to let you rest.'

'Can we not stay, Dad?'

'Don't worry, Charlie,' Declan replied, 'we'll be in and out seeing Mum all day long.'

John

JOHN WATCHED THE SEAGULLS SWIRL OVERHEAD, sounding as if they were in mock celebration, as if they already sensed things that no one on the police marine boat could possibly know. Desperation can leave a person without hope, he thought, and a belief that nothing you can do will change anything. That was how he'd felt when Sarah left.

He listened to the loud hum of the engine as the boat cut through the water, amid furious high winds. The sounds harnessed his anger – a warped, twisted knot of rage that things could come to this.

He tried to ignore the others moving about on the craft, shouting across at one another against the savage wind. None of them understood what he felt or the hate he had for the madness that had taken his wife away. He could still see her as she had been on that last day: the day he had turned his back on her, and she had slipped away.

He remembered how she wore her hair, wild and loose. Over the previous months it had grown to waist-length, as it had been when she was a young girl. He'd always liked it long.

He wondered for the umpteenth time how slim the chance was that she was okay, and how long it would take her to become his Sarah again.

The detective, DI O'Connor, called his name, then raised both hands in the air, his fingers wide apart, telling John that in ten minutes they would be there. He clenched his fists. There were tears in his eyes. A hand rested on his shoulder, and when he turned, it was O'Connor.

'Are you okay?' he asked, standing close enough to stop John jumping overboard.

'I'm fine.' His words had been quick and false.

He looked to the island and the unknown. The boy had said people had died in a fire, that Sarah and others were in danger. With his feet stuck to the deck, he kept staring at the water. The waves were creating changing sheets of white foam. What if he hadn't been so angry? What if he hadn't given up? What if he hadn't let her go or had somehow made it possible for her to come home?

Adam

HE HAD SENT JUST ONE HELICOPTER TO FLY overland, not wanting to raise suspicion. The report back was that everything looked quiet on the island. From the air, it all seemed normal, and Adam hoped that was exactly how he would find it when they got ashore. He knew, from the overhead report, the location of the commune buildings, which he assumed would be where most of the people on the island would be found.

When the boat pulled in, he despatched four different crews to approach the buildings by foot from the north, south, east and west, all with dogs. He told John Sinclair to remain on the boat until he knew what was going on. If he needed more backup, there were officers on standby on the nearest main island, Valentia. They could be there within minutes by helicopter.

With the buildings in sight, he told his own crew to stay back, as they watched the four police groupings come within metres of the target area. So far, they seemed to have got there unnoticed, but it was all too peaceful. Something wasn't right.

He signalled his crew to move forward again, and when they reached higher ground, he could see the old church to the left of the commune building.

'We'll need to check that,' he said, as if thinking out loud.

'Sir?'

'What is it, McGarry?' Adam turned to face one of the female officers.

'I think I saw something.'

'What?'

'I don't know, but it looks like someone's in there. I saw something move past the front door.'

Switching on his walkie-talkie, he made contact with each of the four lead officers of the crews up ahead, telling them not to move in until they had checked the church.

∞

'Did you hear something?' Addy asked Donal, as they scurried to hide behind the granite boulder in front of the altar.

'No.'

'Maybe help is here already.'

'Addy, do you think so?'

'I don't know, but let's get that phone either way.' He hoped it was still there. He reached in, felt it under his fingertips, and heaved a huge sigh of relief.

They jumped when the door swung open, and a female voice shouted, 'Police! If anyone is here, show yourselves.'

Addy dragged Donal up to stand beside him, putting his arms up in the air as he had seen done on television, and Donal copied him. When Addy saw Adam's face, he couldn't believe it.

'Shit! Addy, is that you?'

Adam ran over, signalling to his crew to check the rest of the place. He reached out and grabbed Addy, hugging him tight. Then he stepped back and asked, 'What's going down?'

'There's some kind of mass suicide planned,' Addy told him, breathless. 'Donal overheard some of the members talking.'

'The members?'

'The cult followers.'

'What about this Saka guy?'

'He's dead. He wants the others to follow him.'

'Jesus.'

'Dad, what do you think?'

Even in the mayhem, Addy realised it was the first time he had referred to Adam that way. The look in his father's eyes told him he

405

had registered it too. Adam didn't reply for a couple of seconds, but then said, 'I don't know, son, but I don't like how quiet everything is. How long have you two been in here?'

'Only a few minutes,' Addy replied, 'but it took us a couple of hours to get out of the commune buildings through the water-pipe chambers.'

'How many are inside?'

'I'm not sure.'

'Who's in charge?'

'The leaders, like Stephen. They're up to no good. We haven't seen Jessica, but she's the next in line from Saka.'

'Jessica?'

'Yeah.'

'Shit.'

'What is it?'

'Don't worry, I'll explain later. What about that woman Sarah? You said her life was in danger. Where is she?'

'She's with Chloë, Donal's friend. They're in the infirmary.'

The Game Changer

Kate will suffer. She will know fear, taste it.

It wasn't simply because she was the one who got away, or that Valentine, the Game Changer of my life, protected her instead of me. If it was only that, I could have walked away.

Knowing I was of his flesh and blood was the final outrage. No amount of money would let me turn away from that.

The Game Changer has carried hate before, waiting for the right time, ensuring all the components were in place, where revenge could be aligned with ultimate power, but now Kate has proved to be the final atonement for our father's sins.

Valentine made a choice. He saved Kate. He turned his back on me, his other daughter. I have no doubt that, in his eyes, I wasn't deserving of his love. Instead I received his disdain.

At some point, someone was going to have to pay the price.

(Page 1 of 1)

Adam

THE NUMBER OF PEOPLE NEEDING IMMEDIATE attention at the commune was in excess of a hundred. Adam recognised Amanda Doyle and Robert Cotter from their missing-person photographs. At least a dozen people were dead, but the number could still increase if the medics failed to pull some others through. The scale of what had gone down was too enormous for Adam or any of his crew to take in, at least not fully.

It hadn't taken long to round up the senior members, those who had facilitated the suicides, following Saka's final instruction to the letter. John Sinclair had identified the dead cult leader, but not before he had been reunited with his wife.

Looking at the two of them together, and how much love John obviously had for Sarah, Adam wondered how things between them could have gone so wrong.

Aoife would pull through, and the medics were hopeful about Chloë, too.

'Are you all right, Dad?' Addy asked, standing by his side.

'I should be asking you that, not the other way around.'

'I'm sorry.'

'Why?' Adam looked at his son, confused.

'For not giving you a chance when you were trying so hard.'

'I walked away from you. That was unforgivable.'

'I thought that for a while, but you never gave up on me, not completely. Mum said you used to stay in touch, making sure I was okay.'

'But I wasn't part of your life.'

'That doesn't matter now. When I needed you most, you came.'

'I would have come regardless of who made that call.'

'But it wasn't anyone else. It was me.'

Adam grabbed his son, hugging him even harder than he had before, and longer than he'd ever thought possible. When Addy's body started to shake with tears of relief, Adam still held him, determined to hang on to him for as long as it took, even if that meant the rest of his life.

Kate

KATE KEPT FALLING IN AND OUT OF SLEEP, RELIEVED every time she saw Charlie come back into the room. She hadn't heard anything from Adam yet, but she didn't mind. Everything would happen in its own good time. Pulling back from work all those months ago hadn't meant she had pulled back from life. Despite all the upset over the last few weeks, and everything she had remembered from her past, the harassment notes, the wrongs that had been visited on Jessica Baxter and others, she was grateful for all the love she had been lucky enough to receive.

Charlie was with her, and soon Adam would join him. With the new life fighting for survival inside her, they would forge forward and create a future.

When the door opened, she looked up, expecting to see Charlie and Declan, but a woman came in. She walked over to the bed, and placed a police ID card in front of her. Immediately Kate thought something had happened to Adam.

'Is everything all right? Is Adam okay?'

'Everything is perfect,' the officer replied.

'Sorry, when I saw you I thought something had happened to Adam.'

'Don't worry about him, Kate. It's you and me now.'

'Do I know you?'

Kate stared at the woman. There was something about the way she looked at her, with revulsion, loathing, that unnerved her … and there was something else. She had seen her before. Where? Her features were familiar, and as one thought crashed into the next, her mind flashed back McDonald's, when she had scanned the room for someone watching her and Charlie. Could it be the same woman? And what was it about her that had stayed with Kate? Whatever serenity Kate had felt a few moments earlier was disappearing fast. Suddenly all she could think of was the notes, and the woman who had given the statements to the PIU, the woman who had rented her old house from Malcolm Madden, Kevin Baxter's sister, close to her in age, but that wasn't all of it. There was a familiarity of features. Kate looked so much like her.

'You're not stupid, Kate. I'm sure you've pulled most of this together, and don't be thinking that the police officer outside will save you. I'm very good at convincing people of things I want them to believe. He believes Adam has sent me to talk to you, and that we're not to be disturbed.'

Kate took a closer look at the ID badge. The photograph was perfect, the name immaterial, the division, the Paedophile Investigation Unit.

'What do you want?' Kate asked.

'The same thing I've always wanted. To change the rules of the game.'

'I'm not part of your game.'

'That's where you're wrong, Kate. You've always been part of it.'

'I don't understand.'

'I thought your mind maps were impressive. It's a pity you got knocked down before more of the jigsaw pieces came together.'

'You were responsible for that, weren't you?'

'I wasn't behind the wheel.'

'That doesn't matter.'

'No, it doesn't.'

'You're Jessica, aren't you?'

'I can be anyone you want me to be, even the man who abducted you, although he died a long time ago.'

'Why?' Kate asked, the pain in her chest worsening, as she tried to hide her fear, knowing that somehow she had to buy time.

'You kept looking in the wrong place.'

'For what?'

'For the person responsible.'

'I don't understand.'

'No, you don't. You never did.'

'Jessica, I'm sorry for what happened to you. I wish I could have changed things but I couldn't. I was only a girl like you.'

'WRONG, WRONG, WRONG. You were never a girl like me. Princesses who live in ivory towers cannot know anything. Which is why, very soon, you won't.' Jessica moved her face closer. 'Don't you see the family resemblance?'

'What are you talking about?'

'We're sisters, half-sisters, to be precise. Our father treated me the same as he treated that dead blackbird when he fired it into the skip.'

'You're lying.'

'Tut, tut, tut … It seems I'm a disappointment to you as well as Daddy!'

'We can't be.'

'I keep telling you, Kate. I can be anyone you want me to be, but right now, I'm the woman who's going to take your precious life away, the same way mine was taken from me. I only wish our father was here to share in the joy.'

The stab of the needle in Kate's upper arm happened so quickly, that she had no time to defend herself, and no matter how hard she tried, she couldn't keep her eyes open.

'I'd wanted you to suffer more, but I'm a pragmatist at heart. It's partly why I've survived for so long. Your death will be far less painful than I would have liked it to be, but knowing your foetus will die with you is an added bonus.'

Charlie

THE CANTEEN WAS FULL OF PEOPLE EATING, TALKING, laughing, reading newspapers and all kinds of stuff. Charlie didn't like being away from his mum for so long.

'Dad?'

'What?'

'Can we go back to Mum now?'

'It's only been twenty minutes. You heard what the doctor said.'

'I don't care. I know Mum wouldn't mind.'

'It's not a question of her minding. It's a question of what's best for her.'

'I'm going back down.'

'No, you're not.'

'I am.' He stood up, defiant.

Declan couldn't help but laugh. He knew when he was beaten. 'All right, but if we get into trouble, I'm blaming you.'

'Deal.'

In the lift, they watched the numbers move from floor five to floor two. When the lift doors opened, a woman walked into it, smiling at both of them before they left.

'There's that woman again,' Charlie said, heading towards his mother's door.

'What woman?'

'The woman Mum and I saw a few weeks ago in McDonald's. She used to come to the school too. She looks a bit like Mum, doesn't she?'

'Charlie, are you sure?'

'What's wrong, Dad? Why are you shouting at me?'

Declan took a number of steps forward, getting nearer to Matthews, pulling Charlie with him.

'That woman,' he shouted at Matthews, 'the one who got into the lift. Was she with Kate?'

'DI O'Connor sent her.'

Before Matthews had time to say any more, Declan opened the door to Kate's room. 'Jesus!' he yelled. 'Get help fast.'

One Week Later

Adam

ADAM STARED STRAIGHT AHEAD OF HIM. THE LAST
few days had felt like a lifetime. They had caught up with Jessica
Baxter at Dublin airport. If she hadn't delayed to get to Kate, she
might well have been able to make her escape. But, thankfully,
she was behind bars, as was Malcolm Madden for interfering with
justice. Stephen and the other senior members of the cult were also
under arrest, each suspected of multiple murders, including those
that the police had found buried on the island.

'I never had a chance to meet Lee Fisher,' Kate said.

'You will. He's going to be back in Dublin for the trials.'

'How's Addy coping with everything?'

'He's doing okay.'

'That's good. He and Charlie have gotten very close.'

'I know.'

'Has he spoken to Aoife yet?'

'Not yet. His head is all over the place at the moment.'

'These things take time, Adam. There's a whole programme of
rehabilitation that needs to happen for everyone involved. Aoife, like
the others, will be caught between indoctrination and an uncertain
future. With counselling, hopefully, most of them, including Aoife,
will be able to find their way back.'

'You know that boy, Donal, the one Addy befriended on the
island, is now in state care, along with the little girl Chloe.'

'Let's hope not for long.'

'Addy visited both of them.'

'You should be very proud of him.'

'I am, Kate, really proud. What do you think is going to happen to Sarah Sinclair?'

'Sarah is a special case. Despite the passing of time, she is still traumatised over the loss of Lily. The real world isn't a place she wants to be right now. She has a far bigger battle to conquer than the grieving process or the indoctrination. The cult gave her what she wanted, an opportunity to encourage the denial of her loss, but the real question is, does she want to make a future for herself without Lily?'

'I understand she's not able to have another baby.'

'No, she's not, but John loves her deeply. He will have been changed by this experience too. Everyone needs a rock in their life at moments of vulnerability. I doubt he'll let her slip away from him again, and the heart is a mighty adversary.'

He turned to face her, putting his hands around her waist, turning her to him and looking down at her stomach. 'How's our little survivor doing today?'

'She's taking it one day at a time.'

'You still think it's a girl.'

'I do, and she's a fighter.'

'She's like her mother then.' He laughed.

'Adam, I was thinking we might call her Eva. It means "life" or "living one".'

'I like the sound of that,' he said, then turned to watch the officers below them. Both of them looked down at the enormous hole being dug out of the earth. The anthropologist, Victoria Hunt, from the size of the frame and the shape of the pelvic bones, had already confirmed that they were dealing with the skeletal remains of a young boy.

'Victoria Hunt certainly knows her stuff,' Adam said, as he watched her carefully and meticulously record each discovery.

'It will be a slow process, Adam, but an anthropologist can read a skeleton the way you or I can a book.'

'We'll know soon enough how and when the boy died, and if Peter Kirwan is down there.'

'Buried secrets,' she whispered, as if thinking out loud.

'Kate, do you believe your father had any part in Peter Kirwan's death?'

'No, I don't. But he knew where he was buried. Otherwise, my mother would never have brought me here that night. I feel such shame.'

'You have no reason to. You did nothing wrong.'

'Maybe not, but it's a bitter pill to swallow, that my parents, especially my father, could have taken Peter Kirwan's family out of their misery, and didn't.'

'Who knows, Kate, why people make decisions like that? All we have are fragments of the full story.'

'What about the abuse, Adam? Denying his daughter, my half-sister, what about that?'

'I don't know, but if what you say is true, he did regret the decisions he made. At least he told you he was sorry and that he loved you. That was something.'

'Do you think Victoria will give us enough evidence to find Peter Kirwan's killer?'

'I've been at this game long enough to know that all new evidence offers hope of solving a crime.'

'It feels like a heavy weight inside me, a burden. I thought I wanted answers. I thought what had happened to me all those years ago was a puzzle, that one day I would resolve it. I had no idea that the truth would be harder to take than the not knowing. If I could turn the clock back, I wouldn't want to know any of it. But if Peter Kirwan is down there, his family will at least have some kind of closure. Although I've always hated that word, "closure". These things never have closure, not completely.'

'I guess, Kate, this is how mysteries are solved. A seemingly harmless piece of information remembered, appearing unimportant at the time, but suddenly being the breakthrough needed.'

'Do you know the irony of it all?'

'Tell me.'

'Something struck me when I was in hospital.'

'What?'

'All my life, I hated being an only child. I used to dream about having a sister.' She turned to face him. 'Some dream that turned out to be.'

'We have to be careful what we wish for, Kate, but if you hadn't been her Achilles heel, she might have got away with it.'

'Adam, I thought of something else in the hospital.'

'What was that?'

'No matter how awful all of this is, imagine if I'd had her life.'

'She's not you.'

'I was the lucky one, which is why I'm going to change. From here on, I'm going to focus on all the good bits, and the life I'll share with you, Charlie, Addy, and our future fighter.'

'I'm looking forward to that too.'

Acknowledgements

WRITING IS ALWAYS AN EXPLORATION, AN ENTRY into a world that doesn't exist until you create it. It is a challenging, rewarding and at times daunting experience, and one in which you never know the full extent of the journey unless you have travelled the entirety of it.

Like my previous novels, *Red Ribbons*, *The Doll's House* and *Last Kiss*, *The Game Changer* started out with an impetus of an idea. I was intrigued by the manipulation of the individual in group environments and how the innocent are not always best prepared for this.

Writers study people. It is part of our DNA. Which is why over the last few years, looking at group behaviour has fascinated me. Like a lot of things in life, being part of a group can be both a positive and negative thing depending on the dynamics of the grouping, the people involved, and how an individual fits in. This was my starting point for *The Game Changer* and it certainly framed the story. However, as the writing progressed, the novel became so much more than that.

Our parents are one of the biggest influences in our lives, and within this story, the sins of the father rippled through the narrative in a way that as the writer I didn't expect. This book is dedicated to my mum and dad, two people who are forever foremost in my mind, despite having passed away a number of years ago. I recognised early on in life that human beings are complicated souls, and this has certainly influenced my writing and this story, which I hope you enjoy.

I want to give sincere thanks to my mother and father, Sarah and William Ray, who travelled a difficult journey in life, but one in which they loved their children dearly. I also want to thank my husband, Robert, for his patience and understanding, especially in those moments when I paced the floors working on character and storyline. Huge thanks to my daughters, Jennifer and Lorraine, for their love and support, and special thanks to my son Graham, who helped me with so many aspects of this story.

It has been a real pleasure working with my editor Ciara Doorley and all the team at Hachette Books Ireland, and also Hazel Orme, copy editor, and Ger Nichol, my agent. Their words of encouragement meant a huge amount to me.

While writing this novel I spent some time at the Tyrone Guthrie Centre in Monaghan. I want to thank everyone there, both staff and visiting artists, for creating an environment where creativity can flow.

Finally, I would like to thank Dave Grogan for his support regarding some of the psychological issues explored in the story, members of An Garda Síochána, especially Detective Tom Doyle, for helping with my research, Shirley Benton for asking her daughter lots of questions, all of which helped me to develop the child voices in this story, Mary Lavelle for reading the first draft, Sheila Stone for introducing me to the concept of the raven, Carolann Copland for giving me a wonderful location in Benalmadena to finish editing, and all my friends, who have made the journey all the more pleasurable, and lastly, but most importantly, the readers, who have brought me more encouragement and joy than I ever thought possible.

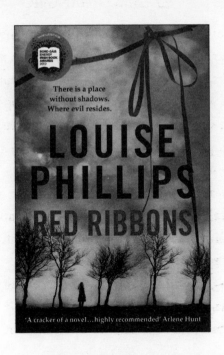

RED RIBBONS

There is a place without shadows. Where evil resides ...

A missing schoolgirl is found buried in the Dublin mountains, hands clasped together in prayer, two red ribbons in her hair. Twenty-four hours later, a second schoolgirl is found in a shallow grave – her body identically arranged. The hunt for the killer is on. The police call in profiler Dr Kate Pearson to get inside the mind of the murderer before he strikes again.

But there's one vital connection to be made – Ellie Brady, a mother institutionalised fifteen years earlier for the murder of her daughter Amy. What connects the death of Amy Brady to the murdered schoolgirls? As Kate Pearson begins to unravel the truth, danger is closer than she knows ...

Also available as an ebook

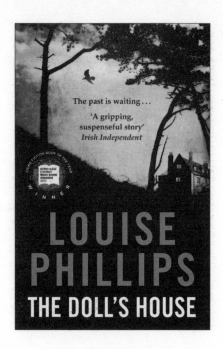

THE DOLL'S HOUSE

The past is waiting …

Thirty-five years ago Adrian Hamilton drowned. At the time his death was deemed a tragic accident but the exact circumstances remain a mystery.

His daughter Clodagh now visits a hypnotherapist in an attempt to come to terms with her past, and her father's death. As disturbing childhood memories are unleashed, memories of another tragedy begin to come to light.

Meanwhile criminal psychologist Dr Kate Pearson is called to assist in a murder investigation after a body is found in a Dublin canal. And when Kate digs beneath the surface of the killing, she discovers a sinister connection to the Hamilton family.

Time is running out for Clodagh and Kate.

And the killer has already chosen his next victim …

Also available as an ebook

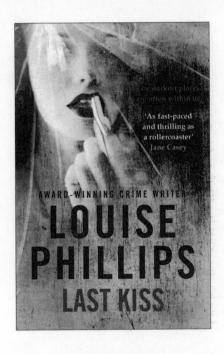

LAST KISS

The darkest places are often within us …

At a hotel room in Dublin, the butchered body of art dealer Rick Shevlin, arranged with artistic precision like the Hanged Man from a Tarot card, is discovered.

Meanwhile, in a quiet suburb, Sandra Regan clings to her sanity as a shadowy presence moves through her home.

What connects them?

Criminal psychologist Dr Kate Pearson is sure that the killer has struck before and will again – soon. As Kate and DI O'Connor are plunged into an investigation which spreads to Rome and Paris, they uncover a vicious trail of sexual power and evil. But will they uncover the killer's identity before she claims another victim?

Also available as an ebook